*ere*

'A gorgeous book. Life-affirming, clever and packed full of emotion'
**ANSTEY HARRIS, bestselling author of**
*The Truths and Triumphs of Grace Atherton*

'A courageous story, beautifully told, full of hope and heart.
I was invested from the very first page'
**HEIDI SWAIN**

'A compelling story about family love at its most complicated ...
Will go on existing in readers' heads long after
the last page has been turned'
**DAISY BUCHANAN**

'Alice demonstrates yet again a remarkable ability to open
up her readers' hearts and draw us into her story
as if it were our own. I loved it'
**KATE FURNIVALL**

'A beautiful story about making difficult choices,
but ultimately – about choosing to live'
**RACHEL CULLEN, author of** *Running for my Life*

'An unforgettable rollercoaster of a book'
**AMANDA BROOKE**

'Stunning and captivating'
**KATIE MARSH, bestselling author of** *This Beautiful Life*

'A beautifully structured, big-hearted novel which ultimately
explores how true love – be that romantic, familial and everything
in between - conquers all ... Utterly life-affirming and just gorgeous'
**KATY REGAN**

... fiction with humour
an... uplifting, but her
pr... adversity. This is based
on ... of a professional tennis career cut
short at the age of eighteen, when she was diagnosed with
rheumatoid arthritis.

Alice has written two non-fiction titles and nine novels,
and is currently living in West London with her handsome
Lucas terrier, Mr Darcy.

Find out more about Alice at www.alicepeterson.co.uk
or follow her on Facebook and Twitter: @AlicePeterson1

*Also by Alice Peterson*

# ALICE PETERSON

# If You Were Here

**SIMON &
SCHUSTER**

London · New York · Sydney · Toronto · New Delhi

A CBS COMPANY

First published in Great Britain by Simon & Schuster UK Ltd, 2019
A CBS COMPANY

Copyright © Alice Peterson, 2019

The right of Alice Peterson to be identified as author of
this work has been asserted in accordance with the
Copyright, Designs and Patents Act, 1988.

1 3 5 7 9 10 8 6 4 2

Simon & Schuster UK Ltd
1st Floor
222 Gray's Inn Road
London WC1X 8HB

Simon & Schuster Australia, Sydney
Simon & Schuster India, New Delhi

www.simonandschuster.co.uk
www.simonandschuster.com.au
www.simonandschuster.co.in

A CIP catalogue record for this book
is available from the British Library

Paperback ISBN: 978-1-4711-5352-5
eBook ISBN: 978-1-4711-5354-9

Typeset in the UK by M Rules
Printed and bound by CPI Group (UK) Ltd, Croydon, CR0 4YY

*To all those whose lives have been touched*
*by Huntington's Disease*

# Prologue

**Peggy**

*July 2012*

I clutch the letter, my hand shaking.

Deep down I always knew. I was just waiting for Beth to tell me, gearing myself up to be strong for us both all over again.

There were times when I sensed she was distant and anxious. Often I wondered why my daughter hadn't married since any man would have been lucky to have her by his side. Yet I allowed myself to believe her excuse that she simply hadn't met the right person, that she wanted to focus on her art, her teaching career and being a mother to Flo.

I have skated around the subject for years, too much of a coward to ask the question I dreaded the answer to. I locked my fears in a box and threw away the key, instead forcing myself to believe she'd escape the odds.

Looking back over the past few years, I was beginning to notice signs, small things, like Beth forgetting our regular weekly call. Once, she locked herself out of the house and had to drive over to get my spare set of keys. I was determined to put it down to her being scatterbrained. Yet there was this persistent voice inside my head.

*She could have it.*

A voice I chose to ignore.

I look down at the letter once more.

*It would kill me.*

I wish now with all my heart that I could take back those selfish words. All I wanted was to protect Beth – and myself – from further pain.

I wipe the tears from my eyes.

Right now, I'd give anything to be able to hold my daughter one last time and tell her how sorry I am for letting her down. And what I wouldn't give to be able to ask her the questions I need answering now like never before.

Did she ever intend for her daughter Flo to see this letter? Maybe, in the end, Beth agreed that none of us should know our future, that we're better off letting fate take its course.

I can't tell my granddaughter.

She is far too fragile, not only to discover that this has been kept a secret from her, but to understand the impact it could have on her own life. She is grieving for her mother and it's taking every ounce of her strength just to get through each day. Showing her this letter would only rake up the past and make Flo fear her future. Yet the decision to keep on hiding the truth doesn't rest easy either.

I tear a small corner of the letter, tempted to rip it into shreds and pretend I'd never seen it.

I wish in so many ways I hadn't.

If I show Flo the letter it could break her heart.

But if I don't . . .

What a fool I have been to think that the past never catches up with you.

# 1

## Flo

### *Five years later*

As I walk down Fifth Avenue, to the mystery place where I'm meeting Theo tonight, I think back on the past week, wishing I didn't have to pack my bags and return to London tomorrow, back to my job and familiar old routine.

My boyfriend Theo has been based in New York for six months.

'Long distance relationships can work, Flo, if we see it as an opportunity,' he'd said, when he broke the news that he was needed over here for a year, possibly more.

And he was right. There is something magnetic about this city. It buzzes with energy, like a party that never stops.

The first time I flew over to see Theo, we visited all the major sights and did all the things you're supposed to, like taking a trip to the top of the Empire State Building and hopping on a ferry over to Staten Island. Now I'm happy to do my own thing, whiling away the hours with my sketchpad in Central Park, or finding hidden gems off the beaten track, like the original piece of the Berlin Wall I discovered in a small plaza at Madison Avenue.

Each time I visit – mainly for long weekends – Theo takes me to a new exhibition or restaurant that has just opened.

Nothing stays the same here. Nothing stands still.

And everything is so tall. Theo works in just one of the thousand dazzling skyscrapers that grace the Manhattan skyline.

I dodge out of the way of a group of tourists taking pictures of the Empire State Building. Another thing I love about this place is it keeps me fit. There's no point hailing a cab and spending a fortune sitting in traffic. Everyone here walks for miles.

As I continue down one of the most famous and elegant streets in the world, I think of Granny, hoping she's all right. It's the anniversary of Mum's death today and it's the first time we've spent it apart. When I called her earlier this evening, she told me she was fine and that she'd laid some flowers on Mum and Granddad's gravestone and would later light a candle.

I promised to light one too.

In many ways Mum's death feels a lifetime ago, but in others as if it were only yesterday. What tormented me most is the fact I didn't have the chance to say goodbye. My last conversation with her was over the phone, while I was at the airport in Venice about to board a plane. I was blissfully happy in a steady relationship and I'd just been offered a job designing sets for a small theatre company in Copenhagen. The only problem was my scatty old mum.

'What now?' I'd snapped, annoyed at having to repeat the conversation we'd *literally* just had about what time my plane landed and whether I'd be home in time for supper.

I never saw her again.

I didn't even tell her I loved her.

That's what I miss most: picking up the phone to talk to her; hearing her voice.

Her death had seemed so avoidable. One moment she was alive, but the next . . .

'It was an accident,' Granny had stressed. 'A tragic accident that makes no sense.'

Losing Mum will be the hardest thing I'll ever go through. At one point I didn't even want to live, oblivion seemed preferable. I don't know what I'd have done without Granny picking me up and piecing me back together again, especially when her grief must have been just as raw.

I can't tell you when I began to feel less broken. I don't recall a turning point. All I know is that food began to taste of something again. Slowly I noticed the sunlight streaming through my bedroom window. I heard the birds sing. My steps began to feel lighter.

And then along came Theo.

We met eighteen months ago in the business lounge at Gatwick airport, when I was heading out on a work trip to southern Spain. I was busy stocking up on all the food and glossy magazines the business lounge had to offer, when I sensed someone watching me. Discreetly, I turned to see an older, fair-haired man drinking a cup of coffee, a flicker of amusement in his eyes. Everything about him spelt success, from his designer suit to his leather briefcase and expensive watch. I returned to my seat, thinking he must have been looking at someone else, or recalling a funny joke he'd just been told.

But then he approached my table.

'Theodore Holmes,' he said, sitting down opposite me, as if it were the most natural thing in the world to introduce oneself to a stranger. Before I could say a word, he continued, 'I don't know your name yet, but what I *do* know is I'm going to spend the rest of my life with you.'

It's not often I'm lost for words. I felt out of my depth, and as if he could read my mind he leaned closer towards me and said quietly, 'Listen, I'm sorry to come on so strong. You don't have to agree to spend the rest of your life with me just yet, but how about dinner?'

He handed me his business card. We parted with a handshake, almost as if we were in a boardroom.

'Deal,' I was tempted to say.

For the next few days, I imagined our perfect first date with flowers and champagne, the conversation flowing freely, the evening ending with a romantic goodnight kiss. When I returned home, however, I began to lose my nerve, that little voice of doubt creeping in.

After Mum died, I broke up with my long-term boyfriend and I hadn't been in a serious relationship since. I felt out of practice.

*As if he's really going to be interested in you, Flo. It meant nothing. He probably says the same thing to every woman he meets and he won't even remember you.*

But despite that voice in my head, I couldn't throw away his business card.

James – my flatmate and best friend's brother – looked him up online with me one evening after work.

'Good-looking,' he said when we saw a picture of Theo smiling broadly into the camera, 'but knows it. Mind you, I'd be smiling like that too if I had his teeth *and* his bank account.'

James is a vet, which, according to him is 'not a job you do for the money'.

He urged me to give Theo a call. 'What's the worst that can happen? It's one night, and if he's a knob, move on.'

I smiled. James always had a way with words.

Anyway, I took his advice and called.

Theo picked up instantly, and when I said my name, asking nervously if it was a good time for him to talk, he replied, 'I've been waiting for days. Ever since I first set eyes on you.'

I was still hesitant to go on a date. I wasn't sure I trusted his smooth talk, but I listened to James again, who told me I had nothing to lose except one evening of takeaway, Netflix, and James's charming company.

On our first date, Theo booked a table at a restaurant on the 32nd floor of the Shard, and over dinner I discovered he left school without any qualifications, but through hard work and self-belief he was now CEO of a company called ASPIRE, one of the biggest global marketing agencies in the world. I tried to ignore that little voice again that wondered why he'd want to go out with someone like me, a mere travel agent, when surely he could have the pick of anyone in this restaurant.

When Theo asked me for a second and a third date, that voice still wouldn't go away. I kept expecting something to go wrong; I was waiting for the fall. Yet my fear has been pointless, and after eighteen months together that little voice has almost disappeared.

*Almost.*

I rummage in my handbag to retrieve the note Theo left on my pillow this morning, with the exact address of where I'm supposed to meet him.

'It's a surprise,' he'd insisted. He's aware it's Mum's anniversary today and wanted to do something to honour it, so I suggested we do something fun: drink cocktails, go to a nightclub and dance until the early hours of the morning.

'Mum loved dancing,' I said. 'She used to dance in the kitchen and sing in the shower.'

I told him I wanted to remember all the happy times we'd shared and celebrate her life tonight, because for the first time in five years I haven't only been thinking about Mum today. This morning, when I woke up in Theo's apartment and read his note, I realized that time does slowly heal, and that right now, despite everything, I am truly happy.

As I arrive I see no sign of a restaurant or bar. I glance at my watch. It's past seven o'clock.

Theo's late. He's never late.

For a split second I feel uneasy. I wish I knew why he was being so secretive. He knows how much I hate surprises. But my worries vanish the moment I see him across the street, and soon I'm in his arms, welcoming his kiss.

'Are you ready?' he asks.

'Ready for what? Where are we—'

'Trust me,' he says, a smile spreading across his face as he holds his hand out towards mine.

I know more than most how happiness can be taken away from us as quickly as it was found. But I know, too, that it's time for me to let go of my past and trust in my future once and for all. It's what Mum would have wanted.

I take his hand.

Maybe I'm allowed to be this happy without a catch after all.

# 2

**Peggy**

My husband, Tim, was diagnosed with Huntington's Disease when our daughter Beth was twelve. But that's not the entire story. His doctor told us that Beth had a fifty per cent chance of inheriting the gene too. We didn't discuss the implications of this as a family. Tim wanted to. I didn't.

It remained the elephant in the room.

Today, I lay my bouquet of pale pink roses on their shared headstone.

'I'm sorry I haven't visited for a while. I can't exactly say I've been busy. The truth is . . .' I stop.

I stare at the names of my husband and daughter engraved into the stone. 'Well, let's not talk about that just yet. But please don't think for a minute it's because I don't think about you both or miss you. Because I do. All the time.'

*Especially today.*

'I'm always asking you to help me out with the crossword, Tim. I can never get the wretched science clues and I still haven't tried the cryptic. I'm too dim.' I laugh faintly.

'Well, what news do I have?' I mull. 'Flo's in New York with Theo; they've been dating for well over a year now. To be honest, I don't know him that well, but they seem happy enough. Remember how I told you he works in branding? Not that I have a clue what that means, mind you. Design, I think, or marketing. I don't sense he's strapped for cash: he owns a flat with a private gym in Canary Wharf. Enviable teeth, too, nice and straight.' I shrug. 'Not like mine. Or yours, Tim. Well, we didn't have orthodontists in our time, did we? You'd love his snazzy car. A *Jaguar*. I think I've told you this before, but he's ten years older than Flo. Thirty-seven. Maybe that's a good thing, he can take good care of her,' I say. 'She's still an assistant manager at the travel agency. I think she enjoys it, although sometimes I wish she'd . . .' I stop again, thinking of Tim and how he hadn't chased his own dream.

'Well, I think that's about all my news,' I wrap up, dreading the long day ahead. 'I'll go home and reheat the quiche: leek and bacon, Tim, your favourite. Flo persuaded me to sign up to Netflix. I'm rather addicted to *The Crown*. The woman who plays the Queen – I forget her name – she's frightfully good. Sounds just like her. Well, I must be off now,' I add, looking down at Elvis, my eleven-year-old Jack Russell. 'Elvis needs his din-dins.'

I look up to the sky, an ominous dark grey that threatens

a storm. I take in the rows of gravestones, flowers and toys left behind for their loved ones. No one wants to belong to a club that has lost a husband or a child – or both – and normally there is a certain comfort being here knowing I am not the only member. Yet nothing can take away my pain today, not on the anniversary of Beth's death.

*Don't cry, Peggy, not in front of them.*

I urge myself to go home, but I find myself kneeling on the grass.

'Oh Beth, what should I do?'

I see that letter again, from the hospital, marked 'confidential'. The letter that stated Beth had tested positive for Huntington's Disease. It's now hidden in an old shoebox in the bottom of my desk, haunting me every single day and night. I promised myself I would tell Flo once the time felt right, but I fear it never will, and the longer I leave it, the harder it becomes.

I'm terrified of telling Flo the truth about Tim and Beth and being seen as the enemy. I'm frightened she won't be able to forgive me. How can I expect her to when I have kept the contents of that letter a secret for almost five years?

'What do you want me to do?' I ask Beth again. 'Should I tell her? I'm the only person Flo has left now and I can't let her down. Talk to me. *Please*, give me some sign.'

I wait, but hear only silence, and the rapid beating of my heart.

# 3

## Peggy

It's ten o'clock on Saturday evening, the day after Beth's anniversary. I'm at home watching the news, though I haven't taken in a single word. There could be an earthquake coming to Hammersmith and I wouldn't realize until my entire house was reduced to rubble.

I couldn't eat supper tonight, not even a boiled egg. Nor could I concentrate playing cards this afternoon. I made one mistake after another. My bridge partner got ever so ratty when I kept trumping his winners. Thank goodness we weren't playing for money. It's lucky I'm not a gambler.

Restless, I lift Elvis off my lap before pacing the room.

I have an unshakeable feeling that something is about to change, that something is in the air.

I stop. Stare at my reflection in the mirror.

After the shock of Beth's death, I turned grey almost

overnight, but I'm rather fond of it now. I shall never dye it. Age is an honour – why try to hide it? Along with the lines and crinkles around my eyes, they tell a story.

My hair is short with a natural curl, though it's thinning out now. I like it when the hairdresser poufs it up. Flo says I look like the Queen for a day.

I've never been much of a beauty, unlike Beth and Flo. Tim used to say to me, 'You can look positively intimidating, Peg, with that steel in your eyes and your determined old chin that juts out when you're ticking me off. But I know you're as soft as they come'.

I pick up the framed photograph of Tim on the mantelpiece. He's smiling at the camera, a cup of coffee in one hand, a cigarette in the other and binoculars around his neck, dark hair blowing in the wind. It was taken on our honeymoon. They were such happy years, raising Beth, Tim climbing the advertising ladder and I loved my job working in the admissions department of Beth's primary school in North London.

We travelled each summer. Tim wanted to hike up mountains and camp, even in the wind and the rain. 'It makes it much more fun, Peg!' he'd say, gleefully zipping up his hooded raincoat. I remember one holiday he taught Beth and me to windsurf in Cornwall. I couldn't stand upright on my board even for a second, preferring the comfort of the sand and a Georgette Heyer novel – you can't beat a good old romance.

I was always Little Miss Cautious and Tim was Action

Man, but when I was with him, somehow he brought out the youth in me again.

I look at his faithful recliner in the corner of the sitting room, close to the television. Tim used to sit in it day after day. It was the one thing I couldn't let go of, even if I don't sit in it or allow guests to.

*Oh, how I miss him.*

Even when our home had begun to resemble a war zone – the chairs threadbare, the carpet stained and the furniture a victim of his accidental kicks – he taught me that these things aren't important. These days, people strive for perfection, not realizing that all they really need is health and happiness. A spotless kitchen isn't going to cut the mustard. A meal in a Michelin-starred restaurant won't either. It's the people sitting around your kitchen table who count.

I put the picture back in its place before returning to my armchair to watch the weather forecast, Elvis settling on my lap again.

In a way it was a blessing that Tim didn't suffer the loss of our Beth. That he didn't know what I know.

In the past, Flo has asked me if I thought it odd how Beth died, simply walking across a busy street, not looking, not paying attention. It made me think of Tim in the early years of his diagnosis, when he'd go to the shops for cigarettes and forget where he was. I didn't want to nanny him; understandably he wanted to cling on to his independence for as long as possible, but eventually I would have to go out and find him. Sometimes he'd be in the pub, watching sport, oblivious to the fact he'd been gone for hours; other times he'd be wandering the streets, lost and disorientated. I once had to run across a busy road to help him reach the other side safely, a horn blasting and an irate driver yelling at us.

*If I'd been just a second later . . .*

The news has come to an end now. I haven't the foggiest what the weather will be like tomorrow. I switch off the television, almost jumping out of my skin when I hear knocking on my front door.

Who on earth would be calling at such an unsocial hour?

'Hello?' he calls out in a deep voice. 'Hello? Are you there?'

I tiptoe to the door and take a look through my peephole. I stagger back.

Good grief. It's my new neighbour who moved in a few weeks ago with his partner and their squawking baby. I must admit, I do find him rather intimidating; he must be well over six foot, with that funny matted hair.

'*Dreadlocks*, Granny,' I recall Flo saying to me, rolling her eyes. 'You can't say "funny hair".'

I suppose I should invite him in, but he could be an ex-prisoner for all I know. A real baddie. After all, why would he be knocking at this time of night?

I wait, holding my breath, hoping he'll get the message, which thankfully he does. I breathe again, before stealthily sliding the chain across the door, double locking and pushing the bottom bolt across too.

You can never be too careful.

After letting Elvis out for a piddle, the two of us head upstairs. If Tim were here, he'd be shocked I allow Elvis to sleep in our bedroom.

'That dog lives the life of Riley,' he'd say.

As I undress, retrieving my nightie neatly folded underneath my pillow, my mobile pings. It's a text message from Flo. My heart lifts.

**Granny, I'm on my way home. Have some exciting news!** ☺ **Can I pop over to see you tomorrow evening? Want to tell you in person! Missed you this weekend. Flo x**

I freeze.

I sit down and reread the message, my heart thumping in my chest.

Theo must have proposed. What else could it be?

I want Flo to get married and have children, of course I do. There is nothing I'd love more than to see her happy, but . . .

*Keep calm, Peggy.*

*Breathe.*

If it is what I think it is, I'll deal with it. In many ways it forces my hand. It doesn't have to change her plans. Flo's life doesn't need to stop.

I shut my bedroom door, but it's optimistic to think I'll get any sleep tonight. I wish Tim were with me, to hold me in his arms and tell me everything will be fine.

I even start to believe it will be. *So long as Theo is the right person . . .*

From the little I know about him – aside from his wealth, his age and his Jaguar – I believe he's wedded to his career. The first time he came over for dinner, his BlackBerry was treated like a fourth guest. He's driven and ambitious, and there's no doubt he's easy on the eye, nor is he running low on confidence. Tim was confident too, but the kind of man who also wore odd socks with holes in the big toe. Or jumpers that I'd darned more times than I could count because he didn't like spending money on clothes.

I can't somehow imagine Theo wearing socks with holes in them. But who knows, I might be wrong.

Often I am.

Anyway, all that matters is whether he will stick by her, knowing she could possibly inherit HD. If he will then that's good enough for me.

As I undress and brush my teeth I recall a conversation I had with Beth, when she told me, out of the blue, that she was pregnant. Of course I was furious. *Livid!* She was far too young; how irresponsible to bring a child into the world without a father.

I thought she'd thrown her life away until the day Flo was born.

I fell in love with this little bundle of joy the moment I held her in my arms and she wrapped her little finger around mine, looking up at me with the biggest, most innocent eyes. Being a granny was a wonderful distraction from everyday life, too. She awakened our home with her toys and games, her baking and painting at the kitchen table. She'd sit on her granddad's lap and tickle his chin.

I sink into bed and close my eyes reassuring myself, yet again, that all will be well. But really, how did I let it get to this stage? I should have learned from my mistakes with Beth. So much remained unsaid between us. Hiding something from someone you love, keeping it locked inside, is like drip-feeding yourself poison.

Hours later I sit up in bed, still wide awake. The past is well and truly backing me into a corner now, telling me loud and clear that if Flo's news is what I strongly suspect it to be, it's time I told her the truth.

# 4

## Flo

'I'd have said yes too,' James says, admiring my diamond and aquamarine ring again. Theo went for the bold modern option. 'That's quite a knuckleduster.'

I smile. In fact, for the past forty-eight hours, I haven't been able to stop smiling. I was grinning like a clown throughout the plane journey, attracting the attention of my American neighbour who said as the drinks trolley stopped at our row, 'I'll have whatever she's having.'

'Have you told Maddie?' he asks me.

I tell him his sister shrieked down the telephone late Friday night, though I urged her not to say a word until I returned home.

'Come here,' James says. 'Congratulations.'

'Thanks. I'm going to miss you though.'

'Yeah, right, when you're drinking margaritas in a

swanky rooftop bar you'll be wishing you were here, with me, eating beans on toast.'

'I love beans on toast. I love this flat; it's my home. You and Maddie, you're my family.'

'Flo?' James stands back and looks me in the eye. 'You're not having any doubts, are you?'

'No, it's just—'

'Granny Peg?'

I nod, knowing it was an easy guess.

With every rose comes a thorn, and the thorn is leaving her. I'm looking forward to telling her the news just as much as I'm dreading it.

'She'll be happy for you,' James assures me as his mobile rings. From the look on his face I can tell it's Kate, a woman he met while out running a couple of weekends ago.

'Take it,' I urge.

Alone, I unpack and throw a load of clothes into the washing machine. I glance at my ring again, still wondering if it's all a dream. I know Granny will be happy for me, but I also know how much we'll miss one another. No matter how many times Theo assured me she could visit, it won't be the same.

Granny and I have always been close. Some of my happiest childhood memories are of decorating cupcakes and making strawberry jam in her kitchen.

I didn't know Granddad so well; I was only little when he died. He had some form of Parkinson's, I think. I remember him always being in a wheelchair, watching television, unable to say very much. Occasionally Granny and I took Granddad to the park to feed the ducks.

Our bond deepened after Mum's death. Up until Mum's funeral I thought I was doing fine. Granny and I had kept busy clearing out our old home in Barnes, burning paperwork, putting furniture into storage and arranging the service. It was only afterwards, when there was nothing left to do, that her death truly dawned on me. I gave up the opportunity to work for a small theatre company in Copenhagen. Granny urged me to think carefully before I turned the offer down, saying it could be exactly what I needed, but creatively I felt dead inside.

Besides, Granny was my only link to Mum and I couldn't bear the thought of leaving her, so I asked if I could move in instead.

Much of that period is a blur. I spent most of my time sleeping, only leaving the house when Granny sent me out to buy some milk. This routine dragged on for weeks, until finally she marched into my bedroom, drew the curtains open and said it was time for me to get up and find a job, slinging the employment section of her daily newspaper at me.

The thought terrified me. Being with Granny and staying indoors felt safe. My dressing gown was quite literally my comfort blanket. But Granny meant business; she had fire in her belly. I knew I couldn't stay with her unless I made more of an effort, so that morning I circled an ad in the paper for a sales consultant at a travel agency in West London and applied.

It was an effort to get up and shower, to brush my hair and put on a clean shirt. During my interview I managed to hold back the tears as I described that Mum and I had always loved to travel. During the school holidays we'd trek across Europe on a shoestring budget with Mum's old-fashioned camera and our sketchpads.

When my boss informed me the job was mine, I didn't feel a thing. Was this what it was going to be like, from now on? Numbness.

All I hoped was it would be enough to get Granny off my back.

It wasn't.

She said now that I had a salary, it was time for me to move out and pay rent. The responsibility made me feel sick. But she placed both her hands on my shoulders and said, 'You have a life to lead, Flo. You need to be with your friends and out in the real world.'

I see now that Granny was right. I needed tough love. Left alone, I would have drowned in my own grief.

I called Maddie to see if she knew anyone looking for a lodger. Her family moved to Barnes when she was eight. We were at school together, then art college. In her I found a soulmate who loved to make as much mess painting and drawing as I did. She said my timing was uncanny: James was just about to advertise for someone to move into their family flat in Chiswick.

'If you're brave enough to live with my stinky bro, the room's yours,' she said. 'I don't even need to ask him.'

I wish Theo were here now. He'd be telling me it's normal to feel this way; that Granny and I have been through so much together the prospect of leaving her is bound to be daunting.

He'd also remind me that she'd hate it if I stayed put for her sake. She wouldn't allow it. Granny is the type of person who despises pity.

Though I do find myself wishing she'd open up more, realize it's all right to say she'll miss me. Mum always used to say Granny was a closed book when it came to anything emotional. She feels it, but can't say it.

'I'm heading over to Kate's,' James says, interrupting my thoughts. 'I can give you a lift to Granny Peg's if you like?' By a lift, James means on the back of Vile Vera, his metallic green motorbike. He bought her in a vile colour so that no one would think to steal her, which – to his credit – they haven't.

I decide to do the rest of my unpacking later. 'Yes, please,' I say, taking in a deep breath. 'Let's go.'

'It'll be all right, Flo. She'll be so happy for you.'

He's right. I glance at my ring again, a promise of a new beginning.

Everything will be fine.

# 5

## Peggy

I hear dreadful music coming from next door and that blasted baby crying again. Why isn't it in bed? It's almost eight o'clock. I always had Beth tucked up by seven sharp with lights out, and never once did she cry. And what did that man want, knocking on my door so late last night?

I walk into the sitting room, too restless to watch television, not even *Dragons' Den*. I need to prepare for Flo's news.

In the early hours of the morning I decided I must tell her about her mother and grandfather as soon as possible, but now I'm not so sure. Isn't it cruel to burst her bubble straightaway? Surely I must tell her when the time is right, rather than thinking about myself, and relieving my own guilt at keeping it a secret.

If Flo is engaged, and if she does move to New York, which I imagine is a possibility, I will miss her. Terribly.

No matter how much I want her to live her own life. Shortly after Beth's funeral, Flo moved in with me. While she wasn't much in the way of company, I had someone to care for, feed and nurture. Selfishly, I would have loved her to stay with me indefinitely. I dreaded my own company again, drawing the curtains late at night and locking the door behind me, making a pot of coffee just for one. I was also scared of being alone because I didn't want the time and space to confront my own grief. Without Flo in the house, I had no excuse not to think about the letter and what I should do next.

I hear the sound of a motorbike outside. I peep through my shutters to see Flo climbing off James's ugly bike, the two of them laughing.

She looks happy, positively glowing, which makes my argument for not saying a word tonight, even stronger.

I open my front door, Elvis by my side, wagging his tail at the new arrivals.

'Flo,' I say, immediately spotting the dazzling ring on her finger. It would be hard not to.

She rushes into my arms, just as she always used to when she was a little girl. 'Theo proposed,' she says.

'Congratulations, my darling,' I reply, holding back the tears. 'Now come inside and tell me *all* about it, I want to hear everything.' I nod at James and put on my bravest smile before he waves goodbye.

\*

Over drinks, Flo describes how Theo had taken her to a family-run jewellery shop overlooking Central Park, a room filled with soft pink furnishings and glass cabinets displaying necklaces and earrings that looked too expensive to touch let alone wear.

'Oh, Granny, it was so much fun trying everything on. I felt like Audrey Hepburn for the night. And then he bent down and . . .' She gestures to her ring that already looks at home on her finger. 'And said, "Will you be my wife?"'

'How romantic,' I sigh, thinking back to how Tim had proposed to me six months after we met. We were eating macaroni cheese – our favourite – watching TV.

'I think we should get hitched, Peg, don't you?' he'd said.

'I think that would be a grand idea,' I replied.

'Granny, that's not all,' Flo continues.

'You're moving to New York, aren't you?' I say, wanting to get it over and done with. Better to rip the plaster off than peel it back slowly.

'Theo's been asked to stay on for another year – two at the most. I'd keep in constant touch,' she reassures me, 'and I promise you it's not for ever.'

'This calls for champagne,' I propose, needing to turn my face away from hers, afraid I might give away my fear that Flo still doesn't know the truth about her mother. I walk into the kitchen, feeling unsteady on my pins.

'To be honest, Granny,' Flo says, following me, 'I've been thinking about leaving my job for some time now. I've been stuck in a rut for months and Theo thinks the culture, the theatre, it could all be an amazing chance for me to reconnect with my art.'

'Yes, that would be good,' I admit. I have always thought it a waste that Flo never followed her dream. Tim hadn't either. He had a successful career in advertising, but his true passion was art and building things. He should really have been an architect. He promised he'd design and build us a house by the sea when he retired. He would have done, too. He was a man of his word.

'When would you go?' I ask, wishing he were here with me now to raise a glass to Flo.

'Well, first of all I have to hand in my notice ...' She stops. 'Granny, I hate the thought of leaving you—'

'Now now, I'll be perfectly all right. This is *exciting* news, Flo.'

'I know, but—'

'You can't worry about your old granny.'

'Theo promised he'd fly you out business class.'

*Makes me sound more like a parcel.*

'Flo, I couldn't be happier for you.'

*But you're certain he's the one?*

Flo uncorks the bottle for me.

'Have you set a date yet?' I query.

'No, we need to talk about that. I want to get married here, at your local church. This is my home.'

Relieved, I brush a thread of cotton off my skirt. 'That's a lovely idea.'

'I only wish Mum were here too,' Flo says, as she pours us both a glass of fizz.

I wipe a tear from her eye with my thumb and tuck a strand of her long dark hair behind one ear. No matter how old she is she will always be my little girl.

'So do I. Now let me look at the ring again.' I take her hand. I have to admit, it's quite a statement, and if I'm honest, I'm not sure I like it. 'Do you love him, Flo?' I ask, before seeing the colour flush in Flo's cheeks and wishing I hadn't.

'Yes, and I really want you to like him too.'

'I do,' I claim, hoping I haven't given Flo any reason to pick up on my misgivings. The one and only tiff we had was when Theo claimed illness was all in the mind, and that we had the power to heal ourselves through meditation and diet. I'd had one too many vodka and tonics by then, which always makes me snappy, and told him I thought he was talking rubbish.

'Our lives, our futures, are in the hands of the gods and no amount of chanting and carrot juice is going to change that, young man.'

You should have seen his face. I doubt anyone had ever spoken to Theo like that before.

But in reality, Theo hadn't meant to be insensitive; he just wasn't aware of Tim's HD or Beth inheriting the gene. In the grand scheme of things, what he'd said was hardly a crime.

Theo is older and responsible; he clearly cares for Flo. Yet I can't help but feel something is lacking.

'Is he kind?' I ask, again registering Flo's surprise. But I have to ask, not only for myself, but for Beth too.

She nods. 'He'd do anything for me. I know you don't know him that well yet, but that will change. You don't need to worry, Granny.'

My face softens. I realize I've pushed her enough. I raise my glass to touch Flo's. 'To your future – just don't come home with an American accent.'

And at long last we laugh, before Flo lays the table. We spend the rest of the evening eating supper and discussing her engagement, Flo sketching a picture of the dress she would like to wear and trying to persuade me it's time to go shopping. 'Hats are back in fashion, Granny.'

# 6

## Flo

'Granny said she was happy, but I could tell something was worrying her. It was strange,' I say to James in the kitchen later that night.

James hands me a mug of tea. 'In what way?'

'That's the thing, I don't know.'

There's no reason for Granny and Theo not to get along. Though I can't help but recall the run-in they had when Theo said he believed so much of any illness is preventable – and I agreed with him – which appeared to rattle Granny.

'That generation really don't understand the power of the mind,' he'd said later to me on the way back to his flat. 'They simply take the pills their doc prescribes, but there's endless research now about exercising the brain to beat dementia.' I remember him turning to me with a smile, adding, 'But boy, she knocks back the vodkas, too, doesn't she? She could drink me under the table.'

'Listen, it's her job to make sure Theo's good enough,' James says. 'My mum always grills my girlfriends.'

'She was happy,' I insist, realizing I'm making little sense, 'but—'

'You're overthinking. You're jet-lagged.'

I nod, but I don't agree. I'm certain that, for a split second, in her eyes, I saw fear.

# 7

## Peggy

The following morning I wake up even more exhausted than when I went to bed, and now my head is pounding. After Flo left, I decided to polish off the rest of the champagne under the guise it was medicinal. I'm not too proud to say drink is my crutch. It allows me to park my problems, anaesthetize them for a few hours. The only hitch is that they soon come back once the anaesthetic has worn off, leaving me worse than before.

Another memory comes creeping back, like unwanted ivy.

*Oh, Peggy. You didn't, did you?*

My hazy recollection of marching into the garden with my torch, leaning over the wall and shouting comes flooding back to me.

'Keep the noise down! I am trying to sleep!'

What must the new neighbours think of me?

*Oh, I don't give a flying monkey what they think.*

I swing my tired old legs out of bed and stretch my neck and shoulders hearing an unpleasant crunch, before I head downstairs to the kitchen to make myself a cup of tea and let Elvis out.

'What should I do, old boy?'

I ruffle his ears and give him one of his sausage roll treats. Sometimes I wish I were a dog, my only concern being my next meal or which position to take by the Aga for my afternoon nap.

The kitchen sink is heaped with unwashed plates and glasses. Flo did offer to clear up last night, but I thought she looked exhausted after her flight. I wanted her to go home and get a good night's sleep.

Besides, I needed to be alone, to think things through.

I rinse one of the plates before loading it into the dishwasher, cursing myself yet again for not having had the courage to talk to Beth. My own mother had practically been a stranger, abandoning my father and me on the verge of the Second World War when I was six months old to move to America with her new man. Apparently, she felt trapped in a boring marriage to a stuffy army man, so when she met a much older, wealthier American chap – a banker – who asked her to return to New York with him, off she bolted.

My father joined his regiment, the Black Watch, and I was packed off to live with my spinster aunt, Celia, Mum's older sister, who lived in a small village in Wiltshire.

My father survived the war. I recall vividly the moment his train pulled into the station.

'Go and kiss your father,' Aunt Celia encouraged me, but I had no idea who he was until she pointed out a handsome man striding towards us in his kilt.

I lived with Dad after that, but it was a quiet, solitary life. He hated noise and was allergic to drama. He was kind and never hurt me, but in many ways I was rather intimidated by his silence. I was seven years old when I first met my mother properly. I don't recall it being a happy visit. I didn't know how to act or behave around this glamorous woman wearing a fur coat and high heels. Over the years she would occasionally sweep in and out of my life with little care of how deeply it affected me. Often I was ill with flu or caught some mysterious bug only days before she arrived.

I met Tim through a friend when I was twenty-four and we were engaged and married within a year. Perhaps the cruellest thing my mother ever said to me was that I'd better accept his proposal as no one else was going to ask me. I hadn't expected her to come to the wedding, but I suppose I always kept that flicker of hope inside me that one day my mother might apologize for leaving Dad and me behind.

I load another glass into the machine.

It's simple. I have two choices: I either tell Flo about the letter, or I don't. I just need to decide which option causes the least damage.

Last night, I was certain I should say something soon, but now I'm not so sure. After all, there is nothing she can do to help herself; no preventative measures. We are all going to die; we just don't know when or how.

Maureen, my bridge friend, told me that her aunt died of a mystery virus. One morning she was eating breakfast, happy as Larry, and the next her head was buried in her bowl of cornflakes.

If we all knew our fate, would we ever get out of bed in the morning? I'm not sure I would.

Tim always reflected that he was glad he hadn't known to begin with. He may have lived his life in fear.

I look up to the ceiling. *I could always pretend I'd only just found the letter.*

For a moment that thought brings comfort. Until I realize Flo would still accuse me of not telling her the truth about her grandfather.

The argument for telling Flo is simple: she deserves to know the truth, not only about her grandfather, but about her mother, too. She needs to know the facts before she makes any life-changing decisions.

If Theo is the right man, he'll stick by her.

She's still Flo. Nothing needs to change. She can still get married and move to New York. Her world doesn't need to stop. Surely once I have explained my reasons for not saying a word she'll understand the impossible position I've been in? Oh, who am I kidding? The truth is, I've made a real pig's ear of this. Her faith in me will be shattered. She might never trust me again.

I feel faint.

I need to sit down, I—

I gasp. *What have I done?*

I look down at my leg. Blood is dripping on to the floor.

Elvis follows me upstairs to the bathroom, my right leg bleeding severely. I tug at the loo roll and place a wodge of sheets against the gash.

*How could I have been so careless?*

I find my first aid kit under the sink and open the rusty old tin, but I can't find a plaster or gauze big enough.

I sigh. It's no use. I know what I have to do.

'Morning!' he says, locking his front door at the same time as me. It's my new neighbour with the dreadlocks. 'I'm Patrick.' He shakes my hand. 'I'm sorry about the noise last night; it was Shelley's fortieth.'

'Not to worry.' I wave a hand away, not wanting to encourage further conversation when I urgently need to get to my GP's surgery. 'Bye now.'

I march towards the main road, heading for the bus stop. I refuse to pay for a cab, even in an emergency.

'Wait!' Patrick catches me up. He's staring at my blood-stained trousers. 'What have you done?'

'Just a little knock. It's perfectly all right.'

'You need to get it seen to immediately.'

'Well, I'm off to the doctor's now.' I quicken my pace, feeling more blood ooze down my leg.

'Wait,' he calls. 'I'm a nurse. Why don't I take a look at it? You can't walk with it like that. It's bleeding badly.'

I stop. I'm tempted. But I really don't know this man, towering over me, claiming he's a nurse. I think back to him knocking on my door at all hours of the night, scaring poor Elvis.

'Let me at least clean it up for you.' He bends down, making himself closer to my height. 'Don't be scared of me.'

'I'm not scared,' I reply, knowing he's recalling the same moment I am.

'I was locked out of my house,' Patrick explains. 'I was going to ask if I could jump over the wall from your garden and climb through the back window. Hurdles were my favourite sport at school. Not surprising with these legs.'

'I wasn't frightened.' I brush a loose thread of cotton off my shirt to avoid eye contact. 'I just wasn't in, that's all.'

He tries not to smile.

'You say you're a doctor?' I ask him.

'A nurse, and I've seen this kind of thing many times before. Let me guess, the dishwasher?'

Still I hesitate.

'Please don't be scared of me,' he reinforces. 'The only person I've ever scared is myself.'


'You need to roll up your trousers or take them off,' Patrick says, standing in my bathroom. Clocking my uncertainty he suggests, 'I'll leave you to it. Call me when you're ready.'

Alone, I fling my trousers into the laundry basket. When he returns I feel vulnerable with only a towel wrapped round my waist, presenting to him my mottled leg, skin as thin as tracing paper. My sock is soaked with blood. He asks me if I'd be more comfortable perching on the loo seat.

When Patrick kneels down in front of me, he's more my height again, which certainly does make me feel less intimidated by his sheer physical presence. He assembles his first-aid box, much more impressively stocked than mine.

Wanting to fill the silence, 'My modelling days are probably now over,' I say, laughing nervously. I then ask him the first question that pops into my head. 'How old is your baby?' I don't even know if it's a boy or a girl.

'Mia, she's five months. I have a son, too, Leo. He's ten.' I recoil when I see a flap of loose skin.

'Sorry, this might sting,' he warns, cleaning the wound with a small tube of sterilized water and a pad of gauze. 'You really gave your dishwasher a good old thump, didn't you?'

I jut out my chin. 'I like to do things with style.'

'How many kids do you have, Mrs . . . sorry, I don't know your name?'

'Mrs Andrews. Just one.'

He waits.

'A daughter.'

'Ah, so the woman I often see coming over, she's your—'

'My granddaughter, Florence.'

'What does she do?'

I tell Patrick she works in a travel agency. 'She's just got engaged.'

'How exciting.'

'Yes. Yes, very exciting.'

He looks up at me. 'You don't seem too happy about it, if you don't mind me saying.'

'He's ten years older.'

He returns his attention back to my wound. 'Age is just a number.'

'Yes, but why isn't he married already?'

'I have a girlfriend, but we're not married.'

I cross my arms. 'He's thirty-seven.'

'I'm forty-one.'

'Pah! Why haven't you tied the knot then?'

'Not everyone wants to, Mrs Andrews. I've got loads of single friends. As for me, I love Shelley, but I've never believed in a piece of paper, that's all.'

'I haven't seen Leo before,' I say, watching him carefully applying an iodine patch to the wound. It stings, but I breathe through the pain.

'He lives with his mum in Chelmsford. I see him every other weekend. It's not enough though; I miss him.' He covers the iodine patch with a square of gauze. 'You should still get this checked out, but at least you look respectable now.' He wraps my leg in a crepe bandage. 'I don't want to apply too much tape, Mrs Andrews, as it might tear your skin.' He gets up and peels off his gloves. 'Right, better be off before I'm sacked.'

I stop dead, remembering this was something Tim used to say to me when we were first married. I can see him now in his suit, picking up his briefcase before saying 'Just one more kiss, Peg,' which usually turned into two or three. 'Right, better be off before I'm sacked,' Tim would finish. To my surprise I find I don't want Patrick to go.

'Do you love your job, Patrick?'

'I do. It's a privilege, looking after people.'

'Theo's very successful. You should have seen the rock he gave Flo. Must have cost an arm and a leg.'

'Well, it's not all about the money, is it?'

'Precisely. My husband, Tim, used to say to me, "If the house were on fire, Peg, what would you save first?"'

Amused, Patrick asks, 'What did you say?'

'The dog.'

Patrick roars with laughter. 'You crack me up, Mrs Andrews.'

'I fear Theo is the type of man to save his BlackBerry before Flo. Or one who'd fling his granny in the Thames to make a quick buck.' I can feel my cheeks flush. 'Oh, I don't mean that. I don't know what's come over me.' I pause. 'He works in New York. Flo's moving out there.'

'Lucky thing. It's a place I've always longed to go. But you'll miss her, right?'

I nod. 'It's hard letting go, isn't it? I just wonder whether he'd run for the hills if something bad were to happen to Flo.'

Patrick tries not to smile again.

'I understand you're protective,' he says, 'but maybe you're worrying too much?'

I look away. *He doesn't understand.*

'Mrs Andrews?'

'Ignore me,' I say, at last. 'You're right. I'm being silly. Now you must get to work.'

Downstairs, Patrick puts on his jacket and picks up his rucksack, which he'd left by the fireplace. I catch him looking at a photograph on my mantelpiece of Beth on her graduation day at Camberwell. 'Your daughter?'

I hold back the tears. 'Beth.'

'She's stunning.'

'That's one of her paintings,' I say, gesturing to a pretty coastal scene in Devon, close to Burgh Island.

'And look at you.' He picks up the photograph of Tim and me running across the very same beach hand in hand, on our honeymoon. 'Sorry, I'm being a nosy parker.' He puts the frame down and I lead him to the front door.

Just before he leaves, he says, 'What does Beth think of Flo getting engaged and going to New York?'

'She died five years ago.'

'I'm so sorry.'

'And my husband died many years before that.'

Patrick doesn't have to say he's sorry again. His look says it all.

'You see, I'm all Flo has,' I continue. 'She's all *I* have.'

When Patrick touches my arm I find it comforting. 'If Flo leaves, you won't lose her, Mrs Andrews. She's only a plane journey away.'

I nod.

'Well, goodbye.' He shakes my hand.

'Goodbye, Patrick.'

'Call me Ricky. The only time I'm called Patrick is when I'm in trouble with my mum or missus.'

When I reach for his hand and clutch it in my own, I'm not sure who is more shocked. 'Thank you for coming to my rescue, and please call me Peggy.'

'Anytime you want to talk, Mrs— I mean, *Peggy*, you know where I am.'

After we say goodbye, I close the door and walk into the sitting room. I picture Tim in his recliner, watching the television, and I miss him so much it hurts. When I look again, he isn't here, and it's painfully quiet, except for the sound of the ticking clock, the patter of Elvis's paws, his four feet never far away, and me blowing my nose, moved to tears by a stranger's kindness. A man I dared to judge.

I can't help but think that my dishwasher did me an enormous favour today.

# 8

**Flo**

It's my last weekend at home before moving to New York. I can hardly believe how quickly things have changed. It's just over three weeks ago since Theo proposed, and now I have only one more week left at work before I leave my old life behind.

Maddie's just arrived. She caught a train from Maiden Newton in Dorset, and James should be here any minute. I wanted to cook a special supper for the three of us tonight.

James had suggested taking us out, but I know money's tight for him this month, especially since, while someone didn't *steal* Vile Vera last week, they did decide to slash her tyres instead. *Bastards.* And Maddie rarely has any money.

'Don't be an artist if you want to be a millionaire,' she says. She's a freelance costume designer and has to earn extra cash working shifts at Costa.

As I make the chocolate sauce to go with our pudding, Maddie and I reminisce about the past. We met at school when we were eight and have remained inseparable ever since. Her family had moved from the depths of Wales to West London as her dad was setting up a veterinary practice in Barnes. I remember how funny she looked in her bottle green and gold uniform, her jumper tucked into her skirt – so mean of her mother to insist – tie lopsided, laces undone, and she had this frizzy mop of auburn hair that framed a heart-shaped freckled face.

When our form teacher asked Maddie to introduce herself to the class she said, 'Hello, my name's Madeleine, but everyone calls me Maddie, and I'm always hungry.' Her voice buzzed with energy and her smile was contagious. It was love at first sight.

Luck came my way when, shortly afterwards, we were paired to do an English project called, 'When I'm a grown-up'. We had to write a short story and put pictures together of how we imagined ourselves in the future.

Maddie drew a ballerina. I was a deep-sea diver, because I loved the ocean and drawing sharks.

When she invited me over to her house to do our homework together, I was struck by how different it was to mine. Firstly, it was at least double the size, over three floors, with steep stone steps leading up to a front door adorned with a lion's head door knocker. Their place was also filled with animals – a yellow Labrador called Monty, Dandelion the rabbit, who lived in a hutch at the end of their garden and a fluffy, white cat called Billy the Bastard, who would have made a convincing villain in any James Bond film.

The first thing Maddie's mother, Lucy, said to me, cigarette dangling out of her mouth as she iced a Victoria sponge cake, was, 'Don't go anywhere near him, ducky, he'll scratch your eyes out. The only person he loves is James'. Quickly, I discovered James was Maddie's older brother, the fridge door adorned with photographs of him either playing cricket or standing on a riverbank proudly holding up a large salmon. There were, of course, pictures of Maddie too, licking an ice cream or devouring a doughnut on a sandy beach, her lips coated in sugar and jam. They both shared an easy smile and charm, but they didn't physically look alike; James has my olive colouring – I have Italian blood in me – with thick brown hair brushed forward, partly covering light brown eyes and only a few freckles dotted along his cheeks and nose.

I also noticed that the edge of the kitchen door was lined with pencil markings and dates indicating the growing heights of Maddie and James, along with the names of other family friends and cousins that had visited. I began to panic about returning the invite. What would Maddie think of our house, so shy of family pictures and four-legged creatures? I didn't have a dad; I'd never known him. I didn't even have a goldfish.

I hear a key in the lock. 'Hi, honey, I'm home,' James calls, entering the kitchen with a bottle of wine and some cans of beer. He sticks them all in the fridge before pulling off his shirt, saying 'I need a shower. I've just castrated a skunk.'

'Disgusting.' Maddie pulls a face.

'Who said the life of a vet wasn't glamorous?' he says, before dipping his finger into my creamy white chocolate sauce. He has a lick and is about to do it again before Maddie slaps his wrist and I shove him away from the pan. 'Any news on the flatmate front?' I ask.

He tells us he's only had one response from the ad he placed online, 'The guy had some serious hygiene issues, so I won't be asking him to move in in a hurry,' he concludes, dipping his finger into the chocolate sauce again.

'I'd have thought you two would get on perfectly,' Maddie says.

'Fuck off,' he replies, leaving the room.

We can't help laughing when we hear James singing badly in the shower.

'I swear to God, I don't know how you've put up with him for so long,' Maddie reflects.

It makes me think back to the week I moved in and how much has changed.

'Would you like to have a shower?' James asked on our first morning together. 'No, you go,' I replied.

'No, please, after you,' he said, leaving me thinking that at this rate neither of us would ever wash.

Things began to warm up about a month later, after James's mother called him one evening, when we were having supper together. 'Mum *still* checks up on me to make sure I'm eating my five-a-day,' he'd moaned, before looking at me, realizing how insensitive he'd just been. 'Oh, Flo, I'm sorry. I wasn't thinking.'

I couldn't bear the awkwardness any longer. I knew we'd been circling the subject of Mum's death for weeks, James too scared to ask the wrong question, me still too raw to say a word. Grief was a foreign language to both of us.

So I picked up the bottle of wine and said five words that would soon change everything: 'Shall we get drunk, James?'

James is three years older than Maddie so I never knew him that well growing up. He was just Maddie's brother and he enjoyed playing that role, wielding his power to make us clean out Dandelion's hutch or pick up after Monty again, even when we knew it wasn't our turn. When I moved into the spare room here, Maddie always thought it would be temporary. 'You won't want to live with him for too long.'

*But here we are, five years later . . .*

And I'm going to miss him. Even his bad singing.


'How's Granny Peg?' Maddie asks me over pudding, somewhat absent-mindedly, since James's ex, Emma, has just called.

Emma, the woman James met in his second year at King's University in London, when she was also studying veterinary science.

Emma, the woman he dated for almost nine years until he decided to let her go, and for the past year he has been wondering if that was the biggest mistake of his life.

Obviously James wanted to take the call in private.

'She's been fine. Better,' I reflect. 'Will you promise me to call her every now and then? I know you're busy—'

'Of course I will, Flo.'

'I'm worried she's keeping something from me about her health: you know her heart problem.' Granny has high blood pressure coupled with atrial fibrillation, an abnormal heart rhythm. 'It would be so typical of Granny not to tell me if it's got worse. If you find out anything—'

'I'll let you know, I promise.'

I squeeze her hand. 'Thank you. Any news on the man front?' I ask, wondering why Emma has called James. I don't think they've spoken in months. A part of me always suspected they would get back together.

'A guy came over last night.'

'Maddie! Who? Why didn't you say something before?'

'Ricardo.'

'*Ricardo?*'

'It was delicious. He was delivering pizza,' she confesses, before I chuck my napkin at her. 'Seriously, Flo, I've got way too much work on even to *think* about men and dates.' She turns round, glancing at the kitchen door. 'What's taking him so long? Shall I—'

'I will,' I say, leaving the table, knowing James is more likely to open up to me than his sister.

I find him smoking on our roof terrace. James hardly ever smokes so I always know something's wrong when he gives in to his bad habit.

'So, you're excited about the Big Apple?' he says, staring ahead.

'Want to talk about it, James?'

He turns to me. Smiles. 'Emma's engaged.'

He withdraws when I touch his shoulder, as if he doesn't deserve any sympathy.

'It was decent of her to call,' he reasons. 'She didn't want me to find out on Twitter or Facebook, or through someone else. It's cool. She's moved on. I'm happy for her.'

'You don't have to pretend with me.' I wait for him to say more, watching him stub out his cigarette with unnecessary force.

'Is this what it's going to be like from now on, Flo? Me standing on the sidelines, watching friends get married and have children – you going off to New York, and I'm still here, castrating skunks for the rest of my life.'

'James, it'll get easier, I promise.' I struggle to know the right thing to say. 'Try to remember you broke up with her for a reason,' I suggest, gently.

'Yeah, but right now the reason feels pretty flimsy.' He lights another cigarette. 'I have no right to be jealous or upset,' he maintains. 'I was the one who thought I didn't love her enough to go the whole distance, but what exactly *am* I looking for? The truth is, I had everything, Flo, and I threw it away thinking the grass might be greener somewhere else. Listen, ignore me; it's your last weekend and I don't want to ruin it. She's moved on. It's time I did the same.'

'But you have moved on,' I say, leaning over the railings

next to him. 'It was probably just hearing her voice, remembering the past, all the good times you shared. You're allowed to feel sad, okay? Emma was a big part of your life, and you still care for her. It just feels like—'

'The end of an era?'

I nod. 'Exactly. I know this might sound spoilt – here I am going to New York and getting engaged – but change terrifies me. The thought of leaving Granny, Maddie and you *terrifies* me,' I repeat, reaching out to touch his hand. 'I'll never forget living with you, how much you helped me through one of the toughest periods of my life. And what am I going to do without Justin Timberlake singing in my shower?'

His expression softens. 'The stupid thing is I always imagined we'd live together for ever. How naïve is that?' James laughs at himself. 'Nothing lasts, right.'

'You're going to be fine, James Bailey. In fact, *more* than fine. One day you're going to meet someone extraordinary, you'll live in the country and have an army of mini Baileys along with your two Labradors, and we'll look back on this conversation and know everything happened for a reason.'

'Right,' he says, as if that's enough emotion for one night. 'We'd better go inside otherwise Maddie will be sending out a search party.'

I link arms with his and we return to the kitchen. 'By the way, I don't want an army,' he sets me straight. 'Two at the most.'

I laugh. 'I'm going to miss you, James.'

'I'll miss you too.'

## 9

### Peggy

The only time Beth and I spoke about the risk she carried was in 1993 when Flo was about to turn three. We had heard groundbreaking news that the HD gene had been identified, making it possible for those at risk to discover their fate with a simple blood test.

Yet I begged Beth not to do it.

I thought it better to cling on to the hope that my daughter didn't have HD, rather than allow a test to destroy it. I couldn't cope with losing both a husband and a daughter – and possibly eventually a grandchild – to this disease.

*It would kill me.*

'How can I help?' says a young-sounding woman on the charity helpline after she has introduced herself and snapped me out of my reverie.

*Don't hang up like last time, Peggy. And the time before that . . .*

'Oh yes, hello,' I say, 'I was wondering . . . I have a friend – er – *Maureen*. She's going through a terrible time.'

'I'm sorry to hear that.'

'She has a granddaughter, you see, who could have HD. Her mother was gene positive, but she died without telling her daughter anything about it so now Flo doesn't know—'

'Sorry, could you slow down, please? Who's Flo?'

'Sorry, yes.' Breathe again. '*Maureen* is unsure if she should tell her granddaughter or not.'

'I see. Flo is the granddaughter?'

'That's right.' *Oh, do keep up.* 'So I was wondering what advice I could give her, I imagine this happens all the time? She's particularly anxious because she's about to move abroad with her boyfriend—'

'I'm sorry, I'm not following. Maureen's leaving—'

'Of course she's worried that Flo – sorry, what did you say?'

'Who's leaving? You said—'

I shake my head in a tizzy. 'Flo's leaving! So Maureen is worried that her granddaughter could become pregnant without knowing she's at risk, so it's all very difficult.'

'I think I understand.'

*About time!*

'She's a dear friend of mine and I hate to see her in such distress. But I'm not sure what advice I can give her. I wondered whether I should tell Flo, I mean, whether *Maureen* should tell Flo or not? I think she should, don't you?'

'Maureen is lucky to have a friend like you,' the woman says, 'and there *is* something you can do, Mrs . . . ?'

'*Maureen*. I mean, Mrs Andrews. I'm *Peggy*!'

*Oh dear Lord.*

'Mrs Andrews, do tell *Maureen* to give us a call. We're here to help.'

My heart sinks. 'But what would you tell Maureen? I can pass it on to her. She's nervous, you see, to pick up the telephone.'

'We really do need to talk to her directly.'

There's a long silence.

'Please pass on to Maureen that she doesn't need to be scared of picking up the phone. We are trained to talk to people who find themselves in exactly these kinds of situations – which are very common – and every call is confidential.' She pauses. 'We understand how difficult this must be.'

*You have no idea.*

'She might find it comforting talking to us. It could help her feel less alone.'

She waits.

'Mrs Andrews?'

'Yes, yes, I'm here. Thank you,' I say eventually. 'So, there's no advice you can give me right now?'

'We often advise people to practise the conversation first before talking to someone. Rehearse it in front of a mirror or we will happily go over some role play with you, I mean with *Maureen*, if that would help?'

I jump when I hear a knock on the door. 'Thank you, I'll pass that on to her,' I say, abruptly hanging up and staggering to the front door. I look through the peephole and see Ricky in a red crochet hat holding a bunch of flowers. I haven't seen him since he nursed my wound just over three weeks ago.

I feel so out of sorts that I'm tempted to go back to pretending I'm not in. Or hide behind the sofa.

'Hello,' he says when I open the door. Elvis rushes to greet him as if he's a long-lost friend. 'I was wondering how your leg was, Peggy? I know these wounds can take weeks to heal.'

'I'm much better. The nurse said you did a grand job.'

'Good. Well these are for you.' He hands me the flowers.

'Oh Ricky, how kind, but I'm far too old for you.'

He laughs. He waits.

*I suppose I must*: 'Would you like to come in?'

I put the kettle on before arranging the lilies into a vase. I tell Ricky to sit down, even though my chairs look far too small for him. In fact, everything looks miniature around Ricky. 'How do you like your tea?'

'Black, one sugar, thanks,' he says, arranging his long legs under the table.

'Have you always been a nurse?' I ask, reaching into the cupboard for my teapot.

He shakes his head. 'My dream was to be a famous footie player. I left school aged fifteen, applied to clubs across the country. They wrote back saying I was too old.'

'Oh, what a shame.'

'Maybe it was a blessing. What's meant to be, and all that. Anyway, I stopped dreaming and got a proper job on reception at a medical centre in Ealing. When they began to train their staff to take blood, I was terrified of needles, had to practise at home on an orange,' he says, picking one up from my fruit bowl and playing with it in his hands. 'But it got me interested, you know? People would often come in, I'd take their blood and then they'd whip off their tops and ask me to take a look at the mole on their back or an odd lump under their arm. I've seen some strange sights in my time, Peggy, many I wouldn't like to see again.'

I chuckle at that.

'Anyway, I started reading medical books in the library, I wanted to be better equipped when the next person asked me my humble opinion, so I decided to go to university as a mature student and train as a nurse.'

'How wonderful!'

'It was. I was one of four men out of a hundred and eighty women. What's not to love?' His face lights up. 'Seriously, it's humbling looking after people. When I work on the hospital wards, I see so much suffering and heartache, but there is love and laughter too. Nursing has opened up my eyes to how precious life is. I've seen people dying, Peggy. I've held their hands as they've breathed their last breath.'

I think of my Tim.

'I always tell my son, Leo, that health is a gift. Not that he listens. But one day he'll get it.'

'You're right. Health is a gift.' I look at him, fantasizing about the relief I'd get from someone else knowing my secret. Perhaps Ricky would have advice, especially being a nurse. 'The thing is, Ricky . . .'

*Say it.*

'The thing is?' he repeats.

*Don't say it.*

'So, how long have you lived in London?'

'Lived here all my life, grew up in Stamford Brook round the corner. What were you about to say?'

'But where are you from? Are you a West Indian?'

He seems to find that funny. 'Jamaican. My family moved here for a better life.'

I offer him the tin of biscuits. 'Was it a better life?'

'It was tough, but happy, you know. We lived on a council estate. Everyone thinks they're rough and all that, but it was a community. I think we've lost a bit of that. People like to keep to themselves these days, plugged into their devices or watching TV. In my days, we didn't have computers or mobiles. We had to talk. We looked out for each other. It taught me to help others, not just number one. We were never rich, but Mum had more opportunities with work over here.'

'And your father?'

'Dad walked out on us when I was six weeks old.' His smile doesn't reach his eyes this time.

'And you've never seen him since?'

'Saw him when I was eleven. I was outside playing footie, mud on my shirt and smeared across my face, when someone said to me, "Ricky, your dad's back". I froze, then ran off the pitch, sprinted home, raced up the stairs, and flung myself through the front door. But you know what? I was standing in front of a stranger.' The smile has disappeared completely now. 'He could have been anyone. I didn't feel a thing.'

I get up, overcome with emotion. I take a piece of kitchen roll and dab it at my eyes.

'I'd always had this fantasy that I'd be the next David Beckham and that one day my dad would turn up to a match and watch me score. He'd feel proud of his son and after the game I'd run into his arms. How daft is that?'

'It's not daft. Not at all, Ricky.' My hand shakes as I pour him another cup of tea. 'My mother bolted too.'

Ricky looks surprised. 'Why? When?'

'It was just before the war. I don't remember the day she left. I was only a baby. She met an American, and America was a safer place to be back then, so off she went to start her new life.'

'Why the hell didn't she take you with her?'

'My father told her she couldn't because those journeys were treacherous, and I doubt she argued. My father then went off to war, so my aunt Celia raised me until he came home, which miraculously he did. Celia was the opposite of my mother: quiet, studious, kind, caring, never going to win a beauty contest.' I smile. 'She raised me single-handedly, loved me like her own. I was lucky. It all worked out for the best.'

'Did you ever see your mum again?'

'Occasionally.'

I can hear her now, regaling me with stories of parties she'd been to and all the places and people she'd met on her travels. They were always unsatisfactory visits that didn't help to heal the wound. They only made it deeper. As I grew older, I began to wonder if she were even capable of love. Celia told me much later on in life that even as a child she had never made real friends; she couldn't keep them. She was always selfish, the kind of person who could never share.

'Well, there we are,' I say. 'These things happen.'

'But these things *shouldn't* happen,' Ricky raises his voice. 'You should not walk out on your kids. Don't have them if you don't want them.'

I close my eyes, trying to block out the image of sitting by my mother's side at the hospice, the day before she died. She was in her late sixties by then; her illness and death was sudden, a cancer that claimed her in weeks.

'I forgive you, Mum,' I'd said.

Her face had darkened. 'Forgive me for what, Peggy? I haven't done anything wrong.'

'It is what it is,' I continue, fighting hard not to crumple into tears in front of Ricky.

'What it is, Peggy, is pretty damn crap. You deserved more.'

I look at my neighbour dressed in his crochet hat and football shirt, shocked that I'm telling him things I've kept buried so deep all my life. I never even told Beth how much my mother's rejection had hurt me. Only Tim knew, but he could read me like a book. Yet no one knows about the last conversation I had with her.

'Thank you,' I say to Ricky. 'You deserved better too.'

I head to the sink and stare out of the window. Beth's death is like an ocean of sadness that floods me every day. She must have been so frightened, watching her father deteriorate day by day, and yet I still put myself first. I'm more like my mother than I realize.

I hear Ricky's chair scrape back. 'Well, I'd better be off. Thank you for . . .'

He stops and turns me round to face him. 'Peggy, what's wrong?'

Next his arms are around me, and I don't pull away.

I can't fight this anymore. I have never cried in front of someone. Yet soon I can't stop, Ricky holding me in his arms.

'Say something, Ricky,' I urge, cradling my mug of tea. 'Tell me I'm a useless old woman, that I deserve this—'

'That's hard,' is all he mutters.

'But it's all my fault,' I insist.

Ricky takes off his jumper and places it around my shoulders. 'It's not your fault. None of this is anyone's fault.'

'If I hadn't made Beth swear—'

'Listen, Peggy, hindsight is a wonderful thing, but the

way I see it, the past is gone and the only thing that's up for grabs is the future.'

I inhale deeply, waiting for what's coming next.

'You need to tell her,' Ricky says, 'because keeping this from Flo is tearing you apart.'

'Fourteen years I looked after him. The last seven were ... unimaginable.'

'Oh, Peggy.' He takes my hand. 'I'm sorry.'

I can't speak for fear of crying again.

'I wouldn't want to know if I were at risk or not. I wouldn't take the test,' he continues, his tone gentle, 'but I'd at least want to make that decision for myself. Everyone has that right. And you know what, Peggy?'

'What?' I ask, my voice no louder than a whisper.

'It's not just about Flo anymore. Theo's involved now; this is going to affect his future. And when they get married, they're probably going to want kids too, so ...' He stops, as if I can work out the rest. 'They can still go ahead and have a family, but Flo might want to take the test first, or she might want to get advice from a professional. So much has changed since your husband was alive, Peggy. There's a lot more research going on, more options, but Flo and Theo need to know about them.'

Everything he's saying makes sense, but still the thought of telling Flo terrifies me. I press my head into my hands. 'Have you ever done anything bad, Ricky?'

'Hasn't everyone done something bad once in their life? It's a rite of passage.'

'I mean *really* bad.'

'Robbery. How's that for you?'

'That is bad.'

'I was sixteen, I could have plastered my bedroom walls with rejection letters from footie teams, so one day my best mate coaxed me into playing truth or dare. We'd been out drinking; I was high as a kite. We broke into a house and trashed the place, grabbed cash and jewellery, even the kid's toys. We never got caught, but I still have sleepless nights thinking about what we did. If anyone stole from me now, or from my children, I'd kill them. But Peggy, what you've done, it's not bad in the same way—'

'I've made such terrible choices.'

'To protect the people you love.'

'And to protect myself.'

He pulls his chair closer to mine. 'You say you wish you'd supported Beth, that you'd put her first? Well, now you've got the chance to put it right, to make amends.'

I nod.

'So make the right choice now and be there for Flo.'

Tears come to my eyes. 'If only we knew what Beth had wanted.'

'I may be speaking out of turn, but I don't think she'd have wanted this. I imagine she was protecting Flo, too, but the thing is, you can't protect a child for ever. That little girl has grown up and she's about to make some big decisions about her future, and in my book, keeping her in the dark is the very opposite of protecting her. She may hate you to begin with, but you're going to need to be strong because Flo is going to need you more than ever.'

I realize that Ricky is right, not just about what I have to do, but about Beth. I can only imagine she didn't say a word because she was hoping and praying that Flo had escaped the odds.

After all Tim had it, Beth did . . . surely Flo can't.

She just can't.

# 10

**Flo**

Maddie and I hardly slept a wink. She was snoring and nicking most of the duvet, and I was tossing and turning, waiting to hear the sound of a key in the lock and James coming home. Last night after supper he said he needed some fresh air, some space. Normally when he's stressed after a long day at work, or if something is bothering him, the first thing he does is to go for a run. But last night he never came back. I hope he didn't do anything stupid like take Vera out for an over-the-limit ride.

As I walk to the kitchen, I can see James's bedroom door is wide open, his bed not slept in. He usually lets me know if he's not coming home. It's always been one of our house rules.

'I hope he's all right,' I mutter to Maddie, pouring myself a glass of water.

'Emma's news hit him hard,' she reflects. 'I don't know why he left her. She was perfect for him.'

'I might send him a text,' I say, knowing I'm feeding my fears, but ever since Mum died, I panic, thinking a freak accident has happened to another person I love.

*Relax. He's not lying in a hospital bed attached to wires and tubes, fighting for his life.*

Maddie touches my arm, resigned to my paranoia. 'Don't. He probably stayed over at Kate's.'

Kate's the personal trainer he met jogging in the park who he's been dating now for seven weeks, and Maddie's probably right. So why do I have this awful feeling in the pit of my stomach, as if something terrible were about to happen?

My mobile rings. Please let that be James.

It's Granny. It's early for her to ring.

'Flo, I need to see you,' she says the moment I pick up. 'Can I come over?'

'Right now?'

'Yes.'

'Is everything all right?'

'I'd like to talk to you, face to face.'

'Granny, what is it?' I ask, the pitch of my voice causing Maddie to look over with concern. 'Can't you tell me now?'

'I'll be with you in half an hour,' she says, hanging up abruptly.

'What do you think it could be?' Maddie asks, adding she'd better make herself scarce.

She's unwell. I knew it; it isn't just my imagination. She's been keeping something from me.

# 11

## Peggy

Flo buzzes me in and I march up to the first floor.

*I must not lose my nerve. I can do this.*

*Remember what Ricky said. I am doing the right thing.*

When Flo opens the door, immediately she asks what's wrong, clearly agitated.

'Let's sit down,' I say, trying to keep my voice calm as I follow Flo into the kitchen.

'Do you want a cup of coffee?' she asks.

'Nothing, thank you.' I take a seat.

'Sorry about the mess, I cooked James and Maddie supper last night—'

'Flo, what I'm about to say isn't easy.'

She pulls up a chair and takes my hands into hers. 'You're not well, are you? Is this to do with your heart and you didn't want to say something sooner, because you didn't want me to put my plans on hold?'

*I wish it were that simple.*

I shake my head. 'It's about your mother.'

'Mum?' She lets go of my hands. 'What about her?'

I look into her eyes, hating myself for what I'm about to say, even if I know I no longer have a choice. As Ricky said, Theo is involved now.

'Tell me,' Flo pleads. 'You're scaring me, Granny.'

*I'm scaring myself, too.*

Flo watches me open my handbag and pull out a white envelope. I lay it on the table with a trembling hand.

'What is it?'

'Please read it, Flo.'

She picks it up, opens it.

'Huntington's Disease,' she says, staring at the letter with the NHS confidential stamp printed across it, Beth's name written inside a box, with her date of birth and hospital number. 'What's that?'

'It's neurological. It damages the brain cells and begins to affect your movement, walking, your memory . . .' I stop. I don't want to tell Flo too much too soon.

'Mum didn't have that.'

'She may have developed early symptoms. Often they go unnoticed.' I recall Tim coming home, frustrated because he couldn't play golf, telling me he couldn't stand still for long enough to hit the ball. Beth and I had teased him. We'd called him 'Mr Wobble Legs'.

To think we'd laughed.

'But Mum wasn't ill.' Flo shakes her head in disbelief. 'She would have told me; we told each other everything.'

'Perhaps not everything.'

She looks at me as if I'm the enemy, which I suppose right now I am.

'Yes, everything,' she insists. She reads out from the letter, *'Dear Miss Andrews, following our appointment to discuss the test results* . . . I don't understand. She took this test when I was eight.'

'You were young, Flo, far too young for her to burden you with this.'

'Did you know?'

I look away.

'Granny?'

'I didn't know she'd taken the test, no.'

She stands up and paces the room. 'How long have you had this letter?'

'That doesn't matter—'

'It does. When did you find this?'

I don't say anything.

Her eyes widen in shock. 'You found this letter when we were clearing out Mum's house, didn't you?' she grills me. 'Only days after Mum died! Why didn't you tell me then?'

'I couldn't; you were so vulnerable. I've wanted to tell you for *so* long, Flo, but there has never been a good time.'

Flo laughs derisively. 'Not once in *five years* have you found a good time to talk to me about this?'

'I've had sleepless nights wondering what to do.'

'I had every right to know. This is about my *mother*.'

'I know.'

'So why are you telling me now?'

I twist my wedding ring round my finger, both hands shaking.

'Why tell me when I've quit my job and I'm happy?' she demands. 'When I'm about to go to America? Mum tested positive for this Huntington's thing and she didn't tell me, but what good is it you dragging it up now, raking up the past?' I jump when Flo slams her fist against the table. 'Tell me!'

And then, at long last, the truth comes out, as little more than a whisper. 'Because it's hereditary,' I pause. 'My Tim had it too.'

The colour drains from her face. 'Granddad had this? You said he had a form of Parkinson's.'

'Your mother inherited Huntington's Disease from her father.'

She sits down and places a hand over her mouth. 'Are you saying I might have this?'

I want to hold her in my arms, tell her it will all be all right and that she won't have it. But I can't. 'Yes, Flo, you might. You have a fifty-fifty chance.'

Flo leaves the room.

I don't know what to do. I'm about to follow her when she returns with her laptop and sits down at the kitchen table.

'If this is something I might have,' she says, tapping her keyboard, 'I want to know exactly what it is.'

'I can explain. I can tell you.'

'Movement problems, chorea,' she reads off her screen. 'An individual with HD has no control ... Emotional and behavioural issues ... the individual may experience depression, mood swings, anxiety, apathy—'

'Flo, stop!'

'Caused by an inherited alteration or mutation in a gene called huntingtin. First symptoms generally start in a person in their late 30s, but can appear earlier or later ...' She freezes. 'There's no cure.'

'Not yet, but there's far more research—'

'Look at this.' She turns the screen towards me at lightning pace, showing me a video of a man in a padded cell, tormented in his own body, kicking and hitting the walls.

'No.' I try to take the laptop away. 'Tim wasn't like that. You can't trust everything you see on the internet.'

'No, I can't trust *you*,' she says.

*You can. You can trust me. Oh, what have I done?*

'All this time you've known—'

'No! No, Flo. I knew your mum was at risk, but I had no idea she'd taken the test until I found the letter. You've got to believe me.'

Yet my words mean nothing. They have come five years too late.

'Hold on ... If I marry Theo and we start a family, are you saying what I think you're—'

'If you have HD, your children will be at risk too,' I finish for her.

'No,' she says. 'No. This isn't . . .'

Flo is struggling to breathe; she clasps her stomach as if I have punched her repeatedly, and it breaks my heart.

This is why I didn't tell her. Who would want to inflict this kind of pain on someone they love?

'This can't be happening,' she murmurs, 'this can't be true.'

'I wish it weren't true,' I say, rushing to her side, but she pushes me away.

'Flo, it doesn't mean you can't still get married and have a family, or do all the things you want to do, and—'

'Go, Granny,' she says, quietly, staring at the floor.

'I'm sure we can get advice. Things have changed so much since Tim was alive,' I stress, remembering what Ricky had encouraged me to say. 'We can get through this, together.'

'I need you to leave, before I say something I regret.'

'Flo, blame me, hate me, be angry, but please don't shut me out.'

'Go.' She still can't look at me. 'The fact I might have this is bad enough, but what's even worse is that you chose not to tell me.'

'Flo, please, let's talk—'

'Granny, GET OUT!' she shouts, looking me straight in the eye now. 'I will never forgive you for this. Never.'

I don't even notice James and Maddie standing at the

kitchen door until Flo rushes past me and out of the room. I shudder when I hear a door slamming shut.

Flo won't ever forgive me for keeping her in the dark. Why should she? And the truth is, I will never forgive myself.

# 12

## Flo

It's close to ten o'clock in the evening, and Maddie, James and I have been sitting round the kitchen table for hours, trying to make sense of today. Right now, I feel trapped in a maze with no way out.

'My jaw.' I touch it. 'It's never closed properly. It could be a sign—'

'Look, why don't we book an appointment to see your GP first thing tomorrow?' Maddie suggests.

I chew on my thumbnail. 'And I'm always losing my house keys.' *Just like Mum used to.*

'That doesn't mean anything except you're scatty, like me,' Maddie sets me straight.

*But I used to call Mum scatty.*

James agrees. 'You need to see a doctor. Someone who can give you proper advice about what to do next.'

I stare up at the ceiling. 'I have a week left. I've given up my room, my job. How can I just take off as if nothing has happened?'

'Maybe talk to Theo?' Maddie's tone is soft. 'I know it won't be an easy conversation, but I'm sure he'll understand if you need more time to work things out here.'

'The room's still yours,' James adds, 'for however long you need it.'

I can't contemplate the thought of telling Theo yet. 'Why couldn't Mum have told me the truth?'

'She probably wanted to protect you,' Maddie says.

Once again I feel anger raging within me. 'I wouldn't call it protection; I'd call it denial, wouldn't you? What did she think would happen once she started developing symptoms?' I place my head in my hands. 'My entire childhood has been a lie.'

'Do you know what I think you should do?' James says.

'What?' I ask, a glimmer of hope in my voice.

'Go to bed.'

I laugh. 'There's no way I can sleep, but you go, there's no point all of us—'

'I'm not going anywhere until I know you're going to stop scaring yourself.' Maddie gestures to my laptop, to the videos I've found online about HD.

I turn to James. 'Maybe you could put me down?'

'Stop it,' he says.

'Steal some meds from work,' I go on. 'A shot of something lethal.'

'For fuck's sake, Flo, stop it,' James insists, fear laced through his voice too.

My phone vibrates. I shiver when I see Theo's name.

**Just checking in ☺ Hope all well at home. Can't wait to see you, not long now. Love you xx**

I toss my phone on to the table. 'Maybe I shouldn't tell him yet.'

I notice Maddie and James exchange a look. 'Don't worry about that tonight,' Maddie says. 'This is a massive shock; you need to take your time, think it through.'

'Mum had *years* to tell me. What was she thinking keeping it from me?' I continue to torment myself. 'Maybe that's why she had the accident? She could have been lost, confused. I always thought something didn't add up.' I look at them both. 'What am I going to do?' My voice breaks. 'I'm scared.'

James pulls me into his arms and soon the three of us are holding on to one another, wrapped up in this new world that we are now facing, a world that's so very different from the one I was living in only yesterday.

# 13

## Peggy

I don't know how long I've been sitting here, in the dark.

I close my eyes and see Tim. He is trying to say something to me, but no words come out. All he can do is scratch his face like an animal. I kneel down by his side, desperately trying to work out what it is he wants. I rush to get him a glass of water. The doctor says I shouldn't, not when he's fed and hydrated on a peg, but it's the only thing that seems to give him comfort.

He drinks the water from a straw, I press a little to his lips. 'Tim, it's all right, it's all right,' I say, stroking the burning red lines of frustration and anxiety across his cheeks, wishing I could take it all away. Wave a magic wand and see my old Tim, the Tim who used to come home from work late and slip into bed, whispering, 'Are you awake, Peg?' to which I'd say, 'I am now,' before we laughed, and he'd take my face into his hands and kiss me.

I miss his touch. Being held.

I miss someone needing me.

I continue to sit in the darkness, paralysed.

*Oh, Peggy, what have you done?*

I ignore Ricky's message on my answering machine. I don't eat or drink a thing. Elvis is deprived of his walk. It could be glorious sunshine or the most beautiful full moon outside for all I care. Because what is my life worth without the people I love in it?

It's ten o'clock. Normally I watch the news before bed, but the thought of being cocooned in yet more darkness terrifies me. I unlock my front door and walk outside, with no idea as to where I'm going or what I'm doing. All I know is I can't be alone for a moment longer.

*I need a drink.*

I walk round the block, stopping when I come to a blackboard sign mounted on the pavement outside my local pub: Live Music Tonight.

With no hesitation I buy a ticket on the door and head inside. The pub is surprisingly full for a Sunday evening, although I'm never out on a Sunday night so I'm hardly the best judge. The noise is a welcome distraction. I head straight to the bar and order myself a double vodka and tonic.

I'd anticipated anger. Resentment. I knew she'd feel let down.

But I also thought I'd feel relieved. To have at last told her, once and for all, to have got it off my chest.

Yet I feel nothing but shame.

I wonder whether Flo will still go to America. In many ways, I hope she does. If she puts off her plans, I fear she will resent me even more. If that's even possible.

I pray that Theo will support her, and that her life will go on.

I pay for my drink and fight my way through the crowd to the nearest free table.

'Give it up, please, for The West Brothers,' someone announces, before everyone cheers and wolf whistles. And that's when I see him on the small stage at the other side of the pub, his smiling face shining under the spotlights.

Ricky steps forward, a guitar strap on his shoulder and a microphone in his hand, dressed all in black apart from his eye-catching red hat. He looks at me with shock. I can tell he wants to come over, but I shake my head, encouraging him to do what he came here to do. I even raise a smile and wave at him, because the last thing I want to do is talk.

The music starts.

Someone is on the drums and another member of the band zigzags across the stage in some kind of stupor with his cap worn back to front. I knock back my drink.

*Oh, what a dreadful noise. So dreadful I might just drown myself in it.*

\*

'Peggy,' a distant voice says. I feel someone touching my shoulder. 'Peggy, wake up.'

Slowly I stir. 'Is it breakfast?' I sit up, my throat as dry as parchment, my head as heavy as a brick.

'Peggy, it's Ricky. My music must have sent you to sleep.'

I look around me, noticing I'm the only person left in the pub aside from Ricky and a man drying up some glasses behind the bar. Then I remember with a sinking feeling my conversation with Flo. It wasn't a dream.

'I must get home.' I stagger to my feet.

'I'll walk you back.' Ricky follows me outside. 'I knocked on your door earlier. I left a message on your machine.'

'I was out.'

He knows I wasn't, but he's kind enough to let me off the hook. 'If I'm honest, Peggy, you're the last person I was expecting to see here tonight. I didn't know you were into dub rock.'

'Dub what?'

'Dub music. Reggae? Never mind.' He touches my arm, lightly. 'How did it go with Flo?'

I quicken my pace. *What if she has tried to call me?*

'Peggy?'

We turn the corner into our street and Ricky follows me to my front door. 'Peggy, please talk to me. I can see you're upset.'

'I'm fine. It's over. I said it; it didn't go well, but there we are. It was never going to be easy. Goodnight, Ricky.'

He pushes past me and walks into my house.

'What are you doing? Go home, back to your family!' I

shout, since I've had just about enough of it today. 'You're not my knight in shining armour.'

'No, no, I'm not. I'm your friend.' He follows me into the kitchen. 'And I'm proud of you.'

I frown, undeserving of his praise.

'I'm not just saying that, Peggy. You did a courageous thing today, all right?'

'Years too late.'

'But you still did it.'

I collapse into a chair, my body aching. 'You should have seen her face, Ricky. All the trust between us, broken in an instant.'

'You can get that back.'

'Can I? How?'

'You earn it back.'

'I can't lose her.'

'You won't.'

'How do you know that, Ricky?'

'Because you're going to fight for her. You just have to give her some time first.'

'How long?'

'At least a few days—'

'But—'

'And then you go round to see her again.'

'But what if she won't talk to me?'

'You *make* her talk to you,' he says, as if it's his battle too. 'You knock on her door until she opens it. You talk to her until she listens.'

'I don't know. I'm tired.'

'I know you are, but you can't just curl up into a ball and hide.'

'Can't I? That sounds like a wonderful plan.' For the first time that evening, I smile.

'You're a strong woman, Peggy. Anyone can be a hero for fifteen minutes. You looked after your husband for almost fifteen years. You gave up your job, your life—'

'That's not heroic. I loved him and I'd do it all over again.'

'Exactly, so try to find the old Peggy again, the Peggy who stood by Tim through thick and thin, and the Peggy who lost her daughter but got through all that grief and trauma of losing their child, because that's who Flo needs.'

I take in a deep breath as if I'm about to enter the boxing ring again for another round. 'Ricky, how is it you know all the right things to say? When Beth died, no one knew how to talk to me. I'd hear all the usual "time heals" or "are you feeling better now?" as if moving past your grief was like getting over a cold. As if grief had a time limit. Many of my friends didn't even dare to ask, so in the end I just, well, I lost touch with the world. I think I lost me,' I say, realizing that truth for the very first time.

I look at this man, choosing to be with me late on a Sunday evening, to make sure I don't drink myself into oblivion. This man who, somehow, I feel an extraordinary bond with.

'I lost someone too,' he confides. 'Shelley and I lost a child before Mia came along. Our baby, Rose.'

'I'm so sorry.'

'It was cot death.'

'Oh, Ricky.' I reach for his hand. 'I'm so sorry,' I repeat.

'It was hard. We'd only known her for a few weeks, but there was always this agonizing feeling at the back of our minds, you know. What if we'd done something differently, bought a new mattress or picked her up in time? She died under my watch, Peggy. I was the only one home while Shelley was out with friends, having a well-earned night off. I slept through it all while my little baby girl died.'

I place a hand over my mouth, tears filling my eyes.

'The grief crushes you, you know? Suffocates you. You get to a point when you think it'll never go away. It's why Shelley and I moved here. We couldn't stay at our old rented place. Each time we walked into the nursery we lost her all over again.'

'I don't know what to say.'

Ricky shrugs. 'There is nothing to say, Peggy, nothing that can make it better or take the pain away. But when I picked up that photograph of Beth, I recognized you'd been through it too. I don't know . . . it's like you're part of a club you sure as hell don't want to belong to, but it helps if there are other members you can talk to. It makes you feel less alone.'

I agree. 'Well, I'm here for you Ricky, if you ever need to talk.'

He looks up at me, nodding gently. 'We nearly split because Shelley couldn't stop blaming me. She needed to be angry with someone and I was the easiest target. She packed her bags and left. I kept knocking on Shelley's door and talking to her until she listened to me. Until she understood we're stronger together, not apart, that we'd already lost Rose and we couldn't lose each other too.'

'She's a lucky woman.'

'I'm a lucky man, too. She's my rock.'

'Won't she be wondering where you are now?' I say, not actually wanting him to leave me on my own.

'I'm not going anywhere until I know you're okay.'

'Thank you, Ricky.'

I don't know how long we sit quietly, my tiny pale hand in his, until I break the silence, saying, 'How do you wash your hair? It's so long.'

Ricky throws back his head and laughs. 'Peggy, you crack me up, mate.'

'But isn't it uncomfortable in bed? Doesn't it itch and dig in?' I touch my own hair as if I can feel the discomfort.

'My mum used to try to get me to cut it, especially for job interviews, but there are lawyers and docs with dreadlocks, too. My hair is my identity. It says, "this is me, I'm comfortable with who I am—"'

'So stick it up your pipe and smoke it,' I finish.

'Exactly. Confidence is the best gift you can give your children. And self-belief. It's the best gift you can give yourself, Peggy.'

I hear my mother telling me all those years ago that I'd better accept Tim's marriage proposal because no one else was going to ask me. I see her scowling at me on her death-bed, saying she'd done nothing wrong by abandoning me. I'd walked away, fighting back the tears, saying nothing, not standing up for myself.

*This is me, Mum, this is who I am.*

She never loved me, but it's time I started to love myself.

And then I can stand up, feel tall and finally fight for my Flo.

# 14

**Flo**

'Morning,' I say to James when he joins me in the kitchen, his hair still damp from the shower.

He stares at me as if I'm mad, or a ghost.

'How did you sleep?' I ask, buttering my toast.

'I didn't. Did you?'

*I wish he'd stop looking at me like he's already planning my funeral.*

'I slept fine,' I say. 'Sorry if I kept you up last night.'

James casts an eye over my navy skirt and lilac shirt. 'Are you going to work?'

'Yep. It's my last week; I've got so much to do.'

*Stop looking at me like that, James.*

'I thought maybe you'd want to take the day off?' he suggests. 'I could too? I'm sure my boss would understand if—'

'I don't want anyone else to know about this.'

'Not even Theo?' Maddie says, entering the kitchen.

I shake my head. 'Especially not Theo. I've made a plan.'

'Why do I have a feeling I need to sit down for this?' James says.

'I'm calling my GP.'

'Great, that's good,' Maddie says with relief.

'I want to have the blood test straightaway.'

'*Straightaway*?' both Maddie and James repeat at the same time.

I nod. 'This week, before I go to New York.'

James looks dubious. 'From what I've read, you have to have genetic counselling—'

'I know,' I interrupt, 'but I'm sure in exceptional circumstances you can cut corners.'

James looks doubtful. 'I don't know, the guidelines seem pretty strict . . .'

'Who cares about guidelines?' I snap.

James glances at Maddie for backup.

'I need to know now,' I reinforce. 'I can't have counselling for months. I don't need it. I don't want it. All I know is I can't have this hanging over me.'

I catch them exchanging yet another look.

'I understand,' Maddie says. 'I'd probably feel the same, but I'm not sure you should rush into this. It's such a big decision, Flo.'

She doesn't understand. 'It's not. This isn't going to change my life,' I insist. I wait for them to say something but their silence speaks volumes. 'And I'm not telling Theo,'

I add, 'not unless I have to.' They won't change my mind on that front either. Telling him makes it an issue. Keeping quiet and taking the test puts me in control.

Maddie looks anxious, twisting a strand of her hair around her finger. 'Flo, are you sure you shouldn't tell him?'

'Why? Why scare him?'

'But I'm sure he'd understand,' she continues. 'He'd want to support you.'

'All I need to do is take the test and put this mess behind me.'

'And Granny Peg?' James asks.

'What about her?' I felt fine this morning, great, until James and Maddie came into the kitchen, dragging their doubts with them.

'Flo, she'll be anxious,' he reasons. 'I think you should let her know your plan—'

'You mean like *she* let me know. Like *my mother* let me know?'

'I get you're angry,' James tells me.

'No, you don't,' I fire back. 'You have no idea how this feels.'

'You're right, I don't,' he concedes. 'You have every right to be angry, but I imagine she must feel terrible too.'

'So she should!' I stand up. 'What did she expect, James, for me to just accept this and move on?'

'No, but—'

'She should have told Flo,' Maddie cuts in, trying to calm the situation down. 'To dump it on her now is not cool.'

'I'm not saying it is,' James argues, 'but it can't have been easy for her—'

'James, can you imagine if Mum had kept this from us all this time?' Maddie challenges him again.

'Exactly,' I echo, staring at him.

'I'd be furious,' James admits.

'And what if I'd got pregnant?' I protest. 'I'm going to take the blood test, but by not telling me, they'd have robbed me of that choice, and that's not fair.'

'I understand, but it's not fair Granny Peg lost her husband and her daughter because of it either,' James says, his voice fuelled with emotion. 'None of this is fair, Flo. Life's unfair.'

I have to stop myself from saying life hasn't dished out too many problems to the Bailey family. Idyllic childhood, two healthy, functional parents, both Maddie and James have successful careers . . . Life has given my family a second helping of troubles. But something stops me.

'Fine, but at some point both she and Mum should have—'

'Yes!' James stands up and faces me full on. 'They should have. But when people are terrified or anxious, denial is their biggest defence; often it's their *only* defence.' He lowers his voice, 'just as you're in denial now, Flo.'

I edge away from him. 'I'm not in denial.'

'Look, let's not argue about this,' Maddie intervenes, standing between us like a referee.

'You're eating breakfast and going to work as if this isn't a big deal,' James asserts.

'I'm making a positive plan.'

'But your plan—'

'That's enough,' Maddie warns him.

'I can't believe you're taking Granny's side, James,' I say, close to tears.

'I'll always be on your side, Flo, always,' he asserts. 'But all I'm trying to say is, maybe when you're grieving and terrified of losing another person close to you, things aren't as straightforward as you think. The last thing Granny Peg would have wanted was to hurt you.'

'Well, she should have thought about that sooner. You can't go wrong if you tell people the truth,' I state, 'right from the start.'

'If it's that simple then why not tell Theo?' James says.

'That's not fair,' I say, leaving the room.

'That was harsh,' I overhear Maddie scold him. 'Just leave her. You've said enough.'

I take the bus to work, relieved to be alone and out of the house.

*'You are number five in the queue,'* says an automated voice before I hear Handel's *Water Music. 'Thank you for waiting, your call is important to us'.*

As we approach Hammersmith Broadway: *'You are number three in the queue'.*

My phone warns me I have less than ten per cent battery power. I was so angry with James I forgot to charge it this morning. *'You are number one in the queue.'*

*Come on.*

'Bridge View Surgery, how can I help?' the perky receptionist says.

'Hi, yes, I need to see a doctor, please, today, as soon as possible.'

I hear her tapping some keys. 'Bear with me.'

Handel's *Water Music* returns.

She comes back on to the line. 'Sorry about the wait, the system's been playing up. Right. It looks like we have one last slot left with Dr Harris.'

'I'll take it. What time?' I wait. 'Hello?' I shake my phone. 'Hello?' My mobile screen goes black.

I stare out of the window, trying not to scream, especially when I realize I have missed my stop.

# 15

## Peggy

It's twenty-four hours since I last spoke to Flo. I'm cleaning the house – like I always do on a Monday morning – but for once it's not a chore, more of a welcome relief to keep busy. Yet nothing can stop me from thinking about Flo.

*Did she sleep?* I hope better than I did. *I can't imagine she went to work?*

I turn off the vacuum cleaner, the sitting room carpet now spotless. My furniture has never looked so glossy and new. I tackle the bathroom next.

*I know Ricky is right*, I think, as I polish the taps until they are gleaming. *I must give her some space.*

Next I move on to the sink, bath, mirror and the floor, and before I know it I'm rifling through the kitchen cupboards, chucking out cans of tinned peaches that expired back when Tim was still alive. They were his favourites.

I used to love baking cakes for Tim and Beth, and cooking with Flo. In fact, I used to love cooking full stop, but there seems little point when there is no one across the table who's going to say 'This is delicious, Peggy, what's in the sauce?' When Beth was growing up, Tim used to say to her, 'Your mother is the best cook in London, isn't she?'

'No, Papa, in the *world*,' Beth would finish.

After I have finished in the kitchen, I decide to tackle the bookshelves in the sitting room, rearranging my novels into alphabetical order. I fetch the mini ladder out of the downstairs broom cupboard and soon books are scattered across the floor.

I come across a collection of old edition Daphne du Maurier novels that Tim gave me one Christmas, not long after we married. He knew I was beguiled by her stories and he used to read them to Beth, too, when she was a young girl. I can see Beth now, sitting cross-legged by the fireplace with her dad after a fun day on the beach building sandcastles and burying him in the sand, listening to every word of *Rebecca* intently.

Those days were precious.

I stop when I see an old copy of *To Kill a Mockingbird*. I recall Tim saying to me one night in bed, in the early years of his HD diagnosis, 'Peg, when I can no longer read, will you read to me?' I imagine I'd reproved him for bringing up such a time, but he'd continued, 'I want to read all the classics like *To Kill a Mockingbird* or *Catcher in the Rye*. Promise me, Peg.'

And so I did. I spent hours reading to Tim, and those days were precious too.

I take a deep breath.

Time is an odd thing. When Tim was unwell and at home day after day, time often crawled by. My husband rushing out the door to get to work or to the airport with barely a second to kiss me goodbye seemed as if it had happened in another life. The idea of me working in an office seemed impossible while I was shaving my husband and dressing him for another day in front of the television, or a trip to the park in his wheelchair. And yet, here I am, almost twenty-five years since his death, wondering where the time has gone. In many ways, those days I spent reading to Tim feel like yesterday.

# 16

**Flo**

When I arrive at the office I head upstairs immediately, barely acknowledging Simon and Natalie who work on the ground floor sales desk. We're only a small team – six in total. I sit down and pick up the telephone. Thankfully, my boss, Harriet, who sits opposite me, hasn't arrived yet.

'Bridge View Surgery, how can I help?' says the receptionist again, this time not sounding quite so perky.

'Oh, yes, I called earlier but we got cut off.' I hear someone coming upstairs.

'I'm afraid we're fully booked now.'

'It's an emergency.'

'Right. What's the problem?'

Natalie approaches my desk. Natalie is twenty-eight and is originally from Poland, her long, iron-straight blonde hair sweeping down her shoulders. She wears dark-rimmed glasses for fashion rather than for need, having always fancied that sexy librarian look.

'It's private,' I say to the receptionist, 'but serious.'

'I'm fine,' I mouth to Natalie.

'Can you describe your symptoms?'

'I don't have any, but I'm anxious to have a blood test, just in case.'

'Are you pregnant?' Natalie mouths back.

'A blood test for what?' the receptionist continues, clearly confused by my cryptic code.

'When's the next available slot?' I ask.

'I suggest you ring back first thing tomorrow.'

'Can't you book me in now?'

'I'm sorry, the system doesn't allow me to do that. What I can do is put you down on a list and ask the duty doctor to call you.'

'I need to see someone now. I just need a test.'

Her patience is wearing thin – like mine. 'Would you like me to put your name down on the list or not?'

It's almost the end of the working day and I'm helping out downstairs since we're short-staffed, talking to a client about a possible trip to Cambodia and Vietnam.

'The ancient temples are fascinating,' I tell the woman who looks in her mid-thirties, dyed red hair.

*What am I going to do?* The duty doctor called back and said I needed to see a genetic counsellor before I can take the test. I can just hear James saying 'I told you so'.

'Yawn,' says the woman, rolling her eyes.

'How about a river-cruise, then?'

'Seasick. I also get really nervous flying,' she says. 'Can they upgrade me to First Class?'

*There's nothing Rodney Sinclair can't do*, I recall Theo saying to me the last time he was unwell. *He's a genius. Sorted out the mole on my back in no time. I'll give you his number.*

I spring out of my chair. 'Natalie, can you ...' I don't even finish my sentence before I'm outside, calling his number. There's no queue, no Handel's *Water Music*. I'm put through to his secretary, who gives me an appointment straight after work.

Natalie joins me outside. 'Flo, that was rude,' she reproves. 'We're not supposed to have our phones anywhere near us when we're with a client.'

'I know. I'm sorry.'

'You look exhausted,' she says, clearly noticing my distress.

'Listen, I might go home, do you mind?'

'You're *my* boss.'

'Not that you'd know it.' Finally I smile.

'I'm worried about you,' she says as she follows me back into the office. 'Are you nervous about leaving?'

'I'm fine, honestly, just tired. I'll do some work from home. Is she going to Cambodia?' I ask, gathering my jacket and handbag.

'I suggested ten days in the Caribbean instead and suddenly she wasn't nearly so nervous about flying.'

'Funny that,' I say, leaving the office, strengthened by the hope that Rodney Sinclair will be able to solve all my problems and give me a blood test tonight.

# 17

## Flo

'Come in,' says Dr Sinclair, tall and lean, dressed in a suit and a dapper navy and white spotted tie, his silvery grey hair giving him a note of distinction. 'I gather you know Theodore? A wonderful chap, fit as a fiddle. I think he only comes here for the fatherly advice and the gin and tonic.'

Everything in the room is plush, from the chintz curtains to the ornate chandelier hanging from the tall moulded ceiling. Dr Sinclair's mahogany desk is at the far side of the room, overlooking Harley Street.

No wonder Theo likes it here. If you have to be ill, at least be ill in style, he'd say. Dr Sinclair gestures for me to take a seat in the leather armchair. 'Now, how can I help you, young lady?'

My appointment is only twenty minutes so I waste no time in telling him. It's surprisingly easy telling a stranger, especially if you need something from them in return.

'Huntington's Disease' he repeats, narrowing his eyes. 'I haven't come across anyone at risk for a while.' He swivels round to his bookcase, filled with heavy volumes of medical books. He produces one of them and leafs through the pages.

'I was hoping I could take a blood test today.'

He looks up at me. 'Today?'

I nod, determined to appear calm.

'If I recollect, most people don't get tested for it. Why do you want to know?'

'Theo and I are engaged.' I show him my ring.

'Wonderful news; many congratulations.'

I smile. 'Thanks, it's all very exciting. Anyway, we want a family at some point so I'd rather know now than put it off.' Somehow I feel involving Theo will help my case. 'I'm joining him in New York, so it would be great to find out before I leave.'

'Right. I see.' He takes a sheet of cream headed paper from his leather in-tray. 'You seem to be of sound mind.'

'Yes, absolutely.'

He picks up his gold fountain pen and says out loud as he writes, 'You want to be tested because you want to be able to make an informed decision about planning a family.' He stops writing, peers at me again. 'And you are aware of the implications of either a negative or positive result?'

I nod. 'Yes. I've spoken about it in depth to my grandmother. You see, my grandfather and my mother had HD. Nothing can change the result, but at least if I know I can plan.'

He looks at me as if that makes complete sense. At last someone understands.

With relief, I watch as he continues to write. 'So does this mean I can take the test today?' I ask.

'I see no reason why not. "*I, Dr Rodney Sinclair,*' he says, jotting it down, '*have discussed the various considerations of genetic testing with Ms Florence Andrews. I can confirm she is of sound mental state to go ahead*". Voila!' I watch him sign his name on the bottom of the piece of paper before asking me to approve the following:

I, Florence Andrews, consent to the genetic testing for Huntington's Disease. I am aware of the implications of this test, but wish to proceed.

He hands me his pen.

I don't allow myself to dwell on what Maddie or James said to me this morning. Or what Mum would think.

*Did she have genetic counselling?* I don't care if she did or not. No one in my family has any right to judge the choices I make anymore.

Dr Sinclair puts on a pair of plastic gloves before he attaches a tourniquet around my upper arm. Gently he taps the inside of my arm to feel for a vein before the needle pierces my skin, blood filling the tube.

He places cotton wool over the injection site, telling me to press hard to stop the bleeding. 'When do you think we'll get the results?'

'I'm writing "Urgent",' he informs me, before folding the consent form into two and adding it to the clear plastic bag with the purple-capped blood test tube. 'It should take no more than a couple of days, Florence, maybe less.'

'Will you call me the moment you hear?'

'I'll call, but I'd also like you to come to the clinic to discuss the results.' He leads me towards the door. 'Please send my regards to Theodore.'

'Of course.' I nod. 'And please could you keep this appointment confidential.'

'But Theodore surely knows you're here?'

'If you could keep it between us I'd be grateful,' is all I say, in a voice I hardly recognize as my own.

On my way home, I touch the plaster on my arm, reassuring myself, not for the first time, that if I don't find out if I'm gene positive or not, I'll always assume the worst. I'll wake up every single morning wondering if this is the day I might get symptoms, and I don't want to live like that.

I'm going to get the results. They *will* be negative. And then I can pack my bags and begin my new life in a city far away from here.

# 18

## Peggy

Dr Amanda Harding leads me into her office, dressed in an elegant cream summer blouse with tailored linen trousers. She sits down at her desk. She's in her late fifties, or perhaps even early sixties – I find age hard to tell.

We look at one another inquisitively. I imagine it takes a certain type of person to be a genetic counsellor. Having to meet people like my Beth on a daily basis, people dealing with life-changing decisions and the prospect of living with HD or any other condition.

I'm certain she is assessing me just as much as I am her. She must have heard a fair amount about me from Beth, which I find unnerving. Surely she often wondered what kind of a dragon I was that Beth couldn't confide in me.

With shame, I glance at the empty chair next to mine,

thinking of all those lost years when I could have been here holding my daughter's hand.

*The past is gone*, I hear Ricky's voice inside my head. *The only thing that's up for grabs is the future.*

'It's kind of you to see me at such short notice,' I say, realizing how lucky I am that Dr Harding gave me an appointment less than forty-eight hours after I called her secretary to explain, in detail, my situation.

The idea to see Dr Harding came to me, as clear as daylight, when I was rearranging my novels into alphabetical order on my bookshelf. *That's it!* I'd almost fallen off the ladder wondering why on earth I hadn't thought about it before! I knew Beth *must* have confided in Dr Harding so if anyone knew my daughter's intentions it would be her. Perhaps she could answer the questions that kept me up at night, the most pressing being had Beth ever planned to tell Flo and me the truth.

I explained my plight to Dr Harding's secretary, my normal reserve going out the window. The secretary had understandably been most wary of me, saying she'd have to talk this through with Dr Harding, that this wasn't a run-of-the-mill situation. *You can say that again.* However, she warmed up considerably when she spoke to me for the second time, saying Dr Harding would like to see me, and as fate had it, there had been a cancellation.

'I'm glad I tracked you down.' Five years ago, Dr Harding moved from London to a hospital in Oxford. 'Do you mind?' I gesture to my notepad and pen. I was frightened I wouldn't remember to ask all the questions I had, so I jotted down a list with Ricky last night.

'Of course. How can I help?' Her voice is calm, her manner poised.

'Well, I wonder if you could talk to me about my daughter, Beth, and her sessions with you. There are things I need to know.'

'Generally, that would be confidential, but in this case, now that Beth is no longer with us' – her expression is full of compassion – 'and knowing how much your daughter would want me to help you, in whatever way I can ... is there anything in particular you'd like to talk about?'

I decide to tell her everything, cutting no corners.

'So, you see, Florence is terrified of her future, and although I'm in no position to judge Beth for keeping secrets, how do I begin to explain to Flo why her mother, the only person in the world she believed she could trust, never told *her*?' I stop to catch my breath and compose myself. 'Did you encourage Beth to say something to Flo?' I ask, trying not to sound too critical.

'Yes. We generally encourage people to talk to their close friends and family.'

'So why didn't she?'

'Fear. I see this far too often, Mrs Andrews. Fear drives a person to silence. I stressed to Beth that, in our experience, honesty is usually the best way forward. I told her that research suggested young people cope far better when told earlier about HD in their family.'

'So why didn't she listen to you?' I ask, before asking the question I'd been longing to hear the answer to. 'Dr Harding, why did she take the test? Why find out?'

Dr Harding inhales deeply. 'Because she wanted to tell you it was over. She longed to be able to say that you didn't have to worry about her future, or Flo's. Most people who take the test crave release, for themselves and for their family.'

I press a hand against my chest. The guilt eats away at me.

'How did she cope, getting the results?' I ask. It's a question I dread hearing the answer to, but I have to know. It breaks my heart imagining Beth sitting in this chair, watching Dr Harding open the envelope, her future mapped out on a piece of paper. 'Was anyone with her?'

All my worst fears are confirmed when Dr Harding tells me she was alone.

'The first thing she said to me was that she'd always known she had HD. She felt it was "in" her. This is quite common, especially with those who know from a young age that they might carry the gene. If they have grown up with a mother or father with HD, as Beth had, it almost becomes a way of life if that makes sense. Strange as this seems, some are disappointed to discover they're gene negative.'

My reaction must convey how impossible that is to conceive because she continues, 'They feel part of their identity has gone. Others have survivor's guilt. They might be gene negative, but their brother or sister isn't. With Beth, it wasn't the result she'd prayed for, but there were no tears, at least not in front of me. She was calm, she thanked me and she left.'

'And she was alone,' I say, my voice almost a whisper.

'She was alone, Mrs Andrews, but we'd done months of counselling to prepare her for the results. Beth was determined to find out from the very beginning. If she'd had her way, she'd have skipped the counselling process altogether and gone straight to the blood test, which goes against all our guidelines because, as I said, you have to be emotionally ready to hear the results. If you aren't, the result can be devastating.'

I twist my wedding ring round and round my finger. 'Yes, yes, I can see that.'

'Beth wanted to have another child. She could have decided to have a baby without taking the test,' Amanda claims, 'many couples do. It's an intensely personal choice and no one judges. But for Beth, she felt it was important to know if she was at risk before she went ahead.'

It makes me wonder about the alternative life my daughter could have lived.

What if she hadn't taken the test? Would she have married her fiancé, Graham, a man Beth had met when Flo was six, and had another child? Flo would have had a baby brother or sister and I'd have had another grandchild. Flo wouldn't be facing this alone.

It could have been a much happier life.

We search for the truth; we are determined to discover our fate — but at what cost?

'There wasn't a single thing you could have done or said to make Beth tell her family? I'm her mother,' I stress again.

She shakes her head. 'I can't force or demand anything of

a patient. Ultimately, it's their choice. It's something I have to respect.'

'So she was never going to tell Flo, or me, *ever*? She was going to wait until we worked it out for ourselves?'

*Peggy, calm down. This isn't Dr Harding's fault.*

'She thought about it constantly, but would always come up with reasons to put it off. All valid to her, but they allowed the fear to grow.'

I nod, knowing about that only too well. 'You must be sitting there thinking I'm a terrible mother—'

'Not at all.' Her voice is firm. 'Beth talked about you with so much affection and love. She admired you hugely.'

'She did?'

'She talked a lot about her father, too, and what you did for him. You and Beth were obviously close.'

*But not close enough.*

Sensing my despair, Dr Harding says, 'Do tell Florence her mother was going to tell her the truth—'

'She was?'

'Yes. Absolutely, but her priority was always to give her as carefree a childhood as possible.'

For the first time since I broke the news to Flo I feel an overwhelming flood of relief that Beth had at least wanted Flo to know, that I didn't speak against my daughter's wishes. 'Did she say when she was going to tell her?'

'After Florence's finals. Beth had become symptomatic,' Dr Harding confesses, before describing things to me that are all too familiar. 'I'd observed her fidgeting with her

hands, the restlessness in her legs. And she was beginning to fall.'

*My darling Beth.* I look away from Dr Harding, dangerously close to tears.

'I understand this is hard for you, Mrs Andrews.'

I shake my head, unworthy of her sympathy. 'Please go
on. I need to know.'

'She was also finding the simplest things difficult, like
shopping and cooking a meal or planning a journey. She
would often get muddled with order and sequences. We
talked about medication and planning her future care. We
both knew the time had come to tell Florence.'

Dr Harding opens her brown file and scans her notes as if
she's just remembered something else. 'She said she'd written
Florence a letter.'

'Really?' I rack my brain, going back to that day when I
found the hospital letter, but I don't recall seeing anything
else. 'Had she definitely written it?'

'Yes.'

My pulse quickens. 'Did she show it to you? What
did it say?'

'It would have explained everything to Florence.'

'Oh, where could it be?' I say to myself, understanding
Dr Harding couldn't possibly know the answer.

Sensing my struggle, she confides, 'I wish I could do more
to help,' and for the first time I see emotion in her eyes. I
hear it in her voice when she says, 'It's my job, but it was
always a pleasure seeing Beth. Please tell Florence that she

can always come to see me,' Dr Harding adds. 'Things are very different now from when your husband was diagnosed. Research has moved forward and there is a lot of support for people in Florence's position. Our doors are always open.'

I close my notepad and put it back into my handbag, before shaking Dr Harding's hand.

'Hang on,' she says, as if unlocking another memory. 'Beth used to write diaries. She wrote them when she was seeing me, *religiously*. I'm guessing you haven't found them?'

'No, but I will,' I vow, already planning where to look first and to recruit Ricky to help me lift some heavy boxes tonight.

'I wish I could have done more, for you and for Beth,' Dr Harding says, leading me towards her door, her professional guard slipping again. I like her for it.

'You were there for her and that's all I could have asked for.'

She nods, appreciatively. 'Give her time,' she says, her tone gentle, 'and when she's ready, she'll come back to you.'

As I'm finally about to leave, 'Mrs Andrews,' she says stopping me in my tracks. 'Beth used to say writing her diaries was like going to confession. They might provide answers for Florence, but I just want to warn you . . .' She stops, as if unsure how to put it.

'Go on,' I urge.

'Florence might find answers she's not yet ready to hear.'

# 19

## Flo

It's Wednesday night, forty-eight hours since I saw Dr Sinclair, and he hasn't yet called me with the results.

He did say it could take up to three days. I'll probably hear tomorrow.

Meanwhile, I have to finish off my packing. I'm determined to behave like nothing has to change.

I look around my bedroom, now sad and bare, the prints taken off the walls, the shelves empty of books, my wardrobe just a shell. The only thing that's left to sort out is my doll's house.

Theo urged me not to bring too much – he's allergic to clutter – but my doll's house means the world to me because Granddad made it.

'Can't it stay with Peggy?' Theo had suggested earlier

this evening over the phone. 'I can't think where it would go here.'

I didn't have the strength to argue. All I could think was, here I am, talking as if nothing has happened, and as if my biggest problem was the future of my doll's house. Maddie called me earlier, too, to check how I was.

I didn't mention the test. I couldn't.

And I haven't seen James since Monday morning. I was relieved he stayed at Kate's on Monday, and yesterday he had an emergency at work and didn't come home until well past eleven o'clock. My heart lifts when I hear the front door opening and the familiar sound of his footsteps. I need to clear the air. I'd hate us to part on bad terms. 'Flo?' he calls.

'In here.'

Seconds later he joins me. 'How are you?' He glances around the bare room.

'Fine. Nearly there with the packing.'

'Needs a good paint,' he says, touching one of the walls. 'I imagine you're taking your doll's house?'

'I'm not sure. Could you keep it here?'

'But Flo—'

'There's not much space, that's all. Just until I have a new home for it? Anyway, how are you?'

'Fine,' he says though I sense he's holding something back.

'How's Kate?'

He sits down on my bed. 'It's over,' he confides.

'Already?' I sit down next to him. 'Why?' I ask, for the first time relieved not to be thinking about my results.

'It's Emma.'

'Does she know about Emma?'

'She does now. Things were actually going pretty well between us, you know. We were keeping it cool and casual, but ever since I heard Emma's news, I've been thinking about her constantly. I knew I had to end it with Kate. It's not fair stringing her along.'

'Oh, James, I'm sorry. What did she say?'

'That she didn't want to be second best.' He shrugs. 'And she's right. She deserves more.'

'Are you still in love with Emma?' I ask, certain he is.

He turns to me. 'Even if I am, it doesn't matter. How about you?' he asks, determined to change the subject, 'How are you doing?'

'Fine. It's all good.'

'Have you spoken to Theo?'

'Yep. So back to Emma—'

'Flo?'

'Not about that.'

'But you're leaving in a few days,' he says, clearly bewildered.

I stare ahead, anticipating his reaction when I say, 'I've taken it already.'

'You've *what*?'

'I should get the results tomorrow.'

James looks stunned. 'Who did it?'

'Theo's doctor.'

'This feels way too rushed. What if—'

'It won't be.'

'You need to tell Theo,' James says, as if I were skating on dangerously thin ice.

'How would you feel if you were going out with me and I dropped this bombshell?'

He doesn't answer.

'Exactly,' I prove my point.

'But you shouldn't be going through this alone. He's your fiancé. If you do test positive—'

'I'll have to tell him and we'll work it out.'

'Flo, he's not going to run away.'

'You run away from women the moment they ask you to hang around for breakfast,' I say, referring to the string of rebound dates he had after he broke up with Emma. I remember James often returning to the flat in the early hours of the morning having made, in his words, 'a quick escape'.

'That's different and you know it. If Emma were in trouble or needed me, I'd be there for her.'

'Look, if I test positive, that's the time to talk to Theo. I won't keep it a secret like Mum and Granny did.'

He breathes in deeply as if he's about to take the test too. 'I can't believe this doctor was allowed to do it.'

'He's private. It works differently.'

'Money talks.'

'I signed a consent form. It's all above board.'

'Are you sure you're not rushing into this?' he presses me again. 'Are you *sure* you don't need more time?'

'Time won't make any difference to the results. It'll be fine,' I reassure him as much as myself, 'I won't have it.'

'And Granny Peg?'

'What about her?'

James looks lost as to what to say, defeated in his argument that I should tell her what's going on. 'It's up to you,' he admits finally. 'You've got to sort this out your way.'


I wake up screaming.

'Flo!' I hear James rushing into my bedroom. 'It's okay. I'm here.' He turns on my bedside light and hands me a glass of water.

'I was in this room,' I say breathlessly, 'it was like a prison cell and I had to make the choice: did I want to know if I had HD, or not. When I told them I wanted to, they said the answer was going to flash on a screen in front of me. A yes or a no.' I take another sip of water. 'I was tied up against a chair, fighting to get away, but I couldn't escape. It was yes. I had it, James.'

'It was just a dream, Flo.'

'What if I test positive?'

'Why don't we call the doctor in the morning? Even if he gets the results, he doesn't have to tell you.'

'No,' I say, trying to calm down. I remember all the reasons why I made the decision. Fears are always magnified at night.

'Try to get some sleep. Make the decision in the morning.'

'Stay.' I grab his hand. 'I'm scared. Will you stay with me?'

# 20

## Peggy

A member of staff unlocks the door of the allocated unit at the storage company in Hammersmith. The room is covered in dust sheets. Chairs are piled on top of one another, cardboard boxes are stacked full with books and Beth's paintings are covered in bubble wrap.

I touch an old lamp on an adjustable stand. It was a special light that Tim and I had given to her for her twenty-first birthday, specifically for her to use in her studio.

'So we're looking for diaries,' Ricky says, wiping some dust off the top of Beth's old television. 'Any idea where they might be?'

Mentally, I return to that day again, only days after Beth's funeral, Flo and I going through the contents of the house, sorting out what to keep in storage, and what to throw away. I recall going through her desk, picking up the file and seeing the official hospital envelope. After rushing to the bathroom to be sick, did I go through the rest of the bottom drawer? I can't think. It's a blank.

'Let's try her desk first,' I suggest, 'and we're also looking for a letter Beth wrote to Flo.'

Ricky begins the search at one end of the unit, while I take the other.

'By the way, Peggy, I hope you don't mind, but I talked to one of the docs today. I didn't mention names, just said I knew someone who was possibly at risk. He says they're working on better drugs and treatments, even a cure.'

'I'll be lucky if I see that happening in my lifetime.'

'But it might happen in Flo's. You've got to have faith.'

If only our faith remained bright, even on the darkest day. If only our faith remained constant. Often mine disappears, but makes a return when I least expect it to. Like the day I bumped my leg into the dishwasher and met Ricky, this man who is now giving up his evening to help me. Days like that restore my faith in humanity.

'Thank you, Ricky,' I say. 'For helping.'

He laughs. 'Gets me out of nappy duty.'

I come to a box filled with Beth's old photo albums.

'Here it is,' Ricky says, after pulling off another dust sheet. I watch as he opens each drawer of Beth's desk. My heart stops when he gets to the bottom one.

'Sorry, nothing,' he says.

'Bugger.' My hope was that some of her diaries might have been kept in a drawer with her sketchpads. I rack my brain again, remembering taking some of her old novels and art books to a charity shop. What if the diaries were lost among them? What if some stranger is reading about our family?

'Oh, Ricky, they must be here somewhere.'

'We'll find them Peggy; don't worry.'

For the next hour, Ricky and I search high and low.

'Peggy, come here, quick!'

Ricky shows me a leather suitcase that used to belong to Tim. Inside the case are several books, some with stickers on the front.

'You brilliant man,' I say, my heart in my mouth as I open one. It's dated 1979, when Beth would have been ten. Seeing her familiar writing makes me feel choked.

*That was weird. I just walked into the kitchen to get a pack of crisps and Mum and Dad stopped talking. They looked spooked, as if they'd just seen a ghost, until Dad laughed, saying he'd lost a golf ball up a tree.*

I stagger to my feet and wipe the dust off my skirt, vividly recalling that night. It was the night after Tim had seen a neurologist and he'd feared the worst.

Ricky puts an arm around my shoulder. 'Are you all right?' he asks.

I nod, before looking at my watch. It's close to ten o'clock at night. I need to get home and work out my next plan of action. I need to give Flo these diaries as soon as possible. After all, she is leaving on Sunday morning.

Ricky lifts the case, making it look as light as a feather in his arms. I feel so shaken I wish he could carry me home, too.

It's no use. I turn on my bedside light and get out of bed. Earlier this evening, I placed the diaries in a box in the corner of my bedroom, certain Flo should be the one to read them first. Yet I can't get Dr Harding's voice out of my head.

*Beth used to say writing her diaries was like going to confession. Florence might find answers she's not yet ready to hear.*

I take in a deep breath as I dive back into my past.

*Mum then asked me what I wanted for supper: quiche or toad-in-the-hole. I said toad-in-the hole. I left, but then decided I wanted juice, too, so was about to go back into the kitchen when Dad mentioned my name, although I couldn't hear the rest. Mum told him to keep quiet.*

*'Don't tell Beth,' she said.*

*She told Dad I was too young to worry about all this.*

*What were they talking about? I wonder if it's to do with money or something?*

I daren't go on reading. Tim and I had argued that night. I was determined not to say a word to Beth until the time was right.

If only I'd listened to Tim and done it his way. If only I could have learned that there never is a right time.

Try to find the right time and you'll put it off for life. You just have to dig deep to find the courage to say it, and even more importantly, the courage to face the consequences.

# 21

**Flo**

I have two days left at work before I leave. I stare at the mess on my desk. I have a mountain of paperwork to sort out and yet the only thing on my mind is Dr Sinclair. The results must be in today.

I jump when my mobile rings, though my heart sinks when I see Granny's name on my screen. I can't talk to her. Not yet. I'm not ready and I certainly can't tell her I've taken the test.

She leaves a message, and just hearing her voice makes me feel emotional. I hate what she did, but I obviously still love her.

'Flo, my darling, I need to see you. I know it's difficult between us, and I understand you can't forgive me, but I have something for you; it's something very important. Please call me as soon as you can. It's urgent.'

'It's really quiet downstairs,' Natalie says, breaking my thoughts about what could be so urgent. 'Do you need a hand with anything?'

'I'm fine,' I reply.

There's a part of me that longs to tell Natalie what's been going on these past few days, but I can't trust myself not to break down. I have to hold on until Dr Sinclair calls. It can't be long now.

I feel as if I'm standing dangerously close to the edge of a cliff, and the one thing I can't do is look down at the sheer drop.

'Another coffee?' she asks.

'Yes, please.'

'And cake?' Natalie is always bringing in her mother's special homemade cakes.

'Just coffee, thanks.'

'Since when haven't you room for cake? You must be ill.'

'Oh, go on then,' I say, thinking I can always take it home for James. 'I'm going to miss you, Natalie, and your mum's baking.'

'Me too. I can't believe you're leaving me here with Ginger.' Ginger is our affectionate name for Simon. We smile, overhearing him say to a client downstairs, 'Shall I put you in the front of the plane and your husband at the back?'

'Just a small slice though.'

'Got to keep your slim figure, right. Have you gone shopping for wedding dresses yet?'

My mobile rescues me just in time. 'Sorry, got to take this.'
I rush downstairs and head outside, into the pouring rain.

'Florence,' Dr Sinclair says.

*I don't like the way he said my name.*

'Do I have it? Tell me.'

'Not over the phone, we need to talk.'

# 22

## Peggy

I stare at the telephone, waiting for Flo to call me back. It's been at least an hour since I left my message.

I couldn't read much of Beth's first diary last night. I had to stop, too upset to continue. I didn't want to see all my failings and flaws through Beth's eyes. Besides, deep down I still believe Flo should be the first person to read them, not me.

It's no use. I can't sit here twiddling my thumbs any longer. I pick up the phone. 'James, it's Peggy,' I say. 'How is she?'

'Has Flo called you?' he asks, on guard immediately.

'I wish she would.'

There's a pause.

'I need to see her tonight, it's important,' I insist. 'Can you help me get through to her?'

'Granny Peg, I can't—'

'Please. I have to see her before she goes.'

'She's taken the test.'

'She's *what*?'

'She's on her way right now to see the doctor. Sorry, Granny Peg, I can't talk—'

'Wait!'

'I'll call you the moment I get news.'

I feel lightheaded and giddy, my heart racing as the line goes dead and the phone slips from my fingers.

# 23

## Flo

'It's bad news,' I say, when James joins me in the kitchen after getting home from work. 'They sent the blood back.'

'Oh, bloody hell, Flo,' he bursts out. 'I thought you were going to tell me you'd tested positive.'

'Sorry,' I say, realizing it was clumsy of me. 'The lab wouldn't process the results.'

'Why not?'

'They wouldn't accept the consent form. Apparently, there are strict guidelines I have to go through, which can take months. You can say it, James. Say "I told you so".'

'I'm sorry, Flo.'

I look at him gratefully. 'Dr Sinclair was sorry, too. I don't know what to do next.'

'Well, what are the options?' He pulls up a chair and sits down next to me.

'Delaying New York to see a counsellor, or getting on that plane and working it out later.'

'I think you need to talk it through with Theo.'

That's an option I don't want to take yet. This could destroy us.

'The longer you wait to tell him, the harder it'll become,' James warns me, just as Maddie had earlier this evening.

'I know,' I admit.

*Look how long it took Granny to tell me.*

'He loves you, Flo. Don't shut him out.'

'I will talk to him, of course I will, but not over the phone. I think I want to tell him face to face.'

James nods.

'Want to hear the good news?' I say.

'Yes, please,' he replies, as if we could both really do with a pick-me-up.

'Dr Sinclair didn't charge me so I bought us a bottle of fizz,' I say, just as the buzzer rings. 'You're not expecting anyone are you?'

'Shit,' he mutters. 'Flo, don't hate me.'

'Why? What have you done?'

'I spoke to Granny Peg this afternoon.'

I freeze.

'I told her you took the test.'

'You *didn't*! *Why*?' Slowly, I recall the message she left me, too.

'I'm sorry, Flo. What could I do? She sounded desperate.'

'She shouldn't be calling you behind my back—'

'If you won't talk to her, somebody has to.'

'She had so many chances to talk to me before,' I say, realizing my anger isn't subsiding. If anything it's getting worse. 'The test was my business.'

The buzzer rings yet again. 'You're family; you're all she has left.'

Exasperated, I say, 'Exactly, James. And if I can't count on my family, who can I count on?'

'Christ, Flo! She's punishing herself enough already. She's nearly eighty. She has a heart condition. She's not going to be around for ever.'

'I can't deal with her right now,' I say, fighting back the tears.

'I understand, but don't go to America without at least saying goodbye. Imagine if something happened to Granny Peg while you were away. It would break your heart and you'd never forgive yourself.'

I pace the room. Deep down I know he's right. 'Fine,' I say, giving permission for James to let her in.

My phone rings. It's Theo. I reject his call, bracing myself for whatever it is Granny has to say first.

James and Granny walk into the kitchen, James carrying Mum's old suitcase. 'I told her the test couldn't be processed,' he says.

And to my relief, Granny doesn't condemn me for trying in the first place. Instead, all she says is, 'It's good to see you, Flo.'

'What's Mum's suitcase doing here?' I ask her, confused.

'I went to see her genetic counsellor yesterday,' she tells me.

'You did?' I ask, trying to remain calm, though I want to hear more.

'Dr Harding told me your mother had written you a letter explaining everything.'

'She had?' Tears come to my eyes.

'Yes.'

'Where is it?'

Granny explains that she and Ricky went to the storage unit last night. They looked everywhere for it. 'I'm so sorry, Flo. It must have got lost or burnt.'

I sit down and bury my head in my hands. The very last piece of her has gone. But at least I know she was going to tell me.

'We found something else, Flo. All your mother's diaries.'

'Her diaries?' I didn't know she'd written any. 'Is that what's in that case?'

'Yes.'

James opens the case for us. Inside is an assortment of coloured hardback books. I pick one up. 'Have you read any of them?'

'I've glanced at one or two,' she replies, visibly shaken now. It takes all my willpower not to put my arms around her. 'I wanted you to read them first. It might be hard, Flo, but I hope you'll find some answers. Well, I'll leave you to it,' she says, turning away.

James stares at me, urging me to say something, *anything*, before he escorts Granny out of the room.

I rush out into the corridor. 'Granny?' I call out.

Immediately she turns round, leaning heavily on James's arm, and I notice how pale and exhausted she looks.

I kiss her on the cheek. 'Thank you.'

'I hope one day you can forgive me,' she says. 'I'll always be here for you, Flo. Always.'

# 24

**Flo**

I skipped supper, James saying he'd leave some in the oven for me. Alone in my bedroom, I turn another page, holding my breath as I read.

*Beth's Diary, 1981*

*I'm so embarrassed. Last night Tibby and I went to see For Your Eyes Only – soooo good. I love Roger Moore! Anyway, I told Dad we would get the bus home – he didn't need to pick us up from the cinema – but he said he didn't want us coming back alone in the dark.*

*So we're driving, Tibby and me on the backseat, and Dad goes this funny route. 'Why are we going this way?' I say to him, 'remember we're taking Tibby home first.'*

*Dad gets all flustered, misses the next turning, and*

*then shouts at us, switching off the radio, saying he can't concentrate with all the noise. So I tell him again that he needs to turn round, before Tibby says, 'It's red, Mr Andrews!' and the next thing I know, a police car is following us, flashing lights, siren blaring, telling Dad to pull over.*

*I notice Dad's hands are shaking when he turns off the engine. The cop asks Dad to step out of the car, like they do in movies, then asks him to walk in a straight line. And Dad's straight line does not look straight to me.*

*'Has your dad been drinking?' Tibby asks, mouth wide open, and I'm just shrinking, right. All I want to do is disappear.*

*Finally, we get home and I go straight to my room. Then the phone rings.*

*'He wasn't over the limit,' I overhear Mum say firmly.*

*She comes upstairs and asks me if I enjoyed the film. I close my diary and hide it under the duvet. She says it's late, and then tucks me up in bed (she still thinks I'm 3, not 12!).*

*As she's about to shut the door I ask if everything is all right with Dad.*

*'He's tired. A stressful day at work, that's all,' she says.*

*'I told him he didn't have to pick us up.'*

*'I know. But he wanted to. Don't be cross with him, Beth.'*

*I couldn't sleep last night. I kept on thinking about that time I overheard them in the kitchen, Mum saying 'Don't tell Beth.'*

*Don't tell me what? What if something is wrong, and
I mean really wrong? Dad doesn't play golf anymore,
and he used to love that game. Mum and I used to tease
him, saying he loved that little white ball more than us.
But when I ask him why he doesn't play, he dodges the
question. Also, he hardly ever paints at the weekends or
makes anything in his studio. These days he prefers to
smoke in front of the TV.*

*I know he has a busy job and travels and everything, so
it's good for him to relax, but there's something else going
on. I'm not stupid.*

I keep on reading, one entry after another. I have to
know when Mum found out about Granddad. *When did
they tell her?*

*Beth's Diary, 1982*

*I don't know where to begin. I can hardly write this. For
a while now I've noticed how Dad can't sit still watching
the TV. His legs and hands twitch all the time – and he's
beginning to get stressed out about everything.*

*He was in tears the other day because he couldn't find
his passport! It was the first time I'd ever seen Dad cry and
it freaked me out.*

*When I helped him look for it, he sat on the bed and
said, 'I don't want to go, Beth'.*

*He looked like a little boy scared to go to big school,*

*not the dad I knew, a director of an advertising firm. So anyway, when Dad finally found his passport and left for the airport, I asked Mum to tell me what was going on.*

*'I'm a teenager now,' I said, 'I'm a grown-up. I can take it.'*

*I knew Dad wasn't just tired. She told me that he had 'senile chorea'. I'd never heard of it before, but it sounded serious. When I asked Mum to tell me more, she said all it meant was he had jerky movements in his feet and hands, which is why he gets restless legs and occasionally knocks into things, or spills his tea.*

*'But it's nothing for you to worry about,' she said, before sending me back upstairs to do my homework, stressing that school was the only thing that mattered right now. 'And don't say a word to your father when he comes home; he doesn't want you to worry.'*

*So I didn't say anything, but then it happened a week later.*

*After school, I came home and found Mum and Dad in the kitchen. Dad is never home in the afternoon! Anyway, they did that thing again – stopped talking the moment I entered the room.*

*'We need to tell her, Peg,' he said. So Mum told me Dad had lost his job; that he'd been made redundant. She turned away. I thought she was going to cry.*

*'We have to tell her,' Dad said again. 'Everything.'*

*So I sat down and said, 'Is this about your senile chorea?'*

'My what?' Dad asked.

'Mum said you have senile chorea.'

Dad stared at Mum as if I were speaking Chinese. 'We've been in denial for too long, Peg. This is happening, whether we like it or not, and it's only going to get worse.'

Mum's face crumpled as she left the room.

'Beth, I don't want you to be scared,' Dad said, reaching for my hand.

Just him saying that made me, though.

'There's no easy way to say this . . . I have Huntington's Disease.'

'What's that?'

He put on his brave Dad face. 'It affects the brain, my movements. It's the reason I'm a bit clumsier these days, getting a few bruises.' I was too nervous to smile back at him. 'But we're going to be okay, Beth. Now that I'm not working we can travel more, I can spend time with you and your mother. Your mum is going to keep her job, and they've paid me a decent redundancy package so we'll be fine, absolutely fine, all right? Nothing needs to change. I'm still your goofy old dad.'

It was hard to understand. What did it mean? Why had Dad said it was only going to get worse?

'Why didn't you tell me before?' I asked.

'We wanted to protect you for as long as we could. One of these days, when you have your own kids, you'll understand that.' I watched Dad get up and walk across the

*room. He picked up the notepad by the kettle. 'I'm going
to write a list, Beth. A list of all the things you and I are
going to do together before . . .' He stopped. Dropped the
pad, picked it up again.*

*'Before what?'*

*He sat down, acted as if he hadn't heard my question.
'We're going to Florence to see the Botticellis. We'll take
our sketchpads, paint and eat chocolate gelato! We could
take a trip to Venice, ride in a gondola, what do you
think? And we could go to Egypt – I've always wanted to
see the Pyramids, haven't you?'*

*'Before what, Dad?'*

*He looked up at me, tears in his eyes. 'Before I
die, Beth.'*

*'You can't die, Dad, not yet. Not ever.'*

*The next day I found a book in the school library on
Huntington's Disease.*

*They say it's hereditary, which means I have a
fifty-fifty chance of getting it too. It's like the toss of a coin,
heads or tails.*

*I wish I didn't know.*

*I wish Dad hadn't told me.*

*I preferred my life before.*

I don't even notice how late it is until my mobile rings. It's
Theo, again.

I can't talk to him. My head is too full with Mum's diaries. I can't pretend everything is fine, but equally I can't

explain what's been happening over the last few days. I let his call go to voicemail again.

I glance at Mum's diary.

*How can it be that less than a week ago I was planning my future with Theo?*

'I preferred my old life too,' I whisper, missing not only Mum, but also the old Florence Andrews.

# 25

**Peggy**

Flo is a little girl, wearing her poppy dress with matching red tights, and she's out on her scooter, alone, heading towards a busy main road. As she gets closer and closer to the traffic, she isn't slowing down. In fact, she is going so fast that she has no chance of stopping in time. There are cars and lorries racing past, and Flo on her baby scooter. I am trying to catch up with her, but my feet won't move. I'm stuck. Paralysed.

'STOP' I cry out. 'Flo, stop!' She looks over her shoulder and then her face changes and she merges into Beth.

I wake myself up screaming, my body shaking.

I think of Flo reading the diaries, praying it's not going to scare her even more.

'I'm frightened, Tim,' I whisper in the darkness, hugging my arms around my chest, wishing with every part of my being that he was lying next to me.

# 26

**Flo**

Somehow I get through my last day at work without a glitch, running on adrenaline and caffeine alone. It's business as usual, until I'm called downstairs by Natalie at the end of the afternoon, who presents me with a chocolate cake, a bottle of champagne and a pale pink cap, embroidered with the letters 'NY'.

As the champagne is poured and my boss, Harriet, thanks me for everything I have done for the company, I can't bring myself to let on that I might not be going to America quite as soon as I'd planned. However, I maintain the pretence, as it's by far the easier thing to do. It's the *only* thing to do if I want to leave here tonight without dissolving into tears.

As Natalie grills me on all the things I'm going to do in New York, and asking if she can come out and stay, it becomes increasingly clear that I'm not ready to get on that plane in less than forty-eight hours. I'm not ready to begin my new life because there's so much in my current one that I don't understand.

Later that day, back at home, I glance at my watch. It's eight o'clock our time, which makes it three in the afternoon for Theo. James wishes me good luck before heading out to see his old friend, Stu.

'Call if you need me,' he says, 'we're only round the corner.' Sensing my fear, he adds, 'You're doing the right thing telling him now. I'm proud of you, Flo.'

I nod. He's right. I'm going to be brave. Tell Theo everything and suggest I stay home for a few more weeks to process the news and see my GP for advice.

The moment I hear James close the front door, I pick up the phone, my heart thudding in my chest.

'Flo,' he says, immediately picking up, 'I was about to call you. I was getting worried; you've been so quiet these past few days.'

'How's everything going?' I ask.

*I can tell him. Just be honest.*

'Manic. How did your last day go?'

'It was great.'

'Can you believe it, Flo? You're a free agent. You'll never have to book anyone's flight again – except your own.' He laughs. 'You all packed?' He waits. 'Flo?'

'I'm here. Actually, there's something I need to talk to you about.'

'You're making me nervous. You haven't changed your mind, have you?'

'No, no, it's nothing like that.'

'Is this about Granny? Flo, she can't make you feel guilty—'

'Yes,' I say, despite myself, 'she's in hospital.'

'Shit, is she all right?'

'We don't know yet. It's her heart. She has really high blood pressure so she's being monitored. I'm so sorry, Theo, but I can't leave her, not yet.'

'Oh, Flo. Of course, you must stay.'

Theo's understanding makes me feel even guiltier for lying.

'How long will she be in hospital for?' he asks.

'Probably a week or so.'

'Okay. You can probably claim insurance?'

'Insurance?'

'Your ticket, sweetheart.'

I hadn't even thought about that.

'If you need me to give you some extra cash—'

'No, it's fine,' I say, my guilt growing. 'I'll sort something out.'

'So when do you think you can come out here?'

'I'm not sure. Until I know what it is—'

'Right. I understand.'

'I'm sorry,' I say once again, registering his disappointment.

'Stop saying sorry; it's not your fault. I'm sad, sure – the flat feels lonely without you – but we've got our whole lives ahead of us, Flo, our entire future, so stay with her for as long as she needs you.'

*

140

Alone in my bedroom, I feel increasingly uneasy. I may have bought myself more time, but the truth is I've just lied to my future husband. I've blamed Granny and Mum for keeping secrets and here I am doing exactly the same thing.

I think of James, dreading telling him I bottled out.

*Why couldn't I tell Theo the truth?* I had it perfectly rehearsed on paper. Maybe I couldn't tell him because I don't even know myself what it means to be at risk.

I pick up Mum's diary, opening it to the last page I'd reached last night. Mum was seventeen then.

I touch her handwriting. I thought I knew her inside out. It's like believing you know every single nook and cranny of your home, then discovering there was another room, on a secret floor, a room that was permanently locked.

It will always hurt being shut out, but at least these diaries provide a key, and now that I've entered, there's no turning back.

*Beth's Diary, 1986*

*I wish I could tell people not to stare. If only I had the courage to walk over to their table and tell them how lucky they are that they can blend into a crowd, eat their meal at a restaurant without panicking that a storm is about to hit. Not worrying that plates, knives and glasses will crash on to the floor, that water will be thrown over burning candles to kill the flame.*

*That's what Dad's HD has done.*

*It has killed the flame of our family life, snuffed out any sense of normality.*

*I wish I could articulate myself in front of people, maybe even explain our situation to put them at ease. If only I could talk to Mum, tell her how I feel, that it's more upsetting going out these days than staying in watching Dad smoke in front of the TV with his bottle of beer.*

*People's stares are like kicks in the gut, reminding me that as each day passes, my father is fading in front of my very eyes, and there is nothing I can do to help him.*

*All we can do as a family is carry on through the storm.*

*I picked up Dad's glass and mopped up the red wine with my napkin, while Mum called a waiter over, saying with her usual false cheer, 'Oh dear, look what a mess we've made! We're so sorry!'*

*I don't know what I'd do if I didn't write a diary. I wouldn't know how to make sense of anything. I've always been much better with a pen or paintbrush in my hand. Words get stuck in my throat.*

*The sad thing is today I should be feeling happy. This morning I found out I've been accepted into one of the best art schools in London – Camberwell – to do a fine art degree in painting. I listened to Dad's advice not to take a gap year, even if I'm only seventeen and a year ahead, but to get on with art school. There will be plenty of time to travel in the holidays.*

*Since Dad told me he had HD, we've had many more*

*heart-to-hearts, Dad stressing we only get one life, one shot, so I was not to waste my time doing something that didn't make me happy.*

*Dad always wanted to be an artist. He would have loved to have been a sculptor, or maybe an architect, but he was never encouraged to dream or aspire. So I listened to him, not expecting to get into Camberwell, especially after my interview when the woman asked me what made me think my portfolio cut the mustard and why was I so buttoned up and polite?*

*'Art can never be buttoned up and polite,' she said. But what did she expect — me to be rude and spit?*

*When she asked me who had influenced me the most, I think she imagined I'd say Cezanne or Picasso, but I said, 'My father'.*

*I found myself telling her about my childhood: Dad and me lying on the floor in his study, opera music playing, working on our doll's house together, him telling me his dream was to design and build a house by the sea in his retirement, somewhere Mum could have her own veggie patch, and he'd build a swimming pool, too, for all his grandkids to play in.*

*'I'm relying on you, Beth, to give me as many as possible, no pressure.' Dad had always wanted a larger family; he would have loved for me to have had a brother or sister, but after my traumatic birth, Mum was warned against trying again.*

*As I was holding back the tears, all I could think was*

*how we make plans and God laughs at them. But we can't
stop making plans or having dreams, can we?*

*We can't stop living.*

*Dad's speech isn't so good now: his words are slurred, as
if he's had too much to drink, but Mum and I understand
him because we know him inside out, so when I waved the
letter in front of him today, saying, 'I got in. They picked
me!' he said he wanted to celebrate. He wanted to go out,
just with Mum, me and my best friend, Tibby, to toast
my future.*

*These days, Dad doesn't like socializing with people
who don't know about his HD. He doesn't want them
to see the way he walks, or the way Mum sometimes cuts
up his food to make it easier for him to swallow. He's lost
touch with his golfing friends, their diaries suddenly full.*

*Anyway, Dad was determined we go out, and when he
gets set on an idea, he's like a dog with a bone. So we go
to a restaurant that doesn't have too many steps, somewhere
we can park right outside. When the waiter shows us to
our table, people stare as Dad bumps into somebody's chair.*

*They probably think he has Parkinson's.*

*We sit down and look at the menu. Dad picks
something that is least likely to end up down his shirt.
Spaghetti is an enemy. He loves steak. How wrong can
you go with that? Until Mum is shouting, 'Is anyone a
doctor!' and I'm helping Dad to his feet, Mum standing
behind him, her small frame no match for Dad's, but she
is wiry and strong, and somehow she's doing the Heimlich*

manoeuvre to remove that bolus of meat that's made itself
at home in Dad's oesophagus.

The restaurant seems to freeze, the chatter dims, until
Dad is back in his seat. I can feel his frustration, his pain,
as he picks up his glass of red wine, Mum, Tibby and me
watching in slow motion to see if it reaches his mouth.

Of course it doesn't, and Dad's plate – his steak and
chips – are soaked in red wine and knocked to the floor.
And the restaurant hushes again, a few stifled giggles
this time.

If it weren't so tragic it would be funny.

I'm ashamed to say I might have laughed if it
weren't my dad.

When he tries to pour himself another glass of wine, he
pushes Mum's hand away, shouting, 'I can do it!'

I can almost hear the other diners thinking 'He
shouldn't be allowed out.' The sort of people who think
children should be seen but not heard.

But do you know what the worst part of this is? It's
only going to get worse. I looked at Mum tonight, so
wonderful and brave, but at some point this disease is going
to defeat her, because she won't let anyone help, except me.
She's too proud. Too stubborn.

Very soon, Mum will have to give up her job to be a
full-time carer. How can I skip off to art school when Dad
is only going to need more and more support?

I realize that one day Mum and I will look back and
think a spilt glass of red wine and the stares were nothing

*compared to what we're facing now. We'll think these days were good, days when we could still get out of the house and toast my future.*

*Because that's what we did. Mum ordered the best champagne on the menu, which received yet another odd look from the waiter, who no doubt wondered what on earth we had to celebrate. But Mum poured the champagne into four flutes, giving Dad a tiny amount to cause minimal waste.*

*'To my Beth,' Dad said. I shall always remember that look of pride in his blue eyes.*

*Sometimes, I get these panic attacks. They come on when I'm alone, at night, when I think too much about my own future, and darkness overtakes light. Tibby says I should talk to my GP. Maybe she could prescribe me some anti-depressants and something to help me sleep.*

*'What you're going through is traumatic,' she says, 'it's okay to ask for help'.*

*Mum and Dad must know that I have a fifty-fifty chance of inheriting the gene, too, and yet none of us have spoken about it. How can we? It's too frightening. It's like the elephant in the room.*

*I'm seventeen. I can head off to art school this autumn, I can toast my future, but the thundercloud over my head, the threat of a storm, will follow me like a shadow wherever I go. The truth is, I have a potential bomb in my bag, and who knows when or if it will go off.*

# 27

**Peggy**

'What are you going to do when she's in New York, Peggy?' Ricky asks me over a cup of tea.

James called me last weekend to say Flo had delayed her flight. A part of me felt relieved. Another part felt overwhelming guilt at being the person who had thwarted her plans at the last minute.

*Impeccable timing, Peggy.*

I longed to ask James what Theo had said, praying he'd been understanding and supportive, but couldn't in the end.

I shrug. 'As long as she's happy.'

'Yes, but what about *you*?'

'What about me?'

'You can't just sit here day in, day out, staring into space, wondering when Flo is going to forgive you.'

'Why not? I'm perfectly all right. I don't feel like seeing anyone anyway.'

'Not even me?'

'You're different.'

He smiles recognizing that's a compliment. 'When my baby girl died, I was given compassionate leave and I needed that time, but I'd have gone mad if I hadn't had my job to go back to. Seeing other people and talking to patients kept me sane.'

'Ricky, I'm retired.'

'Yeah, but you're not retired from *life*. And you can't live through Flo's. Now is the time for you to take up a new hobby.'

'I'm seventy-nine, for goodness sake. I'm an old bag.'

'There must be something you've always longed to do?'

'No. Nothing.'

'I don't believe you, mate. I want to learn the saxophone and my dream is to buy a beach hut for my kids, a place where we can talk and play music and dance by the sea.'

'I'm not about to swan off to knitting classes or ballroom dancing, not when everything's still so up in the air.'

'Maybe not right this minute.' He's smiling again. 'Sorry, I'm just imagining you doing the waltz, Peggy. Or the tango.' He pulls me out of my chair and starts to tango with me around the kitchen floor.

'Stop it, Ricky, honestly!' I say, though a smile is reluctantly creeping on to my face.

'God forbid if anyone stepped on your toes,' he says, carrying on. 'Ouch.'

'Ricky! Enough!' But I find myself laughing with him. We must look a ridiculous pair.

'I'm more at home on a footie pitch,' he admits, both of us sitting down again. 'All I'm saying is—'

'I know what you're saying, and I'll think about it once this is sorted,' I promise, wondering how many of Beth's diaries Flo has now read, praying that no matter how hard reading the truth is, it will help her.

Ricky catches me staring at my mobile again, willing it to ring.

'Flo will go to America,' he states. 'She will live her life, and that's what you need to do, too.'

Later that night, when I'm tucked up in bed, my mobile rings. It's James.

'Hello,' I say, sensing immediately something is wrong.

'I'm sorry to wake you, Granny Peg.'

'Never mind. Is Flo all right?'

'That's why I'm calling. She hasn't come home.' I glance at my clock sitting on my bedside table. It's one in the morning. I sit up abruptly. 'Well, where is she?'

'I was kind of hoping she was with you,' James says.

# 28

**Flo**

'A glass of white wine, please,' I say to the man behind the bar. It's Monday night and I've spent another full day alone in the flat reading Mum's diaries.

I hate thinking about what she went through, seeing her father suffer, watching helplessly as he lost his job and was left unable to do all the things we take for granted.

It hurts me to think she carried this burden alone.

If only she had talked to me about it. I'd have hated anticipating the same thing happening to Mum, but I would have been there for her.

*Why couldn't Granny and Mum talk about it? Why did they have to pretend everything was all right?* The ironic thing is the only person who wanted it to be out in the open was Granddad.

As I drink my wine, my mind flits to James and Maddie. I

couldn't bring myself to tell them I'd wimped out of telling Theo the truth. Instead I'd pretended that he'd taken it in his stride. Maybe my instincts were right in the first place. I *should* talk to him face to face, not over the phone.

As I sit, slumped at the table in the far corner of the bar, all I can hear is my mother's voice inside my head, speaking the words from her diary.

*I can head off to art school, I can toast my future, but the thundercloud over my head, the threat of a storm, will follow me like a shadow wherever I go. The truth is, I have a potential bomb in my bag, and who knows when or if it will go off.*

I don't even notice a man taking a seat next to me until he says, 'May I get you another?' He gestures to my empty glass.

'Thanks.' I hiccup. 'Yes.'

'Nate.' He shakes my hand. He's well over six foot, fair like Theo, and has a smile that would make you agree to pretty much anything. 'What's a beautiful woman like you doing on her own?' he asks.

*But he needs to work on his chat-up lines.*

He waits, a flicker of amusement in his eyes that again reminds me of Theo. 'Do you have a name?'

'Rosie. Rosie Chambers.'

*I don't want to be Flo Andrews tonight.*

*Or tomorrow.*

*Or the next day.*

\*

The moment he heads towards the bar I take off my engagement ring and hide it in my wallet.

# 29

*Beth's Diary, 1987*

*You wouldn't believe the day I've had. It's close to two in the morning. I should be sleeping, but I need to write everything down.*

*So, I dragged myself into college this morning, make-up smudged, my skin sore and red, irritated from kissing Ben, who, despite my protests, is still experimenting with growing a beard. I prayed I wouldn't bump into Mark on the way to my studio, but of course I did.*

*'I've signed you in. Again,' he said, and for a moment I had to turn away, unable to stomach the disappointed look in his eye.*

*This time, when I told him I didn't need another lecture, not even from my favourite tutor, my smile didn't win him over. Instead I should have apologized for letting him down – again – but I was practically on my hands and knees after another late night working at Ben's pub, always packed with students after the cheapest beer in town.*

*I met Ben six months ago, when I'd just started my second year at Camberwell. I caught his eye as I was about to order and there was an instant attraction – he didn't have a beard then. I told him I was looking for a new job, like pretty much everyone else here who needs to pay for their digs and art stuff, and he offered me one there and then, saying it didn't matter if I didn't have any experience behind a bar as I'd learn to pull a pint in no time. I could save money by staying with Mum and Dad, but I need to have a healthy distance from home right now.*

*But nothing about my life is healthy right now, is it?*

*I was standing in front of Mark, looking as if I'd been in a punch-up and smelling like a pub. Each day I intend to give myself a night off from the student union bar. Go home, run a bath, make some decent food and get an early night, and wake up without a hangover.*

*As I was about to walk away, he asked, 'Is everything all right?' which is a question I always dread.*

*Mark knows about Dad's HD, but the answer was still no, nothing was all right.*

*Mum had called last night, upset that Dad had broken her favourite sugar bowl, the one Aunt Celia had given to her. I knew things must have been bad since Mum rarely calls to complain about Dad. I felt guilty that last night*

*I'd been partying like there was no tomorrow, while Mum
was mopping up spilt orange juice, putting another basket
of laundry into the washing machine and wrapping yet
more broken mugs and plates – and now her precious sugar
bowl – in newspaper.*

*'Beth, you look a mess,' Mark continued.*

*'Thanks.' I touched my hair self-consciously.*

*'If you need to talk—'*

*'I'm fine.'*

*'I'm here.'*

*'I'd better go,' I said. I was in no fit state to work on
anything today, just the thought of the smell of paint made
me feel sick.*

*'Take the day off,' he advised, 'sort yourself out and
come back fresh tomorrow.' I knew I'd used up most of
my lifelines. Mark was being kind and giving me one
final chance.*

*So I went to St Martin-in-the-Fields, in Trafalgar
Square, where they have free lunchtime concerts. I love this
place; it's my sanctuary. It's a space where I can close my
eyes. Often I drop off, allowing the music to wash over me.
It was Beethoven today, 'Moonlight Sonata'. It reminded
me of Dad. He used to play this in his study. I knew he'd
love to be sitting by my side, listening too.*

*In the early days, when he was first diagnosed, he could
still go out to enjoy an opera or concert, or a film, or he'd
drive us out of London to the coast and we'd paddle in
the sea and eat fish and chips watching the fading sun.*

Mum, Dad and I packed our bags and made the most of my long summer holidays, ticking off places to see on Dad's bucket list, like India and Egypt. When Dad lost his driving licence, it was a massive blow to his confidence and freedom, and one more nail in the coffin of his independence.

As I was listening to the music, tears were streaming down my cheeks as I thought of Dad and how much of the outside world was now passing him by.

After the concert I had such a strong urge to go home and give him a hug. Hold his hand. See Mum, and say sorry for not visiting for a while . . . and sorry that Dad had broken her precious sugar bowl.

When I arrived, I had to let myself in with my set of keys. There was no sign of Mum, the house eerily quiet. I thought maybe they were at the hospital. I honestly can't count the number of times Dad has tripped over in his determination to try to do things independently. Mum says Beverley, in the minor injury unit at their local hospital, has become a firm friend.

I thought they must be out until I heard footsteps on the landing. When I looked up, I knew at once Dad was in trouble.

In a split second he lost his balance and grabbed the spindle of the banisters, and I screamed as I watched him tumble down the stairs, taking the whole of the banister rail with him. I called an ambulance, too frightened to try to move him in case he'd injured himself badly. As *soon as I put the phone down, Mum returned with a pint of milk, only to find that, after being gone just five minutes, Dad was sprawled on the floor along with half the banister rail.*

*To our relief and astonishment Dad hadn't broken a single bone and didn't need to go to hospital. He's stronger than he looks, his figure solid and sturdy, but it still took me and one of the paramedics twenty minutes to get him back upstairs, standing either side of him, helping him with each laboured step, his brain unable to send the right message to his legs.*

*When finally Dad was undressed and lying down, I knelt by his side and told him about the concert I'd been to, and that one of these days I hoped he could come with me, too, though that day seemed so far away now, as if in another world.*

*I almost broke down kissing Mum goodbye. How I hate leaving her knowing that tomorrow is only going to be worse than today. All I could think was that I shouldn't be going. I should be at home, helping out, not trying to be the next Damien Hirst.*

*After seeing Mum and Dad I decided to go back to my digs, but hours later I found myself propped up against the student union bar, finishing off the dregs of my beer, before ordering another. I was talking to a few friends on my course as if I'd had a perfectly normal day.*

*When they called it a night, I was about to order another drink, but stopped when I caught Mark's eye. As* he sat down on the stool next to mine he told me to put away my wallet, saying he'd order me a coffee. He didn't say a word until I couldn't hold it in any longer.

I didn't just cry, I sobbed, my head resting on his shoulder.

Finally, when I was ready, I told him what had happened to Dad today. I told him the same could happen to me, and that I'm going mad trying to lead this double life, pretending I'm fine when I'm anything but.

Mark encouraged me to open up to the friends I was making here, saying that I should give people more credit. He asked me if Ben knew about my father. I shook my head, eaten up by yet more guilt that I was denying Dad's very existence to my boyfriend.

'It's hard,' I confessed, 'I just want to be normal. I want to fit in. I don't want pity.'

He then asked me what I assumed 'normal' to be, and whether I thought he'd led a normal life.

I looked at Mark, reckoning he was in his mid thirties. Scruffy trousers and trainers, yet he has an air of sophistication. He wears glasses that make him look professor-like, but there is nothing arrogant about him. I could see from the ring on his finger he's married. His life seemed pretty normal to me.

'I lost both my parents within a year of each other when I was seventeen,' he confided. 'I raised my siblings. My brother suffered from depression. He killed himself two years ago.'

*I didn't know how to respond, except to say how sorry I was.*

*'My wife wants to have children,' he continued, 'but if I'm honest I'm frightened of the responsibility, of not being there for them. Beth, every single one of us walks around with a mask. Every single student here is probably scared of something, and sometimes we need to take our masks off and talk about our fears.'*

*In that moment I wanted to reach out and hold him and take his pain away. It was the first moment I noticed how blue his eyes were, and the first time I realized he had a life outside of teaching and signing us in each morning.*

*I wondered if it would be wrong to hold his hand.*

*I risked it.*

*'I'm sorry,' I said again. 'I can't imagine how tough that must have been.'*

*He held my gaze until finally he removed his hand from mine. 'Don't run away from yourself, Beth, or your problems.'*

*'I feel so alone,' I admitted. 'I don't know what to do, how to handle it. I can't talk to Mum,' I added, wishing with all my heart that I could.*

*'I understand, but the answer doesn't lie in the bottle. The answer comes from having the courage to be yourself and let others in.'*

# 30

## Flo

I come home, praying I won't bump into James. With any luck he'll be asleep. As I rummage in my handbag, trying to find my house keys, the door opens, but James's face is far from welcoming.

'Where the hell have you been?' he demands before I've even stepped inside.

'Out,' I reply, immediately on the defence, 'having a good time, thanks.'

'All I wanted was a text, Flo. It's nearly two in the morning.'

I walk past him, aware I must look a mess, and no doubt smelling of alcohol and smoke.

'I'm taking a shower,' I say, needing to wash away the memory of my night. 'Why are you still up?'

He grabs me by the arm. 'Why am I still *up*?'

'Let go, James. You're hurting me.'

'I've been worried about you.'

'I'm fine.' I take off my heels, my feet aching almost as much as my head.

'Where have you been all night?'

'I needed some time alone to think things through.'

'Where did you go?'

'Does it matter?' I raise my voice, not wanting to think about Nate's touch, his lips pressed against mine, me pushing him away, him shouting at me, saying I was a fucking tease.

'Well, wherever you were, I've been out trailing pubs and clubs trying to find you. I even woke up Granny Peg, who's also sick with worry, so thanks, Flo, thanks a lot, so long as you've had a good time, so long as *you're* fine.'

He walks away. I follow him into the kitchen, shame creeping in. 'I'm sorry, James, I should have called.'

He looks a fraction more forgiving until he says, 'Where's your ring?' He eyes my hand suspiciously.

And it's only then that I notice my bare wedding ring finger. With sheer terror, I empty the contents of my handbag on to the kitchen table. 'Why did you take it off?' he asks.

'Not now,' I say, unable to cope with any more questions or his disappointment.

I've lost it. Oh my God, I've not only lost my mind, but my ring too.

*I put it somewhere.*

My wallet! It was at the pub. Just before Nate bought me another drink . . .

The relief when I see it's still there is so enormous that I burst into tears. I look at it, shining like a star. Yet I have no right to put it back on, not after what I did.

I place it on the table.

'James, I'm so sorry,' I repeat, crumpling into a heap on the chair. 'I'm not fine. I'm far from fine. Please don't hate me because I hate myself enough already.'

'Oh, Flo, what have you done?' he says quietly, though of course he has a pretty good idea.

I fall into his arms, sobbing on his shoulder, and when finally my tears subside, I tell James everything. I tell him I lied to Theo, using Granny's health as an excuse not to go to New York. I tell him I've been reading Mum's diaries and that I'm terrified by what I'm discovering. And finally, I tell him about dancing with Nate and heading back to his flat, and then . . .

'We kissed, that's all, and it meant nothing.'

*'Stop.'* I'd said pushing Nate off me. *'I'm engaged.'*

*'So what? I wouldn't care if you were married.'*

'What happened next?' James asks.

'I told him that I did care, and that this was a mistake. He was angry, threw me out into the hallway, slammed the door, and here I am.'

'At least you didn't . . . I mean, for a moment I thought you'd—'

'But I could have. What was I thinking even going back to his flat?'

'You weren't thinking, not clearly.'

162

I press my head into my hands. 'I gave myself a made-up name. I was Rosie Chambers.' I turn away, unable to look at James. 'I'm not sure who I am anymore.'

'You're Flo, and right now you're terrified, and that's understandable. Anyone in your position would be finding this hard, but we'll find a way through this.'

James and I are talking in my bedroom, both of us in our pyjamas. I feel better now I've had a shower, my head clearer.

'Does it help reading these diaries, Flo?' James asks, after I've described what I've read so far, Mum now in her second year at Camberwell.

'Yes and no.' I smile. 'I hear her voice. It's interesting reading about her old tutor Mark. He knew Mum was at risk. At least someone did. She wasn't alone.'

'Where is he now?'

'No idea. I remember he and Mum were good friends when I was growing up; he'd come over for coffee or they'd see an exhibition together, that kind of thing. I often wondered if he and Mum might get together – there was a real spark between them but he was married. I think his sister lives in France,' I recall. 'I'm not sure he even came to the funeral.' I turn on to my side to face James. 'I want to carry on reading, but it's going to get even harder.'

'Take your time. But please, Flo, promise me you'll stop drinking heavily. I don't want to sound all righteous, but it's not the answer.'

'I know,' I say. 'I'm going to tell Theo, too,' I add. 'What happened with Nate was such a mistake. It meant *nothing*, but how am I going to tell him this on top of everything else?'

'Don't. No one needs to know about it, least of all Theo. Just focus on telling him what really matters. Do you know what you want to do, whether you want to take the test or not?'

'No idea.' I inhale deeply. 'But I need to talk to someone about it. I'm going to ask my GP if she can refer me to see a genetic counsellor.'

He nods. 'You're not alone, Flo. We're all here for you.'

'Even when I screw up?'

'Especially when you screw up.'

After James has gone back to his own room, and I'm finally drifting off to sleep, I find myself thinking not just about Theo; what have I done to deserve a friend like James, trailing clubs and bars looking for me?

They say you know who your true friends are in a crisis, those you can call at three a.m. who will drop everything to be with you.

If I do go to New York, and Theo and I do get married, I'm going to miss James far more than I could ever imagine.

# 31

*Beth's Diary, 1989*

*I was just in the canteen with Mark, reminiscing about
the past three years I've spent at Camberwell. When I
first arrived, it seemed far too hip and cool for me, all these
students driven by concepts, the idea that a bag of rubbish
was a work of art. All these weird and wonderful people
with dyed hair and body piercings living in squats or sofa
surfing. And then there was me, painting a bowl of lemons
or a view from the River Thames.*

*That's not to say I haven't learned anything since
coming here. We were given so much free rein from the
beginning that I used to wish we'd had more direction,
instead of hours of time alone, simply told to paint subjects
that inspired us. Hours that were often squandered going to
the pub – until Mark gave me that serious pep talk.*

*And thank God he did, because I needed to leave Ben and find a new job that wasn't anywhere near a pub. I'll miss working for Connor's florist business – instead of getting high on dope and booze, I've spent months feeling high from the smell of beautiful flowers. I'll miss my early morning trips to the flower market in Covent Garden, before drinking black coffee and listening to music while working in Connor's garage, designing table arrangements for marquees and parties.*

*Over the past few years, Mark has given me the confidence to find myself, and I can now see how his teaching has made me grow as an artist. I see London in a whole new light, how the traditional well-to-do, old terraced houses sit next to the rougher parts. I've become obsessed by how small I am, how small we all are, compared to the city around us.*

*We can be surrounded by people and still feel lonely, and I want my paintings to reflect that.*

*I told Mark about my break-up with Nick, how impossible it was going out with someone obsessed with perfection. I can't count the amount of times he has ripped his paintings up in front of me, saying he can do so much better, before cancelling all our plans so that he could work instead. Nick has been unbelievably stressed in the run-up to our final degree show, to the point where I couldn't take it anymore. We argued when I said there were more important things in life than results, that our degree wasn't a matter of life and death. The final straw was when I suggested he take the weekend off to spend some time with me, that maybe we could visit my parents – just pop in for a cup of tea. Well, that was it. With no emotion he told me that he couldn't focus on our relationship as well as his work, and that it was over.*

*When Mark mentioned I didn't appear too upset, I confessed I'd been unhappy with Nick for months. We'd drifted apart some time ago.*

*Nick and I had fun together, he's been supportive of my family and Dad's HD, and he can charm the birds off the trees, as Mum would say, especially when things are going his way. But he likes things to be just so; he needs to feel in control and when he's not, a darker side to him comes out.*

*I don't regret our time together, but deep down I always suspected it was going to come to a natural end, even if we'd said many times that we loved one another. Now I realize how easy it is to say those three words without meaning it or knowing if it's real or not.*

*Mum loves Dad. Dad loves Mum. However tough their life, their love is true.*

*The last time I went home I found Mum and Dad lying down in their bedroom, Mum's arms wrapped tightly around Dad's waist. She didn't know I was watching them through the crack in the door; she didn't realize what I heard her saying through muffled tears.*

*'I'm so sorry for losing my temper, Tim. Please forgive me. I didn't mean it, any of it. None of this is your fault.*

*I'm not sending you away. I promise you I'll never do that. I love you so much.'*

*And even if Dad couldn't say anything back, I knew he felt it and is grateful each day for Mum's unconditional loyalty and devotion.*

*I'm looking for a love like that, a love that can survive no matter what tests it.*

*The truth is, I'm not going to miss Nick. I'm going to miss Mark. He is my tutor, my friend and my counsel. He is the man who saved me when I was sinking, and I shall never forget his kindness. Mark knows every single thing about me, warts and all, which has only strengthened our friendship. I have discovered much more about his parents and his siblings. He likes to talk about his brother, to keep his memory alive. His sister lives in France. She's artistic like him and illustrates children's books. They write to each other regularly. Mark isn't scared to ask me questions about Dad, whereas many of my friends still skirt around the subject, clearly uncomfortable. He knows I still haven't talked to Mum about what HD means for me, but it helps me telling him my worries, even if there is no solution. In fact, if I think too much about the hole he is going to leave in my life I feel desperately sad, because I know that no one can replace him.*

*Occasionally, I have wondered if there is anything between us, whether he feels this bond too. Even if he does, he'd never act on it. He and his wife are trying for a baby. I think they've been trying for some time. He doesn't talk*

*too much about that, and I don't push him. Some things
need to remain private.*

*When he stood up saying he must go, I thanked him.*

*'For everything,' I said. Modestly, he claimed it
was his job, yet I could have sworn he wanted to say
something more.*

*Instead he shook my hand, adding, 'Have fun in
Amsterdam.'*

*I'd told Mark that a few friends and I were going
there to celebrate the end of exams before we found out
our results.*

*'Don't do anything I wouldn't do.' He smiled and
was about to leave, before I plucked up the courage to
call out, 'I'll miss you.' I sensed maybe I'd gone too far,
perhaps even crossed a line, so I added, 'Even when you
tell me off.'*

*He looked at me, as if hesitating with how to respond.
Finally his expression relaxed as if he was giving himself
permission to say it back. 'I'm going to miss you too,
Beth,' he said. 'I've never known anyone quite like you.'*

*I fought back the tears as I watched him leave, a piece of
my heart walking out with him.*

## 32

**Peggy**

'As Elvis is here, I might as well take a look at him,' James says, poor Elvis quivering on the examination table, nothing the matter with him except for his owner who has brought him in under false pretences so she can interrogate the vet. 'Has she told Theo?'

James feels under Elvis's tummy. 'He could do with losing some weight.'

'Couldn't we all.'

'Elvis has some serious love handles, Granny Peg. Ironic, isn't it, when he's been castrated.'

'What did Theo say?' I press James again.

'I think the time has come to feed Elvis lighter food, for the more mature dog.'

'James!'

'I feel uncomfortable talking about that.'

'But I need to know,' I beg. 'Ricky says I must be patient, but waiting is killing me, James, and that's very bad for my nerves. I have a bad heart, you know,' I try. Emotional blackmail is sometimes the only way to go. 'I promise I won't say a word.' I mime zipping up my lips.

He shakes his head. 'No, not yet.'

'Why not?' I ask, though I'm in no position to judge.

'She's seeing her GP today, who will hopefully refer her to a genetic counsellor. She's planning to work out her options before she tells him, okay? She wants to feel in control.'

I stick out my chin. 'So what's she told him in the meantime?'

'I don't know.'

I place my hands on my hips. 'You do.'

'It's up to Flo to tell you.'

'Is she reading the diaries?'

'Crikey, Elvis, you win the gold medal for smelly breath.' He looks up at me. 'Go to the butcher's and get Elvis some marrowbones to chomp on, and his teeth could do with a clean. Use a cloth and salt water.'

'*James!*'

'*Yes*, and she's finding it tough,' he concedes, 'but I think you did the right thing giving them to her.'

'Is she still drinking?'

'Enough,' James says, his tone sharp. 'She's safe. She's doing well. She's working through this, and she'll call you when she's ready.' James lifts Elvis off the table and attaches the lead to his collar. 'Take your old boy for some nice long

171

walks,' he suggests. 'If anything critical happens, I will let you know, I promise.' He opens his door.

'How are you, James?' I ask, not leaving.

He looks thrown by the question. 'I'm good.'

'It can't be easy for you, all of this. I didn't just come here to fire questions at you. I also wanted to thank you for looking out for Flo. She needs a friend like you.'

His guard finally drops before he closes his door and leans against it. 'I'll always be there for her. She's like family.' He pauses. 'If I'm honest, Granny Peg, it's made me put things in perspective. If I've had a bad day at work, it's just a bad day, but what you and your husband went through, what Flo is now going through, I've realized I'm lucky to be alive and to be well.'

'Thank you, James, I appreciate that.'

He touches my shoulder with solidarity. 'I promise I'll keep in touch. Try not to worry.'

'That's like asking me not to breathe.' I compose myself. 'But you're right. I must keep busy. I'll go home . . . and brush Elvis's teeth.'

I chuckle. 'I can't wait. Lucky old me.'

# 33

**Flo**

It's Thursday, less than a week after my last day at work, though in many ways that feels like a lifetime ago. My GP peers at her computer screen. We've had a good appointment. She's going to refer me to a genetic counsellor at a hospital in Tooting. I stressed the sooner the better, explaining my situation. She was sympathetic, understanding it must have been a shock to find out I could be at risk of HD in my twenties, and she thought it would be a good idea to speak to a counsellor, but the referral could take anything between six and eight weeks.

'And health-wise, everything else is okay, Florence?' she asks.

'Yes, fine,' I reply, thinking I really couldn't handle any further complications right now.

'Last time I saw you, goodness, almost a year ago now,

you were having particularly heavy periods and I gave you some tablets for that. Have they helped?'

'Yes,' I mutter, suddenly trying to recall when my last period was and realizing it's late. 'Though sometimes they can be later than usual. That's normal, isn't it?'

'How late?'

'A couple of weeks.'

'Do you think you could be pregnant?'

'I hope not.'

'Are your periods often late?'

I shake my head. 'But I can't be.' I feel sick. 'I've been stressed; the last few weeks haven't been easy, that could be a reason, couldn't it?'

'Don't panic. There could be a number of reasons why. Some people skip their periods entirely when they're on contraception, although that hasn't been the case with you, so perhaps it's worth taking a test, just for your peace of mind.'

I leave her office abruptly, before heading to the pharmacy attached to the surgery to buy a pregnancy test.

On my way home, I stare out of the bus window, reassuring myself Theo and I have been careful. As my GP said, there could be a number of reasons why I'm late. Stress. No sleep. Secrets. Lies. More stress. More lies. Heavy drinking.

My mobile vibrates. It's a text message from Theo. I still need to tell him, but constantly find reasons not to, unable to risk possibly losing him too.

**How's Peggy? Am missing you. Call me with the
latest news. Tx**

I want to have a child, a family; of course I do. Theo and
I have talked about it. We both agreed we'd like to have a
few years to travel and be married without kids, if possible.
I'm only twenty-seven, there is no particular rush, and what
with everything else going on right now, and the idea that
my baby could be at risk . . .

No, I can't even go down that road.

*I'm not pregnant. I can't be.*

# 34

*Beth's Diary, 1989*

*Oh, Beth, you really do know how to make your life
complicated, don't you? I have no idea what to do, and this
time I can't go running to Mark.*

*I'm not at college anymore. It's not his job to clean
up my mess.*

*The last time we spoke was when he congratulated
me on my 2:1. I was staring at the board in case I'd
got it wrong. Later, I discovered I'd missed a First by
just one mark.*

*The owner of the gallery in South Kensington where I'd
mounted my degree show called me, saying he'd like me to
work for them in the future.*

*'If that doesn't give you the confidence to go out into
the world and be an artist, I don't know what will, Beth,'*

*Mark said when we met up for a coffee, Mark unable to wipe the proud smile off his face.*

*Well, I didn't exactly plan to go out into the world and be knocked up by some stranger only weeks after getting my results.*

*What an achievement.*

*I went to see my GP. I told her I'd skipped a couple of periods, but not once did I think I could be pregnant because I'd taken a test a couple of months ago, after returning from Amsterdam. She told me that, occasionally, this does happen; pregnancy tests can initially show up negative, people can have no early symptoms and hardly any weight gain. She sent me to the hospital to have a scan.*

*I am four and a half months pregnant. I have the image to prove it.*

*He was Italian. I'd say early thirties, around Mark's age. He was on a stag weekend. Not his thing, he said, unnecessarily expensive with all that pressure to get drunk. He said he could slip away, none of the lads would notice as they'd been drinking since noon.*

*'The groom has already passed out,' he said with a smile, his eyes flirting with mine. We headed back to my hotel room and raided the mini bar. I felt young, carefree and happy. The memory of Nick, Mark, of home and Dad, seemed a million miles away.*

*He left the following morning, no note on the bed, no romantic gesture of meeting up again. I knew nothing about* him – not even his name – and the funny thing is I didn't care at the time. We'd danced. We'd laughed. We'd had sex, and it was amazing. It was exactly what I needed to try and forget about the man I could never have.

I don't know what to do.

I know, when – or if – I tell Mum, she'll be disappointed in me. She longs for me to have a successful career like my father and have all the opportunities she never had. She grew up without a mother and always said her life felt incomplete with only one parent, no matter how kind her aunt was. I also dread to think what she'll say when I tell her I have no idea how to trace the father.

It's at times like this I miss talking to Dad. I know he'd never judge and he always used to give me good advice. It's impossible to know how much he understands now. Mum and I talk to him as if he does, even if his eyes are glazed over and he doesn't answer back.

I could book myself in for an abortion. But what if I regret the decision for the rest of my life? The doctor advised me to take my time, although I don't have that much to spare.

Do I want to be a single mum? Is it fair to raise a child without giving them a father?

I realize the more important question is: is it fair to bring someone into a life of uncertainty?

If I have inherited this gene from Dad, it isn't his fault because he never knew his father, who died fighting in the Second World War, had the condition. There is also doubt

*as to whether he really was Dad's father – he's always
suspected he could be the result of an affair. We know
Dad's mother had no signs of HD. She died of cancer in
her early fifties.*

*For me it's different. I know that if I have this little boy
or girl, I might be putting him or her at risk. Can I really
do that? Equally, how can I live with myself if I abort a
perfectly healthy baby?*

*I wish the right answer would come to me, a message in
the sky, a sign, anything. Even if I were still at college, I'm
not sure I could tell Mark, however tempting it might be to
rush into his arms.*

*How I'd hate to see his pride turn to bitter disappointment.*

# 35

**Flo**

I'm not pregnant. I took the test the moment I arrived home, before collapsing into bed and sleeping deeply for the first time in days, the relief so overwhelming that I can now return all my attention to telling Theo and deciding whether to take the other test.

I'm hoping I'll find out soon through Mum's diaries if she dithered or not. Was she certain she was doing the right thing? *Is* there a right thing? I imagine not. What's right for me or Mum isn't necessarily going to be right for the next person. I can't imagine anyone finds this decision easy.

I pick up the photograph on my bedside table that Mum took of me in our back garden. I'm wearing my favourite poppy dress and my hair is styled in two long plaits, tied with red velvet ribbons. I remember Mum taking this as we were about to visit Granny and Granddad for tea.

I longed to have a father. I longed to have a normal family, whatever normal was.

I pick up a new diary. I'm now four years old. It's strange reading Mum's diaries now that I'm in them. Growing up you never think your parents had a life before you came along. You also don't imagine they had any problems.

I keep looking back, wondering how I never noticed the signs, although I was only little. I never questioned why Granddad was in a wheelchair. I was only interested in how fast it could go, and whether I could ride on it too.

I loved going over to Granny's for tea. We'd play games or I'd sit at their kitchen table and paint and draw. Often I'd help Granny bake a cake or a batch of scones.

'Splat!' she'd say when Granddad dropped his slice of Victoria sponge on the floor, and we'd all laugh too. I didn't think their set-up was odd at all, or the fact Granny and Granddad rarely went out or visited us at home.

Occasionally, I'd see someone on the television in a wheelchair and point to the screen saying, 'Look, Mama, he's in a chair like Granddad!' There was only one time I remember thinking something was wrong. It was the first and only time I saw Mum cry. I asked why she was so sad, but she never told me. It's only now I'm close to guessing.

# 36

Beth's Diary, 1994

*I hadn't planned on seeing my parents today, but when
Mum said she needed to talk to me, I knew it must be
important. Mum rarely demands my time, especially
since I've had Flo. She understands it's not easy being a
single mum.*

*Initially, when I told Mum I was pregnant and wanted
to keep my child, she was furious. How could I have let
myself down? How could I have saddled myself with a child
without having a job or even knowing the father?*

*I understood her anger. It was only when Flo was born
that she changed. The moment she held her in her arms
she was in love, and since then she has wanted to do
everything in her power to support us. This is where Mum
is so kind, so good. In order to help me financially, she was*

*determined to move into a smaller space that would give her some capital to help me invest in a property. 'Please, Beth, let me do this for you and my grandchild. I know it's what your dad would want too.'*

*So Mum and Dad moved to Hammersmith and Flo and I moved to Barnes, close to Flo's primary school where I now teach art.*

*As I helped Flo put on her poppy dress and tie her plaits with red ribbons, my little girl was wondering with great excitement what games we might play, whereas all I could do was worry about what it was Mum needed to talk to me about. It had to be something to do with Dad.*

*It's hard now, visiting Dad at home. When I look into his eyes I long to see a glimmer of life, anything to suggest he knows who I am. Yet his body is no more than a shell; his soul has gone. Both Mum and I realize that, in many ways, we have been lucky. He has suffered severe frustration and anxiety, who wouldn't? But he has never, once, become aggressive towards us.*

*Dad's doctor had warned Mum that very often behaviour can change, people can become intensely depressed and angry, occasionally violent, but we haven't seen any of this.*

*He has only faded, if that's the right word, day by day.*

*I don't know how Mum has managed to look after a man who can no longer walk, talk, swallow, is fed through a peg and wears incontinence pads. She does have a nurse who comes in three times a week, but I still worry about the physical toll it takes on her, with no break, and I'd already suggested several times the moment has come for Dad to go into a nursing home.*

*And tonight, Mum felt it too.*

*She struggled to talk to me, but I knew what she was trying to say. While Flo was next door, lying on the floor watching television with Granddad, Mum took me to one side in the kitchen. She cleared her throat, composed herself.*

*'Beth, your father is heavy, I'm not strong enough to lift him and—'*

*'Mum.' I touched her arm. 'Let's give the nursing home a call.'*

*'I've done it already, Beth. I'm taking him tomorrow.'*

*And for the first time in years, Mum pulled me towards her and hugged me, and she cried. She cried for all these years that she has cared for him painstakingly, and all I could do was to hold her, saying no one could have loved Dad like she had, so devotedly.*

*Mum dried her eyes and then finally looked at me, and again I knew what she was thinking, which gave me the confidence at last to say it.*

*'There's a test I could take. I've spoken about it with my GP.'*

*My doctor told me it became available over a year ago, in 1993, and I've done nothing but think about it ever since. All it takes is a blood test to determine my fate. How I long to say, after everything Mum has been through, 'It's okay. I tested negative.'*

*Mum shook her head and moved away from me, as if I was about to cause her physical pain. 'Don't, Beth,' she said, 'please don't.'*

*'But Mum—'*

*She turned round to me. 'Promise me you won't.'*

*She didn't need to give me a reason why, and I knew this wasn't exactly the best timing on my part, Mum feeling so upset at the thought of sending Dad to a home, 'But this could affect Flo,' I said, my voice small.*

*We both looked into the sitting room, where Flo was still watching television, happy, oblivious.*

*'You don't have it, Beth. You can't,' she said, as if ordering reality to obey her words. 'It would kill me.'*

*'Why are you crying, Mama?' Flo asked, standing by the kitchen door, holding her fluffy owl toy. I hadn't even realized I was until I wiped the tears away. 'Mama,' Flo said, looking up at me, 'why are you so sad?'*

*Of course I couldn't tell her, and Mum immediately took her away, saying it was time to play a game, before glancing over her shoulder and mouthing at me again, 'Promise me you won't, Beth.'*

# 37

## Peggy

'It's hard to believe I did the right thing, when Flo still won't speak to me,' I say, laying flowers on their grave. 'But there we are. I can't go back now. I saw James today. He told me she's well and wants to see a counsellor. I'm glad she isn't alone.'

Tears fill my eyes at the thought of Beth, who was always there for her father and me, despite herself being alone to care for Flo. I remember all those times she rushed over, day or night. I can see, vividly, both of us trying to lift Tim back into bed after he'd fallen out in the middle of the night, something that was becoming a habit.

'Mum,' she'd said, 'we can't go on like this. He needs to be in a home.'

'He needs to be with *us*,' I'd replied, still unable to let him go, until I too realized it was for the best.

Then I see Beth rushing over to my house in the early hours of the morning, one last time, still in her pyjamas.

Tim had had a terrible night. He was sweating, shaking and his breathing had become rapid and shallow. The duty doctor had said Tim had pneumonia, and that the best thing we could do now was to keep him comfortable at home. All I could do was to hold his hand and stroke his forehead.

*Had he known he was about to go into a nursing home? Does it work like that?*

I remember vividly, Beth saying goodbye to her father. 'To me you'll always be my dad who used to run into the sea in your baggy blue shorts, dragging Mum and me with you. I remember all those times we'd go for long walks in the countryside and you'd stand in front of a stream and say, "Do you think I can make it?" and so often you didn't, Dad. You fell in and ended up caked in mud.'

I smile at the memory myself, of my Tim. How he loved to play the fool.

'I've learned so much from you, Dad. You taught me to look at how things are made, that there is beauty in everything. I loved all the time we spent painting and drawing together. You were ...' Beth stopped. 'You *are* clever, talented, kind and I have been so unbelievably lucky to have had you in my life.'

By now, both Beth and I had stopped trying to fight off the tears.

I picked up when Beth could no longer continue. I knelt down on the other side of the bed and held my Tim's hand. 'I'm so sorry you've had to endure this,' I said, 'something you didn't deserve. No one deserves this, but you've done it with dignity and courage, and I couldn't be prouder of you . . .' My voice was breaking. 'You are the bravest man I know.' I stroked his hair and kissed his forehead. 'But Tim, let go.' I pleaded. 'Please let go.'

In the end, it was the right thing to do. I had to say goodbye. He needed to go to a better place.

A place where I hoped he'd be free, where he could be his old self again.

Beth had returned with Flo. She knelt down beside him and told her there was nothing to be afraid of.

'Darling, say goodbye to Granddad,' she'd said calmly to Flo, who was only four at the time. Beth held on to her hand and she stepped forward and kissed her Granddad on the cheek.

Then my Tim stopped breathing.

Beth looked at me. The room was silent. We both held his hand, willing him together to let go, for all of us, now. And he listened.

Now, I touch his name, engraved into the stone.

TIMOTHY GEORGE ANDREWS,

24 OCTOBER 1938 – 8 MAY 1994;

BELOVED HUSBAND, FATHER AND GRANDFATHER.

REST IN PEACE.

I have to believe Tim's in a better place now, where he and Beth are together again.

# 38

**Flo**

'I'm going for a run,' James calls. 'Need anything while I'm out?'

*Don't cry.*

'Great,' I say closing Mum's diary and holding it close to my chest.

'Flo?' He sticks his head round the door. 'Hey, what's wrong?' He enters my room and sits down, but I can't speak. 'Have you told Theo? Is this about your appointment with the GP today?'

'Granddad just died,' I say, dissolving into tears. Mum's diaries have opened a door to a whole new world I didn't know existed. A world of pain, loss, guilt, fear and secrets. But they have also shown me human resilience, spirit, courage, unconditional love and kindness. Granny stood by Granddad until the very end. Mum held his hand until his very last breath.

I wish I'd had the chance to tell Mum how sorry I am that she had to watch her father die slowly, day by day. How I'd have hated watching her suffer in the same way. And how I wish I'd known what a brave and wonderful person Granddad was.

Why is it we only find things out about the people we love when it's much too late?

'Go, I'm fine,' I say, knowing how much James needs a run to unwind after work, even if I can't think of anything worse.

'Are you sure?'

I take a deep breath. 'Go, James,' I insist this time, before I crack again. 'I want to see Granny.'

Gently he wipes away my tears with his thumb. 'I couldn't be prouder of you.'

'Don't be too nice,' I say, laughing through the tears, 'you'll make me cry even more.'

He holds out his hand. 'Come on, I'll give you a lift. My run can wait.'

Just as we reach the front door, I turn round. 'Did you forget something?' he asks.

'Yes. This.' I kiss him on the cheek. 'Thank you, James, for being one of the best people I know.'

# 39

## Peggy

I'm planting some basil and parsley in the two new pots I bought from the garden centre today, after walking Elvis back from the cemetery. I frown when I hear someone knocking on the door. It can't be Ricky because he and his family are on holiday. They hired a camper van and went to Poole, by the seaside.

I'm tempted to leave it as it's such a bore taking off my dirty gardening gloves. Unless you're Paul Martin, the dishy presenter of my favourite antiques programme, *Flog It!*, please go away.

Whoever it is knocks again.

'All right, I'm coming!' *Keep your hair on!*

I look through the peephole and open the door at once.

'Hello, Granny,' she says.

It's not often I'm lost for words, but when I open my mouth

nothing comes out, and when Flo embraces me, I break down into uncontrollable tears, my heart finally beating with hope again, that the person I thought I'd lost has come back to me.

'I'm so sorry for all those things I said to you that night,' Flo says as we drink our coffee in the kitchen.

'I deserved everything you said, and more.'

'But I had no idea how hard it was for you, looking after Granddad. If I'd known—'

'How could you have known? We should have told you years ago. I should have handled it better; it's something I'll always regret. Your mother and me, if *only* we had talked.'

'Reading her diaries, I longed to bang your heads together,' she agrees.

'I let her down,' is all I can say, the shame refusing to go away.

'She wanted to talk to you, but was too scared because you'd already suffered enough.'

'After your granddad died I was empty. I had no fuel left in my tank so I refused even to consider the possibility of your mother having HD. I was weak,' I admit.

'You weren't weak. You were human.'

'I was weak,' I correct her, not allowing Flo to let me off the hook so easily. I have to own my mistakes. 'I understand it's going to take a long time for things to go back to the way they used to be but—'

'Granny,' Flo says, her voice crumbling, 'I need you now more than ever before.'

'Well, I'm here, and I'll do whatever it takes for you to trust me again.' I wait, sensing Flo is holding something back. 'What is it, darling?'

'I haven't told Theo yet.'

'Ah, I see,' I say, feeling in no position to offer any advice on how or when to tell him. 'But you must have had to explain why you're still here?'

'I said you were unwell.'

'Unwell?' I stick out my chin. 'What's wrong with me?'

'You're at hospital having tests.'

'Don't you dare put me in the departure lounge just yet,' I say with a hint of a smile, though Flo remains distant, lost in her thoughts. 'Flo, are you scared of telling him because you think he'll be frightened off?'

She turns to me. 'Maybe. I'm trying to imagine how I'd feel if it were the other way round, if Theo were at risk. But I'm going to have to tell him soon,' she concedes. 'I spoke to him today, but he was in a rush. It wasn't the right moment, but I feel terrible for lying. I feel so guilty, and I miss him.'

'Do you still love him?'

'Yes.'

'You want to marry him and have a family?'

She nods, slowly. 'Nothing's changed,' she says, 'but everything was straightforward a few weeks ago. I was about to start this new life.' She glances at her ring, 'But how can I when so much of my past isn't . . .'

She stops, unable to articulate her feelings, but I think I know what she is trying to convey. How can she start a

193

new chapter in her life when the previous one has been completely rewritten?

Flo clears her throat. 'Do you think Mum's HD was the reason Graham left?' Graham was Mum's fiancé. Flo adored him. He was the father she'd never had. But then, overnight, he disappeared.

'I don't know,' I say, though strongly suspect it's a possibility. 'Maybe Beth wrote about it in her diary?'

'I haven't reached that part yet. I hardly dare. I always suspected there was more to it too. None of it made sense at the time.'

'I think you'll feel better once you tell Theo. He loves you,' I say, praying to God he doesn't let her down. 'Get on that plane, Flo, don't stop living your life.'

'I'll miss you.'

'And I'll miss you. But we can Skype.'

Flo stares at me as if I've just said I can do a bungee jump. I smile. 'Ricky taught me.'

She smiles back. 'Did you notice Mum had symptoms?'

'Perhaps. Yes,' I confess. 'I tried not to see them at first.'

'I keep thinking I should have seen the signs.'

'But you were away at college. You wouldn't have noticed because Beth was still able to lead a fairly normal life.' I take her hand. 'Do you think you want to take the test, Flo?' I have to ask.

She shakes her head. 'I don't know. I realize last time I rushed into it. I didn't even understand what HD was; it was just this thing I didn't want to have. But now I've read

Mum's diaries . . .' She pauses. 'I want at least to see a genetic counsellor and talk about it.'

'Have you made an appointment?'

'I'm being referred. I want Theo to come to my first one because we'll need advice about having a family.'

'I understand. I think that's very sensible.'

'Tell me more about Granddad,' Flo asks with renewed strength in her voice.

'Well, he loved his red wine and dark chocolate.'

'But how did you meet?'

'I was living with a friend who was going out with Tim at the time.'

'Granny, did you steal him from your friend?' she teases, and it's good to see her smile again.

'Well, they'd only been on a few dates. The poor girl had eaten something dodgy and had terrible diarrhoea so she asked me if I could go to the opera with him instead – La Traviata – so off we went, and we got on like a house on fire.'

She leans her elbows on the table and cocks her head to one side, just as Beth used to. 'Was it love at first sight?'

'In a way it was. He was funny, kind, interesting, creative, all the things I'm not. I couldn't believe my luck when he asked me if I'd like to go out with him again.'

'What happened to your friend?'

'She didn't seem to mind. We were engaged and married within a year. It was so different in my day: you'd meet a nice man, he'd ask you out for dinner and then he'd pop the question.'

'Theo said he knew he was going to marry me on the day we met,' she reminds me.

'Well, he was right.' I sigh. 'I fell in love with Tim over the years in a way I could never have imagined. He used to kiss me first thing in the morning and last thing at night.' Gently, I stroke my cheek as if I can still feel his touch. 'I never thought I'd get married, Flo.'

'Why not?'

'I don't know. When I tried to imagine the kind of man I might meet, all I could picture was a blank face. I think that's the moment when you know you're in love. You see your life together,' I reflect. 'The moment he shook my hand, I saw our children, adventure and a new home. I can't explain why, I just did. We may have been unlucky in many ways but we were so lucky in others. He was one of the best people I've ever known.'

'Is that why you never met anyone else after he died?'

I nod. '"When I'm gone, Peg," he used to say to me, "move on with your life, meet a new chap, don't be alone".'

I can see his generous smile that reached his eyes, the smile I fell head over heels in love with. 'The idea of meeting another man, of starting over again', I continue, 'hasn't once crossed my mind. Can you imagine me going on a date? Besides, no one would put up with an old boot like me.'

'They would.'

'Much easier to have a dog, Flo. They don't argue back.'

'How *did* you cope with his HD?' Flo asks. 'I mean, it seems a lot for Theo to take on if—'

I can't let her finish her sentence. 'You have no choice,' I interrupt. 'You dig deep and find a strength you never realized you had, and all I can say is if I had to live my life all over again, I'd make the same choices. I don't know what Beth wrote, but it wasn't all bad Flo. When he was made redundant his colleagues did a collection and presented him with a cheque for five thousand pounds. It was a blow to his pride not working, but our doctor advised Tim to think of it in another way, saying that if he had been diagnosed with a terminal illness, would he want to carry on sitting in an office or would he prefer spending time with his family and ticking off all the things on his bucket list? Until that moment, Tim and I had thought we might put any savings we had into a new kitchen, but in the end we used that money to go travelling while we still could.'

'Where did you go?'

'Where *didn't* we go! We visited the Pyramids, as Tim had always wanted to. We went to Rajasthan and Jaipur. It had been a dream of your granddad's to take his easel to India. I remember the delicious breakfasts we had on the balcony. It was a lovely family-run hotel. Tim would have his usual two fried eggs.'

'What about you, Granny?'

'I think I just had toast and fruit. I can't really remember.'

'No, what's on *your* bucket list?'

'Oh, goodness, I never made one.'

'Why not?'

'I don't know. I didn't need to. We did other things,

too, like going on long cycle rides or driving to the coast. Tim loved the sound of the sea, so we'd have picnics on the beach.'

'It all sounds much more fun than a new kitchen,' Flo suggests.

'I'd have liked both. But we made the right choice. You can't hold on to the memory of a new oven. I'd have lived in a tin hut if it meant banking more memories with my Tim.'

'Do you know what we should do? Make a bucket list.'

'What a good idea.'

'You too, Granny.'

'Oh no, I'm too old for that.'

'No, you're not. You just told me not to put you in the departure lounge just yet. There must be something you long to do?'

'Nothing,' I say, reminded of the conversation I had with Ricky. 'I just want you to be happy.'

'Oh, Granny.' Flo looks away, as if scared she'll cry again.

'I'd like to go back to Burgh Island,' I reflect, 'in Devon. It's where Tim and I went on our honeymoon.'

Flo's face brightens. 'Well, we should go!'

'I'd love to go to Rome, too. Eat ice cream in that famous square. And you, Flo?'

'I'd like to do something I never imagined I'd be capable of,' she thinks out loud. 'I don't know what that is yet, but I'll work it out.'

It's moments like this when I see Beth in her. She certainly gets her strength from her mother. 'I'm sure you will,' I say.

'You never once wanted to leave him? It didn't get too much?' she asks, gently.

'Occasionally,' I confess.

'You looked after him like a saint, Granny.'

'Oh, Flo, that's not true. I used to shout at Tim for breaking yet another plate or forgetting that he'd left the oven on and burning our supper. Then there was the time when Tim left the bathwater running for three hours and I came home to a flood. I knew none of it was his fault, but you'd have to be a saint not to get frustrated, and believe me, I was far from one. Sometimes I had to go into the garden and scream. Other times I had to take the dog out for a walk to calm myself down and hear myself think. Often I dreamt about packing my bags and never coming home.'

'Why didn't you?'

'Love.' I realize that's not a good enough answer. It goes deeper than that. 'A sense of duty and commitment.'

'If I did take the test, and tested positive, or if things did become . . . well, I wouldn't want Theo to feel he *has* to stay with me out of duty.'

'I didn't mean it quite like that. Oh, how can I put it?' I look at Flo, understanding what concerns her. 'It's not until you truly love someone Flo, that you realize you'll do anything for them, no matter what. Tim was my world, my rock, my best friend, and in the years when I couldn't turn to him for advice, when I had to care for him full-time, he was still there for me, Flo. He was always the man I married, just hidden under the blanket of HD. The love never went away. If anything, it grew.'

'It's a lot to ask of anyone, though, isn't it?'

'There was never a question, Flo.'

'Even to live with someone who could possibly be gene positive?'

'Give Theo the chance to make that choice. There's so much more help out there now,' I add, 'much more than there was for Tim and me. There are better treatments and new drugs in the pipeline. There may even be a cure one day.'

'Do you really believe that?'

'Yes,' I reply, because I have to now. Deep down I couldn't face Beth taking the test because I didn't want anything to steal my hope that she didn't have the gene. 'None of us know what's round the corner. Anything is possible, Flo.'

'How would you tell Theo, Granny?'

I reach for her hand. 'I'm not the person to ask.' Still, she waits for me to continue. 'You have to tell him in your own way,' I suggest, 'but if there's one thing I've learned, and probably your mother learned it too, is that the longer you wait, the harder it becomes.'

# 40

*Beth's Diary, 1998*

*I've had quite a day. I told Graham I was taking the afternoon off work to see my dentist for a root canal filling. I couldn't tell him I was seeing a genetic counsellor because he doesn't want me to take the test.*

*Amanda Harding is in her forties, auburn hair, slim build, dark rimmed glasses and a nametag around her neck. The first thing she asked me was why I wanted to come to the genetics clinic. I was shocked to find out that about eighty per cent of people at risk don't want to find out if they have the gene or not. Amanda said often they think they do, but counselling can change their mind. Yet this still didn't sway me. I told her I wanted to take the test sooner rather than later, maybe even today if possible? She didn't answer, instead telling me to go to back to the beginning, that it helped to draw a family tree.*

*We talked about Flo, and how she was a big reason why I felt I needed to know. Surely finding out I was negative would release her from the burden I was facing now? She agreed, telling me release was the biggest reason people took the test.*

*We also talked about Graham and how we'd been together for almost two years now, and were beginning to talk about having a family. I told Amanda he knew all about my father's HD and was very supportive. What I didn't let on was that I was seeing her behind his back. As far as he's concerned, he's prepared to take the risk that I might get HD. He's determined to believe I'll be okay.*

*'Sure, there's a fifty per cent chance you have it, but there's also a fifty per cent chance you don't,' he says.*

*I fibbed to Amanda yet again and said that if Graham and I were to start a family we both wanted me to get tested. She understood, but did ask if I'd thought about the repercussions if the results weren't what I hoped for.*

*She had to feel sure I could face either result. She stressed I needed time.*

*'I've had far too much time to think about it already,' I protested. 'And time isn't going to make any difference to the test.'*

*'But time will make a difference as to how you respond to it,' she said, her tone challenging.*

*The mood in the room dipped further when she*

*suggested I bring my mother or Graham to my next*
*appointment. I lost my cool then, saying both of them*
*worked, but supported me one hundred per cent.*

*One lie can easily breed another.*

*Amanda said she wasn't trying to put barriers in my*
*way, that it may well be the right thing for me to find out,*
*but she was obliged, under international guidelines, to give*
*people at least three appointments before they made up*
*their mind. The counselling process normally took months,*
*for some it took longer, even years. Everyone is different.*

*'What would you do, if you were me?' I asked*
*eventually.*

*She took her glasses off and rubbed her eyes, saying*
*she couldn't answer that. 'All I can say is if you did test*
*positive, Beth, there is support. I am always humbled by*
*how families pull together. I have seen some truly amazing*
*things in my time working here.'*

*When I returned home, Graham and Flo were cooking*
*brownies, Flo laughing as she licked the wooden spoon.*

*'How did the dentist go?' he asked, giving me a hug,*
*before I opened the fridge – anything to avoid eye contact –*
*and reached for a bottle of wine. 'As both my favourite girls*
*are with me, I have something to say,' Graham continued,*
*'well, something to ask. I was going to wait until our*
*anniversary next week,' he said to me, before I watched*
*him dig into his pocket to retrieve a small black box. He*
*knelt down on bended knee. 'Elizabeth Andrews,' he said,*
*'will you marry me?'*

I almost dropped the bottle of wine. I didn't know what to say.

'Say yes, Mummy!' Flo said, jumping up and down with excitement.

'I didn't think you believed in marriage?' was all I could utter.

'Nor did I until I met you. I want us to be a proper family and have kids of our own.' He turned to my daughter. 'What do you reckon, Flo?'

What a silly question to ask her. She was already sitting at the kitchen table designing her bridesmaid dress.

As for me . . .

All I could think about was the joyful day Graham turned up on his motorbike to fix my nasty grey computer. I was so relieved that I didn't have to buy another one that, without thinking, I gave him a hug, before asking how much I owed.

'Dinner?' he had said. And now, almost two years on from that dinner, we have the chance to share our future together.

So I said yes.

I'm going to arrange my second appointment with Amanda. I have to find out, and then I can put this behind me, once and for all.

# 41

## Flo

'Good luck,' says Maddie down the telephone. 'Theo will understand. You're doing the right thing, I promise.'

I take a deep breath, wishing I felt stronger.

Maddie must pick up on my nerves because she asks if James is home.

'He'll be back around nine.'

'Good. I don't want you to be alone.'

'I'm cooking him supper.'

She laughs. 'What's he done to deserve that?'

Something tells me to keep quiet about the fact he has slept in my bed for the past few nights; that he has been the rock I have clung on to since I found out the news.

'How did the interview go by the way?' I ask, suddenly remembering Maddie was meeting the director of *King Lear* this week.

'I got it,' she says quietly, as if she's ashamed to have good news.

'Oh my God!' I gasp, 'Why didn't you say something before?'

'Because it's not that important—'

'It *is* important,' I argue, resolutely telling myself to send her some flowers tomorrow. 'Whatever shit is happening in my life I always want to hear your good news, okay?'

'Fine,' she says, with a smile in her voice. 'I am pretty chuffed.'

'So you should be. Congratulations, Maddie.'

I glance at my watch. It's eight thirty, so it will be mid afternoon for Theo. When I called him earlier today he was in yet another meeting and asked me to call him back around this time. 'Go,' Maddie says, sensing I need to get this call over and done with. 'And if you need me, I'm here, at the end of the line, or I can jump on a train.'

'You're the best,' I say, touched. 'I don't know what I'd have done without you Baileys.'

After I end the call with Maddie, I dial Theo's number.

*I can do this*, I say to myself.

Besides, I can't keep on lying to him. My time is up. My heart is in my mouth when I hear the international dialling tone.

'Flo,' he says. 'Sorry about earlier, it's been crazy busy recently. How are you?'

'I'm good,' is my kneejerk response.

'And Peggy?'

'Theo, we need to talk.'

'This sounds ominous.'

'It's important; it's something I should have told you sooner.'

'You're still coming, right?'

'Yes.'

'For a moment I thought you were about to call the whole thing off,' he says, relief flooding his voice. When he notices I'm not laughing with him, 'Flo, what is it? What's wrong?'

'I don't know where to start.'

'You're scaring me,' he says, which is something I suspect Theo has never confessed to anyone.

'I'm sorry.' I take another deep breath. 'I wasn't entirely honest with you. Granny isn't unwell.'

'Sorry? What do you mean?'

'She hasn't been in hospital.'

'I'm not following.'

'Please don't be angry.'

'Flo, just tell me.'

He waits.

I glance at the piece of paper in front of me with the notes I made. 'Granny told me that Granddad died of Huntington's Disease.'

'Right,' he says, clearly none the wiser. 'What's that?'

'It's a neurological condition,' I say, trying to keep my voice level and calm. I hear him tapping some keys. 'I'm sorry, but what's that got to do with us?' he asks. 'Ah, here it is.'

'Theo, don't look it up.'

'It says here it's hereditary. Did your mum have it?'

'Yes. I've only just found out.'

'I don't understand. How come you didn't know any of this?'

'Granny kept it from me, and so did Mum.'

'Why?'

'I don't know.'

'It says here there's a fifty-fifty chance . . . oh my God, Flo.'

'I could have it too,' I say quietly.

'Why didn't you tell me this instead of making up news about Peggy?'

'I wanted to, but—'

'You should have told me, right from the start, instead of—'

'I wish I had,' I interrupt, 'but I could hardly explain it to myself, let alone to you.'

There's a long silence.

'I'm sorry, Theo. You have every right to be cross, but please try to understand: this came as a massive shock and I needed time to get my head around it.'

'I understand,' he says, his tone finally softening, until he adds, 'but I still can't believe Peggy didn't tell you this until now. How fucking irresponsible.'

'It was hard for her,' I say, surprised by how quickly I rush to her defence.

'You had a right to know. In fact, so did I.'

'She's desperately sorry.'

'Sorry? It's a bit too late to say sorry, isn't it? This is unbelievable,' he says, as if he's still reading something off his screen. 'So where does this leave us?'

'I still love you. I want to be with you.'

'Right,' he states matter-of-factly.

'But obviously, like you said, this does affect you too.'

'I don't know what to say.'

'Let's talk about this when I'm with you. I've been look-ing into flights. Theo?'

'It says here—'

'There's a lot of scaremongering online,' I warn him, recalling what James had said to me.

'What if you test positive, Flo?'

'I'm not sure I will even take the test, but if I do, it doesn't have to be the end. There are new treatments, more support and research,' I say, echoing Granny last night. 'Look, I'm packed and ready. I miss you.' He doesn't say he misses me back, so I continue, 'we can talk this through, together. I just had to tell you everything now. I couldn't keep it from you any longer.'

'This is a lot to take in. Not now!' I overhear him shout. 'I'm on an important call. Leave it on my desk. Sorry, Flo. I have to go.'

'Can we talk later?' I say, noticing the desperation in my voice. 'Theo, I was right to tell you, wasn't I?'

'You had to, but—'

'But what?'

'This is a lot to take in,' he repeats.

I wait for him to say something positive and reassuring, something that tells me we're in this together. 'I know,' I say, filling in the painful silence. 'But I need you. I can't do this on my own.'

*Please say something. Anything.*

'Listen, I'll call you back,' he says.

'Theo?'

'I can't think straight. This is huge, Flo. I need time, okay? Give me time.'

'I love you.'

'I love you too,' he says, offering me a tiny crumb of hope that we still have a future, before he hangs up.

# 42

*Beth's Diary, 1998*

*What have I done? Oh my God, what have I done?*
*Graham grabbed his bike helmet and left, and I have this*
*awful feeling that it's over, that he's not coming back.*

*I can't believe how angry he was when I told him*
*the news.*

*It's been a week after getting the results and I've*
*been motionless, operating on autopilot the entire time;*
*I've spent half my time in bed. Graham thought I had*
*some nasty virus. He even began to wonder if I could be*
*pregnant. But when he suggested ringing a doctor, I knew*
*my time was running out. I had to tell him.*

*So I did, tonight, while Flo was having her first*
*sleepover at Maddie's house. I bought a bottle of his*
*favourite red wine and cooked his favourite meal. I*

*reassured myself repeatedly that at least we know now,
that it would be okay, as long as I was brave for Graham.
This world I was bringing him into is familiar to me, but
foreign to him.*

*I could do this. Be strong, for both of us. After all,
hadn't I told Amanda unequivocally that I was ready for
the results?*

*'I'm gene positive,' I said to him, my heart racing, still
unable to believe it myself. I said how sorry I was that
I'd taken the test behind his back, that the last thing I'd
wanted to do was to hide anything from him but I'd needed
to put my mind at rest, especially if we were going to
have children.*

*He didn't say a word. He just stared at me.*

*'I can't live my life without a map,' I stressed.*

*'You need a map,' he said slowly, 'but what about
me, Beth?'*

*'I know this must be a shock—'*

*'A shock?'*

*'I understand it's a lot for you to—'*

*'In this world none of us know what's going to happen
next; we don't have a crystal ball. Isn't that the beauty of
life, the unknown, the adventure?'*

*'But—'*

*'Beth, I was ready to marry you but now . . . now we
know exactly which way we're heading.'*

*'I know it's not the result we hoped for, but at least we
can plan, we can make every day count, and—'*

*He stood up, shouting, 'I didn't want a fucking map!
Why did you have to find out? Can't you see this ruins
everything?'*

*'Don't say that,' I begged, rushing to his side. 'I need you.'*

*But he backed away, as if he couldn't bear to be
anywhere near me.*

*'We can work this out. I can't do this on my
own,' I said.*

*'You went behind my back,' he replied, his tone as cold
as stone. 'You chose to find out, Beth, but you're not the
only person this affects, you know.'*

*I was crying by then. 'I wanted to be able to tell you
we'd be okay. I was doing this for us.'*

*'You weren't doing this for me! You didn't think of me
once, did you?'*

*'I did.'*

*'Why didn't you at least ask me what I thought, then?
All these appointments you've been going to secretly,
pretending you were at the dentist. How can this work if I
can't even trust you?'*

*'I'm sorry, I really am. I should have said something,
but I wanted to have a family knowing they weren't at
risk, can't you see that? I wanted Flo to be free.'*

*'Well, now you know she's not. Well done.' I was
taken aback by the scorn in his voice. 'You have your map
and Flo has hers too.'*

*'But surely she has a right to know? Don't you think I
have a responsibility—'*

'What are you going to say to your mother?' he said, refusing to listen. 'How are you going to drop that bombshell?' He turned away from me. 'Oh, Beth, what have you done?'

## 43

### Flo

Theo doesn't call me later that night, and I barely sleep, tossing and turning. One moment I'm reassuring myself that he just needs time, that we'll get through this, then the next I'm replaying our conversation over and over again, and rereading Mum's diary, believing it's over, that Theo will walk away just as Graham did.

I imagine Theo sitting in his office, continuing to look up HD online and thinking this isn't what he signed up for.

In the morning, I feel relieved that I no longer have to fight to fall asleep. I feel stronger and ready to face the day ahead.

Darkness can often rob you of hope. Light gives it back.

I find James in the kitchen. He picks up his house keys and bike helmet.

'I hope he calls,' he says, kissing me on the cheek before

I hear the front door shut and the flat falls deathly silent. It makes me realize that I don't want to spend any more time on my own here.

Without a job, the day stretches out in front of me, like a never-ending road. However much I'll miss James and Granny, I need to book my flights and begin my new life. I need to make Theo see this doesn't have to be the end. I'm determined to fight for us.

For the rest of the day, I keep myself busy finishing off my packing and looking into the best flights over the next few days. I go for a long walk to clear my head and find a café in Chiswick to have lunch, though I can hardly eat, spending every minute instead checking my emails and staring at my mobile, stopping myself from calling him back.

Theo keeps me waiting until the evening. James is home and we're cooking supper together when at last he rings. I leave the room promptly, James mouthing 'Good luck'.

'I'm sorry it's taken me so long,' Theo says. He sounds calmer, which is a good start.

'It's fine, you needed time.'

'I love you, Flo.'

'I love you too,' I say, the relief immediately overwhelming.

'But you shouldn't have lied to me.'

My fear returns instantly. 'I know, but—'

'This can never work if we can't be honest with one another.'

'I know, and I feel terrible, but I'm telling you the truth now.'

'Is there anything else you're hiding?'

'That's not fair, Theo,' I say, though I feel another stab of guilt as I remember the night I'd spent drinking, ending up at Nate's flat, thinking I'd lost my ring.

'How can I trust you?'

'You can, Theo, you know you can,' I say, sensing this isn't what it's really about. 'I need you, Theo. I need us to be strong. There is such a good chance I don't have the gene.'

'But what if you do?'

'We'll get help and support.' *Please say something positive.*

Yet his silence says it all.

'You should have told me before,' he repeats, using his only weapon of defence to end our relationship.

'You're scared, and I get that, so am I, but maybe you can come with me to my first genetic counselling appointment—'

'Flo, I can't do this. I can't.'

'I'll fly out. We need to see each other. We can't throw away what we have over the phone. Don't we owe it ourselves to at least talk, face to—'

'But no amount of talking can change the facts. If you inherit the gene I can't look after you, Flo,' he confesses. His tone is brutally direct.

I feel a lump in my throat. 'But I might not.'

'I can't take that risk, don't you understand? It would only be hovering over me, over us. All the time I'd be wondering when it's going to happen, when you're going to get symptoms. And what about us having a family?'

'Once we get advice—'

'Flo, I can't. I'm sorry. I can't be the man you want me to be.'

'Don't, Theo,' I beg tearfully. This can't be it. I feel as if my entire life is crumbling into pieces around me.

'I think it's better to be honest right from the start.'

'But I love you.' *Doesn't that count?*

'I'm sorry Flo. It's over.'

'No Theo, please.'

'I'm sorry,' he says quietly.

The line goes dead.

Numb, I return to the kitchen. 'Flo,' James says, rushing towards me, before I throw my mobile against the wall and scream.

Soon everything is blurred.

I can't stand up. My legs feel weak.

Soon it's dark and quiet.

*It's over.*

My entire life has stopped.

## 44

**Peggy**

It's two days after Flo spoke to Theo, and I'm at James's flat preparing her breakfast in the kitchen. She won't want to eat, but I have to keep trying.

James went out for a run the moment I arrived this morning and has been gone a good few hours. It's not easy for him, all of this. I've told him he mustn't take days off work or cancel seeing his own friends. His life must go on. But it must be difficult living with someone at the end of his corridor who has completely shut down.

It's hard to ignore a closed bedroom door when you know your friend is suffering behind it.

They say you only see people's true characters in a moment of crisis. If you were on a bus and a person pulled out a knife, would you rush to the defence of others or would you get off the bus as quickly as you could?

I'm angry with Theo for ending it so abruptly, but I suspect he's not the only person who'd walk away. It is a daunting prospect knowing someone you love could possibly have HD, and I don't hate him for the choice he's made. I only hate how it's made my Flo feel. I wanted to believe so much, for Flo's sake, that Theo would stand by her, even if, deep down, I feared it would end this way.

Gently, I open her bedroom door and place the tray on her bedside table. She's lying on her side, motionless. Her eyes are open, but she is little more than a shell. A body.

Something has died within her; some light has gone out.

For the past few days, I believe she has been in deep shock, everything finally catching up with her, including now the end of her relationship.

'Good morning, darling,' I say. 'Try to eat something, even half a piece of toast. I bought you some special honey in a comb, the kind you love.'

'Later,' she murmurs.

'Here, you need to drink.'

I help Flo to sit up in bed, rearranging the pillows, and to my relief she takes the mug of hot ginger and lemon and has a few sips.

I walk over to the window to open the curtains. The sun is shining, the sky a clear blue.

'Don't,' she says, as if frightened to let any light into the room.

*Should I open them anyway? Isn't it worse to be plunged in darkness? Should I be firmer with her?*

I leave the curtains shut, before asking if she needs anything else.

She shakes her head.

I perch on the edge of her bed and hand her a small quarter of toast. 'If I eat this, will you let me sleep?' she says. 'I'm so tired, Granny.'

'I know.' I stroke her hair, just as I used to do with Beth when she was a little girl. 'Why not try to get up later on today? We could go for a short walk around the park with Elvis.'

'Maybe.'

I understand how cruel Theo's rejection must have felt, but thank goodness she is here with James and me. Maddie is also coming to stay. Her train arrives tonight.

I'm relieved she didn't fly out to break the news to him. The idea of her being rejected in a city miles away from home is unthinkable.

'I've got nothing, Granny,' she says. 'Nothing.'

I reach for her hand, wishing I could think of the right thing to say, or something that would make her feel better. 'That's not true. You've got your friends and you've got me.'

When Flo stares up at the ceiling, asking 'What's the point of going on?' I realize I am out of my depth, since indifference is even harder to deal with than anger.

It's late afternoon when James arrives back home and finds me in the kitchen, preparing a chicken salad for supper. 'Did you run a marathon?' I ask, chopping some tomatoes.

'My legs feel as if they did. It's hot out there.' It's the middle of August and for once we've had a decent summer's day. He opens the cupboard, picks up a glass. 'I had lunch with Stu. Didn't you get my text, Granny Peg?'

'I haven't checked. I only keep my mobile on in emergencies.'

'How is she?' he asks.

'Much the same,' I reply, hating killing that flicker of hope in his eyes. 'But I was given some good advice,' I go on, before the buzzer rings. I pick up the intercom, telling James it will be Ricky. 'He's a nurse. Make yourself useful,' I add, 'put the kettle on. He likes Earl Grey, one sugar.'

'Yes, ma'am!' he calls back.

When I open the door, Ricky bounds inside, almost tripping over the rug in the hallway. He kisses me on both cheeks before I lead him into the kitchen.

'All right, mate,' he says, shaking James's hand so hard that I'm certain he'll have a bruise in the morning. 'I'm Ricky. You're the vet dude, right? Cool bike outside.'

James can't help but grin as he looks up at this man, tall enough to be a professional basketball player, taking in the hat, the dreadlocks, the white T-shirt with an image of Bob Marley printed on the front and the neon-coloured trainers.

'How's Flo?' Ricky asks with concern.

'Not good,' James replies. 'It's as if her whole body has gone into shock.'

Ricky nods. 'That can happen, delayed trauma.' He takes a notepad out of his work briefcase. 'Well, I went online,

Peggy, as you asked,' he says. 'She's a bossy old thing, isn't she?' he directs at James, 'and there's a lot of info out there on research and drug trials. This looks interesting.' Ricky shows us both an article he printed out about a drug — with a name I can't even pronounce — that can be used to help control the jerky dance-like movements that Tim used to have.

'This is great,' James mutters, scanning over the piece, 'but I'm not sure Flo's going to be interested in reading any of this right now. She needs some medicine to mend her broken heart.'

'If only I could invent that,' I say.

Ricky adjusts his hat. 'What I think she needs more than anything is a goal, something to get out of bed for, right?'

I agree. 'That's a good idea. She needs some fresh air.'

Ricky shakes his head. 'She needs a focus, a real project.'

'Not working probably doesn't help,' I reflect, recalling how Flo spent weeks in bed after her mother died, until I forced her to get a job. 'She'll need the money, too.'

'Work is good,' Ricky muses, 'the last thing she needs is hours alone in this flat, and we all need to earn, but it'd be good if she had something outside of work, too, something more than just earning a living, something that'll make her believe life is worth fighting for. My music is a passion, you know? My band, we're only amateurs, right, as Peggy will no doubt tell you.'

'I take my hearing aids out,' I whisper to James.

James and Ricky laugh. 'But that doesn't matter,' Ricky

continues. 'My guitar has helped me through some serious dark times.'

I tell James Ricky lost a child to cot death.

'I'm so sorry,' James says.

'Thanks.' Ricky pats him on the shoulder in a fatherly way. 'These things happen, right, and you never think you'll be able to pick yourself up off the ground, but somehow you do.'

'I wouldn't know,' James responds with refreshing honesty. 'I've never had to deal with anything like that, or what Flo's going through.'

'Flo said she wanted to do something she thought she'd never be capable of,' I reflect, thinking back to our conversation about bucket lists.

'The bigger the challenge the better,' Ricky says, 'she needs something to get herself up and running again.'

'I've got an idea,' James says, a smile slowly spreading across his face. 'Ricky, you're a *genius*.'

## 45

*Beth's Diary, 2000*

*I haven't written in my diary for months because I'm
happy. Yes, happy! It's hard to believe it was almost two
years ago when Amanda opened the test results and said to
me, 'You're positive'. The most surreal and life-changing
moment, and yet my life hadn't changed at all. I left her
office the same person, I drove home the same person and I
cooked Flo's supper as I do every single night.*

*But I knew the person I would become.*

*After Graham walked out on me, I went straight to bed.*

*And if it hadn't been for Flo, I'm not sure I'd have ever
got up again.*

*But I did.*

*As Amanda advised I gave myself time to grieve and
adjust, time to be kind to myself, and gradually darkness*

gave way to light. I realized my life hasn't stopped. If anything, I'm the happiest I've been for years.

Graham came back to the house a few days after that fateful night. He was calmer this time, loving even. I didn't beg or plead with him to stay, as I knew, deep down, it was over. We both cried when he handed me his set of house keys, saying he'd pick up the rest of his stuff when Flo wasn't at home.

What hurt the most was when Flo asked me if Graham had left because he hadn't liked her bridesmaid dress. Was it something she'd done? I almost told her there and then about the HD – I nearly blurted it out – but I'm so relieved I didn't. I must find the right time.

I'm still certain that taking the test was the right thing for me. In so many ways it has lifted the burden of uncertainty off my shoulders. Now that I know, I'm determined to see the time I have left as a gift, and that has been truly liberating. I'm not going to put anything off until tomorrow, since there is no promise of tomorrow. It's the moment that counts.

About six months after getting my test results, when I began to feel human again, I called Terry Simpson, the gallery owner in South Kensington who discovered me at my degree show. I reminded him he'd asked me to do some work for him, all those years ago. I asked if he remembered me, and if he was willing to give me a second chance.

When he suggested I visit his gallery to show him my latest work, I warned him my style had changed.

'I wouldn't expect anything less,' he replied.

I have become obsessed by shapes and textures in my art and have begun to make the oddest things. Flo came home from a sleepover the other day, only to find me making a ceramic egg out of broken plates.

'What's that, Mum?' she'd giggled. 'That's weird, even for you.'

But Terry didn't laugh when I visited him with my portfolio, describing how I love to work with things that others would put straight into the bin, things that are no longer useful: broken china, jewellery, feathers, rusty old nails, damaged shells and bones.

'I find beauty in things that can be easily overlooked,' I said, thinking about Mark, and how he always used to teach us to look at everything around us, and breathe life into all we see. Art is about storytelling, he said.

The following day, Terry called to say he'd love to give me my own private show. I screamed with joy and started dancing around the kitchen table, not even noticing Flo and Maddie enter the room until they laughed and fled as quickly as they'd come in.

'She's bonkers,' I overheard Flo say.

'Not as mad as my mum,' Maddie had replied.

Anyway, I was so happy that I decided to call Mark. Mark is always the first person I want to talk to when I get good news. He was thrilled, and suggested we go out for lunch to celebrate.

He and I have continued to stay in touch. He wrote

to me shortly after my father had died, saying he was thinking of me, and would I like to meet for a coffee. We hadn't seen one another for almost five years, not since our painfully awkward exchange, when I told him I was pregnant with Flo and he wished me luck.

I felt nervous, but the moment we met, it was as if nothing had changed.

'Teaching is an admirable profession,' Mark said when I told him my life wasn't quite so fancy as some of the other students I'd lived with, who'd gone on to own galleries and work in Paris and New York.

My ex, Nick, runs his own gallery in Berlin.

'Only the very best teach,' he claimed, making me smile.

I've met his wife, Eve, and she and Mark have two boys, Anthony, who is eighteen months younger than Flo, and Ben who is seven. I like Eve.

Soon after Mark and I met for coffee, he suggested I pop over for some supper. I understood why she wanted to meet me. I wouldn't like my husband regularly meeting up with a former student. Initially, she was on guard, it felt rather awkward, everyone on their best behaviour, but as the dinner progressed, and more wine was poured, we loosened up. I told her about the support Mark had given me at college with my father's HD, and how I too was at risk. I wanted to be as open and honest with her as possible, and over the past few years we've become good friends.

As to relationships, I have decided not to put myself through rejection again. I can't have another man abandon

*Flo and me. Both Mark and Eve keep on telling me I mustn't be cynical about love and give up on finding the right person. I'm thirty-one; I'm still young with so much to give, they say.*

*Amanda tells me she wishes I'd listen to my friends. She sees men and women with HD marrying and having families all the time, yet I know it takes one hell of a person to do what Mum did for Dad. I reassure them I'm happy focusing my energy on Flo and my career. I have goals, and that's what matters.*

*Since my first exhibition with Terry, and through word of mouth, I receive regular commissions now. I don't earn a fortune, but with my teaching salary it's enough.*

*Mum owns one of my paintings, a landscape of Burgh Island in Devon where she and Dad honeymooned. She jokes, says I get all my talent from her, before she gives me a hug, which I know is her way of saying how much she misses Dad too, and that he'd be proud I'm finally following my dream.*

# 46

**Flo**

I sit up in bed and throw off the covers, Mum's diary falling on to the floor. Mum didn't lie in bed wishing her life away. She got up. She made plans. She rebuilt her career.

*I'm not going to put anything off until tomorrow, since there is no promise of tomorrow. It's the moment that counts.*

I can't spend another day, a day I'll never get back again, under the covers.

I'm going to work out whether I want to take the test or not, but either way I'm not going to let Theo's rejection or any test result beat me.

I draw the curtains. I have no idea what the date is. I've lost all track of time. I'm aware James, Maddie and Granny have been in the flat most of the time, like shift workers. I feel guilty that everyone is putting their life on hold for me, that they're trying to piece me back together again. Maddie even mentioned she's been in touch with Natalie. They haven't found a permanent replacement yet; my old job is still mine if I want it back.

I look down at my ring, a constant reminder of what I've lost.

I take it off my finger.

If I have any kind of chance of moving on, the ring has to go. I'll send it back to Theo.

Now I know exactly why Mum chose not to meet anyone else. Who would want to go through this twice?

I'm never going to let any man break my heart again.

# 47

**Flo**

It's now September. Three weeks since I forced myself out of bed and back to life.

'What are you doing?' James asks, before I turn round, gasping.

'You gave me a shock.'

James is standing in my bedroom in his black Nike shorts and T-shirt. I hadn't even heard him come in from his run. He must have been up at the crack of dawn this morning.

His discipline makes me feel guilty. I must sign up to a gym.

'I'm going through my stuff,' I tell him, taking out of my suitcase all the things I'd packed for New York, including the red silk dress Theo gave to me a year after we got together. It was an anniversary present. I try not to remember the night I'd unwrapped it from its tissue-lined box, or recall the look on Theo's face as he watched me try it on before I felt the touch of his hand as his fingers played with the back zip.

I snatch it off the hanger and chuck it into the black bin bag, along with the memory.

I wish I could stop thinking about him. When I don't hate him, I miss him. And when I miss him, I hate both him and Graham for giving up on Mum and me so easily.

James sits down on the edge of my bed. 'Why are you throwing that away? You could wear it to the Oscars.'

I raise an eyebrow. 'You want it?'

James crosses his legs and pouts, saying 'It's not my colour, *darling.*'

I laugh, as James continues to watch me chuck more tops and dresses into the black bag at a frightening speed.

'You're not going to have anything left to wear at this rate, although that's fine by me,' he says, masking his fear of my erratic behaviour with more humour.

'It's time for a new start,' I declare.

'That's great, but you still need clothes for that.'

'Out with the old and in with the new; I mean, I've had this jumper for *years*,' I exclaim, tossing it into the bag. 'And when am I ever going to wear this again?' I hold up a black cocktail dress with a healthy slit up one side, that I wore to one of Theo's work events.

'You'll wear that again, won't you?'

'Theo gave it to me,' I say, as if that's all he needs to know.

'Flo, are you all right?'

I sit down on my bed, suddenly exhausted by the mess I've made, clothes strewn across the floor.

I thought I was doing fine. Yesterday was a good day, a happy one with Granny. We walked to the cemetery to visit Mum and Granddad, and then we went to see a movie in the evening. Granny spent half of it asleep, mind you, mouth wide open and treating me to the occasional snort, before telling me at the end how much she'd enjoyed it. In the past few weeks, I've been feeling better, much more in control: my boss, Harriet, gave me my old job back, and I have a date to see a genetic counsellor next month.

'What's up?' James persists.

I look at him, unsure how to explain. I think back to my first day in the office just over a week ago. I'm exceptionally lucky to have been given a second chance, even if my shattered plans to go to America, my break-up with Theo and the risk to my health had all been showcased in spectacular fashion to my work colleagues.

When I entered the office there was a painful silence, the kind of awkwardness you might feel on a first date, when you're not sure whether to shake hands or kiss on the cheek.

All I could think was, Natalie, *please* still be nightmarishly chirpy and tell me to sod off if I ask you to make me a coffee with frothy milk. And Simon, don't look at me with that awful sympathy in your eyes, as if my dog has just died.

Finally, Natalie gave me a hug, saying, 'Nice to see you back on your feet, boss,' before she'd glanced at my skirt hanging off my hips. 'But bloody hell, you need cake,' she added, which finally made us all relax.

When I thanked Harriet for keeping my job for me, she said, 'I didn't keep it for you, Flo, I just didn't happen to find anyone else half as good,' which was my first compliment from her in five years.

I know, despite everything, I'm fortunate. I could easily be out of work, and the one thing I need right now is security and routine, and company, and money to pay my rent. As much as I love James for not finding a new flatmate, I can't abuse his kindness by not paying my way. Besides, my pride won't allow it.

Look at what Mum went through. Look at how she pulled her life back together. I'm so relieved she felt this positive *after* taking the test.

'You're bound to feel restless,' James says, bringing me back to reality.

'I feel like I need something new,' I confide, 'but I'm not sure what I'm looking for.'

'Flo, I've been thinking.'

'Uh-oh.'

'Don't call me crazy. I wanted to mention it a while ago, but needed to pick the right moment.'

'Go on.'

'You should train for the marathon.'

I laugh. I must have misheard. Yet when I look at him, I realize he's not finding it as funny as I do.

'You said you wanted to get fit in America, right?'

'Yes, but—'

'Why not get fit here?'

'I meant eating less chocolate and more kale, and going to the gym a couple of times a week.'

'Who wants to eat kale? And why join a gym when running is free?'

'James, this is insane.' I laugh again. 'I'd rather miss the bus than run for it.'

'Listen, I'm not saying it's easy, you'd need to be tough and fit like me.' He flexes his muscles. 'It's a commitment, Flo, but when you cross that finishing line—'

'*If* I cross it.'

'Flo, running is the best release for stress. It helped me through my finals, when my head was exploding from too much time cooped up indoors revising. I never thought running twenty-six miles in a rhino suit would be one of the most memorable days of my life.'

I smile. 'But I can't run.'

'Everyone can run,' he says, refusing to listen. 'You could run for a charity. Hang on, you should do it for HD.'

'James, this is crazy.'

'Why? I can help you train. Seriously, Flo, this could be the perfect way for you to throw yourself into something new and do something positive while you're trying to work out if you want to take the test or not. Running is a brilliant way to think, to put things in perspective. You're too late for the ballot, but you could probably still grab a charity place, so long as you can raise some serious cash.'

'I could sell some of these clothes on eBay,' I begin to think out loud, 'and put the money towards—'

'Exactly.'

'Have you got a place?' I ask, warming up to the idea if we could run together.

'I entered the ballot; I should know by early October.'

That's next month.

'You need to get on to this quickly,' James advises. 'It's really competitive. Believe it or not people are queuing up to run twenty-six miles. I know someone who has signed up to the ballot five years in a row and still hasn't got a place.'

'Wait here,' I say to James, before rushing into the kitchen and returning with my laptop. Granny gave me some articles that Ricky had printed about research and new drugs and treatments for HD, and information on the HDA, the Huntington's Disease Association. I haven't read any of it yet, but maybe it's about time I did.

I perch on my bed next to James and log on to the charity website.

I can't believe I'm seriously considering this, although I have to admit there is something about the idea that is waking up my senses.

'You'd really help me train?' I ask.

He nods. 'I can't wait to haul you out of bed on a cold, wet day and make you run five miles with me.'

I smile at that, even if I hate the idea. But it's better than lying in bed, worrying about my future.

'My father ran the New York Marathon a year before I

was born,' James continues, 'Mum called it his last run for freedom. Honestly, Flo, Dad said it was one of the most incredible moments of his life, so I knew I had to do it too. I was one of those weird kids at school who loved cross-country training more than football.'

'That's lovely, but you're a natural at sport. I was the girl who finished last in every race. You really think I could do it?'

'Well, you won't know until you try. What have you got to lose?'

'Nothing,' I realize.

Nothing at all.

# 48

**Peggy**

I take the pad of paper from the person next to me, a man young enough to be my grandson, and write down my email address. He's looking at me as if he drew the short straw, turning up late to class and finding the only free seat was next to an old, grey-haired biddy.

*What am I doing here?* Italian for beginners seemed such a good idea at the time.

The idea came to me after Flo announced she was running the marathon. I recalled something Ricky had said, about me not being retired from life, so I decided it was time I too had some goals.

I was writing my bucket list when Ricky knocked on my door. As we sat down to chat, I quickly shoved my pad of paper under the nearest cushion.

'What's that you're hiding?' Ricky asked, sharp as a pin.

'Nothing,' I said, blushing like a teenager.

'Peggy Andrews! Are you writing a dirty novel?' He roared with laughter.

'If only I could. I'm glad you find yourself so amusing.'

'Well, what is it?'

'I took your advice.' I retrieved my list and showed it to him.

'Ballet,' Ricky read. 'Men in tights don't do it for me, but if they rock your boat, Peggy,' he said, clapping me on the back. 'Bravo!' he added when he came to my dream of learning the most romantic language in the world.

'If you aren't able to make a lesson,' says Maria, our young Italian teacher, bringing me back down to earth, 'please email me. But it helps if I have all your names and addresses so I can email you the notes from the lesson and your *compiti*. Homework,' she translates.

'Homework? We don't have to take an exam, do we?' I mutter, before passing the pad on.

'First things first,' says Maria. 'Welcome everyone. *Salve a tutti.*'

'What does that mean?' I ask without thinking.

'Hello everyone,' Maria answers for me.

'Yes, of course.' I laugh nervously. 'I knew that.'

*Oh dear Peggy! There's always one dud.*

'Hello. *Salve,*' I repeat to no one in particular, before looking down at my hands.

'*Ciao* is another way to say hello,' Maria informs me, before addressing the whole class. 'It's less formal.'

She perches on the edge of her desk, exceptionally pretty, dressed in leopard print leggings and purple suede ankle boots. 'But before we get stuck in, I thought, as an introduction, we could take turns and tell the others why we all want to learn Italian,' Maria suggests, making English sound such a romantic language when spoken with her accent. 'And what you hope to achieve by the end of term one. You can see the topics we'll cover, on the sheets I've given you, like saying hello, travelling on public transport and going to the bar.'

'That's the most important,' says the man sitting opposite me, leaning nonchalantly against his chair, arms crossed, everyone around the room agreeing.

'Or booking a room in a hotel—' Maria continues.

'For a dirty weekend,' the man adds, laughing, and to my horror winking at me, but I suppose I am in his firing line, sitting directly opposite him.

Maria gives him a look. There is always one who brings the tone down.

'For your *vacanza*,' she corrects. 'But if there is something you specifically need to learn, now is a good time to tell me, so I can add it to the list.'

I scan the class, all of us sitting behind tables arranged to make up a square. There must be at least twelve of us, maybe sixteen, I think, nodding as I count everyone.

'Why don't we begin at this end,' Maria says, thankfully choosing the end opposite mine. She looks at the pad. 'So, Nigel, would you like to go first?'

Nigel looks as if he's in his mid fifties and dressed for a boardroom meeting. 'I was recently made redundant from my City firm,' he says. 'Don't feel sorry for me, it was a blessing in disguise because my wife and I are now looking to buy a place in Italy. It's time for a new start.'

'Ah, that is exciting,' Maria says. 'Where?'

'Just outside of Florence. San Casciano. In Val di Pesa.'

'Beautiful.'

Maria has to stop Nigel from showing her the numerous photographs on his iPhone, and telling her about all his plans to renovate a property and set up a bed and breakfast, and how learning Italian would help him read and understand property contracts.

I suspect he's expecting too much from a beginners class.

'Sarah, you next,' Maria says. Sarah looks as if she's in her mid sixties, with dyed blonde curly hair, glasses and a bright smile. 'When my husband finally retires, we want to move to Florence,' she says.

'I have an Italian girlfriend, she can't speak much English,' says the next chap, 'so it would be no bad thing for me to learn her lingo, you know,' he says, which receives a few smiles and raised eyebrows.

'Don't,' advises the man who made the comment about the dirty weekend. 'Once you communicate that's when it starts to go wrong, trust me,' he advises, before realizing it's his turn, and I think we're all fascinated to know what this man does.

He's rather handsome in that grubby unshaven kind

of way. 'I'm an antiques dealer,' he says, which I sense rather disappoints everyone except me. I wonder if he enjoys *Flog It!*.

'I travel round Europe and can speak Spanish and French.' He shrugs.

'So you have saved the best language until last,' Maria suggests.

It's getting closer to my turn and I'm still unsure what to say, my stomach churning at the thought of having to say anything at all.

'I'm an art dealer,' says the next person.

'A chef.'

'A writer and I'm setting my next book in Bologna.'

'I work in TV and our next project is in Sicily.'

'My daughter's fiancé is Italian so I want to surprise everyone on the big day by giving a speech in Italian,' claims Iris. 'I haven't told a soul I'm doing this course.'

'Peggy?' Maria says.

*There's nothing wrong with putting myself first once in a while, is there? I'm doing this for me, for Peggy. Not for Tim, not for Beth or even Flo, but for me.*

'Peggy?'

The room hushes, everyone looking at me expectantly.

'I need to get out of the house more,' is all I end up saying, which to my absolute astonishment receives the best laughter of all.

'Couldn't agree more,' says the writer. 'I stare all day long at my screen, and it's not good for my eyes.'

'Being cooped up in editing studios isn't good for the soul either,' says the TV man.

'My wife is delighted I'm out of the house,' admits another, 'and not hanging around asking what's for lunch.'

But Maria is looking at me, as if waiting for something extra.

'Peggy,' she says once more, this time her tone gently challenging, and I'm twisting my wedding ring round and round my finger. I've never enjoyed the limelight; that was always Tim's place, a place he actively sought. At school I used to dread the teacher asking me to come to the front of the class to read out loud.

'Well, it's a beautiful language, something I've always wanted to do,' I say, disappointed with giving such a bland response, though Maria, sensing my discomfort moves on to the next and final person.

'And it's never too late,' I say, before the young man has had a chance to give his reason.

Maria encourages me to go on.

'Life is short,' I continue, the room deadly quiet, 'but it's never too late to start living again.'

'Respect, Peggy,' says the man next to me, holding up his hand towards me to do a high five, something I've never done before in my entire life either, but it's never too late to start.

# 49

## Flo

I watch James walk towards the reception desk with a woman in her seventies, carrying a slate-grey cat in a cage. 'Flo,' he says with surprise when he sees me sitting in the waiting room. 'What are you doing here?'

I hold up a form. 'It came today.'

'Hang on,' he says to me, before placing the cage on the desk and helping the woman settle her extortionate bill. I still don't understand why James is so broke.

'Lovely to see you, Mrs Rogers, and Smokey,' he says, before gesturing to me to follow him into his office. He closes the door behind us and takes the form.

'Huntington's Disease Association, Virgin Money London Marathon, Sunday 22 April 2018 Gold Bond Application Form,' he reads out. 'That's great, Flo.'

'I spoke to Helen in fundraising,' I tell him. 'They only

have nine places. Apparently, they had over thirty applicants last year. She said shortlisting and turning people down is the hardest part of her job.'

'You have as good a chance as anyone else,' James reassures me.

'I need your help. It says I need to present them with a fundraising plan and everything.'

'We can work on it.'

'Tonight? The deadline's only a week away.' Noticing his hesitation I add, 'Sorry, you're probably going out, aren't you? Stupid of me, I should have called, but I fancied the walk anyway. Need to get fit, just in case.' I laugh at myself.

'I'm only going out with Stu and Jane.' Stu and James went to school together, ended up in the same veterinary college, ran a marathon side by side, shared a twenty-first birthday party, and they were both engaged at the same time, Stu to Jane, James to Emma, Stu relieved that he wasn't the only one waving goodbye to his single days. They did everything together until James lost his nerve and pulled out, and for the first time in their lives, they were no longer in step. Yet they're still close.

'Go,' I insist, putting the form back into my handbag. 'I can make a start on my own.'

'Why don't you come and then we can all chat about it?' James proposes, ushering me out of the door, already late. 'Stu's run more marathons than I have. He can give us a few tips. And if you buy them a drink, I'm sure they'll sponsor you.'

\*

'So this afternoon, this woman comes in with her pug,' James tells Stu, Jane and me over drinks, 'and says, "Alfie smells."'

I laugh so hard that I spit out some of my wine, making everyone laugh even more.

'So I say,' James continues, '"Well, dogs do smell, I'm afraid". And she says, "What can I do about it? I shampoo the life out of Alfie every day, but nothing works."'

'But dogs smell of dogs,' Jane says, rolling her eyes. 'Alfie smells of Alfie.'

'Exactly. Elvis doesn't exactly smell of Jo Malone,' I chip in. 'If only he did.'

'You try telling her that,' James suggests, finishing off his beer. 'Honestly, sometimes I don't know what to say.'

'You'll like this one,' Stu predicts. 'A lovely dog called Bertie comes into my clinic today, a golden retriever, but the mother and daughter are distraught because they've found a lump.'

'This isn't going to be sad is it?' Jane challenges him.

'I don't want a sad story either,' I agree.

'Just wait,' Stu says, holding up his hand. 'So, I lift poor Bertie on to the table and run my hand along his coat, and I can feel something, a lump, and then when I look more closely, I see this suspicious black stripe.'

I wince.

'It gets worse, Flo,' Stu warns me with a deadpan expression. 'I feel something very sticky. It doesn't look good.'

We wait for the verdict in fear. Except for James. He seems to find this funny.

'Bertie didn't have a tumour,' Stu says, 'he had a humbug stuck in his fur.'

Later that evening, after returning home from the pub, James and I are lying on my bed working on the marathon application form. We've completed the easy section. Now we're on to the fundraising.

The HDA charity specifies applicants need to aim to raise a minimum of two thousand pounds to be in with a chance for a place, and I need to demonstrate a plan as to how I'd raise the cash.

'Well, Stu and Jane promised you fifty quid,' James says, 'so you only have one thousand nine hundred and fifty to go.'

'Not helpful.'

'And I'll give you a fiver, so that's one thousand nine hundred and forty-five.'

I hit his arm. 'Your generosity is truly touching.'

'I'm training you,' he reminds me, 'pro bono.'

'I'm sure my office would get behind me,' I think out loud. 'They'll be amazed. Harriet might even match my sponsorship money.'

'No harm asking,' James agrees.

'I'll carry on flogging some things on eBay, too,' I suggest. 'Little does Theo realize that his dress sold for a hundred quid, so thanks Theo, for that. It's going to HDA,' I say, wishing I could get rid of the tremor in my voice each time I say his name.

'Where did you hear about running for HDA?' I continue to read off the form, before ticking the box beside 'friend'. 'Shame they don't have a "mad flatmate" category. Have you had any experience of HD?' I turn to James again. 'Where do I start on that one?'

'From the beginning.'

'James,' I say, nudging him. 'Wake up.'

'Sorry. What's the time?' He sits up, his hair messy, his cheeks creased with sleep. 'It's almost one in the morning,' he moans. 'I need my bed.'

'Wait. I've only got one section left,' I say, grabbing his arm, 'the additional info part. I need to tell them why I want to run, don't I. What can I say?'

'Why do you want to do it, Flo?' he asks. 'Imagine sitting round a table and everyone is giving a reason – what are you going to say that's going to stand out?'

'I want to get fit and do something new.'

'You can get fit in a million ways and do anything new any time.'

'It's difficult,' I sigh. 'It would be good to raise money for charity, for HD.'

'Why?'

'To raise awareness.'

'Good.'

'I want to do something I never thought I could do, to prove to myself that whether I have HD or not, life goes on.'

'Keep going. Why do you want to run twenty-six point

two miles?' he presses. 'Why do you want to inflict pain on your back?'

'I don't.'

'Why inflict grief on your hips, knees and ankles?'

'I won't, will I?'

'You'll need a lot of hot baths, put it that way. Why do you want to cut down on wine and cake?'

'Really? I can't have the odd glass—'

'Why do you want to kiss goodbye to your social life?' James keeps on pushing me.

'Well, I haven't exactly had much of one—'

'You can also forget lie-ins on a Sunday morning and you'd better save up for all those sports massages you'll need—'

'Stop!' I insist at last, unable to listen to any more reasons not to do it. 'I want to run twenty-six miles for all those people affected by HD in some way,' I say, 'like children at risk, or parents with the gene, for grandparents who have lost a son or daughter, or for people who have HD but haven't told anyone. For people who feel desperately alone, who believe there is no one they can turn to who will listen or understand. I want to raise money so that maybe one day there'll be a cure. But on the day itself, I want to run it for my mum and granddad, and for Granny.' I take in a deep breath. 'I want to run it for my family.'

'You don't need my help, Flo,' James says, standing up and leaving the room as if his work is done.

I glance down at the form, the last section still blank.

'How did I put it? Oh James, how did I say it?' I laugh as I order him to come back. 'I need to write it down.' I follow him into his bedroom.

'I need to sleep. Remember to set your alarm for five,' he says.

'*Five*?'

'Training starts tomorrow, so you'd better get used to it. Just a gentle ten-mile jog to begin with.'

'James!'

'Night, Flo.' He pushes me out of his room, both of us unable to stop smiling.

# 50

*Beth's Diary, 2000*

*It was Flo's sports day today so I left work early, not wanting to miss her one-hundred-meter race. When I arrived, I saw her fooling around with Maddie. They are such a funny pair, Maddie with her bright red hair and Flo's as dark as liquorice.*

*Maddie has a figure like a runner bean. Flo still hasn't lost her puppy fat and I have to restrain myself from kissing and squeezing her chubby dimpled cheeks, especially out in public.*

*Anyway, I joined Maddie's mum, Lucy, who's mad as a box of frogs, wearing denim shorts and wellies, having rushed from the garden to the school, confessing she'd forgotten all about today until her husband reminded her. He had come along, too, joking that he didn't want to miss the sports event of the year.*

*As we were all chatting away with the other parents, drinking our cups of tea and eating slices of homemade cake, I didn't feel at all bothered by Flo's race until I actually saw her and Maddie taking their positions behind the line. I don't know what came over me – I've never thought of myself as remotely competitive – but I pushed and barged through the cluster of mothers determined to get a good view.*

*'Go Flo!' I shouted, pumping my fists, noticing Flo look away, her cheeks as red as Maddie's hair. When the whistle blew, I was screaming out her name, but it was clear from the very start that my Flo isn't a natural, and just reaching the finishing line would be a result.*

*Maddie came first. She makes running look effortless. I know her brother James is a demon runner too, both of them taking after their father, but I continued to call out Flo's name, hoping she didn't come last. No one wants to come bottom of the heap.*

*She came second to last. The girl who came last tripped just before the end. Yes!*

*As soon as it was over and I saw a dejected Flo trailing back to her class friends, I longed to rush over and say 'Well done for taking part anyway,' but I had to stop myself, knowing I'd caused enough embarrassment for one day.*

*Instead, I returned to the pack of mothers, slightly in shame that they had witnessed me pumping my fists.*

*'Anyway, so what were we saying?' I asked Lucy, who*

was looking at me in a new light before we both burst out laughing, and she handed me another slice of lemon drizzle cake.

When it came to the mothers' race, I took off my shoes and gave it my best shot.

I came joint last with a woman who has just come off crutches after a knee injury.

Honestly, I think these mothers eat cake in public but train in secret. Clearly, I spend far too much time on my backside painting and teaching. I've made a vow to join a gym.

I think it's safe to say running doesn't run – excuse the pun, ha ha! – in our family, and that night Flo was low. She told me she hated sport, always came last and that she shouldn't have eaten her packet of cheese and onion crisps before the race because they gave her a stitch.

'I'm not taking part in any stupid race ever again,' she declared, sticking her chin out defiantly, reminding me so much of Mum.

'We can't be good at everything, darling,' I said. 'My dad always used to say success isn't about winning. It's about not being scared to fail.'

'Whatever.'

'It's about giving things a go,' I gamely continued.

'Maddie's lucky she has a dad,' she said, the change of subject abrupt, and I wasn't sure what to say except, 'I know.' Whenever I pick Flo up from Maddie's house there is a twinge of jealousy that the Baileys seem to have it all.

*They are the family every little child paints at nursery, the family that lives in a house with climbing roses, a mum and a dad who stand proudly outside the front door, flanked by two perfect children – a boy and a girl – along with a dog and a cat.*

I'm aware Flo has been bullied for not having a father, and I have always told her to come to me if anyone upsets her, but what I can't do is bring Graham back or meet someone else who'll break our hearts all over again.

There is one particular ringleader called Samantha, who I know has it in for Flo.

Soon after Graham left, Flo used to be scared of going to sleep. Night after night I'd find her sitting at the top of the stairs in her pyjamas, when it was hours past her bedtime.

'Flo, this has got to stop,' I'd said. 'Why aren't you in bed?'

'Because Samantha says you'll leave me too, just like my dad and Graham.'

'Maddie's dad has run a marathon, too,' she continued, bringing me back to reality. 'It's no wonder she won.' Finally, she looked up at me. 'Maybe one day I'll run a marathon, Mum.'

I tried not to smile at how quickly she had changed her mind, so relieved the subject was off fathers.

'Maybe,' I said. 'Who knows what the future will bring, Flo.'

# 51

## Peggy

'Why don't you tell me your name now,' the recorded voice says, 'and where you live.'

I clear my throat and sit up straight. '*Mi chiamo* Peggy,' I say. '*Abito a Londra. In* Hammersmith.' I laugh at my accent, but it's quite hard to make Hammersmith sound Italian and romantic.

Before I reach the next exercise, there's a knock on my door.

*Who could that be?*

Reluctantly, I get up and look through the peephole, only to see Ricky and Shelley carrying baby Mia. Goodness, the whole family have descended on my doorstep.

'Peggy,' he says as he steps inside.

'Where are you off to looking so smart? You could be the next James Bond,' I say, glancing at his hair tied back in a ponytail, his white shirt ironed, wearing a tie with bright blue kingfishers on it. 'Hello, you must be Shelley,' I add, before she kisses me on the cheek.

It's funny that we haven't met before. In a way I think my friendship with Ricky has been so unexpected and special, that we've kept it selfishly to ourselves. Shelley is as fair as Ricky is dark, a splattering of freckles across her nose.

'And I know who you are, Mia,' I say. 'I hear from you often.'

'I'm sorry, Peggy, does she keep you awake?' Shelley asks.

'No,' I pretend. 'She's adorable. Anyway, what are you doing?' I ask, trying not to sound rude, but I really do need to get on with my homework.

Ricky holds up a pair of tickets. 'He's going on a date,' Shelley tells me.

'A date?' I reply. 'Do you need me to babysit?'

'A date with *you*,' Ricky says.

'With *me*?'

Shelley nods. 'I thought it was about time I met the woman he's been spending so much time with before I get jealous.'

'I still don't understand,' I say, peering at the tickets. Until I do.

'*Swan Lake*,' I gasp, a hand flying over my mouth before I look closely at the date. It's Wednesday 27th September 2017. 'Tonight?'

Ricky's face breaks into a smile. 'Go and get ready, Peggy. We're off to watch the men in tights.'

# 52

## Flo

I'm back at work, planning a forthcoming promotion for winter breaks. The office is quiet: Harriet is at a conference and Natalie and Simon are working with the sales team downstairs.

Two weeks have passed since I sent my application form back to the charity, and I've been living in limbo land waiting for their response, which James assures me is normal. He is also anxious to know if he has secured a place in the ballot. We should both find out at about the same time.

I'm unsure whether to start dieting seriously yet, though so far I've been unable to give up the cappuccinos and the homemade Polish cakes that Natalie brings into the office, along with the occasional glass of wine after work. I've also been far too weak to turn down Granny's fish and chips on a Friday night.

It comes to my attention that I have as much discipline as ... well, a person with no discipline.

I should be getting fitter, marathon or no marathon, so today I bought my tracksuit and trainers into work with me, and come what may, I'm going to run home. On Google Maps it says running from High Street Kensington tube station to Turnham Green Terrace is roughly three miles, which seems fairly manageable to me.

I look out of the window. It's not raining.

*I can do this. Three miles isn't that far.*

How hard can it be?


'Coming for a drink, Flo?' Natalie calls up the stairs at the end of the day as I'm getting changed, and for a moment I'm tempted. There's a tug of war inside my head – drink or run – heading for its inevitable conclusion, but at the last moment there is a surprise victory.

'I can't, not tonight,' I call, heading downstairs.

'What are you doing?' Natalie stares at me as if I'm wearing something from outer space. I haven't told anyone in the office about my plans to run a marathon yet, just in case my application is rejected.

It's like a driving test. Why tell friends until you've passed?

'I'm going for a run,' I announce as if it's nothing unusual.

'I can see that. *Why*?'

'To get fit.' I jog up and down on the spot, wondering if I should do some warm-up exercises first, or eat something, though I had quite a late lunch.

'Got to go,' I say, before I can change my mind, heading out of the door in record speed. 'See you tomorrow!'

And I'm off. I'm running.

*Oh God, how long have I been running for?*

I glance at my watch. Not even for a minute and already I have a stitch.

I looked up a few tips online and James suggested I run for a minute then walk for two, but that seems like cheating to me.

I shouldn't have eaten that tuna melt for lunch. It's sitting in the pit of my stomach like a log.

I need to stop. Can't breathe.

I also need a wee. *Why didn't I go to the loo before I left?*

My rucksack feels heavy, my shoes and jacket weighing it down. My back is aching. I walk for a short stretch, my legs shaking as if in shock from the sudden exercise.

*I'll walk to that lamp post*, I tell myself, *and then I'll run again, and this time I'll try to run for longer.*

And I'm off again, though I've barely run to the end of the road before my heart is hammering in my chest. But I carry on with gritted teeth. I turn a corner.

*Keep going*, I tell myself. Don't think about that glass of chilled wine. Don't think about sitting on a nice comfy chair or relaxing in front of the TV with a takeaway.

This is fun. I *am* enjoying myself.

*Oh my God, I can't be this unfit.*

I swim. Occasionally I walk to work. I play tennis and I walk Elvis around the park with Granny. *I must not stop.*

But I have to. My knees hurt.

I stop to remove my rucksack, crammed with everything except water.

*Clever.*

I decide to grab a bottle from the next shop I pass. I imagine I've run about half a mile, maybe three quarters. I'm still on High Street Kensington. This road is never-ending.

Once I've recovered my breath, on I go, this time at quite a pace, passing a newsagent, but deciding I won't stop and weigh my rucksack down further with a bottle of water. Best to keep going.

The knees and thighs are getting vocal again: upset, shocked, tearful. My trainers are rubbing, but I'm going to run home if it kills me.

Eventually, I make it to the last stretch, about a mile to go.

*Stop running, Flo.*

The voice inside my head is getting louder and more insistent, but I can't stop now. I have to push myself that extra mile. This is what it's all about. If it were easy, everyone would be running marathons.

I can't breathe. I'm going to have a heart attack or a stroke.

I feel sick, so sick that the voice inside my head is screaming at me to stop, but it's too late.

My tuna melt makes a reappearance behind a tree.

Someone walks past me and pulls a disgusted face.

I am a disgrace.

With any luck, my application has been rejected.

\*

The washing machine is on, I'm showered and dressed and eating some toast and Marmite watching *MasterChef* when James comes home.

'Good day?' he asks, before handing me my mail. I felt so ill by the time I reached the front door that I couldn't even bend down to pick up the post.

'Yes, not bad,' I fudge. 'You?'

'I didn't get in, Flo.' He sits down and kicks off his shoes.

'Didn't get into what?'

'The marathon.'

I sit up straight. 'No! You didn't? Why?'

'It's not a huge surprise, they only accept one in five.'

'I can't believe it,' I murmur, before thinking this must be another sign, a message from the universe that this marathon business was not meant to be. I certainly can't do it without James. I need to think of a new goal.

'You know what? I was thinking of other ways I could raise money for charity.'

'I can still train you, Flo.'

'I could bake some cakes, hold a few coffee mornings or I could do a knitting challenge—'

'A *knitting* challenge?' he repeats open-mouthed just as my phone rings.

It's Helen, calling from the HDA charity.

'Take it,' James urges, 'or I will.'

'I'm sorry it's late, Florence, I tried calling you earlier,' she says, 'but I didn't want to leave you a message.'

She sounds far too perky for my liking.

'I thought you'd be excited to know you have a place. Your application has been accepted.' She waits. 'You'll be running the London Marathon next April.' She waits again. 'Isn't that great news? Florence? Hello? Are you still there?'

James takes the mobile from my hands. 'Hello,' he says, 'this is her flatmate. That *is* great news. She's absolutely thrilled, so thrilled she can't talk. She's in shock.' He hands the phone back to me, willing me to say something.

'Thank you,' is all I can say eventually, 'but are you *sure*?'

'Positive! Congratulations, Florence.'

Numb, I hang up.

'You take my place,' I suggest to James. This is the perfect solution. 'We could call Helen back to explain?'

James shakes his head. 'Explain what?'

'That I can't run after all. I'll come last.'

'You won't. But even if you did, someone has to.'

'I probably won't even get to the end. I'll be wheeled off to hospital.'

'Flo, what's going on? You were dying to get a place. You put so much effort into your application form. What's changed?'

I hide my face in my hands before telling him about my run home, and how I threw up like a drunken teenager after a night out in the pub.

'Flo, I warned you to go slow.'

'I know.' I shrug. 'I'm sorry, James. I'm obviously not cut out for this. I'm not a runner. I'm not an athlete.'

'You don't have to be the next Mo Farah,' he says. 'Listen, we'll draw up a programme. You have six months to get fit, which is more than enough time. We can do this, okay? Providing we do it properly.'

I draw comfort at the word 'we'.

'Three miles was way too much to attempt on day one,' he stresses. 'In week one, you should just be doing steady walking, a few easy jogs, not sprinting to and from the office like a maniac.'

I nod. I can do steady walking.

'Perhaps it's just as well I didn't get in this year,' James decides, a smile never far from his face. 'I can focus all my attention on you. We're going to get there, Flo. Your form impressed them. You were chosen above many other applicants, and you know as well as I do you'll only regret it if you don't grab this chance. You can do this. Say it, say "I can do this".'

'I can do this,' I repeat.

'Louder.'

*Maybe one day I'll run a marathon, Mum.*

'I can do this,' I repeat, the shock and fear beginning to thaw. 'I earned my place,' I remind myself.

I must have done something right.

# 53

## Peggy

I never knew buying a pair of trainers could be this complicated, I think, listening to the sporty-looking salesman, who looks as if he lives in the gym, explain to Flo the importance of investing in the right running shoe. I'm rather fixated on the bulging muscles of his arms, which seem to have a life of their own. 'If you overpronate—'

'What does that mean?' I ask him, standing next to Flo.

'Pronation refers to the way your foot rolls inwards for impact distribution upon landing,' he says, his eyes still remaining firmly on my granddaughter's.

Pah! You're invisible when you're my age, though I should be used to it by now.

'Overpronators roll their foot inwards,' he goes on, 'so they need a more structured cushioning shoe. Supinators need a lot of cushioning to avoid impact injuries, and neutral pronators can wear a variety of shoes.'

'Do you understand a single word he's saying?' I nudge Flo, who is nodding up and down with puppy-like enthusiasm as he speaks.

This is harder than learning Italian.

'*Granny*,' she blushes, before she relegates me to a chair in the far corner of the shop, making me feel like a child who has been given a time-out. But I have to say, it is a relief to sit down.

'Right, let's get you on to the treadmill, Flo,' Mr Muscleman says, leading her towards a hefty-looking running machine.

As I watch Flo have her gait analysed, I feel absurdly proud that she is going to run the marathon for the Huntington's Disease Association charity. I have already bought a diary for next year and firmly put 'FLO'S RUN' on Sunday 22nd April.

While running twenty-six miles isn't on my bucket list – and never will be – I understand Flo's passion to do this. It's a project. Already Flo has a detailed chart on her bedroom wall: an eighteen-week programme devised by James, with instructions for each day. It was James who also insisted she buy the right kit, so Flo bought some running leggings and tops to replace the tracksuit she'd bought almost a decade ago.

Once she's off the machine, I watch her try on a pair of bright orange trainers and walk up and down in front of the long mirror.

I imagine choosing a pair of trainers is rather like choosing a mattress. Given we spend a third of our life sleeping, it makes no sense to buy a nasty old cheap mattress. So if Flo is going to be running for the next six months, she needs a decent pair of shoes.

I watch Flo try on another pair.

'I'm running for Huntington's Disease,' I overhear her tell Mr Muscleman.

'I've never heard of that,' he replies, and as Flo explains exactly what it is, it feels surprisingly liberating knowing it's out in the open now. Flo hasn't crawled under a rock or given up, and with each day that passes we are healing the damage I caused, and Flo is slowly getting over Theo. I know it will take time, but we're good friends again, shopping together on a Sunday afternoon. As I watch Flo walking towards the till with the salesman, the two of them laughing and flirting with one another, I realize both Beth and I should have given this girl far more credit.

'How much?' I ask, jutting out my chin, as I join them both.

'One hundred and sixty pounds,' he says to me with a bright smile, waiting for my credit card. I'm not so invisible when he wants my money. *Funny that.*

Flo must pick up on my shock as she says, 'I can pay for them, honestly, Granny.'

'Put your wallet away,' I insist. 'I'm doing this. I'm sure they're worth every penny, and they'll last you for life.'

He shakes his head. 'They'll last for her training and the marathon itself, but if you catch the bug, Flo, which I'm sure you will, you'll need to invest in another pair after that.'

'Right.' I clear my throat, reminding myself it's only money. I thrust my card in his direction.

'Training socks,' he says to Flo, ignoring my card, before leading her off to another section of the shop, while I'm assigned to the chair in the corner, invisible once again.

'*Due cappuccini, per favore,*' I say to the waiter in the café, relieved to be out of the running shop. '*E vorrei vedere il menu del pranzo, per favore?*'

'*Certamente,*' the waiter says with delight. '*Un momento.*'

Flo continues to stare at me, wide-mouthed, until she says, 'When did—'

'A month or so ago.' I didn't say anything to Flo just in case I was rubbish and had to pull out. 'I've also signed up to do Pilates once a week, and I've booked tickets for the ballet this Christmas,' I show off now, telling Flo how magical my evening with Ricky had been watching *Swan Lake*.

Flo continues to look at me with surprise, before that surprise turns to something close to pride. 'To us, Granny,' she says, when the waiter returns with our cappuccini. She holds her mug towards mine. 'And thank you for my trainers and my high-tech socks.'

'Everyone needs a pair of high-tech socks,' I say, before we laugh, and for the next hour or so we eat lunch and talk about nothing important, but it's the best lunch I've eaten in years, because for the first time in a long while I feel completely at peace.

'Granny, I meant to tell you: I have my first appointment with the genetic counsellor next week. It finally came through.' She squeezes my hand. 'I was wondering if you would come with me?'

I hadn't thought about the test for weeks, not since the bust-up with Theo. And then, what with Flo's breakdown and the marathon news taking over, I'd almost forgotten about it completely.

I feel that panic returning, rising in my chest. I pick up my glass of water, my heart racing, my head feeling light. I realize I'm having a wobble.

'If it's too upsetting, I'd understand,' Flo says gently. 'Are you all right, Granny?' She waits. 'I could ask James or Maddie. I can even go on my own.'

'No,' I say, when I'm ready to talk, remembering all those years I wasn't there for Beth. All those times I could have been sitting next to my daughter, while instead she faced it alone. 'I'll be there, Flo, come what may.'

# 54

*Beth's Diary, 2004*

*I saw Amanda today and she asked me if I'd had any further thoughts about telling Flo and Mum.*

*'Flo's just had her first period,' I said. 'She's feeling anxious about that, and Mum has rebuilt her life after Dad.' I told Amanda how much Mum was enjoying her new part-time job working for a charity that built retirement homes for the over-sixties, joking that she'll move into one soon. 'She's doing well, and I don't want to do anything to jeopardize that. I like being normal,' I confided. 'My work is going well, I'm happy.'*

*'But it's a lot to shoulder on your own, Beth.'*

*Mark also tells me I should lean on friends. I guess the truth is I don't want anything to rock the boat. I've got used to the way things are. There's a certain comfort in being in control: it's only my hands on the steering wheel and I'm going in the direction I choose.*

*Amanda understood, but she said that, in her experience, the sooner you talk to your child the better, stressing that if I continue to hide it from Flo, the message she could get is that HD is scary or even shameful. By talking about it, it becomes normal.*

*Amanda wants me to put faith in my daughter. She claims children have an extraordinary ability to deal with difficult situations. She suggested reminding Flo about her grandfather first, asking if she remembers him being in a wheelchair, and then explaining it was because he had HD. By doing that, I've at least introduced her to the name of the condition. Slowly drip feed information to her, like feeding a baby. I know this all makes perfect sense. If I were Amanda, I'd be saying the exact same thing to me too.*

*I told her that Mum had a recent scare with her heart. For weeks she's been getting headaches and chest pain, and when she casually dropped into conversation that she'd also seen some blood in her urine, I took her off to see the GP immediately, cross that she'd kept it from me – not that I'm one to talk.*

*I gatecrashed the appointment because I was anxious Mum would skim over her problems, pursing her lips and sticking out her chin, saying she was perfectly all right.*

*Anyway, the GP sent her off to have various tests, and she was diagnosed with high blood pressure, which doesn't* sound too serious, often people don't feel any symptoms, but it can be a problem if you have a mother who doesn't follow doctor's orders to cut back on alcohol, caffeine and chocolate.

'What's life without a bit of Toblerone?' she snapped back at the poor woman only trying to do her job. 'I have two triangles after supper every night.'

When the GP suggested she learn to manage her stress:

'Stress?' Mum replied, before cackling, 'The only stress I have is if I don't count my trumps or go to bed with an ace!' I turned to the blank-looking doctor informing her that my mother was talking about playing bridge.

Anyway, Mum took away a leaflet giving her dietary and exercise advice, but I imagine it went straight into the bin. She spent so much time caring for Dad that I think she's forgotten how to look after herself.

I stressed to Amanda that, not only do I need to have faith that Flo can deal with this, I need to believe that my mother is strong enough to go through it all over again.

Mum pretends to be a tough old nut, but in reality she's vulnerable like the rest of us. As Dad used to say, 'She's as soft as they come'.

# 55

## Flo

The hospital waiting room is empty, quiet except for the sound of a ticking clock. I glance at Granny, knowing this can't be easy for her, and as if sensing my thoughts she turns to me and says, 'We're going to be fine, Flo. Let's hope she's nice.'

At that moment, a door opens and a petite woman dressed in pastel pink, which looks striking against her short dark hair and olive toned skin, calls out my name.

'Hello, I'm Dr Fraser.' She shakes my hand.

'This is my grandmother,' I introduce them. 'I hope it's okay if she comes in with me?'

'Of course. Would you like to come this way?' She turns on her heels before Granny and I follow her into her office.

'Excuse the mess, I'm always drowning in paperwork,' she

says, referring to the pile of sheets on her desk, alongside her computer, medical books and a mug of tea.

Granny and I sit opposite her. When she smiles, I notice soft eye make-up framing vivid brown eyes and that her fine silk scarf matches her jacket. I imagine she's in her early forties.

The first thing Dr Fraser wants us to do is sketch a family tree, to understand how I have possibly inherited the gene. Granny explains that Tim's mother could have had an affair.

'You'd be surprised how much this happens,' Dr Fraser says. 'Many women had affairs during the Second World War while their husbands were away, and unknowingly gave birth to a child at risk.'

After we have completed the family tree, ending with Mum's diagnosis, Dr Fraser puts her pen down. 'So tell me how you feel, Florence. What have you been thinking about in the lead-up to this appointment?'

'I'm trying to decide if I want to take the test or not. I go round and round in circles, especially at night.'

'That's normal,' she reassures me.

'I was certain I wanted to know at first.'

'Why was that?'

Her tone is soft, but probing. I sense she is watching my every move, expression, mannerism, even the way I am coiling a strand of my hair tightly around my fingers right now.

I stop, placing my hands on my lap. 'I wanted the problem to go away as quickly as it had come. I didn't want to believe it could happen to me, if that makes sense? I was in denial.'

She nods as if this is familiar territory for her.

I look at Granny, fearful I might hurt her with what I'm about to say next, but she nods discreetly.

'When I was growing up, Mum didn't tell me she had HD, not even that her father had it. I had no idea that I could be at risk until a few months ago.'

'How did that make you feel?'

*How do I begin to answer that?*

'Angry,' Granny suggests for me. 'It's fine, Flo, say it. I don't mind. It made her feel very angry,' she tells Dr Fraser.

But Dr Fraser's eyes don't leave mine. She wants to hear me say it.

*Anger barely touches the surface.*

'I was devastated,' I admit, before going on to tell Dr Fraser about the diaries Granny found. 'At least I know now that Mum *was* going to tell me, eventually. If only she'd said something right from the start.'

I want Dr Fraser to agree, to tell me that honesty always pays off.

'Do you understand why your mother may not have told you?' she asks instead.

'To protect me.' I shrug. 'I realize I can't dwell on the decisions she made, but to hear this in my twenties was ...' – I search for the right word – '*shattering.*'

Dr Fraser nods again. 'But how do you tell a child?'

'You tell them the truth.'

'When is the right time? When might they understand?' Dr Fraser asks. 'These were probably some of the questions your mother struggled with, daily.'

'I get it's not easy—'

'It was my fault,' Granny says. 'If you're going to point the finger—'

Dr Fraser stops her. 'No one wants to point a finger.'

'But if only I'd been able to talk to Beth, we wouldn't be in this mess.'

I stare ahead. 'I'd made all these plans.'

'What plans?' Dr Fraser asks, her tone calm but direct.

'I was about to move to America with my boyfriend. My *fiancé.*'

'And you can't still go?'

Somehow my pride can't tell her what happened with Theo, but I sense she's guessed, given I haven't answered the question.

'If you were in my shoes, what would you do, Dr Fraser?' I ask. 'Would you take the test?'

I search her face for any clues, but her expression remains neutral. That's her job, after all. *My* job is to work hard to come to my own decision.

'Florence, there is no right or wrong; it's a deeply personal decision. What I tend to ask anyone in your position is: what is most important to you?'

*I want to be my old self. I want to have normal problems, like laddering my tights just before a meeting or having a disastrous haircut or a disappointing first date with a man who quibbles over the bill, just as Maddie had the other week. I'm terrified that if I don't find out whether or not I have HD, every single day I'll wonder if this is the day I start to spot symptoms . . .*

'Is the fear of carrying the gene worse than knowing one way or another if you will inherit HD?' she asks.

'In many ways.' I inhale deeply. 'It's the unknown, the uncertainty.'

'Would finding out alleviate that fear?'

'Yes and no. I mean, if I found out I was positive I'm not sure yet how I'd cope,' I say. 'Do most people want to know?'

'No. Most people don't,' Dr Fraser says.

'Really?'

'You look surprised?'

I'm unsure why.

'Most people think they want to know, especially right after discovering they are at risk,' Dr Fraser continues. 'They want to rip the plaster off. But genetic counselling can help people to understand that there are choices. It can prepare them not only for the result, but to be able to deal with what comes afterwards. Can you expand on your fear, Florence? Pin down exactly what it is, apart from the uncertainty, that scares you?'

There's another long silence.

*I'm frightened I'll be alone for the rest of my life.*

No matter how much I tell myself that, right now, I'm better off single, it doesn't stop me from feeling alone, and from remembering the days with Theo and how much I miss him. And it doesn't stop me from fast-forwarding to the life that Granddad had, although Granddad had Granny.

What if I have no one? Will I live in a care home, no one visiting me? Or if they do, will they dread coming because they don't know what to say or how to act? I imagine James living in the country with his wife and two Labradors, along with three screaming children and when the phone rings he'll pull a face and ask his wife to pretend he's not in.

I must be smiling because Dr Fraser asks me what I'm thinking about. So I tell her about James.

'Honestly, he does that with his mother too, the lies I have to tell for him.' I roll my eyes, all of us laughing, the tension easing, before I confess, 'I'm scared I'll be alone.'

'You won't be,' Granny is quick to argue, looking at Dr Fraser. 'A beautiful young woman like Flo.'

'I might be, Granny.'

She turns to me. 'You won't.' She turns back to Dr Fraser. 'She won't. I'm here.'

Dr Fraser looks at us both. 'It seems you'll always have your grandmother, Florence.'

*But she knows what I'm getting at, and surely she would feel the same way too?*

Dr Fraser draws me back to the question with, 'Florence, where does this fear of being on your own come from?'

'My mother's fiancé walked out on us, and . . . the same thing happened to—'

'It's his loss,' Granny cuts in, before apologizing when Dr Fraser raises her hand, signalling for her not to interrupt this time.

'The moment you tell someone,' I claim, 'they'll run in the opposite direction.'

'Not everyone will,' Dr Fraser disputes.

'If this is how it feels when you're at risk but haven't had the test, imagine how hard it would be to tell someone new that you are definitely going to get HD,' I insist.

'If you have cancer or any kind of illness, there will be people who will stick by you,' Dr Fraser assures me.

I shake my head. I don't want her to feed me false hope. 'It's a lot to ask though, of anyone, to look after me the way Granny looked after Granddad.'

'Not if you love them, Flo,' Granny says.

'But it was different for you,' I say before she can protest. 'You were already married. There is no reason why anyone would want to go out with me once they find out I could be at risk. It's like walking into a clothes shop. No one is going to buy the faulty dress when they can buy a new one. That's why it's so much simpler not to meet anyone, that way I can't get hurt.'

'You've been hurt already,' says Dr Fraser. 'It's natural you feel this way, but in my experience I have met many people with HD who have gone on to marry and be happy. The right person won't be scared.'

'Where do the right people live?' I ask.

'If I knew I'd tell you,' she says, hinting to the fact that perhaps she needs to meet someone from there too. 'But they live somewhere. They do exist.'

*If only Mum had met the right person.*

'Not everyone is born to be a carer, Florence, and we can't judge them for that,' Dr Fraser says. 'It doesn't make them a bad person. What's important is to surround yourself with people who love you. It's not always about having a husband or partner. Sometimes we can be with the wrong person and feel lonelier than ever. It's about having good friends and goals. It's about not giving up.'

I tell Dr Fraser about running the marathon for HD. 'That's fantastic,' she says.

'But if I were to go on a date,' I say, still fixated on this point, 'how would I begin to tell him?'

'You pick your moment,' Dr Fraser suggests.

'Perhaps it's not the first thing to launch into over cocktails.'

She smiles. 'If you see a future with someone, I believe it's better to let them in. They need to be a part of *all* of you, and you will sense when the moment is right to tell them.'

I know she's right. Our family has been shrouded in secrecy and I'm exhausted by it, but honesty comes with the deep-rooted fear of rejection.

'No one is spared rejection,' Dr Fraser says, as if reading my mind and speaking from personal experience. 'No one is immune to it.'

She writes something else in her notes before asking, 'Is there anything else that concerns you, Florence?'

I nod, knowing I must ask her the question I've been dreading to know the answer to. 'If I were to take the test and discover I'm gene positive, does that mean I can't have children?' I reach for Granny's hand.

It seems an eternity before Dr Fraser replies, 'Of course you can. Since the huntingtin gene was discovered in 1993 we've discovered a great deal more about this disease, Florence,' she reassures me. 'Scientific progress will make a huge difference to you. So much has changed since your grandfather had HD, and even since your mother was tested.'

'But how can I have a baby if I don't take the test?'

'If you decide not to take the test, there are fertility techniques we can use to avoid potentially passing HD to your child. They can be complicated – they carry risk like any pregnancy – but it can be done.' She looks me straight in the eye. 'Florence, life goes on whether you have HD or not. You can be a mother.'

*Life goes on.*

'This is all hypothetical,' I remind her.

'It's good to be hypothetical. You're young and it's highly likely this will come up when you do meet the right person. What you do need to think through carefully, though, is having a child when it's possible you could become symptomatic later on. Having a family is a lot to take on for anyone, so all I'm saying is you and your partner—'

'Whoever the unlucky sod may be.'

'Stop it, Florence!' Granny barks at me, Dr Fraser trying not to smile again.

'Whoever the lucky man may be,' she continues, 'would need to make sure you understand what both of you could possibly be taking on.'

'Maybe I need to work out if I'm going to take the test first,' I reflect.

Dr Fraser nods.

'I know this sounds a stupid question,' I say, though I feel comfortable enough to ask it now.

'No question is stupid.'

'Can you explain to me exactly what HD is? I know what it means and I know what it did to Granddad,' I add. 'I've read up about it online and read Mum's diaries, but I don't understand the gene thing. I don't get the CAG repeats? Science was never my strong point.'

'Nor mine,' Granny admits. 'Always bottom of the pile in physics, no matter how many people were in my class.' She laughs nervously with me.

'How can a blood test give me the answer?' I ask.

'Okay, I'll try not to blind you both with too much science,' Dr Fraser says, picking up her pad of paper and pen again.

# 56

## Flo

'Slow down,' James urges again. He phoned me from work after my appointment with Dr Fraser, suggesting we could take a day off training, or just do a short easy run, rather than attempt six miles again, but I insisted we stick to the training programme. It's early November and already we're coming to the end of week four.

I turn up the volume on my iPod, pretending I didn't hear, my new trainers pounding against the pavement as I try to ignore both James and the cold – and the pouring rain. I realize I haven't eaten enough today, either.

*I know I planned on telling Flo when she was thirteen, but I'm going to wait.*

No, Mum, better not say a word. Just mess up my entire life instead.

'Flo, slow down!' James calls out again.

I pick up my pace.

*Waiting is risky. But this is where I am. I'm going to take that chance. After all, Flo's still very young.*

I wonder if you would have ever told me, Mum? You said you would, but then you said that so many times, didn't you? First, you were going to say something when Graham left, next you planned to tell me when I was ten, then thirteen, so how do I know you wouldn't have bottled out yet again? I'd have come home from my holiday and you would have said nothing.

As I turn another corner, I hear Dr Fraser's voice inside my head. *We all have thousands of genes that come in pairs. We inherit one of each pair from our mother and one from our father.* I don't even know who my father is. Thanks for that too, Mum.

'Flo.' James grabs my arm. 'Let's walk the next bit.'

*Everyone has two copies of the HD gene: one they inherited from their mum, one from their dad. In people at risk of developing HD, one of these copies of the HD gene is changed or mutated in a very specific way. Beth, unfortunately, inherited the altered copy of her father's gene.*

Mum gave birth to me when she knew she was at risk. Thanks again.

'Flo, we need to pace ourselves. You're going too fast.'

'I'm fine!'

'Let's go home. It's nasty out here.'

'I'm fine!' I repeat breathlessly, my legs feeling like lead as I try to go even faster to show James I'm improving.

*When I look back, I realize I was plagued with worry about Dad ever since that conversation I overheard in the kitchen when I was ten. I wished I hadn't overheard Mum and Dad talking, because everything changed after that. I want to give Flo the carefree childhood I never had.*

You know what, Mum, instead of constantly writing in your stupid diary, why didn't you just sit me down at the kitchen table and fucking tell me?

*You had a right to know. In fact so did I,* I hear Theo saying to me now. *I still can't believe Peggy didn't tell you this until now,* Theo's voice continues to taunt me. *How fucking irresponsible! It's over.*

'Flo!' James takes me by the arm again.

'*What?*' I swing round to him, ready to strike.

'If you carry on pushing yourself like this you'll get an injury,' he warns me, his tone as sharp as mine now.

I don't care. I charge off again, down the steps and under the subway and my thighs are killing me as I tackle the steps on the other side, before James pulls me back once more, forcing me to stop this time. 'Is this about your appointment today?'

I don't know; I suddenly feel so angry I want to punch this wall.

'Let's call it a day,' he insists. 'It's too grim.'

For a moment I'm tempted. I look at my watch. We've only covered one and a half miles.

'I don't want to go home, but you can,' I say, turning up my music.

James grabs my arm yet again, but this time it hurts. 'If you keep on stopping me like this, my times will never improve.'

'I don't care about your fucking times.'

'Well, I do,' I shout back at him, exasperated, as a few passers-by glance over their shoulders, not wanting to miss a juicy argument.

'You're not doing this to beat a world record,' James helpfully informs me.

'Can we just carry on?' I say, on the verge of tears, running on. 'I'll never get round in a good time if I don't put the work in.'

'You're not running this for a time!' he calls out to me. 'You're running this for your mum.'

I stop and turn round to face him. 'My mum who never told me,' I say, tears now streaming down my face.

He edges closer towards me. 'I know. Wait, Flo, don't run on.'

I don't move. 'My mum who was always "about" to tell me, James.'

*Will this anger and resentment ever go away?*

'Okay, forget your mum for a minute. Remember what you put on your application form?' he says, standing in front of me now. 'You wanted to help raise money for research? Flo, there's this guy who is certain HD is curable—'

'Stop, James, just stop.' I wipe my eyes. 'I don't need you to tell me it's all going to be fine, because it's not.'

'Let's go home.' He waits. 'Please, Flo. Before you injure yourself. If you do that it'll take weeks off your training.'

'Fine. I'm just . . .' I clench my hands into fists. 'Today, it was good – she was lovely – but it brought up a lot of stuff and I still don't know if I want to take the test or not.' I look at James drenched, realizing he doesn't have to be running with me tonight; he's choosing to. 'I'm sorry. I don't know how you put up with me.'

'Because someone has to.' A small, relieved smile creeps on to his face. 'But can we go home now, before we freeze to death?'

'On one condition.'

'Name it.'

'We stop via the newsagent. I'm dying for some chocolate. And some wine.'

'Hallelujah!' he says, both of us finally laughing as he puts an arm around my shoulders and we make our way home together.


James and I are huddled together on the sofa, chocolate wrappers scattered across the floor, along with an empty bottle of white wine and two empty glasses. I was like some kind of addict, unable to wait until we got home, tucking into the chocolate the moment we left the shop, and pouring the wine the minute we arrived home.

'There are bound to be days like this,' James assures me. 'One moment you're fine, or you're at least treading water, the next a big wave comes along and knocks you sideways.'

'It was talking about Mum, and before we did our run I read some more of her diary,' I admit. 'I can't bear all the

287

constant excuses she used not to tell me. It was just one thing after another.'

'I understand.'

'I really liked her,' I say, referring to Dr Fraser again. I smile, recalling Granny's baffled face when she was trying to explain to us the science part.

'What's so funny?' James asks.

I tell him about our science lesson, admitting that's part of my frustration too. I still don't quite get how one blood test can determine my fate.

'Okay,' James says with renewed energy, as if this is a problem he can fix. 'As you know, our genes are made up of the genetic material DNA, so when you were born, Flo, you inherited half the genetic material from your mum and half from your dad.'

'My non-existent dad.'

'You still have his genes.'

'Right.'

'We all have two copies of the HD gene, and near the beginning of this gene is a repetitive sequence that reads, C-A-G.'

'This is the part where I got lost,' I confess.

'Our DNA is made up of four chemicals: Adenine, Cytosine . . .' He stops. 'Actually, just think of them as A, C, G and T and think of it as code used by scientists to describe DNA, okay?'

'With you.'

'Everyone has this C-A-G repeat for this particular gene,

okay? I do, Granny Peg does, so does Maddie, but what we have inherited is a copy both from our mother and father, each under 20 repeats, which is normal. Whereas your mum would have had one normal copy and one copy with 40 or more CAG repeats. Does that make sense?'

I watch him lean over to the coffee table to pick up a pad of paper and a pen. He writes: CAGCAGCAGCAG-CAGCAGCAGCAG.

It's still another language to me. A language I don't want to learn, but I have to, to feel more in control. 'How do you know all this, James?'

'I learned it at college. Animals have genes,' he reminds me.

'So the reason it's fifty-fifty for me,' I realize, 'is because there's a chance I might have inherited the larger-size gene from Mum.'

He nods.

'But if I've inherited the two normal-size ones—'

'You won't get HD,' James finishes for me. 'The blood test would show two normal C-A-G repeats.'

'And it's the huntingtin protein, produced by the HD gene, which causes harm to the brain cells.'

'Exactly.'

I take in a deep breath, as if I'm about to take the blood test now. 'I can't believe how stupid I was to rush this,' I mutter, thinking of how willingly I'd given my vein to Theo's doctor, when I didn't even understand the process.

'Would you take the test, James?'

'I knew you were going to ask me that at some point.' He helps himself to another chocolate. 'I don't know, Flo, probably not. I kind of see life like a tube map, with all these stops we could get off at, like cancer, a plane crash, falling off a cliff or Alzheimer's here we come—'

'This is cheerful.'

'You asked. Or there's the stop where we die peacefully in our bed at the end of the line with our family around us. Obviously, that's the place we all want to end up, but if nothing can change our route, if we can't turn round or get on another train that heads in a different direction, I'm not sure I'd want to know, because there'd be nothing I could do to change it. If I tested positive, all I'd want would be to scientifically reprogram my fate, and it'd kill me that I couldn't, so I think I'd rather *not* know.'

'And if you met someone like me, imagine we didn't know each other—'

'That's impossible. I've known you since you were seven, Flo.'

'Try to imagine we're strangers on a date and I tell you I'm at risk. What would you think?'

'I'd feel for you. I'd think it was really bad luck.'

'Yeah, but would there be a second date or would you be planning your exit strategy immediately?'

'Flo, it's hard to say when it's you.'

I turn away. 'That's a no to the second date then.'

He turns me back to face him, puts a finger under my chin and tilts my head upwards so that I can't avoid his eyes.

'It doesn't mean no. Besides, I didn't think you were interested in meeting anyone right now.'

'I'm not, well not right now, but we talked about it today, how the right person won't be scared.'

'I'm sure he won't be and when he does come along, I'll be sure to warn him not to become your marathon training partner any time soon.'

I laugh. 'I'm sorry, James. I'm such an idiot.'

'No, you're not. No one can imagine what you're going through right now, least of all me. The only thing I've ever had to deal with was my dog dying and breaking up with Emma—'

'That was bad enough.'

'Yeah, but that's just life, everyone has relationship problems. I know the thought of HD is a terrifying thing to face, but in many ways none of us have a clue what's round the corner. I could get run over by a bus tomorrow.'

I shouldn't smile; it's just the way James said it. 'Please don't.'

'My stop could be sooner than yours, for all I know.'

'Shush,' I plead.

'Anything can happen, Flo, good, bad, ugly, wonderful and everything in between. Isn't that the magic of life, to hop on the ride, and hope for the best? But if you do decide to take the test – and I get that too – I'll be here for you.'

'Thank you.' I rest my head on James's shoulder, feeling safe and lucky to have such a good friend. I don't know how long we sit in companionable silence until finally I break it.

'It's an odd thought, knowing I'm made up of someone I've never met,' I reflect, imagining adopted people must often feel the same way, however close they are to their parents. They must wonder where certain traits came from, peculiarities and mannerisms.

When I look in the mirror and see my olive-toned skin and dark brown eyes, I often imagine what my father might look like. If he's even still alive. I guess that's another thing today brought up: it made me think about Theo and Graham, and how I have always craved a father figure in my life. I think, in many ways, that's why I went for an older man. I believed Theo could offer me not only love, but security too.

'Anyway, how was your day?' I ask, 'apart from being shouted at by your neurotic flatmate?'

Just as he's about to answer his mother calls him on his mobile.

'Take it,' I urge. 'Don't screen.'

I readjust my position on the sofa and listen to the comforting sound of James talking next to me. For a moment I think about Granny. I hope today wasn't too painful for her. She promised me she was fine, and she also swore she wasn't going to be alone tonight. She's having supper with a few friends she has met on her Italian course.

I am no closer to knowing if I want to take the test or not. If anything, I am further away. But this time there is no rush. Dr Fraser suggested I see her again in a month's time.

I shut my eyes, and before I know it, I'm falling into a deep sleep.

## 57

## Peggy

As I get undressed for bed, I'm glad I didn't cancel my supper tonight with two of the women from my Italian course: Sarah who wants to move to Florence when her husband retires, and Iris, a retired teacher about my age, with two daughters, one getting married to an Italian chap in the New Year.

I was close to calling off the night, certain I'd be poor company, only able to think about Flo and our appointment with Dr Fraser today. I wasn't sure I'd be strong enough to hear about their families and their seemingly untroubled lives. I was tempted to sit in my armchair and watch a recorded episode of *Flog It!* eating a poached egg on toast. There is a certain ease and comfort in being alone.

One moment, I'm longing for Flo to take the test. I'm dreaming of her saying to me, 'Granny, it's okay; I don't have it'. But the next I'm praying she doesn't.

Like Dr Fraser has warned, Flo needs to be aware that finding out you are gene positive can remove hope. Once you know, there is no turning back. It's like saying something that can never be unsaid.

For some, it must be like living with a permanent black cloud over your head, just waiting for it to rain. For others, perhaps finding out doesn't remove that hope but allows them to plan. It motivates them to make the most of the time they have.

I believe Beth was in that camp. Not once did she look back and regret. She had a successful career. She loved being a teacher. My only sadness was she never met anyone after Graham. She didn't meet the right person, though I never got the sense she even tried, just as I didn't after losing Tim.

If it were me, I probably wouldn't want to know, simply because I'd rather live in the hope that I will peacefully slip away in an armchair after a delicious glass of champagne and a boiled egg for breakfast.

Some might say that's cowardly. Others might have to know what lies ahead; they need that map. I believe both choices require faith and strength.

I hadn't realized I was being so quiet over the meal until Iris asked me if I was all right, also noticing that I'd hardly touched my pasta.

I was about to say I was perfectly all right, but 'No,' came out instead, before I told them all about my family, ending with my appointment with Flo today.

They asked questions, listened attentively and Iris even held my hand as she said, 'What a brave girl. We must sponsor Florence.'

'We can do better than that,' Sarah claimed. 'We can ask our whole class to sponsor her, and I'll ask all my friends too, and I could come and cheer her on with you on the day, Peggy, if you'd like? I've always wanted to watch a marathon live.'

I get into bed and close my eyes, my head and heart lighter for sharing my troubles with them, and I'm touched by their response. We all shared a pudding too: tiramisu with three teaspoons, and Iris and Sarah clapped when I asked the waiter for the bill in Italian, also adding, '*La pasta era deliziosa!*'

I hope Flo is all right. After the appointment she told me she was fine. I have to admit I thought my head might explode when Dr Fraser started talking about CAG repeats. I still haven't quite grasped what they are. I'll ask Ricky to explain it to me. He can give me a science lesson for dummies. *Lucky Ricky!*

I did think Flo looked tired though, deep circles under her eyes. She went straight on to work after the appointment, saying it was good for her to keep busy. She also promised me that she wasn't alone tonight; she was training with James. She told me how much she was enjoying her running, proud that she'd managed a few weeks without wine or chocolate, or anything naughty like tiramisu.

I admire her willpower. I couldn't last a day.

Theo wasn't the right man, but she will meet someone. I may be biased, but any man that can't see how special she is must be blind.

I switch off the light.

Flo is a brave girl. She takes after her mother and her grandfather.

I'm mighty proud of them all.

## 58

### Flo

'How hungry are you?' I ask Maddie, who has come to stay for the weekend.

'*Starving*. I wonder how James's date is going.'

Three weeks ago, James met Chloe online. He signed up to some dating app. Apparently, she's passionate about vegetarian cooking and writes a food blog.

'He's been trying to encourage me to do it too,' I tell Maddie.

She looks at me with concern. 'It's probably still too soon after Theo?'

'It's been over two months since we broke up, and the sad part is we haven't kept in touch at all. I thought he might at least contact me after I returned his ring, even just an acknowledgement.'

'He probably feels guilty,' suggests Maddie. 'I would.'

Occasionally, in the moments when I miss being with him and think what could have been, I have clung on to the hope that he might change his mind. But I realize now I could never be with someone who was uncertain of our future. He can't take back the things he said. They would always be there, hanging over us.

It's odd to think how Theo was in my life for eighteen months, day after day, and then in an instant, it's as if the two of us didn't exist for each other.

'You're wise not to rush into dating, Flo,' Maddie continues. 'Believe me, you meet some right oddballs online. I'm going out with someone next week. Probably another dud.'

I smile. 'Who's the lucky guy?'

'Jack. He works in property or something.'

'Promise to let me know how it goes.' I add the spaghetti to a pan of boiling water. 'James just worries I spend too much time on my own thinking about everything. He wants to keep me distracted.'

'Are you any closer to making up your mind?'

I shake my head. 'One moment I'm certain I want to, but the next—'

'It's a massive decision, and it hasn't been that long Flo, not really. I bet some people take months, even years to decide.'

'Exactly. What would you do?'

'You're asking someone who reads the last chapter of a book first. I'd *have* to know.'

I could never read the last chapter of a book first. If I

knew the ending before I'd even begun, there would be no twists and turns or surprises along the way. Isn't half the pleasure of reading a book turning the page to find out what happens next?

'More wine, Maddie?'

'Please. But have some too, before I finish off the whole bottle.'

Maddie teases me, just like James does, saying I'm taking my training too seriously. After binging on chocolates and wine the evening of my counselling appointment three weeks ago, I decided to cut both out altogether and plan a whole new diet. I threw out everything remotely unhealthy in our kitchen and replaced them with pulses, grains, oats, mixed nuts instead of crisps, carbohydrate drinks and energy gels, cereal bars, yoghurt, bananas, berries, salmon, pasta and eggs.

I'm now seven weeks into my programme and it's getting harder, especially since it's bitingly cold in the mornings and the temptation to stay under the duvet for an extra half hour rather than jogging to work is strong. It's also dark by three in the afternoon now, but I'm sticking to the programme and my new diet religiously, crossing off each day as I go along. It's the only thing that gives me a sense of purpose and control right now.

'How's the training going?' Maddie asks.

I tell her that James and I meet up most evenings after work. Normally, he picks me up on Vile Vera and takes me home, before we get changed, have a peanut butter bagel, and then go out again. Last weekend we finished our first eight-mile run without stopping.

'A tortoise could move faster,' I said, when we arrived home in the pitch black.

'Train like a tortoise, race like a hare,' he said, which he clearly thought was rather quick-witted of him.

'I'm rubbish,' I admit to Maddie, describing how at the beginning of our runs, I bounce up and down like a child about to open their Christmas presents. I look every inch the professional, with my new trainers and energy tablets in the back pocket of my sleek running leggings, and an iPod strapped to my arm, but it doesn't take long for me to feel like a knackered old warhorse, feet barely lifting off the ground.

'One runner even approached me and asked if I was injured and needed to go to A&E.'

'Good-looking?' Maddie asks.

'He was well into his seventies and fitter than me.'

We both laugh again, before my phone vibrates. It's a text message from James, sending me a link to an article written by a leading consultant neurologist, Edward Wild, about the latest HD drug news.

'What's he doing texting you on a date?' Maddie asks. 'I hate the way everyone sits there glued to their phones in restaurants and bars when they've got company. It's not cool.'

'You know, your brother is pretty special,' I reflect, thinking how he's always trying to keep my hopes up, printing out articles or sending me information online about different drugs and trials. I know he wants to help me, but with his scientific background I think he finds it interesting too.

'He's all right, I suppose,' she shrugs. 'When he's not being annoying.'

I tell Maddie about this one trial in particular that James has mentioned, a gene silencing treatment that could slow down, even prevent, HD. I know it's a long way off, and mention of cures and breakthroughs should be taken with a pinch of salt, but it's reassuring to know there's talk. It would be seriously depressing if I went online and found nothing.

At least there are a group of off-the-scale-intelligent people working in laboratories, day and night, to try to give people like me hope.

If I do take the test and it's positive, perhaps I can cling on to the idea that, by the time I get symptoms, there might be a drug I can take that will help me, and thousands of others in the same position.

When I see Dr Fraser next week I'm going to ask her about this trial.

My mobile vibrates again.

'Is he even *talking* to Chloe?' Maddie exclaims.

'He must be. He says he'll be home late.'

A few hours later, when Maddie and I are tucked up in bed reminiscing about our college days, James sends me another text message saying he's not coming home tonight after all, adding a smiley face.

I set my alarm, ignoring my niggling disappointment

that he probably won't be back in time to train with me tomorrow.

*Come on, Flo.* I'm pleased. It's time he got over Emma once and for all.

It makes me think of my first love. His name was Freddie. FREDDIE & FLO, TOGETHER FOR EVER I wrote on the outside of my pencil case, surrounded by lots of hearts.

James deserves to be happy, but the funny thing is, I've got too used to having him to myself.

Later that night, I still can't sleep. Quietly, I take Mum's diary and go into the kitchen. I'm sweet sixteen now and still blissfully ignorant of the future ahead.

# 59

*Beth's Diary, 2006*

*I can hardly believe my little girl is sixteen. She's taller than me now, (she loves to pat me on the head) and I know I'm biased, but she's beautiful, inside and out, with a smile that could melt the stoniest of hearts.*

*And she has a lot to smile about right now. The end of exams is finally in sight, along with the prospect of hanging out with Maddie and her friends over the long summer holiday, before she goes to college in the autumn to begin her A levels.*

*But that's not the only reason why she's so happy at the moment.*

*'Mum,' she whispered last night, when she came home after an evening out with Freddie. Not only is Flo taller than me, she now goes to bed later than I do, too, and has*

303

*regular date nights, while I'm on the sofa with my mug of tea watching* EastEnders.

*'Are you awake?' she asked.*

*'I am now,' I said, relieved to know she was home safe and sound.*

*'Can I tell you a secret?'*

*I sat bolt upright and switched on the light.*

*'You've had sex,' I blurted out, terrified, especially since I'd recently tried to talk to her about protection and how she must never feel pressured to do anything before she's ready. It must have been the shortest conversation in the world, since Flo hates me discussing anything to do with sex: the moment I mention the word 'penis' she flees the room with her hands over her ears, claiming they've learned about it at school.*

*'No!' she replied, before whispering again, 'Freddie said he loves me.'*

*I tapped the empty side of the bed next to me, and she laid down and told me all about it, the excitement in her voice touching.*

*I'm so relieved that my daughter's first experience of falling in love is with Freddie. He's the perfect boyfriend. Tall like her, sporty unlike her – Flo says he's in the first team in tennis, cricket and rugby. He's polite and kind, even offers to do the drying-up after meals. But the best thing about these two is they're great friends already. There has been none of that 'Why won't he call me, Mum?' or 'I'm not sure he likes me anymore'.*

*With Freddie it's been extraordinarily straightforward. He has been in love with Flo for months but Flo was adamant she only wanted to be friends, until eventually his persistence paid off.*

*They spend most of their time hanging out at each other's houses. When they're here, they play music and chat in Flo's bedroom. They spend a lot of time not chatting too, before coming downstairs for supper with flushed faces, zips undone or buttons skew-whiff.*

*I catch the subtle glances, the little touches, Flo playing with her hair and Freddie reaching for her hand when he thinks I'm not looking. It's a special time for them because they're learning about love for themselves, instead of watching it on TV or reading about it in books.*

*'Who was your first boyfriend, Mum?' she asked, resting her head on my shoulder.*

*How I wished I could come up with an innocent and romantic story like theirs, of a young boy who had also made me discover how love makes the world seem a brighter place.*

*When I feel overwhelmed by guilt that I haven't told Flo about my teenage years, I try to reassure myself that equally Flo hasn't had to worry about me in the same way I used to worry about my father. If I can give my daughter a relatively trouble-free childhood for as long as possible, then at least I'll have done something right.*

*Instead, I confided to Flo that her old mum has been a late starter. I used to go out with a chap called Ben when*

*I first went to art school. He and I worked together in a bar and used to stay up late, chatting, after everyone had gone home. I didn't tell her that I more than made up for lost time by having a series of one-night stands and dating a string of unsuitable men, Ben being one of them.*

'Have you ever loved anyone, Mum?'

'I love you,' I said, which received a 'that's not what I mean' nudge.

'You loved Graham, didn't you?' she persisted.

*I nodded. 'Yes. Very much.' That part of my life feels a world away now, almost like it never existed. Flo has often asked why I haven't met anyone else after Graham, and why he walked out on us. All I can do is give her the same old tired answer, which is that we knew in the end it wasn't right, and that sometimes it takes courage to walk away no matter how painful it is.*

*She then asked me if I ever felt lonely, and why didn't I go online to find a date.*

'Lots of people do it,' she insisted. 'You could meet the man of your dreams. You're not a wrinkly old bag yet,' she added, making me laugh. 'Anyone would be lucky to have you, Mum, and your awesome macaroni cheese.'

*I pulled her into my arms, saying I was lucky to have her, and that seeing her so happy was the greatest gift she could give me. I told her I prayed she'd go on to do art for her A levels, because she was very talented, just like her grandfather. But Flo wriggled from my grasp.*

'Sometimes I wish Mark wasn't married, don't you?'

'He's a good friend, that's all,' I said, realizing I wasn't fooling myself, let alone Flo.

'Freddie used to be a good friend. Now look at us. You've always said friendship is the most important—'

'He's married, darling.'

'I see the way he looks at you when he comes here for coffee, Mum. He can't take his eyes off you.'

'Oh, Flo, we're fond of one another, that's all.'

'You look at him in the same way too.' She crossed her arms defiantly, jutting out her chin. 'It's so obvious.'

'He's married' was the only thing I could say again.

'I know, but I can spot true love when I see it.'

'Flo, that's enough,' I said, not wanting to offer her false hope, even if there have been many times when I've found myself wishing too that things could be different between Mark and me.

I know there is a connection, a spark. Aside from Graham, he is the only person who knows I've taken the test. He is the one person I can turn to when things get rough, and each time we meet our bond deepens. When I'm with Mark, I can truly be myself.

When he kisses me goodbye on the cheek, I feel a stab of regret and jealousy that he is going home to his wife. Alone, I can't help but imagine what it might feel like to be the object of his affection.

Occasionally, I wonder if it would be easier not to see him, not to be around someone I can't have. Yet a

*life without Mark isn't a life I want. I'd rather have his
friendship than nothing at all.*

'Mum, what's wrong with your hand?'

'Nothing,' I said, steadying it immediately. *My legs
have recently felt restless too, but it could easily be this
condition called 'restless leg syndrome'. Apparently,
it's common.*

*I'm thirty-seven. Dad's troubles began when he was
forty, or possibly before that. Symptoms can go unnoticed,
especially if you're not looking for them. I'm probably
looking out for mine too much. I'm sure it's nothing.
Maddie's mother says her legs always feel restless, just
when she wants to sit down and relax.*

'Mum? Are you all right?' *She was still looking
at my hand.*

'All fine, just a twitch,' I lied, *hating myself for it.*
'Anyway, what did you have to eat tonight?' I asked,
*desperate to change the subject.*

*The last time I saw Mark he told me it was natural to
want to keep on protecting Flo for ever. As a father, all he
wants is to iron out every single bump for his two sons.*

'But at some point I'm going to have to let them go over
the bumps on their own,' *he'd said,* 'and hope they make it
to the other side in one piece. You've got to trust her, Beth,
trust that she can find a way to deal with it.'

*He's right. I think of all those times when I've dropped
Flo off at a party and watched her disappear behind the
front door in a skirt far too short for my liking, and I've*

*had to trust that she'll come home by ten as promised, and not once has she let me down. If she goes shopping with her friends, I trust they will stick together, not talk to strangers and take the tube or bus home together.*

*Flo is old enough to fall in love. She's old enough to work part time – she has a waitressing job, and is currently saving up to go travelling across Europe by train next year. She has always been responsible, and in many ways far older and wiser than her years. I know it's time I trusted her with my secret.*

*I'm going to tell her the moment she finishes her exams. I'll pick the right time, and then I'll talk to Mum.*

*The ironic thing is this isn't so much about the HD anymore. It's about not being in control. For years I have become an expert at parking all my worries and concerns. When I tell Flo and Mum, it will feel frighteningly real, and there will be no place for me to hide.*

*'I want you to be as happy as me, Mum. Don't you get lonely?' she asked again.*

*I stroked her hair. Sometimes I feel so lonely it hurts.*

*'No. I have everything I need right here.' I squeezed her hand. 'Now, you haven't told me if you said you loved Freddie back.'*

*She nodded. 'Oh, Mum, it was amazing,' she said, and as she continued, I wished I could press a pause button to stop Flo growing up so quickly, and to stop my precious time with my daughter slipping through my fingers.*

## 60

**Flo**

It's early morning on the second Sunday of December, and I'm on week nine of my training programme, a week that James's chart tells me is all about building endurance. My goal today is to run ten to twelve miles.

'Holy shit,' says Iona, my new running partner, who has just come over to train with me again. She looks out of my bedroom window. 'Is it *ever* going to stop raining?'

James loves to remind me that he's still in charge, but he can't always be jogging by my side, especially since he's now officially dating Chloe, so I've become more involved with a few of the other runners that I've met through the HDA charity. They set up a Facebook group page for all of us who secured a place in the marathon, to say hello and give each other tips and encouragement during our training, and when I discovered one of the runners, Iona, lived close to me, we decided to meet up.

During the past few weeks, we've trained together at weekends and occasionally after work, but the best thing about it is we're as bad as each other. Iona must only be about five-foot tall, so she's unable to take great big strides with her short plump legs, and so far as her technique goes, 'I just keep on running,' she wrote on our page, which immediately made me smile, along with the fact that she also confided that she still eats whatever she likes.

'Swapping doughnuts for Hobnobs is about all I've done so far, but I'm not quitting booze. There is no way I'm not going to have a glass of wine after a crappy day at work,' she'd written with a smiley face attached.

She also wasn't too proud to admit that, when she had her gait tested, she was told it was so tragic she could break her ankles if she kept on running. 'It'll take a lot more than that for me to give up,' was her reply.

Aside from the helpful tips we share, we also share our stories, which has been surprisingly cathartic. My running buddies and I may have nothing in common, yet we are all linked in some way by a rare condition, so Iona doesn't need to ask what I'm going through, nor do I need to imagine how hard it is for her to know that she's gene positive.

She took the test when she was twenty. She's now twenty-two and engaged to be married next year, a few months after the marathon.

'I need to get it over and done with first,' she'd said. 'Fingers crossed I won't be carried up the aisle on a stretcher.'

'Nearly ready,' I say to her, before putting on my turquoise waterproof jacket that I begrudgingly bought a few weeks ago. Practical gear has queue-jumped stylish clothes. Iona is wearing a similar rain jacket, only hers is bright purple, along with leggings and trainers that almost match the colour of her striking red hair.

We set our watches to record our distance, speed and heart rate, though I'm trying not to beat myself up over my times anymore.

Iona's attitude has really helped. She's running for her Dad, she reminds me. Her best friend, who used to be a piano tuner and loves the unlikely combination of classical music and the heavy metal band Iron Maiden, her father who is in a nursing home in the later stages of HD.

I walk past James's room; his bed wasn't slept in again last night. He was at a party with Chloe. For a moment I miss him, wondering what he'll be doing today, and wondering what she's like. Things appear to be getting serious between them.

Outside Iona touches my arm. It's a pat of solidarity. It's asking 'Are you ready?'

And we're off.


I feel sore. Every part of my body aches, but I tell Iona the pain isn't quite as bad as the run before. 'We must be getting fitter?'

'You are, *we* are,' she says, as we grab a table with the comfiest-looking chairs at a café close to Iona's flat where we are to have some brunch together before she visits her father.

'Feels good, doesn't it?' I reflect, finally realizing why people do catch the bug. Exercise really does release endorphins.

What might I be doing otherwise? Sitting at home, worrying. Feeling anxious and depressed. Watching TV. Instead, we've just jogged to Richmond Park, and all the way back to Earls Court. We saw deer, we saw dog walkers also braving the wind, rain and cold, and we cheered on other runners.

Slowly, I'm beginning to feel like I belong in a group. I imagine it's the same for dog walkers. You become part of a pack.

'Dad's expecting me at about half one,' Iona says, as we order two plates of eggs Benedict, coffee and freshly squeezed orange juice, Christmas music playing in the background. 'Not that he'd actually notice if I were late; he doesn't even know what day it is now.'

'How is he?' I ask.

'Happy enough.' She shrugs. 'He didn't want to go into a home to begin with – it terrified him – but he's safe and well cared for.'

Iona found out about her father's HD when she was twelve. Her mum told her, but what she didn't add was that Iona had a chance of inheriting the gene. In so many ways her childhood was similar to Mum's. Both Iona and my mother knew about their fathers, but what was never discussed was how it could potentially affect them.

It was the elephant in the room.

Iona only worked it out after learning about genetics in a science class in school when she was fourteen, but she was still too frightened to bring it up with her mother.

HD was fast becoming this big scary monster that made her father, normally so even-tempered, fly into rages, one time cutting up her mum's clothes before threatening to attack her with the kitchen scissors too.

No one in her family talked about it – it was easier not to – and yet it was there, in bold. It was only when Iona was sixteen that finally she broke down in tears in front of her mum, saying, 'Why didn't you tell me this could happen to *me* too?'

'How are the wedding plans going?' I ask.

'Great. We're keeping it dead simple, Flo. I don't understand these people who get into a right old tizzy planning it. Steve and I are inviting fifty people; it'll be fish and chips, bubbly and dancing.'

'Sounds perfect. How did you two meet?'

She grins, as if I'm going to like this story. 'It was four years ago. I was eighteen and miserable, Flo, in therapy, trying to work out if I wanted to take the test or not. I was just like you, one minute thinking I wanted to, but changing my mind the next. I was all over the shop. You know what it's like.'

I nod, knowing only too well.

'Anyhow, we went out on a date and I told him about Dad's HD, sparing no details. I told him that it was so bad I'd self-harmed.'

'That's brave of you to admit that. Especially on a first date.'

'Nah, it wasn't brave. It was the drink talking. Apparently I said to him, "I'll be the worst mistake you ever make, Steve".' Iona cringes just thinking about it. 'He bundled me into a cab home. "That went well," I thought, thinking another man bites the dust. The thing is, a lot of men had messed me around before that, and I'd always thought it was the HD, but it wasn't. It was either me getting plastered and pushing them away, or they were just arseholes.'

'Back to Steve,' I say, enjoying the story since I know it has a happy ending.

'So he calls me the next day and asks me how my hangover is, and if it's better, would I like to go on another date.'

Steve is surely the mayor of the island where the right people live.

'I know,' she says, clocking my surprise. 'I was as stunned as you are, but he's a decent bloke, a caring one too without being soppy. He came to all my genetic counselling appointments with me.'

'Did he want you to take the test?'

'Yes, but only because he knew I was going mad not knowing. That's what made my decision easier in the end. If I tripped or fell or my legs felt restless, I'd think "Could this be the start of it?" The second-guessing, the paranoia, became impossible to deal with. I felt as if my life was constantly on hold. Finding out was the biggest weight lifted off my shoulders.'

'Even though——'

'Yes, even though. The night after we found out I tested positive wasn't easy, I'm not gonna lie. Steve and I were lying in bed with our eyes wide open, thinking "holy shit" but then we just turned to one another, sat up, switched the light on and began to draw up a list of all the things we needed to think about and plan. My dad got Mum into a whole lot of debt because he couldn't manage his money, so one of the first things I put on that list was to save for the future. I didn't want us to buy a house with a massive mortgage. That's why we're not having a huge fairy-tale wedding either.'

'That makes sense,' I admit, just as our food arrives.

'You think you can't cope, Flo,' Iona says more gently. 'There were days during my counselling when I'd hear this snide voice inside my head saying, "If you find out you're positive, are you sure you won't self-harm again?" I knew I could only take that test if I were the strongest version of myself, and I was lucky too, because I had Steve and my mum and all my friends supporting me. People in Dad's day disowned him. Just years ago we'd have been locked up in a loony bin. I don't regret taking the test for a minute.' She stops, recovers her breath. 'Sorry, I've been rambling on and on about myself.'

'No, it helps talking about it. You're amazing, Iona.'

'Nah, I'm not.'

'You are.' *And so is Steve.* He is cut from a different cloth to Theo.

'Well, so are you then,' she says, as if that's settled. 'How are you feeling about it all? When's your next appointment with Dr Fraser?'

'Next month, just after Christmas.' It will be my third one. 'I still don't know what to do.'

'Do you know what helped me in the end?'

'Go on.'

'Thinking about HD in a scientific way. It's not some big hairy monster that's out to get us. It's a genetic problem. Steve is constantly tweeting the scientists, asking about the latest treatments.'

'James does that too.'

'You talk about him a lot, you know.'

'Do I? I suppose we've been spending more time together recently.'

'That's it? He's just a friend?'

I nod.

'Could he be more?' she pushes.

'No.' I smile at the idea. I know James would laugh too.

'Shame,' Iona says. 'Sounds like he really looks out for you, and blokes like that don't come along too often.'

'He's going out with someone – not that that makes any difference – and I'm not interested in dating anyway, not at the moment.'

I admire Iona's guts, but I don't think my confidence could take another hit. Not yet.

Iona glances at her watch. 'Right, need to go.'

'I'll get this,' I suggest, gesturing to the bill.

'I'll get the next one then,' she says, before we plan to meet next Sunday, to race our first half marathon. 'Holy shit,' we both exclaim at the same time, before laughing afterwards.

After she has left, I'm considering cheating and taking the tube home, before Iona heads back into the café. 'Flo, I was thinking, would you like to meet my dad?'

Iona's father, Ray, is at Sunrise Nursing Home, in Ealing, West London, and his room is on the ground floor, overlooking the road and the pub. When we arrive, a tall man in a hooded sweatshirt waves at us from his window. 'His favourite hobby is people watching,' Iona says, waving back, 'and going to the pub to watch the footie.'

After signing our names in the visitors' book, and saying hello to the member of staff on reception duty, Iona and I approach the sitting room, noticing one of the residents singing to two bright green birds in a cage, and other patients drinking coffee or tea as they stare with glazed eyes at the television.

We walk down another long corridor, before knocking on a door. Iona doesn't wait for a reply. 'Hi, Dad,' she says, as she leads me into his bedroom, dominated by a television, fridge and framed photographs of Iona and her family dotted around the room. He smiles, before he coughs, and then his cough turns into a choking fit, Iona rushing to pour him a glass of water.

'Here, Pops, sit down.' She helps him into his armchair, by the window. He drinks the water slowly, before he glances at me. Tentatively, I step towards him.

'Dad, this is my friend, Flo.'

He doesn't say anything, but I sense he's aware I'm here.

'Sit down,' Iona says to me, gesturing to the chair, whereas Iona perches on his bed. 'Pops, tell Flo about your favourite TV programmes. I'm surprised you're not watching anything now.'

Again he says nothing.

'Dad used to love Jeremy Kyle,' she teases. 'Now it's all cop shows and hospital dramas, isn't it? Oh and footie nights.' She turns to me. 'He sits with all his friends in the lounge and watches the match with a couple of beers.'

I sense it's something he probably loved before, and know how important it is to keep a part of the old Ray alive.

As Iona goes on to tell her dad that we're training for the marathon, I catch a glimpse of his ensuite bathroom with solid white handrails around the loo. I look away.

'It's great news about Iona getting married, isn't it?' I say, changing the subject. I'm taken aback by how young he looks; he can only be in his fifties. When I was little I thought Granddad was ancient, but he would have been about Ray's age too, and it hits home even more how cruel HD can be, shortening lives.

Iona picks up a wedding photograph of her father and mother on his bedside table: he has long hair and a nose ring, and is wearing sandals. 'Do you remember your wedding day, Pops?'

I take a peek at the photo. 'You were a bit of a rock star, weren't you?' I say.

'He was. Rocker Ray.' Iona laughs.

There is a glimpse of a smile from him, as if a memory has been reawakened.

'Mum and I wanted to put up as many pictures as possible,' she tells me, 'so that the carers can see he has a history; he's not just some poor old bloke with a disease.'

Iona digs into her rucksack and produces a card. 'I wanted to show you my wedding invite, Pops. It's next June. We're having the reception in an old converted barn, think oak beams and fairy lights,' she enthuses, but I don't think Ray is thinking oak beams and fairy lights for a second. It seems as if he is just a shell of the person he used to be. Iona continues to talk about all the plans she is making, and where she and Steve are going on honeymoon.

'You will make the most beautiful bride,' Ray suddenly says.

I am so stunned he has spoken and understood that it makes me want to cry. Iona looks tearful too, as she says, 'Ah, thanks, Dad. And remember you're giving me away. You'd better get me to the church on time.'

As we're signing ourselves out in the reception, Iona tells me her father is silent ninety per cent of the time, 'But it's that ten per cent Mum and I cling to,' she confides. 'That ten per cent means the world to us.'

*

Later on in the afternoon, when I arrive home, there are no lights on, the flat quiet and dark. James can't be back yet. There is nothing surprising about that, except for my disappointment.

As I head into my bedroom and get out of my running clothes, I wish he were here so I could tell him that I ran twelve miles today, and not only that, but that I'd vaguely enjoyed it. I didn't crucify myself for stopping, and I didn't look repeatedly at my watch.

As I was running today I heard James's voice inside my head, saying, 'One of these days, Flo, you'll go out for a run and forget you're even doing it. You'll feel as if you were flying.' I can't imagine that. But then again, I never imagined I'd be able to run twelve miles.

As I lie in a deep hot bath, I think about Iona again. She has reconciled her fate with such strength and humour, her spirit seemingly unbreakable. 'Finding out was the best decision of my life. Everyone's different, but for me, no man's land wasn't a happy place,' she said.

She has healed her relationship with her mother. She is getting married and planning on having a family. Her life is moving on.

I wait to hear the key in the lock. I hope James comes home soon.

Iona's right: no man's land is not a happy place to be.

I submerge myself under the water, the warmth comforting. Just like Iona, I don't want my life to be a waiting game.

I think I'm going to take the test.

# 61

## Peggy

'In this lesson, we're going to learn to talk about what we do in our spare time,' Maria says, pacing up and down the middle of the classroom in tight jeans and high heels that are certainly attracting the attention of Colin, the antiques dealer. 'Who in the class likes sport?'

No one puts up their hand. Maria places her hands on her hips. 'No one plays anything? Tennis or golf? Football?' She glances at the men.

'I play cards,' I say, which makes everyone laugh for some reason. 'Bridge.'

'*Peggy gioca a carte*,' says Maria. 'Who plays a musical instrument?'

Again, no one puts up their hand.

'We do bugger all!' says Colin, roaring with laughter. 'Except work.'

'And learn Italian,' I chip in.

'*Studiamo l'italiano*,' Maria says, writing it on the white board.

'By the way, have you heard the news?' Colin asks, for some reason looking at me.

'What news?' I say.

'I saw it on my phone.'

'I only keep my phone on in emergencies,' I tell him.

'Well, that's not much use, Peggy,' he says. 'Someone could be trying to call you right now in a major pickle. Anyway, it was a BBC news alert.'

Iris enters the classroom. '*Buon giorno*, sorry I'm late. Boiler broke down,' she says breathlessly. 'Peggy, have you heard the news?' she asks, taking her usual seat in the corner. We are such creatures of habit.

'*What news*?' I ask with mounting impatience.

'Can we save the talking until the end of the lesson?' Maria suggests.

'They've found a treatment that could prevent HD,' says Colin.

'Exactly,' echoes Iris. 'It made me think of Flo.'

I rummage in my handbag to find my mobile.

'It's plastered all over the papers too,' Colin continues. 'It was hard to miss.'

Well, I haven't seen a paper yet, nor turned on the TV. I was walking Elvis in the park before my lesson.

Maria perches on the end of her desk, aware the lesson isn't going to get very far until I know more about this news.

Immediately, I switch on my mobile. I have several missed calls from Ricky and from James.

It rings once again and Ricky's name appears on my screen.

'Peggy, take it,' Maria insists. 'This sounds important.'

I leave the room in a fluster. 'Ricky?'

'Where are you?' he asks.

'Is this about the drug?'

'It's incredible, Peggy. They've made a real breakthrough. Does Flo know?'

## 62

## Flo

After the meeting with Harriet and the sales team, discussing our last-minute discount off winter package holidays and some of the projects we have in place for the new year, I head back to my desk, before turning the sound back on my phone.

That's odd. I have an alarming amount of missed calls.

The first one is from Maddie, then two from James, two from Iona, and when James calls me yet again . . .

*Oh dear God, please let nothing be wrong.*

'Have you heard?' he asks, sounding as if he's out on a run.

'Heard what?'

'Flo, go online, there's been a massive breakthrough.'

I rush to my computer, tap some keys:

In an announcement likely to stand as one of the biggest breakthroughs in Huntington's disease since the discovery of the HD gene in 1993, Ionis and Roche today announced that the first human trial of a huntingtin-lowering drug, IONIS-HTTRx, demonstrates that it reduces mutant huntingtin in the nervous system, and is safe and well tolerated.

'Oh my God,' I utter.

'Exactly,' he says. 'Let's talk about it tonight? Are you in?'

'Yes, please.' I stare at the screen, still in shock.

The moment we say goodbye I try to explain to Harriet and Natalie what's going on, when Iona calls. I excuse myself, rushing downstairs and heading outside.

'Holy shit! Steve and I are dancing round the kitchen table.'

After our call Maddie rings me again. 'Flo, isn't it exciting? I've been sending you messages on Facebook but had to speak to you.'

'I know, it's amazing, but can I call you back in a minute?'

I hear her dialing tone. *Pick up, Granny, pick up . . .*

'Flo,' she says.

'I know, Granny,' I finish, before we both burst into tears.

# 63

## Peggy

Ricky, James, Flo, Shelley and baby Mia are huddled in my sitting room, empty pasta bowls on the floor, the television still on. It's coming up to the ten o'clock news, and although we've heard it all before, we're still glued to the screen, listening to the presenter.

> *'Tonight at ten, a major breakthrough in the treatment of Huntington's Disease, which could lead to new therapies for Alzheimer's and other conditions. By correcting the defect that causes Huntington's, the new experimental drug is potentially the biggest breakthrough in half a century.'*

I notice James squeezing Flo's shoulder, Flo sitting cross-legged on the floor, her head resting against his knees, Elvis curled up asleep on her lap.

After Ricky called, I asked Maria if I could excuse myself from the lesson.

'I'm so sorry, but my husband, Timothy, he died of it, my daughter had it too, and my granddaughter is at risk but now there is hope—'

'Go,' Colin had said. 'Go, Peggy! Get out of here!'

'Yes, of course,' Maria agreed, and soon the whole class was willing me to go.

'Good luck,' they were calling out as I gathered my textbook, clumsily trying to shove my folder into my bag.

'*Arrivederci!*' I said, before leaving and bolting down the stairs. There is nothing like good news to give your old tired legs a new lease of life.

I grabbed a newspaper from the nearest shop and then devoured the article about the drug as I was walking home. Just as I reached the front door, Flo called, and we hardly had to say a word to one another. We just sobbed, me wondering if it was all a dream.

Yet here we are, and it really is true. Today is the first day in years that I have had hope.

As far as I can gather from the news, forty-six people have taken part in this trial led by scientists at University College London. I watch on the screen as a patient is lying on his side on a hospital bed, about to receive an injection into the fluid that bathes the brain and spinal cord. In theory, this drug reduces the amount of the corrupted huntingtin gene that causes the toxic protein, which destroyed my Tim's brain and was intent on doing the same to Beth, and possibly Flo if it has the chance.

Slowly, I'm beginning to understand that the treatment is designed to silence the gene, or at least lower the levels of the harmful protein.

'*For the first time, we have the potential,*' I watch Professor Sarah Tabrizi say, who is the lead researcher and director of the HD Centre at UCL. '*We have hope for a therapy that may one day slow or prevent Huntington's Disease completely.*'

A family comes on to the screen next, a family blighted by HD, claiming the lives of their mother, uncle and grandmother. My heart goes out to them.

'*The Allen family have made a promise to their children that a treatment will be ready in time for them. Research over the next four years will see if gene silencing can fulfil that promise*'.

If only Tim and Beth were with me now to share this news. It's not a cure, but it's something we can hold on to, and I'm going to cling on to it for as long as I live.

# 64

## Flo

After leaving Granny's, I climb on to the back of Vera. I don't want to go straight home. I'm too wired to go to bed, I'll never sleep. And as if James can read my mind, he turns to me and says, 'I don't feel like going home yet, do you?'

London has a certain magic about it at night, but especially at Christmas. James navigates his way around Hammersmith Broadway, and soon we're on the Cromwell Road heading towards South Kensington, a route we have jogged many times during our training.

I have no idea where he's taking me, all he said was he had an idea. I hold on to James tightly, feeling a mix of emotions that I can't quite figure out.

*Yes, I'm happy. Of course I am. Yesterday I knew nothing about this drug. But also yesterday I was closer to thinking I wanted to take the test. Does this change how I feel now?*

I breathe in the cold night air, grateful to feel the wind whipping against my face. I find the sound of the traffic, the noise, the lights and the warmth of being close to James, comforting. Right now, the last thing I need is to be alone.

James and I take our hot chocolates and watch the ice-skaters at the pop-up rink outside the Natural History Museum. 'Always makes me smile watching people fall flat on their backsides,' James says. He nudges me. 'You've been quiet tonight. How are you feeling about it all?'

I look at him, still unsure how to explain the muddle in my head. 'I know I should be feeling happy.'

'*Should* be?'

'And I am. James, it's amazing. Today has been extraordinary.' I see Granny's face, the hope in her eyes, and remember how she held me in her arms before saying goodnight. And then Ricky hugged me, even Shelley too, who until this evening I hadn't met properly.

'I was thinking if only I were little again,' I continue, 'and Mum were still alive, so she would have a chance.'

James nods.

'And then I was thinking, what makes my life so important, James?'

Confusion clouds his face. 'Flo, this is *crazy* talk.'

'I know, but—'

'This drug could be available to you in time; that's if you have HD.'

'I know it's good news,' I insist again, 'but it just got me thinking, that's all.'

'Thinking that you're not worth it,' he raises his voice.

I turn to him with half a smile. 'Would it be such a tragedy to humanity if I were to die?'

'Flo, stop it,' he says, visibly uncomfortable, shocked and puzzled by my reaction, when he no doubt thinks I should be dancing at the news.

I feel a lump in my throat. I think this is coming from missing my mum, reading her diaries and realizing how much I have let her down because I haven't pursued my art. She was a single mother and she sacrificed so much for me, so that I could go to one of the best art schools in the country, and here I am, with nothing but a failed relationship behind me, wasting my training by not doing what I set out to do.

'Why should I expect the scientists and doctors to work faster for someone as unimportant as me, so I can sit around watching films on Netflix for a few more years?'

James turns me towards him. 'For fuck's sake, Flo,' he says now, disbelief and fear in his voice, 'can you stop putting yourself down like this? The scientists are working hard for you because everyone matters; every single person in this world counts.' He shrugs, 'Well, there are a few exceptions, but every person skating on this ice rink matters. See that girl ...' He leans closer towards me, before pointing to a teenager with long blonde hair, wearing a woolly hat with matching bright red jeans, 'She matters because she's someone's daughter or sister or best friend, and that old geezer over there, who quite frankly is scaring me by being anywhere near the ice,' – he points to a man with snow-white hair, about Granny's age, exceptionally game to be skating on such doddery legs – 'he matters because the whole family will be descending on him for Christmas, and they can't imagine a time when there will be a Christmas without him.'

I fight back my tears. James is right. *What has got into me?*

'Flo, you are the centre of Granny Peg's life. You're my sister's best friend. And I know my existence wouldn't be half as much fun if I couldn't wake you up at the crack of dawn and make you come out for a run with me.'

I smile at that.

'So if you start talking like this again, saying you're not worth saving, I will personally box you round the ears.' He pulls me into his arms before we both wince, watching the man with the snow-white hair, inevitably fall, landing on his bottom, though it's not long before his daughter – or she could be his third wife, as James guesses – holds out her hand and helps him back up. He dusts himself down and they laugh as they continue to skate.

'Want a go?' James asks me.

I shake my head. All I want to do is be here, with James, held in his arms. 'I don't know what I'd do without you,' I murmur into his coat.

'You'd be fine,' he replies, stroking my hair.

'The news has made me think I might look for a new job, finally do something with my art.'

James's grip around me tightens. 'That's a great idea.'

I realize I have been exceptionally lucky to have my current job. It helped me through my grief for Mum. And then, when I needed it most, Harriet welcomed me back with open arms. I shall always be in debt to her, but I want to feel that adrenaline I used to feel when I was in college, working on my mood boxes and designing sets for plays.

I see the passion James has for being a vet. On one of our runs, he told me about the first time he'd drilled a hole into the side of a dog's head after only six months of surgical experience.

'When I was studying, Flo, we did things because some-one told us to,' James had explained, 'but when you're working for real, you have to make these massive decisions on your own. The owner is putting their most precious friend into my hands, and here I am with a drill and it only takes one tiny little mistake ... but when you save an ani-mal's life, it's the best feeling in the world,' he said.

My work wasn't saving lives, but it was something of my own, and I want it back. Going back to my art would be like coming home.

'Maddie will love that too,' James says. 'I'm sure she'd help. You must have spoken to her today?'

I nod. 'She asked me to stay for New Year at your parents.'

'Oh right.'

'Will you be around or are you doing something with Chloe?'

'She's away.'

I sit up abruptly. 'Hang on, weren't you supposed to be seeing her tonight?'

'She cancelled.'

'Oh. I thought you said last night it was her Christmas—'

'She thinks she caught some nasty bug.'

'They're going around.'

'Besides, after the news, it was good to be here with you.'

I rest my head against his shoulder again. 'Well, it was lucky for me.'

'Flo, I know you said last night you were thinking you might take the test now—'

'I don't know. I think I still do,' I say, though I'm wavering again. 'It's not a cure.'

'Sure, though in time they could develop it—'

'But it could take years.' I stop, realizing how selfish I am sounding. I only have to think of Iona's father, sitting in his nursing home, day after day, watching these medical advances slowly unfold while his brain cells are dying, never to return. All those years he has lost with his family. I only have to think about Granddad too, and how he never had a moment like today, with scientists saying this is the biggest advance in their field for half a decade, and that it's of groundbreaking importance to families.

'Maybe it won't be too late for me, James, or Iona.'

'It's never too late, Flo.' He stands up and holds out his hand. 'So come on, get your skates on. If that old man can do it, so can we.'

# 65

**Peggy**

I feel stupidly tearful as I wave Flo goodbye. It's not as if I won't see her or speak to her for weeks.

She's taking the tube to Paddington, before catching a train to Abergavenny, to spend the New Year with James and Maddie at their parents' home. As she's just about to turn the corner, pulling her small suitcase on wheels, she stops and waves. 'See you next year, Granny,' she calls.

I wave back, saying, 'Off you go, have fun!' It's important for her to see the New Year in with her friends, but this Christmas has been the happiest one we have spent together since Beth died.

The two of us went over to Ricky's for Christmas Day lunch. And when I say lunch, we didn't actually sit down until four in the afternoon, after we'd watched the Queen's speech and opened presents.

I smile. Ricky and Shelley did themselves proud. We had roast turkey with all the trimmings, and Christmas pudding with brandy butter. Shelley even lit the pud.

We raised our glasses to absent friends. Mia sat with us in her high chair. She didn't know what the heck was going on, but she loved unwrapping the presents, paper flying everywhere.

I let her open all of mine. Ricky and Shelley gave me a guidebook on the best hotels and bed and breakfasts in Rome, along with a travel journal notepad.

'I'm not sure when I'll go,' I'd said.

'How about next May?' Flo suggested, handing me an envelope. Inside was a card, with our flight information. 'I'm free if you are?'

As I walk back into the sitting room, with only Elvis and the Christmas tree shedding its pine needles for company, I don't allow myself to feel sad for a moment longer.

I am lucky.

To think, this time last year, Flo still didn't know the truth, Ricky and Shelley hadn't moved next door and there was no news about a breakthrough drug. Flo could be in New York, oblivious, and I could be sitting in my armchair, drinking myself silly, not knowing whether it was Monday or Friday.

Flo appears to be stronger by the day, putting her relationship with Theo behind her, though she is still unsure whether or not to take the test. With Beth it must have been an impossibly hard decision, though her driving force was marrying Graham and wanting to have more children. With Flo, she doesn't have that motivation yet, so maybe that's why it's hard for her to make up her mind once and for all.

I thought it would be difficult going to Flo's counselling appointments, that it would be painful to talk about Tim and Beth again, but it hasn't been as hard as I'd feared. In many ways it helps to ease my guilt. At least being there for Flo somewhat makes up for not being there for Beth.

I wonder if there were many times when Beth nearly told me, before changing her mind. Probably just as many as I nearly told Flo. After all, in our own way, Beth and I were close. There must have been occasions when she feared she wouldn't be there for Flo, to see her get married or have children. There must have been moments when she looked in the mirror and saw her father, and needed to talk to someone, apart from her counsellor, about her own fears for the future.

Often it keeps me awake, wondering how Beth faced this alone.

Flo reinforced Beth was great friends with Mark, so at least she had him to turn to. A pity he was married.

She's taking her time reading her mother's diaries, which I think is wise.

'It's like a book, Granny,' she once said. 'A book that's hard to read, so hard that often I need to put it down, but I know I have to finish it eventually.'

Maybe one day I shall be brave enough to read them too. Flo assures me it is helping her, that I did the right thing in finding them for her.

## If You Were Here

I wrap up warm before Elvis and I walk to the cemetery. London is rather beautiful at this time of year, since it's deserted and peaceful. It's probably just as well I'm having a quiet few days, since I had another funny turn on Boxing Day, my heart racing, my head so light I thought I was going to faint.

I don't think all the champagne and wine, or the unusually late nights helped.

Flo made me lie down until it passed, which it did, but nevertheless it's rather scary when it happens, making me think I could have a heart attack or stroke at any minute.

And the last thing I want to do is peg out – excuse the pun.

I've got to stick around, for Flo, and to my surprise I realize I want to stick around for myself too.

# 66

*Beth's Diary, 2009*

*I can't sleep. Not after the day I've had.*

*My diary is the only thing that keeps me sane. I swear I'd go mad if I couldn't write things down.*

*I called Mum today, first thing this morning.*

*'We need to talk,' I said, determined to tell her, once and for all. I have reasoned with myself that Flo is in a good place right now. She's eighteen, her A levels are behind her, she's still madly in love with Freddie, and she has been accepted into a theatre design course in Kent, one of the best drama and art schools in the country.*

*I could make the excuse that I don't want to tell her before she goes, in case she gave up her place, but my conscience is creeping up on me, and so are my symptoms.*

*The other day I drove to the supermarket, got out of*

*the car and my legs literally gave way. I didn't fall over, thankfully, but a few people stared at me as if I'd been at the bottle and shouldn't be behind a wheel.*

*I put on a brave face all the time — no one would ever know — but when I'm alone, I'm consumed with worry that I'll miss out on so much of Flo's life. That I won't be there when she gets her first job, nor will I be sitting in the front seat of the church when she marries. What if I don't have the chance to hold her first baby, my grandchild, in my arms?*

*Something has creatively died inside of me, and I know it's because I need to tell Mum before I go out of my mind. I have to release this burden and ask her to be there for Flo when I won't be able to. I need to feel at peace to sleep at night.*

*I don't think Mum has ever truly understood the impact Dad's illness had on me. Or if she did, she wasn't able to express it. She rebuffed the idea of some counselling sessions after Dad died.*

*'He's gone,' she said, 'and no amount of talking can bring him back.'*

*It's hardly surprising she is the way she is. She had a tough upbringing, her mother abandoning her and her father returning from the war a relative stranger. I don't blame her for being so buttoned up, but things will be different for Flo and me. I can talk to her, guide her, see if she wants to be tested or not. I'd never make her promise not to find out. No one understands like I do what Flo will have to go through.*

So I sat in the café waiting for Mum, playing with the menu, my stomach tangled with nerves. She was late, for starters, which worried me, since Mum is a stickler for time. When she did arrive, she looked pale but typically said she was perfectly all right, nothing that a nice glass of wine couldn't fix.

As we were making the usual small talk all I could think was 'Say it, Beth'. And literally I was about to, I got so far as 'Mum, there is something I haven't told you, something important', when she stood up, scraped her chair back and said calmly but firmly that she needed to go to A&E. She could feel her heart racing. Something wasn't right.

The restaurant called us a taxi immediately and we were driven straight to the hospital. She was seen quickly, since her history of high blood pressure coupled with her age put her at risk of a heart attack or stroke. What made me cross was that I discovered this wasn't the first time she'd had a 'funny turn', as she described them. She confessed to the doctor that they had been going on for four months, saying it literally felt as if her heart was jumping out of her chest – 'racing like a Porsche,' she said – and each time she experienced it, she had to sit down because she felt so light-headed and out of breath.

'Why didn't you tell me before?' I asked, when the doctor left the room.

'I thought it would go away,' she said, her head down, suddenly looking vulnerable.

As the doctor carried out a series of tests, including an

*ECG, I left the room to call Mark. I wasn't sure he'd pick up, since I've been keeping my distance for months, not returning his calls. Friendship is no longer enough for me. It hurts too much saying goodbye. Yet he was the only person I wanted to see today.*

*He did pick up and his tone was aloof, until I told him what happened.*

*'I'm on my way,' he said, and the moment I saw him striding through the double doors, towards the reception area, I got up from my seat and rushed into his arms, where I stayed, feeling safe and loved. He bought me a coffee from the vending machine, and we sat down and talked.*

*'Try not to panic until we know what's going on,' he said, holding my hand, his touch comforting.*

*'Will you stay with me?' I asked. 'Just until—'*

*'Of course,' he said. We sat in silence, until he broke it saying, 'You haven't been in touch for a while.'*

*'I've been busy,' I fudged, staring ahead. 'What with work and preparing—'*

*'Beth.' He looked into my eyes, before taking my face in his hands. 'I've missed you.'*

*'I can't do this anymore,' I whispered, placing my hand over his. 'It's hard pretending. I'm sorry, I know you're married, but I love you.'*

*It seemed an eternity before he replied, 'I love you too, Beth, but—'*

*We couldn't finish the conversation as the doctor*

*appeared, but how I hated the word 'but'. But we can have no future. But I'm married. But I could never leave my children. But you have HD.*

*Mark said he'd leave us to talk in private and that he'd call me tomorrow. He kissed me on the cheek. His hand lightly brushed against mine.*

*As I watched him leave, I felt a fresh wave of grief and regret that he and I could never be. I took a deep breath before turning back to the doctor, who said she needed to carry out more tests, including a twenty-four-hour ECG.*

*'I think your mother could have atrial fibrillation,' she said.*

*'What's that?'*

*'It's an irregular rapid heartbeat that can cause tiredness and symptoms like being out of breath. We need to refer her to a cardiologist.'*

*'This sounds serious.'*

*'Most cases aren't life-threatening – some people can have it without even knowing – but given your mother's history of high blood pressure we need to treat this more cautiously.'*

*'Absolutely. What can I do to help?' I asked.*

*'Well, we'll know more after the tests. She could need an operation. But for now it's important your mother has plenty of rest and no stress.'*

*Mum and I took a cab home. She went straight to bed, saying she was fine and that I could go home. I didn't need to treat her like a toddler.*

*So I came back here, thinking the day couldn't get*

much worse, only to find Flo sitting slumped at the kitchen table, in tears.

'Freddie broke up with me,' she said, as if her entire world was over. I held her in my arms, wishing I could make the pain go away. 'I want to die, Mum.'

'No, Flo, it'll get easier, I promise. It hurts so much right now, but—'

'I can't live without him, Mum.'

I could feel her heart breaking, just like mine.

# 67

## Flo

I wake up on New Year's Eve disorientated, wondering where I am, before slowly remembering. I stretch out my arms. I slept like a log, the mattress as soft as a marshmallow.

James and Maddie's parents moved out of London five years ago. Their mother, Lucy, was longing to return to her roots in Wales, so their father sold his veterinary practice in Barnes and they packed their bags. I remember James saying they were both like fish out of water in London and that Wales would always be their home. The river, unspoilt countryside and wildlife were in their blood. Their new home is close to where Lucy was brought up, a small market town called Crickhowell, and overlooks the Brecon Beacons and Black Mountains.

Reluctantly, I get out of my warm, cosy bed and open the curtains, which look out on to a backyard, home to a rundown caravan, wonky washing line and a family of noisy chickens. It's no wonder they're noisy when I see Rocket, their mad miniature Dachshund, chasing them in a frenzy before Lucy emerges from the kitchen shaking a drying-up cloth at him.

'Shoo, shoo! Morning, Flo!' She waves at me from across the yard, wearing a flowery apron over dungarees. 'Come and have some breakfast, duckie. I've just made some coffee, and the eggs should be delicious as they're freshly laid.'

'Sounds perfect,' I say, thinking that whenever I'm here I feel as if I'm safely back in the palm of the Bailey family.

'Don't bother getting dressed,' she continues. 'You're the first one up. I have a family of layabouts!'

'No, you don't, Mum,' James calls, standing behind me, dressed in his tracksuit and T-shirt. I hadn't even heard him come in. 'Shouldn't you knock?' I ask, trying to sound put out, but failing miserably. 'I could have been in the shower—'

'We live together.' He shrugs. 'I've seen it all before.'

'You haven't.' I hit his arm playfully.

'I did knock,' he adds. 'You didn't hear. You're getting deaf in your old age.'

'That's because of the chickens.'

'They're a rowdy bunch,' he agrees. 'Breakfast first and then—'

'We're on *holiday*,' I protest, knowing it's a lame excuse.

'We need to stick to the programme.'

'Oh come on, James. Can't you smell the sausages and bacon?' I rub my tummy.

I don't feel like sticking to the diet and eating a bagel with peanut butter, or lumpy porridge with berries, or a poached egg. I feel like a fry-up and lots of caffeine.

He looks at me, clearly tempted. 'Flo, we won't feel like running tomorrow morning,' he reminds me. 'Let's have something quick to eat and then go.'

He's right. Stu and Jane are arriving this afternoon. It's only dinner here, low key, but it's still going to be a late night, and if Lucy and James's father, Matthew, have anything to do with it, there'll be plenty of alcohol involved as well.

'Let her have a day off,' Maddie insists to James, suddenly in my bedroom too, dressed in her pyjamas and sloppy jumper, her long frizzy hair tied back in two ponytails. 'Flo, don't let him bully you.'

'Well, I'm going,' he states. 'Need to run off the mince pies.'

I think about my indulgent few days with Granny. If I wasn't sleeping I was eating, and the chart on my bedroom door was ignored. I haven't been for a run since Christmas Eve and I know the longer I leave it the harder it will become . . .

'Okay, fine,' I give in to James. 'Sorry Maddie, I'd better go. You could come too?' I suggest.

Her laugh says it all. 'Just don't be too long,' she adds.

There is something special about running in the countryside, on uninterrupted land, only rolling hills and stunning views for company. James and I head all the way into Crickhowell, which is just over four miles from his parents' home, and it's hard work for me after a few days off, whereas James annoyingly makes it appear effortless. We go at a slower pace on the way home, James taking me off the beaten track, leading me towards a grand-looking hotel in the far distance.

'Shouldn't we be getting home?' I say, aware I'd promised Maddie it would only be a short run.

'I want to show you this place first,' James says.

We walk up some steps and into the hotel reception. 'Hello, James,' a smart woman in uniform greets him from behind the desk, before coming forward to give him a hug. 'Lovely to see you.'

'You too.' He introduces me to Eleanor, a family friend. 'Can I give Flo a quick tour? I know we're not exactly dressed—'

'As it's you,' she says. 'Go on, make yourself at home.'

James leads me into a drawing room with a cosy fireplace and sofas that look so comfortable I want to lie down at once, and a table covered with books and magazines. We walk through a small bar, a few guests drinking coffee and reading the paper.

'When I'm feeling low I shut my eyes and think of this view,' he tells me, walking out on to the terrace that overlooks the river Usk. 'On a summer's day, I love sitting out here, listening to the sound of the river.'

It's too cold to stay outside, but James and I order a coffee from the bar. 'You know we just ran nine miles, Flo? Not bad post–Christmas.'

'But it's nowhere near twenty-six. Do you wish you were running it?'

'Yes,' he admits. 'So you're just going to have to do it for me, okay?'

I smile, suddenly feeling strangely conscious being with James in a bar. It's almost as if we're on a date.

'How's Chloe?' I ask. 'It's a shame she couldn't be here.'

'Yeah, well, I'm sure she'd rather be in Venice.'

'And how was your Christmas?' I carry on, sounding as if I'm interviewing him.

'Pretty much the same as last year: drinks with the neighbours on Christmas Eve, stockings in our parents' room on Christmas Day, then Mum grilling me on my love life; you know what it's like.' He stops. His face reddens. 'Sorry, that was a stupid thing to say.'

'Don't worry,' I reassure him, 'but make the most of your mum and dad. You know what I wish?'

'Go on.'

'That I'd asked Mum more questions. I thought I knew *everything* about her, but since reading her diaries, I realize there were so many things I wasn't curious about.'

'Like what?'

'I learned all about her time at Camberwell. I discovered she'd worked for this decorative florist to pay for her art stuff and her drinks in the student union bar. Some amazing guy set up a business in his garage in Twickenham, and Mum would go to the garden market in Covent Garden in the early hours of the morning, a couple of times a week, to buy the flowers. She ended up having a hot steamy affair with one of the guys she worked with. They'd stick the radio on and smoke pot. She said he helped her forget all her troubles back home.'

James runs a hand through his hair. 'Sex is a good distraction. So what happened to this guy?'

'I don't know; that's my point. Sometimes she'd go for weeks without writing, and then write every day for the next month. I wish I'd had the time to fill in the gaps while she was alive. And then there was Mark.'

'Mark? Wasn't he the older guy? The teacher?'

'Exactly. Her tutor. He was married. I used to think he was interested in her, but she constantly denied it, saying they were just friends. But she loved him and he loved her.' I can't help but feel hurt that it's yet one more thing Mum didn't tell me. 'Why didn't she say something to me, James?'

'I don't know. Parents do keep things from us. I'm sure there's a hell of a lot I don't know about my mum's past. Maybe she didn't say anything about Mark because nothing could happen between them?'

'Maybe. I'm glad she had him in her life. I'm relieved she had someone to turn to. She came so close to telling Granny.' When I read that entry I couldn't help but wonder what might have happened if she had, if Granny hadn't needed to go to A&E. I imagine things would have turned out very differently. Mum might still be alive.

'What stopped her?'

I tell James what happened, before realizing it's getting late and we should be heading back.

'Anyway, that's all I'm saying: talk to your parents,' I tell him. 'Don't screen your mum's calls—'

'I won't, unless *Line of Duty*'s on—'

'Be serious,' I say, unwrapping the mint chocolate that came with our coffee, aware James is watching me closely. 'Have I got something—?'

Before I can finish my sentence, James's thumb is gently wiping away the chocolate that has settled in one corner of my mouth, his eyes making contact with mine again.

'We should go,' I say, pulling away abruptly. 'They'll be wondering where we are.'

He places a fiver on the table and sticks his jacket on. 'Race you back.'

'Wait!' I put my coat on. 'That's not fair!'

'Life isn't fair,' he calls over his shoulder.

'Wait!' I catch up with him saying goodbye to Eleanor behind the reception desk, before we're both outside again.

'Loser has to do the washing-up for the next year,' he suggests.

'I do that anyway. You are remarkably shy of *any* housework.'

'Well, I don't like being too forward. Loser has to unclog the hair in the shower too.'

I attempt to trip him up since that's a job I'd readily give up. Currently James and I take it in turns.

'Foul play,' he says, trying to trip me up now, before I grab his arm to pull him back, giggling, and we're still laughing when we return to the house.

'You've been hours,' Maddie says, with a hint of annoyance, classical music blasting from the kitchen, the dogs rushing to greet us.

'I won,' I declare to James.

'No, you didn't. I did.'

'Children, it was a draw,' Maddie decides for us.

'Fine,' I say, picking up on Maddie's irritable mood. 'Sorry we've been so long but James showed me the hotel—'

'Doesn't matter,' she cuts me off. 'I made a pot of coffee, but it went cold hours ago,' she says, walking away.

# 68

## Peggy

It's early evening when Ricky pops over with Mia, now almost a year old, in her buggy and looking faintly ridiculous carrying a flowery rucksack.

'You're a legend,' Ricky tells me. He and Shelley are going out tonight for a meal, before watching the fireworks on the Victoria Embankment. I'm only too happy to stay in and babysit, and make sure Elvis isn't too spooked by the bangs.

'Shelley has packed her bag,' Ricky assures me. 'There's everything you need, toys, snacks and she's been changed so she should be cool, but there are nappies too, just in case. Can't thank you enough,' he says, giving me a hug and a thumbs up before adding, 'See you next year!'

'Now then, Mia, what shall we do?' I stare down at this little dark-haired girl in her pushchair. 'Hello, little one.' I wave at her and she stares back at me, but on I go, suggesting, 'We could play a fun little game? Why don't we play with your toys?' I ask in a peculiar singalong voice.

She continues to stare back at me with her big round eyes in a rather off-putting way, as if to say 'You're not my mother; you're an old prune'.

Determined not to be put off yet, I lift her out of her pushchair before popping her on to one of Elvis's blankets on the floor, Elvis sniffing her out to see who this is invading his spot by the fireplace.

'Shoo, Elvis,' I say, turning round to unzip the bulging rucksack to see what toys Shelley has packed. I notice a Tupperware box that needs to be put straight into the fridge, along with a bottle of water, a packet of rice cakes and a bag filled with chopped carrots. With any luck, Mia can sit quietly and play before bedtime. I know Ricky is far more relaxed – Mia stays up half the night with him – but I think an early supper, a quick game and then straight to bed.

I head into the kitchen to make myself a cup of tea, only to turn round seconds later when I hear Mia giggling as she tugs Elvis's short stumpy tail.

'No!' I say, bending down to pick her up before placing her back on the blanket by the fireplace. 'You stay here. Look, what a lovely game!' I point to some building bricks but Mia decides crawling around the sitting room floor pulling Elvis's tail again is much more fun.

As I attempt for the third time to settle her back on to the blanket, I smell something distinctly pongy, so pongy even Elvis makes a swift getaway, escaping under the armchair.

'Oh dear, I've made a mistake,' I say to Mia, examining her after changing her nappy, knowing something isn't quite right. Perhaps the picture of the lion's smiling face on one side of the nappy and his tail on the other was a good clue as to which is the front and which is the back.

'Silly Granny, she's made a boo-boo,' I say, amazed when Mia breaks into a smile and laughs. 'Silly Granny,' I say once more. She remains quiet. 'Boo-boo!' I repeat, delighted when she giggles again.

'Now, we'll have some delicious supper – fish pie, yum yum – and then have a little nap-nap,' I say, pushing her buggy into the kitchen.

I really need a high chair. She'll have to eat where she is.

I give her a small piece of raw carrot that's been cut into a neat baton. As I turn on the oven to warm up the fish pie, I hear a gagging sound before I yank the carrot back from her mouth. I don't want her to choke on my watch.

I open the packet of rice cakes instead.

'Here we go.' But she doesn't want to eat a rice cake. I take a sniff and a small bite. Frankly, I wouldn't either. It tastes of sawdust and air.

I take a biscuit from my tin – a chocolate bourbon – dunk it into my cup of sugary tea and see if that's a more appetizing starter. Mia's face lights up as if she has never tasted a chocolate biscuit before.

'Well, it *is* New Year's Eve. I won't tell if you don't,' I whisper, pressing a finger to my lips.

My mobile rings.

'Hi, Granny,' Flo says, sounding relaxed. 'Wanted to say Happy New Year now, just in case I don't get a chance to call later.' Flo knows only too well that I never normally bother to wait for Big Ben to strike twelve times. I've never seen the point of the terrible pressure to pretend you're having a jolly good time, when all you really want is to be in bed with a cosy hot-water bottle. Wake me up when it's all over, please. I tell her I'm babysitting Mia, which she seems to find funny. 'Are you having a nice time?' I ask, hearing music playing in the background and lots of laughter.

'Lovely,' she says. 'You haven't had any more funny turns?'

'I'm as fit as a fiddle!'

'You promise?'

'I promise.'

'Good. I'd better go. I'm needed to lay the table.'

'What are you going to eat?' I ask, wanting to keep her on the line a moment longer.

'Roast lamb.'

'How delicious.'

'I wish you were here, Granny.'

'Oh, Flo. Me too. But I'm with you in spirit.'

'Happy New Year,' Flo says once more. 'I'll raise a glass to Mum and Granddad at midnight. And to you.'

# 69

**Flo**

James's father, Matthew, sits at the head of the table. In his mid-sixties, he has a head of unruly grey hair and equally wayward eyebrows that work well with his craggy features. Though far from conventionally handsome, when he smiles his entire face lights up and the mischievous twinkle in his eyes reminds me of James.

Lucy sits opposite him in a figure-hugging pale-grey dress and knee-high purple suede boots. She cut her hair this afternoon. She is a wonderful no-nonsense kind of woman. If her hair is getting too long she simply takes a pair of kitchen scissors and gives it a good cut. She swims in the river all year round because that's what a wetsuit's for. Maddie and James have often told me about her midnight trips to the river, fishing in waders over her pyjamas, and wearing a lantern strapped around her head.

'I don't care what I look like,' she says, 'that's the advantage of getting old.'

'But Mum, no one's going to see you anyway, not in the dark,' Maddie reminds her.

I'm sitting next to Matthew and opposite James, and Maddie sits on my other side. During our first course we talk about politics and the gloomy state of the world, careful not to discuss Brexit, quickly changing the subject to work.

Stu horrifies us by saying a mongrel dog was brought into his clinic recently, having been found beaten and battered on a motorway.

'Wait, it's got a happy ending,' he reassures us. 'We've nursed her back to health and found her a new home.'

Maddie tells us she has just landed a new job designing costumes for *A Midsummer Night's Dream* at the National Theatre in London. It's her biggest job yet. We all clap at that, me claiming excitedly that she can come and stay with James and me.

'This year has been, well . . . *different*,' I say, when it comes to my turn, before everyone falls silent. Not wanting to drag the mood down, I continue, 'I didn't go to America, but I *have* run nearly fourteen miles,' which receives the biggest round of applause.

'And you've put up with living with my brother for yet another three hundred and sixty-five days,' Maddie says.

'No mean feat,' Matthew adds.

'Oh, he's all right,' I find myself saying, catching James's eye.

Over pudding I talk to Matthew about his childhood in Kenya. 'I had a wild time scampering around in shorts and plimsolls, collecting birds' eggs. Seeing a snake was nothing unusual. That's where my curiosity of animals and wildlife began, Flo.'

'I'm envious,' calls Lucy across the table.

'Why, Mum?' James asks. 'What was yours like?'

'Rigid. Dinner at seven on the dot and polishing school shoes every Sunday evening.'

'Looking back, I was lucky', Matthew continues, 'to be surrounded by beautiful creatures, and to be able to ride and fish. My father made a special rod for me out of bamboo. He was a wonderful vet, Flo. In the middle of nowhere, he had to work on instinct. Young vets these days have a different approach. They rely on equipment, X-rays and blood tests.'

'It's called progress,' James suggests, conceding, 'but I know what you mean. I'd love to work out in the bush like Granddad did.' He looks at me again. 'I wish I'd talked more to him about it.'

'Well, why don't you travel with your job, James?' Lucy says. 'You're free as a bird, no ties. Now's the time to do it.'

'Exactly,' Maddie agrees. 'What's keeping you here?'

During cheese and biscuits we go round the table again, sharing New Year resolutions.

'I've got to lose some weight,' Maddie confesses. 'All I do is sit hunched over my desk and order pizza. And I need to stop drinking.' She refills her glass. 'Oh, and find a boy-friend, but that would be a miracle.'

'No, it wouldn't,' I say. 'It's hard meeting the right person, but it's possible.'

'How about you, Flo?' Lucy asks.

'I don't have any resolutions.'

'No,' Lucy says. 'I meant have *you* met anyone? Don't you young ones go online these days?'

I can feel my cheeks redden. 'No. I haven't.'

'Sorry, darling, is it too soon after Theo?'

Unsure what to say, Maddie helps me out. 'The online dating world is terrifying, Mum. It's a jungle out there and you have to be in the right frame of mind to do it. Half of the guys just want sex and the other half are married. I'm getting another cat.'

'My resolution is positively *not* to meet anyone,' I say.

'I don't believe in resolutions,' James chips in.

'Why? Because you're so perfect?' Maddie asks.

'I'm not saying that. I don't like setting myself up to fail, that's all.'

'I'd like to stop snoring,' Matthew tells us, breaking the odd tension that's formed around the table.

'Now that would be a miracle.' Lucy laughs. 'He sounds like a blooming fog horn.'

'You could sort out your bloody clutter,' he fights back. 'We live in a pigsty.' Lucy hates to throw anything away. There is so much clutter in each room. The kitchen is the worst, every surface covered with pots, pans, bowls, cookbooks, old newspapers and magazines, a sewing machine, paperwork, letters and bills, dog baskets in one corner, and the fridge door plastered with family photographs.

'We'd like to have a family,' Stu says, glancing at Jane. 'Wouldn't we?'

'I'm pregnant,' she confides. 'Fourteen weeks.'

'Oh, dear God, Stu is going to be a dad,' says James, before everyone laughs and we all congratulate them.

'I need to catch more salmon and finish writing my book,' Lucy claims when we're back to discussing resolutions.

'What's it about?' I ask.

'Fishing.'

'Oh, Mum, that's going to be a real page-turner,' Maddie groans.

'It will be when I finish it. Think Jilly Cooper set on the riverbank.'

'Oh, Mum,' Maddie cringes again, all of us laughing. 'Who's going to read it?'

'I will,' I say, wanting to be loyal.

'Fishing is one of the best distractions in the world,' Lucy defends herself and her book, 'and when a fresh salmon takes your fly, boy, there is no better feeling. Believe me, it's even better than sex.'

'Thank you,' says Matthew solemnly.

'If that's the case, sex is wildly overrated,' Maddie states.

'Have you ever fished?' Lucy asks me.

'I'd be useless. I don't really get it,' I admit. 'Sitting on a bank with a rod—'

'You don't sit, Flo,' James corrects me. 'You get in the water.'

'Even worse.' I laugh, Maddie thrilled I'm on her side.

'And you're not useless until you've at least given it a shot,' Lucy says. 'Everyone should try something once in their life.'

'Right,' James says, standing up. 'You're having a lesson with me on the lawn, Flo.'

'What, *now*?' I remain firmly put.

'James, don't be an idiot,' says Maddie. 'It's pitch black.'

'We have lights on the terrace,' Lucy suggests. 'Candles. Oh, come on, where's your spirit of adventure, Maddie? Jane, Matthew can give you a casting lesson.'

Jane looks at her as if she'd rather eat cardboard, or go to bed, but Stu says he could do with a fag, so somehow we are all heading outside fifteen minutes before midnight, James handing me a rod, me protesting this is crazy.

'Go with it, Flo,' he suggests, grinning.

And he's right. For the next ten minutes, all of us are finding our lessons stupidly funny. I've never heard Jane snort so much with laughter, and she hasn't touched a glass of wine tonight.

'Fishing is about patience and faith,' James says, standing only inches apart from me again. 'Okay, Flo, hold the rod firmly. Remember what I said last time?'

'Uh-huh.'

'Enlighten me.'

'Er . . .'

'Flo, the object of the exercise is to cast your fly into the river in such a way that attracts or irritates the salmon to take it.'

'That's right.' I turn to him. 'Exactly.'

'Stop moving; it spooks the fish.'

'There are no fish, James! This is stupid!'

'Just imagine there are.'

'Fine.' I attempt to keep still, but it's hard with James standing so close to me.

'Now try to make the top part of your rod do all the work.' James places one hand against my hip and with his other hand he clasps me around my wrist, guiding the rod upwards, towards twelve o'clock, and in one sharp movement the line shoots forward.

'That's better,' he says, 'I'm going to get you back here in the summer, to do it for real, waders and all. Once more.'

'Very good, Flo!' Lucy calls.

'Flo's probably had enough,' Maddie says. 'Can't we all go inside now? I'm freezing.'

I can feel his warm breath against my cheek as he continues, 'Just raise the tip of your rod and keep the line as tight as you can.'

'Why do you love this so much?' I ask.

'I love the solitude, the sound of the water, the birds. It's a place to think,' James says now sounding remarkably sober. 'When you have a rod in your hand you live in the moment. All that matters is the light, the cast, attracting the fish. There's always hope too. I don't know many sports where you can fish for weeks, months even, and catch nothing, but somehow remain hopeful that the next time will be *your* moment, that you will come home with a ten-pound salmon in your net. When I think about it, fishing is all about hope and faith.'

'Flo! Everyone!' Maddie calls. 'It's time!'

The lesson on the lawn abruptly comes to an end, all of us running inside, before Lucy switches on the television in the kitchen, and Matthew gets out the bottle of champagne. 'Three, two, ONE' – we all call out as the cork pops – 'HAPPY NEW YEAR!'

I feel his hand on mine before he pulls me into his arms. 'Happy New Year, Flo,' James says.

# 70

## Peggy

I stir when I hear noise outside, drunken revellers no doubt.
I leap to my feet, glancing at the clock on my mantelpiece.
It's past twelve o'clock. I have no idea how long I've been
dozing. Quietly, I walk upstairs to check up on Mia. She
looks peaceful lying on my bed, asleep under her soft
cream blanket, her breathing steady, and for a moment I'm
reminded of Beth as a little girl. I kiss her cheek and stroke
her hair. I know I shouldn't disturb her, but I can't help
myself, and when she slowly opens her eyes she treats me to
the most beautiful smile.

Thirty minutes later I open my front door to Ricky and
Shelley, both wearing grins on their faces as they come inside.

'Mia's asleep. What's the joke?' I ask.

'Peggy,' Ricky says, 'you won't believe this, but Shelley
was dumb enough to say yes. We're getting married!'

I look over to Shelley and she nods. 'Wish me luck,' she jokes.

'You won't need it. This calls for a celebration,' I say, rushing to the kitchen to find a bottle of something, Ricky following me, me calling out to Shelley to sit down, that I want to hear all about it. Flo taught me always to keep a bottle of champagne in my fridge, as you never know when you might need it, and tonight seems to call for it.

'I didn't think you believed in marriage,' I whisper, as Ricky reaches for the glasses.

'Nor did I.' He shrugs. 'I think I've realized, more than ever before, we only get one life, one shot. I love her and I want us to be a family. Anyway ...' He claps his hand as if he doesn't want to scare himself by thinking about the commitment, before we join Shelley, talking and laughing until the early hours of the morning, taking our glasses into the garden to watch the local fireworks.

I realize it's the first time since Tim died that I've seen the New Year in, and how special it is to spend it with my new friends.

# 71

**Flo**

It's four in the morning when finally I crawl into bed. James was right. A run was never going to be on the cards today. I smile, remembering us dancing, calling ourselves Ginger Rogers and Fred Astaire.

I hear a knock on the door and for a moment my heart stops, until I hear Maddie whisper, 'Flo? Are you awake?' She enters my room in her pyjamas and flops down on the other side of my bed.

'That was such a fun evening,' I say, realizing it's the first time I've truly let my hair down in months. If I could, I'd rewind and have the night all over again, even the mad casting lesson on the lawn, but nothing surprises me when it comes to the eccentric Baileys.

'I love your family,' I say. 'I might have to borrow your parents from time to time.'

'I think they'd love to adopt you too.' She turns over on to her side, to face me. 'You and James seem close?'

I nod, somehow sensing this conversation was brewing. 'He's been great, Maddie, really supportive.'

'What's Chloe like?'

'Haven't met her.'

She sighs, staring up to the ceiling. She seems restless. 'Sometimes I feel cut off living out of London.'

'But you love it where you are.'

'I know, but when you were going through everything, I felt pretty useless. I couldn't pop over to see you as much as I wanted.'

'I wasn't great company.'

'You know what I mean, Flo.'

'You were on the end of a telephone line.'

'But it's not the same. I've thought about moving back, especially with this new job.'

'And?'

'I couldn't afford it. I work all these bloody hours and get paid practically nothing. People think if you work in theatre it's a privilege, a hobby. Are you sure you want to get back into it?'

I sit up. 'Maddie, what's wrong?'

'Sorry, ignore me. I'm tired, that's all, and my head is hurting. Self-induced pain. I'm a spotty old cow too.'

'I can't see a single spot.'

She points to her chin. 'Here. And I've put on far too much weight.'

'You haven't.'

'I'm single, fat and spotty and I live with a cat,' she laughs at herself.

'You're beautiful and talented and one day you'll meet someone.'

'You sound like Mum. "Your time will come",' she mimics. '"Your boat will come in". Well, I wish the boat would stop chugging along and get a move on.'

'I'm single and live with your smelly old brother,' I remind her.

'You two have become really close, haven't you?' she asks me again.

I realize from the tone of Maddie's voice I need to be clever with my words. 'He's been a good friend when I've needed one. You both have.'

She shakes her head, as if ashamed of herself. 'I'm sorry, Flo. You've had so much to deal with lately, and here I am moaning about not having a man in my life, and a few spots.'

'Moan away. God knows, I've done it enough to last a lifetime.'

'I love my brother.'

I wait.

'He's always been the apple of my parents' eye, the boy who can do no wrong, following in Dad's footsteps. The clever one.'

'You're clever.'

'In an artistic way, but that doesn't count in our family.'

'It does. Look at you! You're only working for the

National Theatre. This year you're going to see your name, "Madeleine Bailey, Set and Costume Designer", in a big bold font in their programme.'

'Thanks,' she says, as if she needed to hear me say that. 'But you and James—'

'There's nothing going on,' I reassure her, 'honestly, nothing.'

'Are you sure? I mean there might not be for you, but I've noticed the way he looks at you—'

'I really meant it when I said I don't want to be in relationship right now, and it's James,' I say, as much to myself as to Maddie. 'He's like family.'

'I know. Sorry. It would be weird, wouldn't it?'

'Very,' I say, wondering what it could be like, because when Lucy mentioned James should travel I noticed I didn't like it. *I hated it, in fact.*

'I'm glad you're not into him,' Maddie continues, 'because I'd be piggy in the middle and I wouldn't be able to forgive him if he hurt you.'

I nod.

'He stuffs up all his relationships too,' Maddie says, on a roll now. 'I don't know why he left Emma.'

'Maybe he didn't love her enough? Sometimes it takes courage to walk away.'

For a moment I think of Theo, wondering if it was brave of him to be honest right from the start, saying he couldn't be the man I wanted him to be. I want to imagine it wasn't an easy decision to call our engagement off, and that occasionally he does think of me, as I think of him. I don't hate him anymore for what he did. Nor do I believe he set out to hurt me. He would have hurt me more in the long run if he hadn't been true to himself, and had deserted me the moment I discovered I tested positive. Or if he'd left me when I could no longer work, or hang on to my independence.

Theo and I spent eighteen happy, carefree months together, months I don't regret anymore, since I now realize it could have never worked between us. I think of Mum and Mark, how she completely let him into her life. He knew everything about her, warts and all, and he still loved her. If only he'd been free to be with her. Selfishly, I wish he'd left his wife.

'Maybe,' Maddie says. 'I just think he's a commitment freak, which is why I don't want him anywhere near you.'

'Stop panicking. It's not going to happen,' I say, trying to disguise my confusion that there was a flicker of disappointment when I realized it wasn't James knocking on my door tonight, disappointment followed swiftly by relief.

I can see why I'd be the last person Maddie would want her brother to date, and the last thing I want to do is play Russian roulette with two of my closest friends.

# 72

## Flo

It's now February, and Iona and I are on a sixteen-mile run this morning, heading towards Hyde Park. We've progressed to an improver programme and have eight weeks to go until we approach the start line. Just the idea of it makes me feel sick with nerves, but at the same time it's the most important thing in my life.

I spend a good chunk of my day, even at work, checking my sponsorship page to see how close – currently 52 per cent – I am to my £2,000 target. If I can do this, surely I can do anything, I tell myself. It's also a big reason why I can't seem to have energy to devote to make a final decision whether I want to take the test or not. My counselling has been pushed to the back of the queue for now, Dr Fraser saying her door is always open when I need to talk about it again.

'How much have you raised?' I ask Iona, as we run through St James's Park.

'About a grand so far. People say they'll sponsor you, but then you check . . . and you can't really ask them again, can you?'

'No. Well, depends who it is, I guess.'

'I'm knackered,' she admits. 'I need to sit down.'

Iona and I are desperately trying not to stop and start anymore. If you walk it only makes it harder to start running again. 'Holy shit, Flo, when does this get easier?' Iona groans. 'I shouldn't have gone out last night. Bet you were in bed tucked up.'

'I stayed in with James.'

'I still don't know why you two aren't together.'

'I do: he's a friend and he's with someone.'

Though in the end I confide to Iona about New Year and how close to him I'd felt at his parents' house.

'I might be paranoid,' I say, 'but I feel as if something's changed: it's almost as if he's avoiding me. Last night was the first time in weeks that we've spent the evening together.' I've also noticed we've been calling and texting each other far less.

'Avoidance is a sure sign,' Iona says. 'He's probably just as confused as you are.'

'I don't know,' I say, begrudgingly admitting that there is a tiny part of me that's jealous of Chloe, even if I have no right to be.

'I'd be jealous too,' Iona insists. 'She's with your man.'

'Oh, stop it,' I say, thinking of Maddie too. I've got to put to bed the absurd idea that James and I could be anything more than friends.

'How are we going to raise the cash?' I ask, changing the subject. I've asked all the usual suspects and they've all been incredibly generous, but I need more.

'If only we had some rich rellies,' Iona sighs.

'If only.'

'Maybe the Queen will sponsor us,' she suggests as we run past the gates of Buckingham Palace. 'Listen, maybe talk to James?'

'No way! I'm not even sure how I feel.'

'You're scared – that's what you're feeling – because this could be real.'

I stop running. 'I'm not scared. I'm probably reading way too much into it. I know he's been busy at work—'

'That old chestnut.'

'It's true,' I call after her. 'His job *is* stressful.'

Iona stops running and turns to face me. 'Admit it, Flo: you're scared.'

'And I've been really busy training and—'

'I get it's a risk falling for your best friend.'

'I'm not falling for him,' I insist. *I can't be.*

'You've got a lot to lose, but if you do or say nothing, in my book, that's a far bigger risk to take.'

# 73

*Beth's Diary, 2011*

*I still haven't told Flo. She's in her second year at art school and seems to have found a real niche in model making. She can make, on a tiny scale, pieces of furniture or other props for the stage. She once showed me a racing car that was smaller than the size of her thumb.*

*'I spent hours hunched over my chair and this is all I have to show for it, Mum, this teeny-weenie little car,' she'd said. The detail was exquisite, from the seats to the steering wheel and the handbrake made out of a filed cocktail stick. Her art teacher has inspired her to dream of working with directors across the globe, designing stage sets for theatre.*

*She has such a promising future ahead of her — what's the point of me bursting her bubble right now?*

*I want her college years to be the happiest of her life,
not filled with dread and doubt that could affect her work.
If I tell her now she might even drop out, and I'd never
forgive myself for that. I don't want anything to jeopardize
her chance of finishing her course. After she's graduated,
that's the time to say something. Or the moment my
symptoms become too obvious to ignore. No more excuses.
All I can do is pray she'll understand, and that she'll
forgive me.*

*Just heading out to meet Mark now for coffee, will write
more later . . .*

*Mark and I just had a huge row. Things have been
strained enough between us; feelings always get in the way
of a friendship.*

*'You're always making excuses,' he said to me over our
coffee. 'If it's not Flo's birthday then it's her exams, or
you can't say anything because she's just broken up with a
boyfriend. What's it going to be next? She lands her dream
job so you can't say a word? Face it, Beth, this isn't about
finding a good time anymore, you're just fucking scared.'*

*I was so angry I could have hit him. 'Yes, yes, I am scared.
I'm terrified. But how about you Mark?'*

*'What about me?'*

*'You say you don't love your wife anymore, that you
love me, but there's always a "but" isn't there? You can't
leave Eve because her mother is unwell or work is stressful
or Ben needs you.'*

377

He slammed his fist on the table. 'That's unfair, Beth. He does. Both my children need me.'

'Face it, Mark, there is never going to be a good time to tell your wife, unless you don't want to.'

'Beth—'

'You're scared too,' I said. 'Scared of change, scared of being with me, scared of taking any risks.'

'Beth, that's not true.'

'Prove it then.'

And I stormed out. He hasn't called me back.

I think that could be it. I think, finally, it's over between us.

# 74

Flo

As I'm about to leave the office to head out for a run, I can't help looking at my sponsorship page one last time, which is now looking considerably healthier since all of Granny's new friends that she has met on her Italian course, including her teacher Maria, have sponsored me, along with James and Maddie's work colleagues. Even some of James's furry four-legged friends: Betsy, a seven-year old bichon frise, whom James nursed back to life after eating macadamia nuts – highly toxic and poisonous for dogs – sponsored me a hundred pounds.

I stare at my screen.

*Holy shit!* as Iona would say.

Thankfully, I am the only person left in the office so I can scream, shout and dance around the room, before finally calming down and looking at my page once again, just in case it's a dream.

I stop dead when I see his name under the donation.

Theo has sponsored me two thousand pounds.

*It's a great cause, Flo, and I wish you all the very best with it.*

It's formal, but I feel strangely touched. This isn't out of guilt; Theo doesn't operate like that. No one told him I was running a marathon. Somehow he found out, and then decided to support me. Perhaps we did mean something to one another, after all.


I turn the key in the lock. I'm home. I must have run at least fourteen miles tonight since it's coming up to nine, and I didn't stop once for a break. For the first time, it felt easy, as if I were floating on the top deck of a double-decker bus, being carried along effortlessly, and it was the best feeling ever.

As I take off my trainers and leave them by the front door, I think back to my first attempt, when I couldn't even run down the road without getting a stitch before throwing up my tuna melt.

To my surprise, I find James in the kitchen eating scrambled eggs.

'Hello, stranger,' I say, pouring myself a glass of water. 'How are you?'

'Good, thanks. You?'

'Great. I've just been on a run,' I say, stating the obvious.

'Good run?'

'Brilliant. Do you remember you said one of these days I'd run without even knowing?'

He nods.

'Well, tonight I did. I'm beginning to think I won't come last.'

I wait for him to smile, but he's quiet, his food barely touched.

'You won't ever guess who sponsored me?' I say, joining him at the table.

'Who?'

'Theo.'

He looks up. '*Theo?*'

'I know. I'm as shocked as you. Two thousand pounds.' The moment I say how much, I wish I could take it back.

He shrugs. 'Well, it's easy for him. He can afford it.'

'Yes, perhaps, but I'm still grateful.'

'It's pocket money to him, isn't it?'

'Maybe, but he didn't have to.'

'He probably felt bad. Guilt money.'

'I was still touched,' I say defensively, getting up to leave the room.

'*Touched?*' he calls out, following me. 'Flo, the guy's a jerk. He dumps you at the first sign of trouble and then you're touched because he tosses money your way to ease his conscience?'

I hesitate as to what to say back, not wanting this to descend into an ugly argument. 'Is everything all right?' I ask him.

'I can't believe he says nothing to you for months – he doesn't even bother to find out how you are – and then he thinks this makes it all okay?'

'I doubt he thinks this makes it all okay. It was just a gesture. This was his way to do something, to show he cared.'

'*Cared*? Christ, Flo, you're gullible.'

'James, stop it. What's got into you?'

'He didn't care. If he did, you'd still be together. Instead, he left *us* to pick up the pieces while he carries on making his millions and driving his Porsche, and probably screwing the next fit woman he meets.'

I walk away, hurt.

'Are you still in love with him?' he asks, following me to my bedroom. 'Flo?'

'Fuck you,' I say, before going into my room and slamming the door behind me.

# 75

## Peggy

Flo just called me in tears to tell me she and James had a big row. I have to say, there is a grain of truth in what James thinks. There must be a part of Theo that does feel guilty. And so he should.

Then again, he didn't have to give Flo a bean, and it's much better for Flo not to waste her time and energy feeling bitter about their breakup. She's trying to move on, and it would be churlish to refuse his donation. What would that achieve? As to James's reaction, it doesn't take a rocket scientist to work it out.

I noticed the way he looked at her the night we heard the news of the drug trial. It was the way Tim used to look at me. I see the way her eyes light up when she talks about him, or if he says something funny.

Over the past few months, I have seen a different side

to this young man. Don't get me wrong, I've always liked James, but I've never thought about him as anything other than Flo's flatmate. Yet, the way he has stuck by Flo through all this turmoil ... Any old fool can see James is hopelessly in love with her, and I'm fairly certain Flo is beginning to feel the same way too. She just doesn't know it yet.

But there's no need for me to tell her.

Love has a funny way of catching up with you, especially when you least expect it.

## 76

Flo

Maddie and I walk down Brick Lane, one of the most famous streets in East London. With only five weeks left to train, I should have gone out for a run today, but when I woke up this morning, my legs were aching and my head was pounding.

'One morning off won't hurt,' Maddie had suggested. 'Use me as an excuse.' I didn't take much persuading.

James wasn't at home. He must have stayed over at Chloe's again. We've barely spoken since our argument. The following morning, before I left for work, he said he was sorry and that he'd spoken out of turn, but something's changed and I hate it. There's a distance between us. I wish everything could go back to the way it used to be, and the ironic thing is I can't talk to James or to Maddie about it.

When we enter the warehouse-type building, immediately

I am struck by the familiar scent of timber. This art shop used to be one of my favourite college haunts, and it still smells like an old, leather-bound book. The sight of shelves, stacked with packets filled with model-making accessories and a wall adorned with paintbrushes of every shape and size instantly lifts my mood and helps me to ignore my stubborn headache and my anxiety over James.

'How are you going to pay for all this?' Maddie asks as we join the queue. My trolley is filled with paintbrushes, a selection of card, and I couldn't resist a box of gold, silver and copper flakes, imitation snow and packets of cork and fake grass.

'Mr Mastercard,' I reply, leaning against the trolley, almost tempted to climb in myself and ask Maddie to push me home.

'Are you okay?' she asks as we shuffle forward.

'Just tired.' I press a hand against my forehead. 'I feel as if I've been in a boxing ring with Mike Tyson.'

'I told you exercise was bad for your health.'

I take off my jacket.

'Have a lie-down when we get home,' she suggests, making me feel ancient, but I think I might have to. 'I need to catch up on some work, so don't worry about entertaining me.'

When Maddie and I return to the flat, my energy has picked up, and I'm far too excited to go to bed. I want to unpack my shopping and make something for my doll's house.

I open my wardrobe. On the top shelf is a large striped hatbox, and with Maddie's help, somehow we manage to drop it on to my bed before I take off the lid, caked in dust.

Inside are earthenware pots filled with paintbrushes. Most of these belonged to Mum.

'That one's made out of real badger hair, Flo,' she'd say when I used to pick them out of her jam jar.

I open the lid of my old bottle of white spirit. It smells of orange liquor. I feel emotional when I see my scalpel covered in masking tape and my mechanical pencil, which cost me more than a month's rent. Maddie and I used to joke that we'd choose our pencil or scalpel over any man.

'We were that sad,' she says.

'And still are,' I laugh.

As I crouch down on to the floor to reach for something under my bed, I feel dizzy again.

'Here,' Maddie says, 'let me do it.' She pulls out a leather suitcase that had belonged to my grandfather. Inside is my old cutting board, scratched and splattered with paint, my orange scale ruler, and the party would never be complete without a pot of cocktail sticks, which Maddie and I used to file down and make into table and chair legs. It reminds me of Mum's diary, of showing her the convertible car I'd designed, the size of my thumb, using a cocktail stick for the handbrake.

Later that afternoon while Maddie is working on some designs in the kitchen, I'm sitting at my table by my bedroom window, transported back to my old college studio that looked out on to a courtyard. Ignoring my headache, I pick up my pencil and draw to scale a small rectangular shape on my mount board card, which is going to be the top of my coffee table. I cut it out, scoring it with my scalpel, enjoying the satisfying sound of the blade slicing into the paper. 'Fancy a cup of tea?' Maddie calls.

'No, thanks.'

'Do you know what's got into James lately? He's been such a moody bugger.'

I drop the scalpel, blood oozing from my finger. Cursing under my breath, I rush to the bathroom and run my finger under the tap.

Maddie joins me, opening the mirrored cupboard to find a box of plasters. 'You're out of practice,' she reassures me, 'that's all.'

'I don't feel good,' I admit, feeling queasy. Maybe it's the sight of blood.

'Have a rest,' she insists, and this time I have no strength to argue. 'I'll wake you up at seven, so you have time to get ready for tonight.'

I don't wake up until nine o'clock that evening, and I don't feel any better.

I feel infinitely worse.

## 77

## Peggy

'Granny, don't catch it,' Flo groans, as I enter her bedroom with a cup of ginger and honey tea.

'Don't you worry about me,' I say. 'The one advantage of being a perky pensioner is I'm allowed the flu jab each year.' I perch next to Flo and feel her forehead, before taking her temperature.

Flo has been in bed for five days, sleeping most of the time, barely able to drag herself to the bathroom, and there are no signs of her getting any better. She could hardly stand up this morning to give me enough time to change her bed sheets, before collapsing under the covers again.

Maddie called me on Sunday morning to tell me she suspected Flo had flu. She said she wished she could stay on to look after her, but she had to catch the train home, and James equally couldn't take time off work, so Elvis and I have made ourselves comfy in the flat this week. Not that there's a lot I can do, except make sure she is drinking plenty of fluids and resting.

While she's asleep I do my Italian homework, and I'm still trying to finish my tapestry cushion. At this rate, I'm sure I'll be taking it to my grave.

'What if I can't run?' she says, when I rest a lukewarm flannel against her forehead. Flo has had a particularly nasty virus that has affected her chest, and Ricky warned me it could take weeks for her to recover. Even then she'd need to give herself plenty of time before she could even put on her trainers, let alone run twenty-six miles.

'I can't afford to miss another week, Granny.'

'I know, but your health is more important.'

'All my sponsors, if I don't run now—'

'Try not to worry.'

'I'll let everyone down.'

'Flo, it's horrible luck,' I say, though deep down I'm not surprised she has fallen prey to this bug. She has had far too much to contend with over the past eight months, but not only that, her training has been gruelling. I feel ill just looking at her fitness programme taunting her from her bedroom wall, a full week without any ticks in the boxes. By the end of this week, she was supposed to be running twenty miles, performing a rehearsal of the big day itself, but she can barely lift a glass to her mouth.

'I'll let my sponsors down, the charity, all those people who applied, who could have run instead of me—'

'Flo, there is nothing—'

'And you—'

'You could never let me down.'

'Iona will be doing it on her own,' she continues, making me realize it's pointless trying to tell her to stop working herself up into a stew.

'We promised we'd be on the starting line together. And James.'

It pains me when Flo's face crumples into tears because there isn't anything I can say to make this better. *If only I had a magic wand.*

'There, there,' I mutter, fearing Flo could be right. All her hard work, all those weeks and months of training with James and Iona, could amount to nothing. People would still sponsor her, but it's not the same and everyone knows it.

'Now what would you like for lunch?'

'I'm not hungry.' She closes her eyes.

'Try to eat something, Flo, even if it's a small bowl of soup.'

'I'll let everyone down, especially Mum,' she continues to punish herself, before struggling to sit up in bed, her eyes now streaming with tears. 'Granny, it's the only thing that's been keeping me going, if I can't run, if I . . .' She's too exhausted to finish the sentence, but she doesn't need to. If she doesn't run it will break her heart.

*And mine.*

'Flo, you will run this race,' I pledge like Cinderella's fairy godmother, 'we will get you better.'

*

Early that afternoon, after I have managed to feed Flo a few spoonfuls of homemade vegetable soup, the soup I used to make for Tim, I am in the local health food shop buying fresh ginger, vitamin C and another bottle of tablets that claim to boost the immune system. I also add to my trolley cider vinegar to splash into herbal teas, more raw honey, a nasal spray, leeks, spinach, oranges and potatoes, and the woman persuades me to buy a humidifier, explaining that it helps people with congested chests and flu breathe more easily.

I almost pass out when she tells me how much the bill comes to, but come what may, Flo *will* run this marathon.

## 78

## Flo

Granny sits in a corner of my bedroom, Elvis lying at her feet, working on her tapestry cushion, which has been a work-in-progress for the past two years.

'Come in,' I call, when James knocks on my door.

'I hope you've had a more exciting day than me,' I say, sitting up in bed, aware I haven't brushed my hair for days or seen any sunlight. Or seen James for that matter. I didn't want him to catch my germs either, and things between us still aren't quite back to normal.

'I've had a shocking day,' he admits.

Granny looks up.

'I lost my cool in clinic,' he says, perching on the end of my bed. 'There's this man, Roger, who has an overweight three-year-old basset hound because he doesn't walk it.'

'How cruel,' Granny says. 'You shouldn't get a dog if you're not prepared to walk it.'

'Exactly, but try explaining that to Roger. He doesn't listen to a word I say. In the end I showed him the door; I kicked him out.'

'Don't come too close,' I warn, when he takes off his shoes and lies down next to me.

'Flo, I don't care if I get your flu; I've probably just lost my job.'

'What did your boss say?' I ask, as Granny gets up and discreetly leaves the room.

'He was furious.'

'You were right though,' I say. 'It's not fair on the dog.'

'I know, but I shouldn't have lost my cool. Talk about unprofessional. Geoff's going to talk to me about it tomorrow when we've both calmed down. Anyway, much more importantly, how are *you* feeling?' he moves on. 'Any better?'

'I ate half a baked potato for lunch.' I give him a thumbs up.

'Have you managed to get some sleep?'

I nod. 'I had this nightmare that I featured on the BBC news headlines as the world's slowest marathon racer, *ever.*'

James smiles, and for a moment I feel like we're the old James and Flo again. Perhaps time and distance was all we needed.

'I had another one too. In this one I was so close to the finishing line, within touching distance. I could see Granny, Maddie, Ricky – I could see you, James – cheering me on, and then I tripped and fell, and the crowds were laughing and throwing things at me, as I was taken off in a stretcher.'

James bursts out laughing.

'It's not funny!' I exclaim. 'What if it's some sign I shouldn't run?'

He sits up and takes both my hands. 'Say this with me,' he begins, '"I, Florence Andrews". Go on, say it.'

'I, Florence Andrews.'

'"Am going to run the marathon and I'm not going to come last."'

I grin.

'Say it with me, Flo.'

'I, Florence Andrews,' we say together, 'am going to run the marathon and I'm not going to come last.'

'Now say it once more like you mean it. If I can't train you outside, I'll train you on the inside; it's just as important.'

'I, Florence Andrews, am going to run the marathon and I'm going to come *first*.'

'Good.' He laughs again. 'Well, maybe not first.'

'You know what, I *am* feeling better. Thank you, James.'

'No need to thank me.'

I pluck up the courage to ask, 'Is everything all right? I mean apart from today?'

'Yes, why wouldn't it be?'

'You've been ... I don't know ... You would tell me if anything was wrong, wouldn't you?'

James stares ahead. 'Chloe and I split up.'

'I'm so sorry. When?'

'A week ago.'

'A *week* ago?' I gasp. 'Why didn't you say something sooner?'

'You've been asleep most of the time,' he reminds me.

'Why did you break up? Was it you?'

He nods.

'I thought it was going well?'

'I had to break up with her, because . . . well, it just didn't work out,' is all he ends up saying.

'I'm sorry, James.'

'Don't be. It was the right thing,' he asserts, his voice overly cheerful. 'I thought it was better to break it off now, rather than . . .' His voice trails off. 'Anyway, it's fine. I'm fine. It's all good. Right, I'm grabbing myself something to eat.'

I touch his arm, not wanting him to leave. 'You're one of the most important people in my life, you know that don't you?'

He looks at me before slowly withdrawing his arm. 'Flo?'

'Yes?'

Finally, he looks away. 'Fancy anything to eat?' He leaves the room giving me no time to answer.

Alone, I lie back down again, even more confused.

I can't deny a part of me feels relieved he has broken up with Chloe, but what kind of person doesn't want their friend to be happy? When he held my hands this evening, I wondered what it might feel like, if he ran his hand through my hair, or touched my cheek. Or clasped both hands around my neck and pulled me close towards him, before we kissed.

But if I were brave enough to tell him I do have feelings, I'd be naïve to think it wouldn't change everything between us. If things were to go wrong, I could lose not only James, but possibly Maddie too, and my home here.

Iona talks about taking risks, but isn't it safer to remain friends? To hope that whatever these feelings are, they'll go away?

'Flo,' James says, returning. 'I know this is bad timing – terrible, in fact – but the thing is . . .'

'What is it?'

He hesitates.

'James?'

'I broke up with Chloe because life's too short to be with the wrong person.'

I freeze, the fear of what he's about to say next overwhelming.

*I'm not ready for this.*

'You must know why I broke up with her. I don't love her.'

*Don't say it.*

'I love *you*, Flo.'

He waits.

'Say something,' he begs.

'James, I care for you, I care for you so much but—'

'Don't say what I think you're going to say.'

'We're friends.'

'No, we're not. We're more than that and you know it.'

'We have too much to lose if it goes wrong.'

'So that's it? We never give it a go? Every single relationship we go into is a risk, but don't we owe it to ourselves to *try*?'

I have never felt this torn, or confused. *Or scared. Exposed.*

'I've wanted to say it for so long,' he continues, 'but, like you, I've been too frightened, but I'm sick of that. I want to look back knowing I told you, that I didn't choke or bottle out, that for once I put my heart on the line.'

'James, you know this makes it complicated.'

'I don't care.'

'But what if—'

'You test positive? I don't care.'

'But you *should* care,' I raise my voice. 'What if I decide not to take the test? Can you really live with the uncertainty?'

'Just tell me if you feel the same,' he says, as if he didn't hear my question.

*Tell him, Flo.*

*Don't tell him.*

'Fine,' he says, leaving the room.

*Look at what you could lose.*

*Look at what you could have.*

'James, wait!' He turns, a tiny glimmer of hope in his eyes. I want to say I love him too, but . . .

*Don't cross that line.*

*Cross it.*

Yet hasn't it been crossed already? I think we both know we went over the line a long time ago.

He walks away.

I get out of bed and run after him. 'Don't go.' I grab him by the arm, not ready to let go of him yet, or the idea of us. 'All I'm saying is I need more time.'

'Time for what?' he asks, his tone gentle. 'Haven't we waited long enough?'

'It's *us*. You and me.'

'What's going on?' asks Granny, joining us in the hallway. 'Flo, you're shivering. Get back into bed.'

'Hang on, Granny,' James and I say together, our eyes not leaving one another.

'I can't. I can't lose you,' I say, wrapping my arms around my chest.

'Theo left you. Graham walked out on your mum. I get you're scared, Flo. So am I. I'm terrified, but we can't live our lives in fear.'

He steps towards me, but I back away. He nods, as if to say he understands. And this time I don't follow him when he leaves.

Minutes later, I hear the sound of his motorbike outside. I look out of my bedroom window and realize I'm crying.

Granny enters my room. I don't have to tell her what's wrong. She holds me in her arms until my tears subside.

# 79

*Beth's Diary, 2012*

*Mark dropped a bombshell today. He called me unusually early this morning, sounding agitated, saying he had to see me. I knew something was up because, since our argument six months ago, we've barely been in touch. Within an hour he was knocking on my door.*

*'I've left her,' he confessed the moment he stepped inside. 'Beth, I'm free.'*

*For the first time in years I felt hope. Was he really saying we could be together at last?*

*I thought I must have been dreaming when he took my face in his hands and kissed me. I hadn't been kissed for so long – not since Graham – that I'd forgotten how it felt to be touched and held in someone's arms. I'd forgotten what it felt like to be desired.*

*I kissed him back, like I have never kissed a man before, wanting to stay in his arms for ever. When finally we parted, he told me to sit down.*

*'I've left Camberwell. I'm moving to France,' he said.*

*'To France?'*

*'To be closer to my sister. It's a new start, a new beginning.' He paused. 'Come with me.'*

*'Come with you?' I repeated, as if it were impossible.*

*'Yes. Why not? This is our chance, Beth.'*

*'But what about Flo?'*

*'Flo's leaving college next month,' he reasoned. 'She's almost finished her course.'*

*'I can't leave her.'*

*'And then she'll be working away from home just like my boys.'*

*'I can't tell her my news and then abandon her.'*

*'You won't be abandoning her.'*

*'She'll need me.'*

*'And she'll still have you. You don't have to be physically here.'*

*'But—'*

*'She's a grown-up, Beth. An adult.'*

*'But Mark, she'll need me.'*

*'She'll always need you, and you can be there for her, no matter where you live.'*

*'It's not the same.'*

*'But maybe that's a good thing,' he argued.*

'I love you. I want to be with you – of course I do – but why can't we stay here?'

'We can't. Well, I can't.'

'Why?'

'I've been offered a teaching job in Carcassonne.'

'Have you accepted?'

Before I'd even asked the question, I knew the answer.

Mark touched my arm. 'You were right, Beth, I have been scared of change and hurting those I love, but isn't this what we've always wanted? To be together? Now we have a chance.'

'But what about when I'm unwell, when I need Amanda, the hospital—'

'I can be with you,' he assured me, 'love you and care for you.'

'My symptoms are getting worse,' I confessed almost wanting to put him off so I didn't have to make this decision. 'I forgot the way to school again, and the other day I fell—'

'I know what's to come, Beth. It's a big step for both of us, but you don't have to be alone.'

'I don't know,' I said. Why does fear always have a nasty habit of creeping in?

'I've put my family first for years, but now it's time for us.'

I looked at Mark, desperately torn. He has been a part of my life for over twenty years and I love every single thing about him, from the kindness in his heart to the lines *around his dark blue eyes that tell a thousand different stories, to the grey in his hair and the old jumpers he wears with holes in their elbows, reminding me so much of my father.*

But France? Leaving Flo? And Amanda? Leaving Mum, too, when she finds out I tested positive? My job? What would I do in France? How can I just pack my bags and leave everything I love behind? Except if I were to stay here I wouldn't have Mark . . .

'I need to go, Beth, get away from here. I need a clean break.'

'When are you leaving?'

'At the end of the week.'

'So soon?' I gasped.

*Say you'll go, Beth. Say it.*

'I love you,' I said instead.

'Then come,' he begged.

'Your life in France will be much easier without me.'

'Stop it. It won't.'

'You do deserve a new start, but I don't want you to be burdened with—'

'Listen.' He grabbed hold of me. 'I love you, okay, and nothing will change that.'

I realized there and then that I have been terrified of living on my own for the rest of my life, but putting your faith and hopes in a new dream, away from everything that is so familiar can be just as daunting.

'It doesn't have to be right now,' Mark continued. 'It can

be later, when you've talked to Flo and your mother. We've been friends for years, Beth. Finally this is our chance,' he reinforced.

'I can't,' I said, turning away, fighting hard not to cry. 'I can't ever leave Flo. I need to be here. With her.'

# 80

## Flo

I stare at my clothes neatly laid out on my bed, hardly able to believe it's happening, that I'm actually running the marathon tomorrow. I was so close to thinking I'd have to pull out, but thankfully my flu didn't drag on. I don't know who was more determined that I run today, me, Iona or Granny, but between the three of us, here I am.

My kit bag is packed, my number is pinned to my red and green HDA running vest and my tag is tied to my trainers so that Maddie and James can track me on their phones during the race.

I sit down on the bed, my stomach knotted with nerves. The forecast for tomorrow is going to be hot, something like twenty-three degrees. Far too hot to run twenty-six point two miles.

'Supper in twenty minutes,' I hear Granny call from

downstairs. She's making us some pasta with pancetta and pesto.

I glance at my phone. I haven't seen James for over three weeks. Not since he told me he loves me. After he left the flat, he texted to say he was staying over with Stu and Jane. The following morning I packed my bags. I thought it was the best thing, for both of us.

I left a note on the kitchen table explaining that I'd moved in temporarily with Granny. I knew the only way I could work out my feelings for him, once and for all, was if we didn't live together. But I didn't want James to feel driven out of his own flat either. It was his home.

He hasn't been in touch once. I shouldn't be surprised. He has given me exactly what I asked for: space and time.

Yet I can't deny that not seeing him has been much harder than I'd expected, and there have been many times when I've longed to pick up the phone. I've yearned to hear his voice. I've missed him as my trainer and flatmate. But most of all, I've missed my best friend.

'Well, *tell* him that,' Iona has insisted during our runs.

'But he wants more.'

'And you don't? Are you mad? Blind? Deaf? Dumb? What's holding you back?'

I dreaded talking to Maddie about it because I knew this was exactly what she'd anticipated, but she was supportive, telling me I'd done the right thing moving out.

'He's in pieces, though, Flo,' she added. 'He wanted me to tell you he was doing brilliantly, but I can't lie.' She laughed sadly. 'Tread carefully. He might be my stinky old bro, but I kind of love him too.'

She's staying with James tonight, but will be here with me early tomorrow morning to catch the tube to Greenwich Park. Granny has suggested coming with me to the start too, but I managed to put her off that idea, as the assembly area is really only for runners and I didn't like the idea of Granny being out all day in the heat.

As I'm about to head downstairs for supper, my mobile rings. When I see his name I feel nervous.

'Hi,' I say, picking up, 'how are you?'

'I'm good,' James replies, doing his best not to sound nervous too. 'You?'

'Great. Well, I'm terrified actually, what's new?'

'You'll be fine. You've done the hard bit getting over flu and finishing your training.'

I'm so affected by hearing his voice that I start to gabble, telling him these past three weeks Iona and I have trained as if our lives depended on it. I bang on about how I completed a mock trial of twenty-two miles, which I finished in five hours, and I've taken my final week easy, just a few short runs.

'Though I find the short runs as hard as the long ones. They're harder to pace, aren't they ...' I stop, sick of the sound of my own voice, especially when all I want to know is how he is. 'How are you?' I ask again.

'I'm fine, Flo,' he replies, his voice now distant.

'I've missed you.'

'Anyway, the reason I was calling,' he says as if he didn't hear me. 'It's going to be hot out there tomorrow, apparently record temperatures. Stop at every drinking station, listen to your body, don't push yourself in the heat, run in the shade as much as you can, and look out for us. I'll try to get to Tower Bridge or Canary Wharf, and close to the end, okay? We'll aim to stick to the left, and Maddie's drawn an enormous picture of you on a banner so you won't be able to miss us.'

'I hope she's edited out the blue tape covering my legs. Shin splint hell.' I long to hear him laugh too, as he normally would. 'I wasn't sure you'd come,' I say quietly.

'I wouldn't miss it for the world. Good luck, Flo.'

After we hang up, I can't stop thinking about him.

James invades my thoughts every minute of the day. Sometimes my imagination leads me to a happy place where we're together, but then doubt creeps in, thinking yet again that the stakes are too high. And do I really want James to place his bets on someone like me, someone with such an uncertain future? Is it fair on him?

'But that's *his* choice to make,' Granny tells me over supper. 'Don't forget, too, Flo, what you can offer someone like James. Don't forget how special *you* are. He sees it, I see it, the whole world does as far as I'm concerned, so perhaps it's time you did too.'

I think of Mark and how I wish things had turned out differently between him and Mum. She had waited so long to find love – she didn't even believe it would ever come along – but then when it did, she backed away in fear and sacrificed her future for my own.

I wish she had done many things, but most of all, I wish she'd packed her bags and gone to France. Perhaps she would still be alive. And I wish, more than anything, she could be there watching me tomorrow.

Later that night, I can't sleep. I switch on my bedside light and pick up Mum's last diary. I'm now in July 2012, only days before she died.

I'm dreading saying goodbye to her all over again.

# 81

*Beth's Diary, 2012*

*I saw Amanda today. I told her I was a proud mum. My Flo got a 2:1! She's currently with Maddie in Venice. Amanda was thrilled, of course, but it wasn't long before I detected impatience. She didn't want to discuss the beauty of Piazza San Marco and what a crime it was that she hadn't been yet.*

*'Beth,' she said, raising her hand to stop me mid-flow.*

*'I know,' was all I could say. I have to tell Flo when she returns in two days.*

*Amanda suggested it might be a good idea for Flo to make an appointment to see a HD adviser when the time comes. My mother might also need to see a counsellor. I think that too would be a good idea. I have always believed Mum has suffered post-traumatic stress, another big reason,*

*aside from her heart, why I haven't wanted to burden
her with my situation. When Dad was really unwell I
suggested Mum should seek counselling, but that went
down like a lead balloon, so somehow I doubt she'll see one
now, but you never know.*

*As I reached for my glass of water, I caught Amanda
glancing at my right hand, the hand that twitches as if
I have a constant itch. It slipped from my grasp, water
spilling across her desk. I made some sort of joke about how
clumsy I am these days.*

*And as to why I was late for my appointment, when I
got off the tube, my mind went blank as to where I was.
This hospital has been my second home for years — I don't
have to think about which way to go or what button to
press in the lift — but today I felt like a tourist following the
signs in a foreign country. It was frightening.*

*'You're right,' I said finally. 'It's time to tell her.'*

*Once Flo knows, will she want to see a genetic
counsellor? I will explain that I believe there is no right or
wrong answer about finding out. People can lead happy
lives not knowing they are at risk. I have lived a happy life
knowing. The important thing is just to live.*

*But am I living? Am I really living at the moment?*

*'What are you thinking about?' Amanda asked.*

*'Mark,' I admitted. 'I didn't go to France because I
always thought I needed to be here for Flo, and I do, but in
a way he's right: she does have her own life to lead. She's
been offered a job in Copenhagen.'*

'That's wonderful,' she said, sensing there was more.

'She told me she wanted to live abroad, that she was looking for work in maybe New York or San Francisco.'

Amanda waited. They do that, these counsellors, they have a canny ability to know when to ask the questions and when to keep quiet.

'I still see her as my little girl, with two long plaits, wearing her favourite poppy dress or her lilac dungarees,' I said. 'The little girl I taught to ride a bike.' I smiled nostalgically. 'But she's twenty-one now. She's a big girl.'

I showed Amanda the card I had bought for her, a pretty one of a woman walking through a field of poppies, carrying a basket of flowers. I read out what I'd written inside.

Amanda doesn't need to convince me anymore to tell my daughter. I am determined to.

I'm expecting Flo to hate me for a while, feel angry, betrayed. I imagine she'll use me as both a punchbag and a shoulder to cry on. But I will be with her, every step of the way, and we will get through this, I'll make sure of that. All I can pray is that she'll forgive me in time.

'I'll stay for however long it takes,' I vowed to Amanda and to myself, 'for however long she needs me, but it doesn't mean I have to put my own life on hold, for ever, does it?'

Amanda shook her head.

'I want to make the most of the years I have left,' I said, thinking of Dad, and how much we travelled as a *family after he retired. We grabbed life by the scruff of the neck and gave it our best shot while we still could.*

*'I think I'd regret it if I didn't give Mark and me a chance. I don't want a future without the man I love.'*

*I tried calling Mark tonight, but he hasn't rung me back. He must be away, or perhaps something has come up with his sister. I don't want to email him or leave a message. I need to hear his voice. I'm longing to tell him that, once the dust settles, I'll pack my bags. I ache for him to know I love him and that I don't want us to spend any more time apart.*

*I'll call him again tomorrow.*

# 82

**Peggy**

I shut the door.

Flo has left. I packed her off with a slice of malt loaf and a banana for the tube journey, and she has gone.

Alone, I switch on the television and see that charming newsreader, Sophie Raworth, being interviewed. I give Elvis his breakfast and make myself a cup of strong coffee. I barely had a wink of sleep last night, and I can't imagine Flo had much either, since we were both terrified of oversleeping.

I set three alarm clocks this morning, all for six. To be honest, it was a relief to hear them go off at once, since I was wide awake anyway.

*What if Flo is sick or has a heart attack or collapses in the heat?*

We had breakfast at six thirty. I made Flo a bagel with scrambled eggs, which she washed down with plenty of water. Like me, she was a bundle of nerves, having spent most of last night panicking about hitting the wall, which she explained was when your body and mind go on strike and you literally cannot run a single step further. But she was also extraordinarily emotional, saying she had read Beth's second-to-last diary entry, which has revealed how her mother had planned to move to France. I realized just how much I'd missed in Beth's life. My daughter, at long last, had found love and was on the verge of moving abroad. If only she'd had the chance to be happy with Mark.

'Why didn't I just do a cake sale, Granny?' she asked, laughing hysterically before bursting into tears. And I hate to admit it, but at that moment, I would have preferred a cake sale too, especially if it were lemon drizzle.

I was relieved when Maddie arrived. I knew she'd be better equipped to calm Flo down and hold her hand before the race. I'm relieved James is coming to support her too. She needs him.

As I wrap my hands around my coffee mug, the warmth comforting, I think about Beth and Tim, and how I wish they were here with me today. Perhaps they will be looking down cheering her on. I cling to that thought as I stroke Elvis, and continue to watch the marathon coverage on the television.

It's almost ten o'clock when Ricky comes over, dressed in his bright green 'I'm supporting TEAM HDA' T-shirt.

'We look like twins,' he says, gesturing to our matching tops, his smile as bright as the sun, lifting my spirits immediately. 'Shelley will bring Mia towards the end,' he informs me. 'And a few of my footie mates will join us too, and maybe Vic from the band.'

'The more the merrier,' I say, marvelling at how relaxed Ricky looks in his cap and shorts, carrying his guitar. He looks as if he's about to spend the day on the beach.

'She'll be fine, Peggy. She's prepared,' he reassures me, my nerves building as we watch the Queen on the television, looking resplendent dressed in pink, with a matching hat and white gloves, preparing to press the button from outside Windsor Castle any moment now.

The national anthem plays, filling me with pride, but the sight of the crowds only adds to my anxiety for Flo. She'll be standing among over forty thousand people.

The Queen presses the button.

'Let's go,' I tell Ricky, switching off the television.

He takes me by the arm, gently. 'Breathe, Peggy. Breathe. Drop your shoulders. They're practically touching your ears, mate.'

I do as he says.

'Over three hundred thousand people applied to run this race,' he reminds me. 'Flo is one of the lucky ones who got a place, and she's going to do us all proud, right? Especially you. She'll be fine. Have faith. Got any brandy?' he adds, making me laugh at last. 'Just a spoonful?'

I laugh again. He's right. This is an experience of a lifetime for Flo. A privilege. And I couldn't be prouder.

Though all that comes out of my mouth is, 'Off we go!' I pick up the picnic basket and hand Ricky my fold-up chair. 'The sooner this race begins, the sooner Flo will finish.'

# 83

## Flo

Iona and I shuffle forward. We must be getting closer to the start line as it's well past ten o'clock now. Since arriving, after being assembled into the right place and saying a tearful farewell to Maddie, it's been a waiting game, runners exchanging stories, crying and hugging, sharing tips of how to survive this heat, dishing out extra safety pins to make sure our running numbers stay secured to our vests; someone even offered me some Imodium tablets, which I took gratefully.

There have been a lot of nervous visits to the loo. Some runners joined mile-long queues; others opted to squat instead, *au naturel*. Iona and I did the latter, looking at one another, both of us wondering what the hell we were doing. But it's easy to remember why we're here when we speak to the other competitors.

I've met a guy in his thirties called Charlie, running for

his wife, Cass, a doctor who has a spinal cord injury and is in a wheelchair. He showed me a picture of their assistant dog – a yellow Labrador called Ticket – who is coming to cheer him on today.

I've met Finn, who has a teenage son with Attention Deficit Hyperactivity Disorder (ADHD). Katie told me about her disabled sister, Bells, and Gilly, who's running for spina bifida, a condition her little sister, Megan, died of when she was two. There's Ward, running for his stepdaughter, Isla, who has cerebral palsy.

Put us together in a tube carriage on a Monday morning and none of us would utter a word to one another, but all barriers are broken down in an environment like this. I found myself telling Charlie about my mother and Granddad, feeling again Mum's pain that after all those years, she never got to be with the man she loved.

I told Gilly I hadn't yet made up my mind whether to take the test or not.

'One day you'll just know,' she said.

Iona and I catch a glimpse of the journalist and writer, Bryony Gordon, running in her underwear. In many ways I envy how much cooler she must feel, though it's still brave of her to be wearing nothing but a pair of black knickers and a bra. I love her spirit; how she raises awareness around mental health and body image. It's only now that I see what a waste of time it is to obsess over such things. It's about being alive, taking risks, and being happy with ourselves – inside and out – that's what really matters.

Iona has talked about her father, who is coming with his carer today, along with Iona's fiancé, Steve, and her mum. We've also bumped into a few of the HDA runners we've chatted with online on our Facebook page. It was like saying hello to family. We hugged one another and shed more tears.

I hadn't expected to feel this emotional before the race. What was I going to be like by the end?

'Have we started?' I ask Iona, as we shuffle forward, but this time we don't stop. She gives me the thumbs up. We're running. We're not stopping this time. We really have begun, though it's not long before I need the loo again.

I stop and bend over, clutching my stomach.

'Go on,' I urge Iona. We're only at mile five. I can't believe it. In my recent training sessions I haven't needed to stop at mile five once, and yet my head is pounding as if it's about to explode, my stomach is bloated and I feel faint.

'Try to walk slowly with me,' Iona suggests, gently taking me by the arm. The sound of the crowds chanting and cheering, along with the thousands of runners, makes me feel giddy.

'I can't go on,' I say. 'Go, Iona.'

'I'm not leaving without—'

But before she can finish her sentence I have thrown up by the side of the pavement.

I am vaguely aware of other runners stopping to ask if I need help. Spectators crowd round me. One hands me their bottle of water.

'I want my mum,' I whimper in a pathetic crumpled heap. Iona crouches down to my level, stroking my back. 'Well, you'll have to make do with me instead. I'm not leaving.'

'But what about your time?' I whisper, holding my stomach, the dizziness slowly subsiding. I know she was aiming to run it in five hours twenty.

'I don't care,' she says. 'It wouldn't be the same without you.'

I look at her, realizing this isn't about a finishing time anymore. It's about surviving the next twenty-one miles in blazing heat, and it will be a lot easier with Iona by my side. I stagger to my feet.

'Thank you,' I say, as the crowds cheer us on. 'You can do it, Flo!' some random stranger shouts as we jog past.

'What a friend!' shouts another. 'Go Iona!'

Iona and I make it to mile eight, the sweltering heat from the pavement and from the other runners intensifying. We have trained in one of the coldest winters, and yet now it feels as if we are running in the Sahara.

At the last water station, we not only drank water but chucked it over ourselves too.

We keep to the left, and when I see James's face among the spectators and Maddie waving her banner, it makes me want to burst into tears again. I rush over to give Jane, Stu, Maddie and finally James, a hug, holding on to him for a second longer. I wish I didn't have to let him go, though I daren't linger, because if I do, I won't be able to start again.

'See you at the next stop,' I say, blowing them a kiss and waving them goodbye. But I have to turn round once more. I need to see his face.

I catch James's eye, 'Keep going,' he calls out. 'You can do it.'

# 84

## Peggy

'Where *is* she, Ricky?' I pester him yet again. He told me he had downloaded some app on his mobile, which can track Flo's progress. All he has to do is put in her name and running number and her location pops up like magic.

Tower Bridge is heaving. Anyone who says the Brits are reserved needs to watch a marathon.

'Here comes the bride!' sings Ricky, strumming it on his guitar too, as a man dressed in white wearing a veil runs past us.

'Get me to the church on time!' sing Ricky's footie mates – before another runner performs a rather wonky cartwheel, everyone cheering and clapping.

'Go, carrot man!' I find myself calling to the person dressed in an orange costume with something green sprouting from the top of his head. Ricky and his friends turn to me in surprise.

'BOB, BOB, BOB!' I chant with the crowds. I haven't the foggiest which one Bob is, but if I'm going to endure waiting for Flo, I'll be much happier joining in. Though it's not long before I gasp, watching a runner stop abruptly, clutching his thigh in agony, hopping on one foot. The poor man must have cramp. I wave my arms and pump my fists when he begins to run again. The crowd applauds him as if he's a hero. And in many ways he is. All these thousands of runners putting one foot in front of another for a person they love or a cause they believe in are heroes, including my Flo.

'Where *is* she, Ricky?'

'She's doing well,' he informs me looking at his mobile screen. 'She should be here any moment now.'

I take a deep breath again before scanning the runners. We are just beyond the bridge. I can't miss her. I can't.

'There she is!' I scream, pointing to Flo running towards us with Iona. I turn to hug Ricky and all his friends cheer.

She's safe. She's well. She's still on her feet, and not only that, she's smiling. She's laughing. Oh, this is wonderful!

'Flo!' I jump up and down before telling everyone standing close to me, 'That's my granddaughter!'

She sees me. She hears Ricky playing on his guitar, 'Here Comes the Sun' by The Beatles, which we discussed would be her special song. She rushes over.

'Keep going!' I say, smothering her with as many kisses as I can. 'You're about halfway there.'

I hadn't expected her to look this relaxed and happy. To be honest, I don't know what I expected, but after seeing

## 85

**Flo**

*This is too hard. You can't do it.*

The voice inside my head taunts me, my feet unable to lift off the ground.

*You still have eight miles to go; you're never going to make it.*

I bend over in pain. I have stomach cramps.

But then I remember what James told me, now challenging the voice in my head, *It doesn't matter if you walk or crawl across the finishing line. All you have to do is finish.*

*I can do this.*

I am promptly sick. Again.

The sight of Iona's family around the eighteen-mile mark lifts my spirits. I watch as she throws her arms around her father, who sits in his wheelchair, his stillness reminding me of Granddad. I watch as she kisses her fiancé, both of them in tears.

'Florence!' I hear someone call. I look around me. No one calls me Florence. Nor do I recognize the voice.

'Florence,' he repeats. I see a man with grey hair waving at me. He looks familiar, but I can't quite place him.

'It's Mark,' he says, as I approach cautiously. 'Your mother's old friend.'

'*Mark*?' I repeat in shock. Of course it's Mark. How could I not have recognized those blue eyes? Reading Mum's diaries and now seeing him standing only inches from me is surreal.

'How did you know? I can't believe—'

'My son, Ben.' He gestures to the tall fair-haired man standing next to him, a younger version of himself, 'He saw your fundraising page. Now probably isn't the best time to chat, but maybe—'

'Did Mum ever tell you? Did you talk?'

'Talk? All the time, Flo. She was my best friend.'

He doesn't understand.

'She made the decision to come to France.'

He shakes his head. 'No, she needed to be with you.'

'She called you. She'd handed in her notice.'

He looks confused. 'She left a message for me, just before—' Colour drains from his face.

'She changed her mind, Mark.'

'I was away. By the time—'

'She was going to tell you she wanted to be with you.'

He turns away, Ben putting an arm around his shoulder.

'I have to go,' I tell them. 'Where are you staying? Give

me your number, or I can give you mine? I can explain everything.'

'I'm sorry.' He faces me again, inhales deeply.

'She loved you,' I say, softly. 'Your friendship meant the world to her.'

'Go,' he says, barely able to utter more, Ben writing down my mobile number on the palm of his hand. 'Go, Flo,' both father and son now urge.

I rejoin Iona, before glancing over my shoulder one last time, to see his face among the crowds.

He waves at me then shouts, 'She'd be proud.'

I look up to the bright blue sky, fighting back my tears, unable to believe I've just seen Mark, the man who appears in almost every page of Mum's diary, the love of her life.

If only I could tell Mum about today, that her message got through to him in the end. If only she knew he was here.

'They're with us,' says one of the HDA runners who stops to talk to me. 'I promise you, Flo, they're with us. You're doing really well by the way,' he adds.

As I watch him run off, I look up to the sky.

'Ready?' Iona prompts me.

My legs, back, knees and feet are knackered, I have no fuel left in my tank, but that thought keeps me going.

*Mum is with me. She* is *here.*

As I run, I see myself standing proudly next to the bicycle Mum gave me for my fifth birthday, wearing my lilac dungarees, my long dark hair styled into two plaits.

'This is a big day, Flo,' Mum says to me. 'Everyone remembers the day they learned to ride their bicycle.'

We're at Barnes Common, an expanse of open grassland, with plenty of space for my bike and me. 'I promise you don't need to be scared,' Mum says, 'I'll be here.'

'I won't fall off?'

'You won't fall off.'

'You won't let me go?'

'I won't let you go, Flo.'

I get on to my bike, immediately losing my balance, until I feel an arm against my back and holding on to my side.

'You've turned into jelly!' Mum laughs. 'Wobble, wobble.'

I'm too nervous to laugh back, intent on concentrating as Mum tells me to put my feet on the pedals again.

'I've got you,' she says, holding on to the back of my saddle and leaning forward to grasp the handlebars to keep me straight. 'Look at the horizon, Flo. Always look straight. Never look back; that's not where you're going.'

Slowly I pedal.

'Go, Flo. Be brave. Let go of the brakes.'

Soon I'm pedalling away with Mum running alongside me, still holding on to the back of my seat and the handlebars. 'Keep going!' she encourages.

*Don't let me go. Don't let me go.*

'Mummy!'

'Look out!' she calls as I almost swerve into a bush. Fear kicks in again until I see Mum running alongside me again. 'Keep pedalling, Flo! Keep straight!'

'Hold on to me,' I call back.

'I am.'

'Are you still there, Mummy?'

'Yes, I'm here.'

But her voice seems further behind me than before. 'Mummy?' I look over my shoulder and see her metres behind me now. She is not holding on.

*I must have been doing it on my own.*

I turn back round and keep on pedalling, my fear now overtaken by adrenaline and excitement, especially when I hear Mum saying, 'You're doing it, Flo. Look at you! You're off to the moon. Tell me what it's like when you get there!'

*I am off to the moon! I'm flying!*

If I can do this, I can do anything, I think, hearing Mum clap when I cycle back towards her.

'You've done it,' she says with a smile as big as the world.


Mum carries me all the way to the twenty-five mile mark, to Birdcage Walk. I am tantalizingly close to Buckingham Palace and the finishing line on The Mall.

My heart soars when I see Granny, Ricky, Shelley, Mia, James, Maddie, Stu, Jane, Natalie from work, Maddie and James's parents and a few others I assume must be Granny's new Italian friends, all clustered together wearing their green HDA T-shirts, waving their banners and shouting out my name and Iona's.

I wave at everyone before hugging Granny.

'Oh, Flo,' she says tearfully. 'You're almost there.'

I hug Maddie and then, finally, before Iona and I tackle the very last stretch, I walk over to James.

'Not a cool look,' he says rubbing his eyes, close to tears himself, 'but I don't care. You've done it, Flo.'

'Only because of you,' I say, unsure how I can even begin to thank James.

'No, you're here because of you.'

I try to imagine a world without James in it. It hurts even to think of such a place.

He touches my shoulder. 'Go, Flo.' His eyes remain on mine, his expression softening. 'What are you waiting for?'

I think of Mark, of Mum's message, and the years they could have spent together. The years they never had.

I take James's face in my hands, saying, 'You.'

A small smile surfaces on his lips. 'Are you … is this … what I think?' he murmurs, our foreheads touching, our mouths only inches apart.

'Yes.' I nod, 'If I'm not too late.'

'Never too late,' he says quietly.

'I love you, James.'

As we kiss, time stands still. I block out the sound of the crowds. I forget where I am. It's just James and me. No longer am I imagining James holding me in his arms. I am feeling his touch, his kiss and his hand running through my hair. I'm not going to waste another day worrying about what the future may bring, because the only certainty we have is right now, in this moment.

'Go,' he says when we finally part. He wipes away my tears. 'Go, Flo, finish off what you started.'

'I will,' I say, kissing him once more before Iona grabs my hand, forcing me to leave James's side. 'You've got plenty of time for all that mushy stuff,' she says with a mischievous smile. And we're off again to further cheers from the crowds.

'About bloody time,' she adds, 'what changed your mind?'

'Mark.'

'*Mark*? Who the heck's he? Blimey, I can't keep up with your love life, Flo Andrews.'

When I see the sign that reads '200 yards to go' I turn to Iona, 'Well you don't have to, all you need to do is keep up with *me*. Come on. You ready?'

She nods, as if she's thinking exactly the same as me, that this is our moment.

From out of nowhere, somehow, we have the energy to sprint down The Mall, towards the finishing line, holding hands, our arms raised in the air, the two of us sobbing like idiots, receiving rapturous applause for our final effort.

We cross the line.

After six hours and two minutes, we have finished.

Yet we don't care about our time. It's more than enough to receive our medal and know we have raised thousands of pounds for the Huntington's Disease Association. It's more than enough to have been a part of this day. This race has been everything I could have hoped for and more.

A marshal comes over to give us both a hug. He says, '*You are the spirit of London.*'

# 86

**Flo**

*Three months later*

'Florence Andrews,' Dr Harding says. She smiles when she spots me in the waiting room. 'I could have guessed it was you. You look like your mother,' she says. 'Do come in.' She gestures to her office.

I sit down opposite her desk. Her frame is so slender that you'd be forgiven for thinking it's impossible for her to carry the responsibility of many people like my mother, people who have walked through her door with similar stories of secrets, loss, fear and abandonment, coupled with the angst and uncertainty of whether to take the test or not.

I only have to think of Iona's family to know she has no doubt witnessed great courage and human spirit, too.

'How can I help?' she asks, though I think she already knows.

'I wanted to talk to you about my mother, Dr Harding.'

'Oh, please, call me Amanda, Florence,' she says, as if she knows me already. And in many ways she does. I feel as if I know her too.

I relax, immediately understanding why Mum liked her.

'In that case, call me Flo.' I clear my throat. 'You were the only person Mum confided in. I've read her diaries, every single entry.'

*Except the very last one . . .*

Somehow I can't bring myself to read what Mum wrote on the day she died. It's like watching someone you love walk slowly into the ocean, knowing they are going to drown.

'That must have taken some time.'

'Months.'

'I hope they gave you some answers, Flo.'

I nod. 'I just wanted to say thank you for being there for her until the very end. Mum clearly trusted and loved you.' Amanda doesn't offer me the box of tissues on her desk. She takes one for herself instead.

'I constantly encouraged her to talk to you and to your grandmother,' Amanda assures me, as if this is all-too-familiar territory, 'but she was determined to do it her way.'

'That must have been frustrating for you.'

'It can be, but we can't force anyone. We have to respect our patients' choices.'

I may well have argued my case when I first found out,

but there is little point now. At the end of the day, Mum was the only one who could have told me her reasons.

'She *always* talked about you, Flo,' Amanda continues, putting us in danger of crying again. 'She'd come into my office, sit down ...' She gestures to the empty seat next to mine, 'and then take out a picture from her wallet to show me how much you'd grown since the last time we'd seen one another, or she'd tell me how well you were doing at school. I remember one time she was ever so chuffed that you'd won a competition for something like the best Easter hat, first prize, no less.'

I smile in awe of Amanda's memory, remembering myself the hat she must have meant. I'd made a sculpture of a chicken with eggs when I was ten. I still have the picture.

'What are you doing now, Flo?'

'I gave up my art,' I confess. 'I had all these ambitions to work in theatre, but when Mum died something died in me too. I couldn't do it anymore. Does that make sense?'

'Yes. I should think that's common.'

'I'm finding my way back to it now, though. I'm looking for a new job,' I say, crossing my fingers. 'I have a couple of interviews coming up.'

'Good luck.'

'Do you think Mum's accident ...' I stop, unsure how to phrase the question.

'Do I think her accident had anything to do with her HD?' Amanda suggests.

Slowly I nod. This is something Granny and I have talked

about too, although Granny hates to think about it, and I don't like to upset her.

'It's impossible to say. It may have played a part. Beth was showing symptoms, but it wouldn't have been the whole cause. I still believe it was a terrible accident.'

'I probably shouldn't have even asked,' I say, feeling stronger than I thought I would. 'It won't bring her back.' I also know Mum would hate me to dwell on the past. 'Is there any more news about the trial? Are you encouraged?'

'Yes. I think it will be at least five years until we know the results of the next phase of the trial but the data we've received so far indicates it's safe and it lowers the levels of the huntingtin gene, so it's extremely promising. It's not a cure, and there are no guarantees, but it's a big step forward.'

'Five years is a long time.'

'It could be more, Flo. Or less, but it's not weeks or months. I know the wait is frustrating, but a drug like this is very different from a drug that just targets symptoms.'

'Is it changing people's minds about wanting to take the test or not?'

She considers this. 'On the whole, no, but we are getting many more referrals. People are coming to see us because they've heard the news about the trial. I don't think that it's changing people's minds about taking the test but even if they decide not to, they can still take part in research studies. People tend to make a decision to test or not when something comes along, like meeting someone or getting married or wanting a family. They can do all these things with HD or not, but for them it's important to know, and in my experience, a drug in the pipeline isn't going to convince them to wait. Others never want to know. So much depends on timing and what is most important to you.'

'Do you think, deep down, Mum regretted taking the test?'

'I have a theory, a non-scientific one, you'll be relieved to know,' Amanda says. 'I believe, in this life, we are born either glass half full or glass half empty. That whatever is thrown at us, however frightening or punishing or unfair it may be, we always, over time, return to the person we used to be. Some people will never find peace or happiness. Even if the most wonderful things happen to them, they don't see the sunshine, only the rain; others, who have known nothing but strife, smile through it all. You know which category I'm going to put your mother into, don't you?'

I nod, urging her to go on.

'It wasn't easy for Beth to begin with. It took her months to accept the results and it was important for her to take that time. But I can recall so clearly seeing a certain peace in her during one appointment, an acceptance. It was in her eyes. In the end, she chose never to look back, but to embrace life. She chose to make every single moment with you count.'

Now I'm the one reaching for the box of tissues.

'How about you, Flo, have you had any thoughts about finding out or not?'

'Yes,' I say with conviction, before blowing my nose and laughing nervously.

*Is it best to live your life with hope or live your life with fear?*

'I don't want to find out yet,' I tell her, 'if at all.' The marathon played a huge part in my decision. Seeing all those people running for HD, all of us wanting to make a difference in some small way, how could I not have faith that one day our efforts will pay off?

Days after completing my run, I woke up knowing I didn't want to find out one way or another. I resolved that I was going to put my faith in science, and hope, but I kept my decision to myself for a few days, just in case I changed my mind again, but this time I haven't once wavered or had any doubts.

Challenging things that come along often make us stronger, even if it's hard to see it at the time. I'm not saying everything happens for a reason, or that this is the way I wanted life to be. I'd bring Mum back in an instant if I could, and I wish Granny and Granddad hadn't suffered so much. Yet at the same time, I wouldn't want to go back to the woman I used to be. I hate to imagine what might have happened if the private blood test had been processed and I'd tested positive. Equally, if I'd tested negative, I would have packed my bags, relieved that the nightmare was over, and set off to New York to be with Theo.

I'm ashamed to say I'd have only thought of myself. I wouldn't have made amends with Granny, since I wouldn't have understood her past. Iona and I would be strangers. I certainly wouldn't have been mad enough to run a marathon. Nor would I have met Mark for dinner and had the chance to reminisce about his friendship with Mum and how much they loved one another. We have promised to keep in touch.

I wouldn't have discovered Mum's past.

And I wouldn't have fallen in love with James.

'Would you want to know?' I ask Amanda, purely out of interest.

She takes off her glasses. 'After all my years working in this field, I still don't know,' she admits, which surprises me almost as much as it does her. 'One day I think I would, the next I'm not so sure, but either way, Flo, we're in a new dynamic age of research, and I do believe anything could happen. But remember, we're not just here to talk about whether or not to take the test. Whenever you need to see me, or Dr Fraser, we're here.'

As I brace myself to leave, I find myself heading over to Amanda's side of the desk and wrapping my arms around her.

'Goodbye,' I say, 'and thank you again. This hug is from Mum,' I add.

'Goodbye, Flo,' she responds, touched, 'and good luck with your interviews.'

I walk towards the door before I turn, realizing I have forgotten one of my most important questions. 'I know Mum wrote to me; a card that she said she'd read out to you?'

'I can't remember exactly what she said,' Amanda replies. 'But she explained her reasons for not telling you sooner, hoping you'd forgive her in time.'

I nod. I hadn't expected to find out anything more. I walk towards the door again.

'Flo?'

I stop and turn round.

'She also said she hoped you'd meet someone.' Amanda pauses. 'That's right Flo,' she says, as if she can hear Mum now, reminding her. 'She said she hoped you'd meet someone who loved you, *no matter what*.'

I think of James and our first date.

We met at a restaurant, James insisting he wanted to do it properly. He was wearing a pale blue linen shirt that I hadn't seen before, and I realized he'd bought it especially for our evening. After our meal we walked hand in hand to the Natural History Museum, home to the ice rink where we'd skated on the night we found out about the trial.

'I wanted to bring you back here on our first date,' James said.

'Why?'

'Because I realized that night that I was in love with you.'

I linked my arm through his, recalling that evening too, James and I laughing on the ice, especially when we both fell over.

'How about you, Flo? When did you know?'

'At your parents over New Year,' I told him. 'When Maddie and your mum suggested you should travel with your work, I hated the idea of not seeing you.'

'Well, I'm sticking around, test or no test, positive or

negative. I'm sticking around to sing badly in the shower, to snore and nick the duvet off you, and to eat cereal out of the packet. I'm sticking around, Florence Andrews, to annoy you for the rest of your life.'

'Flo?' Amanda prompts, bringing me back to reality.

*She said she hoped you'd meet someone who loved you, no matter what.*

'I have,' I say, realizing I am strong enough, at long last, to read Mum's final entry.

## 87

*Beth's Diary, 14 July 2012*

*I can hardly believe I've written a diary for thirty years.
You should see the boxes in the loft. I have often thought
about throwing them away, what use are they to anyone?
I'm not sure I could ever reread them. It would bring back
too many painful memories of Dad. But something always
stops me from taking them down to the tip. It would feel
like throwing part of my life away.*

*I'm cooking Flo roast beef tonight, her favourite, but
stupid me, I forgot to go to the butcher's after I'd been to
the supermarket so I had to make two trips. I feel anxious.
I keep looking at the clock and thinking, in only a matter
of hours Flo will know the truth.*

*I'm glad she has Maddie. She'll need good friends.
I wish Mark was here to calm me down. I still haven't*

*managed to talk to him. He must be away. I just want to hear his voice.*

*I also miss my father. I've been thinking about him a lot today. If only he were here to wrap his arms around me, to stroke my hair and read me a story with a happy ending.*

*I've never been particularly religious, but I found myself going to church this afternoon and saying a prayer that Flo, Mum and I will survive, that we'll come out of the debris stronger than before and ready to face this together, that Flo will forgive me, and Mum will understand the choices I have made, too.*

*Every day I marvel at Flo, how she is growing into a beautiful young woman. One day I hope I'll still be here to see her fall in love, marry and have children, and I pray there will be a cure for HD, so that Flo's life, if she is gene positive, will be very different to my father's and to mine.*

*Wish me luck.*

*I'll write more later.*

## 88

**Peggy**

I lay my flowers on Tim and Beth's grave.

TIMOTHY GEORGE ANDREWS,
24 OCTOBER 1938 – 8 MAY 1994

ELIZABETH SARAH ANDREWS,
12 MARCH 1969 – 14 JULY 2012

My Beth died six years ago today. Barely a day goes by when I don't recall the doctor telling me she was involved in a road accident, and that her condition was critical. I only have to close my eyes to see myself rushing to the hospital, but I was too late.

'We're so sorry, Mrs Andrews,' a doctor said. And the

nightmare was far from over. I had to pick up the telephone and somehow tell Flo that her mother had died.

It was the most painful telephone call I ever had to make; one of the hardest things I ever had to do too, aside from breaking the news of the hospital letter years later.

I used to cry in my sleep, recalling holding Beth's lifeless hand in my own, kissing it, willing her to wake up, and hearing Flo cry out in pain when I told her the news, the grief shocking and raw.

I wished more than anything I had died, not Beth.

Not a day goes by that I don't wonder what might have happened if Beth hadn't burnt the beef the night Flo was due to fly home. What if she hadn't rushed out to the shops, no doubt wondering what else she could buy for their evening meal instead?

I imagine her mind was in turmoil since, not only did she have to worry about food, but finally telling Flo the news. She must have felt confused, lost and vulnerable. A witness said Beth ran across a busy road, not looking, and she fell or tripped over something. *My Tim used to fall.* There was absolutely nothing the driver could have done to prevent the crash.

I think about Beth every day, but no longer does the grief crush my heart and stop me from breathing. Now I can think about my daughter with nothing but love and happy memories. She wouldn't want me to dwell on the past, only celebrate her life.

Of course, I shall always regret making Beth promise

not to take the test, but no longer will I torture myself for mistakes I made in the past. Finally, I feel a certain peace.

If Beth were here, with me now, I'm certain she would be reassured knowing everything is out in the open and that the truth has brought Flo and me closer together, and has also brought new friends into our lives. I know how happy she'd be to see Flo and James deeply in love, and also to know that her daughter is spending time with her beloved Mark.

If Tim were here, standing by my side, he'd never call me a stubborn old so-and-so who should have listened to him all those years ago when he told me to be more open with our daughter. That wasn't his style. I'd like to think that he'd be proud of me. Finally.

I recall the past few weeks, telling Beth and Tim that Ricky and Shelley got married last weekend and that Ricky introduced me to his mother. When she told me with a mega-watt smile that Ricky thought the world of me, I couldn't help but feel ashamed of my initial prejudice towards him.

To think I didn't open my front door that very first time he knocked, thinking he was a baddie with a hammer.

'Your son is one of the best people I know,' I told her, overcome with emotion.

Ricky has proved to me how friendships can spring up in the most unexpected of ways, and I shall be forever grateful that after our first encounter, he didn't judge me in return as some stupid old buttoned-up biddy not worth the time of day.

I often think about the day Flo ran the marathon, too. It is something I shall never forget. On the tube home, a man offered me his seat. He was a father with two teenage sons and a daughter.

'Congratulations,' he said, when he saw Flo's medal hanging round her neck. When he asked her why she was raising money for Huntington's Disease, she looked at me, as if it were my story to tell. But it isn't, not anymore. It is *our* story. Mine and Tim's. Beth's and Flo's.

And so we told him, from the very beginning.

I jump when I feel Flo's hand in mine. It takes me a moment to leave my memories behind and to be here again with her.

She kisses my cheek, her touch comforting. To think this time last year Flo was in New York with Theo. To think I nearly lost her too.

We stand in companionable silence until finally she removes her hand from mine. She retrieves something from her handbag, wrapped in tissue.

'I wanted to give this to Mum and Granddad,' she says. 'I thought today was the right time.'

And I watch with pride as Flo lays her medal on their grave.

Often, I have asked myself: if I could have my time all over again, would I have married Tim and made the same choices? But my answer remains the same: marrying someone who didn't have HD may well have been easier – it could have been harder, too, who knows – yet all I am certain of is that there is no one else I'd have wanted to spend my life with more than my Tim.

I remember him watching me walk down the aisle towards him. I can still feel his breath on my cheek as I stood by his side and he whispered, 'You look beautiful, Peg'. I can picture us now, running across a sandy beach in Devon on our honeymoon, hand in hand, laughing and kissing, mad fools in love, excited to have a whole new life ahead of us.

Without Tim, I wouldn't have held our baby, Beth, in my arms and watched her grow up into a beautiful, talented, courageous woman. I wouldn't have my granddaughter, of whom I grow prouder by the day.

Even during the hardest of times, Tim lived with such dignity. He was brave and uncomplaining. His love was a gift, even if it was taken away too soon. I would rather know true love and feel grave loss, than feel nothing at all. So I know my answer.

I wouldn't have traded the life I had, not in a million years.

# Acknowledgements

Firstly, thank you, Jackie, and Jenny Fraser, for giving me the idea to write about Huntington's Disease, to raise awareness of the condition and the impact it has on families and relationships. Thank you, Jackie, for your courage, and thank you, Jenny, for your support. *If You Were Here* would not have been possible without you both.

There are many more people I need to thank. When I started this book, I knew very little about HD so relied heavily on those in the medical profession and the HD community to help me with my research. I cannot thank Dr Nayana Lahiri enough for giving me such a vivid insight into her work as a clinical geneticist and the predictive testing process. Nayana was endlessly patient with my questions over the past eighteen months and was always there to read over my work, which was reassuring. Her dedication to her job and to her patients is inspiring.

Warm thanks also go to genetic counsellor, Dr Rhona

MacLeod, who encouraged and supported me from the beginning. To Cath Stanley, chief executive of the Huntington's Disease Association (HDA) (www.hda.org. uk), the only charity in England and Wales dedicated to supporting people affected in any way by HD. Cath kindly put me in touch with various people who work for the charity. To Mandy Ledbury, who described in detail her role as a HD specialist adviser. To community fundraiser Hannah Longworth and former HD specialist adviser, Fiona Sturrock. Hannah and Fiona introduced me to some of the incredible team who ran the marathon in 2018 for #TeamHDA: Rosie Allen, Charlotte Blake and Emma P. These women are amazing! Each of them told me about their training programmes and how HD had touched their lives and the lives of their loved ones. They spoke to me with humour and courage about the highs and lows of running twenty-six-point-two miles, and how it felt crossing the finishing line. I was there on the day itself, cheering them on as loudly as I could.

I would also like to thank Matt Ellison and his mother Norma Ellison. Matt grew up with a father who had HD and tested positive himself aged nineteen. Matt saw the urgent need to set up a charity that supported children and teenagers who had had similar experiences to his own. The Huntington's Disease Youth Organization (www.en.hdyo. org) is a lifeline for young people affected by HD. Norma gave me an honest account of what it was like for her caring for a husband with HD. She relayed her pride for everything

Matt has achieved despite the odds. Both are exceptional people for whom I have nothing but admiration.

To Ellie-May Sanders. Thank you so much for talking to me about how your family has been affected by HD, and what it was like, for you, making the life-changing decision of do I, or don't I, take the test? Huge thanks also to Sam Herreid for telling me your experiences, which I found profoundly moving. To Fran Smith, thank you for sharing with me the reasons why you chose to find out if you were gene positive or not. I owe much to you all for telling me your stories.

There are friends I want to thank who have helped me in many different and important ways: Silvy Weatherall – a talented artist who helped inspire Beth's art. To Rosie Motion, an equally talented set designer and model maker, who gave me the idea for Flo's passion in theatre. To Angela D'Agostin, my Italian teacher at the Macbeth Centre in West London. To Simon Felger and Andrew Carmichael, both wonderful vets, who told me about their work. To Janie and Justyn who showed me that best friends can fall in love. To Matthew Jevan, David W, Monika Cholewo, Edward Lucas, Mark Tredwell, Tiggy Pettifer, Anne Pease, Sarah Petherick, my sister Hels, my cousin SJ and the indomitable Molly – all of you have contributed in different ways, making this book what it is.

To Mum and Dad – as always – my rocks. To my Lucas terrier, Mr Darcy, who keeps me company as I write and makes me go for walks when I need to think over the plot

line. To all my readers, and blogger friends on social media –
and my fellow writer friends – thank you for continuing to
support me, and my books. It means a huge amount.

To my publishing team, I owe more than I can say. Firstly,
my agent and friend, Diana Beaumont, always by my side.
Wise, kind and fun, she is someone I can turn to for advice
and support. I couldn't do this job without you.

To Alice Rodgers, SJV, Becky McCarthy, Amy Fulwood
and everyone else involved with my book at Simon &
Schuster. It is great to be part of such an enthusiastic and
talented team. Enormous thanks to Jo Dickinson. Jo is an
extraordinary editor who constantly challenges me to look
at things differently. Praise from Jo means the absolute world
as I know I have really earned it.

And finally, to my editor, Rebecca Farrell, who has been
a joy to work with: passionate and hardworking – she has
put her heart and soul into all the characters that live in
*If You Were Here*. This book simply wouldn't be the same
without her.

# Inside Huntington's Disease:
# Genetic counselling in the real world

*by Dr Nayana Lahiri, Consultant Clinical Geneticist & Honorary Senior Lecturer at St. George's University Hospital, London*

When Alice Peterson first told me she was writing a book about Huntington's Disease, I was so pleased to be able to help in what little way I could. Spreading awareness of HD and how it affects not only those diagnosed, but their families too, is something I continue to support.

Most children are taught about HD when learning about genetic disorders at school, but it wasn't until I first met a patient with the condition, five years after qualifying as a doctor, that I began to learn about how it affects individuals and their families in everyday life. I learnt how easy it is for people with HD to fall through the gaps in medicine because their symptoms are so varied; how they can be misunderstood within social care because people aren't properly informed about what HD is and how challenging it can be to take care of those affected.

The symptoms of HD – involuntary movements, personality and behavioural changes – often force patients to hide the disease, for fear of discrimination and unfair treatment. It is these symptoms, and people's reactions to them, that have led to the breakdown of families and relationships. Despite the fact that there is medication and some interventions that can help with certain symptoms, living with someone who has HD is not always easy, nor is growing up as a child with an affected parent. Add into the mix the hereditary nature of the condition and you can see why fear, shame, guilt and denial are a common theme for many. Nobody wants to believe that their life will end this way, or that their children and grandchildren may be at risk because of a condition they have unintentionally passed on. People do not want to become a burden on their families or for anybody's perception of them to change. When HD is hidden in a closet, it can be hard for a person to open the door and let it out.

Although HD is a condition caused by one genetic alteration in one gene, no two people have the same experience. Coupled with that the fact that there is currently no way of preventing the condition or slowing down its progression, this makes the decision to have – or not have – genetic testing unique to each person. As genetic counsellors, we help people to think through their options carefully and support them throughout the decision-making process, and for the years that follow; from starting a family to the start of symptoms in loved ones, or even themselves.

Before the gene for HD was discovered, the vast majority of family members said they *would* opt to take a test to find out whether or not they were going to develop the condition. However, when that test became available, only 20% of people actually decided to take it, a figure that has remained almost the same over the past twenty-five years. In my experience, this is largely because, when faced with the prospect of a definite result, the idea of finding out isn't nearly as simple as previously imagined. In *If You Were Here,* when Flo first learns about HD she immediately wants to take the test to know for sure, one way or the other, whether she will develop HD. But in reality, she only wants to learn that she *won't* develop the condition— a reaction which is understandable and common. She simply wants the problem to go away. Over time, many realise that a genetic test can give you an answer, but it can't guarantee it will be the one you want. For some people, taking the test isn't worth the risk of losing hope. I have seen many patients change their minds during the counselling process, wondering if they truly could cope with knowing the outcome. They also want to protect their families, fearing the knowledge that the result won't only affect them, but their loved ones too. This is why genetic counselling remains so important, because a result cannot be undone. Many people will take the test further down the line, when the uncertainty of not knowing becomes greater than the fear of what the result will be.

Of course, this will change when there is real treatment, specifically for HD, and even now, participation in research can play a hugely positive role in how some people live life 'at risk'. I spent several years working with Professor Tabrizi and her team at University College London and with HD families in research. I was blown away by the dedication of the families involved, hoping for and being part of the search for a cure. Not only people with symptoms, but also those at risk, even unaffected partners, brothers and sisters gave up their time to take part in an exhausting schedule of physical and mental tasks, MRI scans and blood samples. They were being observed closely, but there was nothing in it for them aside from the fact that their participation may help advance knowledge of HD and, in the future, might help other people at risk.

Research studies like this have now led to the possibility of real treatments for HD. News reports, like the one Flo saw in December 2017 reporting the results of a 'Huntingtin lowering therapy'.This drug may prevent the altered copy of the HD gene from doing further damage in the brain. The next pivotal phase of this potential therapy (the catchily-named RG6042) was announced by Roche Pharmaceuticals in December 2018 – almost a year after the announcement that Flo heard. In this next clinical trial, 650 people world-wide affected with HD will receive spinal fluid injections over a two-year period to see if the drug is helping treat signs and symptoms of HD and possibly even slowing down pro-gression of the disease. And there are several other clinical trials from different companies in the pipeline.

When I was talking to Alice Peterson about *If You Were Here*, the first question she asked me was one I'm often asked: How do people cope if they test positive for the HD gene?

Obviously each patient is different, but in the past twelve years I have witnessed great courage, resilience and humour at the very darkest of times. People don't give up or feel that life isn't worth living anymore. Humans have an extraordinary capacity to cope with adversity, and I continue to be in awe of their strength. It is always a privilege to be a part of their journey.

# FIRST CLASS
## HOLIDAYS

**Booking your dream holiday is not a decision to be taken lightly, whether that be a touring holiday, a luxury honeymoon or a holiday to celebrate a special occasion.**

That's where award-winning First Class Holidays come in. Specialising in tailor-made holidays to Canada & Alaska, America, Australia, New Zealand, South Africa and the Pacific Islands, they take away the hard work when it comes to planning the trip you've always imagined and provide an outstanding level of service while doing so, and with over 750 years' experience between the team, over 100,000 satisfied customers and 23 years delivering exceptional service, they'll plan your journey to absolute perfection, offering first-hand advice with the knowledge they've garnered throughout their own travels.